In Time of War

THE ALEX BALFOUR SERIES BY ALLEN APPEL

Till The End Of Time

Twice Upon A Time

Time After Time

ALSO BY ALLEN APPEL

From Father to Son: Wisdom for the Next Generation

Hellhound (written with Craig Roberts)

Thanks, Dad

Thanks, Mom

In Time of War

AN ALEX BALFOUR NOVEL

ALLEN APPEL

CARROLL & GRAF PUBLISHERS
NEW YORK

IN TIME OF WAR
AN ALEX BALFOUR NOVEL

Carroll & Graf Publishers
An Imprint of Avalon Publishing Group Inc.
161 William St., 16th Floor
New York, NY 10038

Copyright © 2003 by Allen Appel

First Carroll & Graf edition 2003

Library of Congress Cataloging-in-Publication Data is available.

ISBN: 0-7867-1162-0

Printed in the United States of America
Interior design by Simon M. Sullivan
Distributed by Publishers Group West

For Bhob Stewart

Time, like an ever-rolling stream,
Bears all its sons away;
They fly, forgotten, as a dream
Dies at the op'ning day.
—Isaac Watts (1719)

"Time is the fire in which we burn."
—Star Trek

introduction

ALEX BALFOUR HAS a gift. Or perhaps it's a curse. He is able to move from our present into the past. This is the gift. The fact that he cannot control these movements, cannot initiate them when he wishes, or terminate them when he has had enough, is the curse. He does not travel through time. He is *taken* by time.

Alex, like the last four generations of all male Balfours, is a historian. He is not a scientist, and has never been able to explain or understand the how or why of his time traveling. But he has learned that there are certain rules, certain conditions that seem to at least prompt the time shift. This list of what he knows is short. The list of what he does not know—the questions, the mysteries—is long.

Here is what he knows:

His father has the same ability.

He seems to be taken to times that he is particularly interested in and has extended knowledge of: He has been to Russia, 1916; the United States, 1876; the Far Eastern theater of World War II, 1945.

He has seen and participated in history; smelled, tasted, and felt the glories of the past. He has also been starved, wounded, beaten, and almost killed on many occasions.

He is now trapped in the past.

The lifeline that has connected him to the present, a necessary condition for returning to it, has been broken. Molly Glenn, his love, his bond, is dead. A year before this time she had gone to Japan to research a story she was writing for her employer, the *New York Times*, and was killed there. She died in Alex's arms, and he was then drawn back to the past. His anchor was lost, and he is now adrift, unable to return to the present.

Love is the gravity, the force that pulled him back to the present, and with death has come the end of love. For death is unassailable.

Or is it?

Shhhhhh. Listen. Is that thunder?

BOOK ONE

chapter one

A LEX BALFOUR BLINKED against the bright morning sun. He was standing on a steep hillside in knee-high rough brown grass. His thudding heart and sudden fear told him he was not where he had been, that he had gone once again to a new place. A new time.

He heard a low roll of thunder in the distance and looked up. The sky was blue and clear. *No, not thunder. Something else.* Behind him he heard a horse stomp. He turned. Just within a line of trees at the crest of the hill he could see movement.

General George Custer sat on his horse inside a line of trees at the head of three thousand Union cavalrymen stretched along the brow of a long hill overlooking a swath of grassy valley. For two hours Custer and his men had listened to the rumble of cannons and the growl of nearby battle as thousands fought and died. Now the battle was approaching and soon it would be Custer's turn to throw his men at the Rebel army.

The lush Shenandoah Valley of Virginia in the autumn of the year 1864 was one of the world's most beautiful places. Custer was aware of the beauty, and his blood sang with the electric pleasure he knew was soon to come. And so when a man flickered into view halfway down the rolling hillside he was at first not sure if what he saw was real, or if it was some phantom presaging the coming battle.

When he saw other men looking at him for orders, he knew that they too had seen the lone man appear.

Custer held up a gloved hand. "Not yet," he said, quietly. "Soon."

Whoever the man on the hillside was, enemy or friend, it did not matter. He was quite probably about to die.

Alex saw movement, a half mile down the slope and across the floor of the valley. Men carrying rifles appeared out of the trees. They hesitated, as if readying themselves in their minds, and then stepped forward together, firmly, in succeeding ranks, almost as if being birthed by the forest. More men followed until the far edges of the field surged and roiled with hundreds of men in brown and gray, hundreds that became thousands, a mass that edged forward, toward him. Alex turned, thinking he could climb the hill and disappear into the trees.

He flinched as a cavalry bugle sounded, and hundreds of men on horseback burst from the row of trees and underbrush above and thundered down the slope toward him. Bugles brayed. The charging men shouted over the rumbling hoofbeats. Alex recognized the rider in the very front: long flowing blond hair, elaborate blue uniform—George Armstrong Custer. In this terrible second Alex knew where he was—caught between a ground-trembling Union cavalry charge and a horde of keening Confederate infantrymen.

He ran at an angle, toward a line of trees bright with fall color at the side of the field. The horsemen were almost on him. Ahead, the infantrymen suddenly knelt and pointed their rifles and Alex dove to the ground as gray smoke erupted. A horse leapt over him, and others crashed to the shaking earth, throwing cursing, shouting men into the grass and dirt that spat upward as another volley of shot poured into the wild-eyed horses, into the ground, into the men. Cannons boomed, dirt geysered upward, and gray smoke rolled over the battlefield. Alex stood and ran, now behind the first rank of horses as another row burst from the trees behind, and thundered toward him.

Cannon-fire roared from where the horsemen had come, firing down the hill over his head. The air was filled with buzzing, shrieking, wailing chunks of hot iron. Alex hit the ground again and rolled, as horses reared trying to avoid stepping on him. He got to his feet and ran to the right as the next rank of horsemen appeared from the trees.

The valley was swarming with soldiers who knelt and fired into Custer's cavalry. The lead horsemen smashed into the foot soldiers, the infantry firing up at the riders, gutting horses with bayonets as saber blades slashed down onto unprotected heads and shoulders.

Alex was closer to the safety of the trees when men began to appear there as well, men who went to one knee and fired into the line of horsemen from the side.

A bullet knocked him off his feet and slammed him into the grass. He lay for a moment, stunned, not understanding what had happened. He tried to rise and fell heavily. He pushed himself up and looked at his leg, as bright blood appeared just above the knee and spread alarmingly across his rough brown pants. He began to crawl blindly, hoping to become lost in the high grass—by not being able to see, he would then become unseen.

He dragged himself forward. The grass was taller here and he burrowed, mole-like, on and on until he hauled himself into the trees and brush. He kept on crawling until the mad scene behind him disappeared. He concentrated on forward movement, concentrated on breathing, his eyes fixed on the ground directly in front of him. The grass soon became dirt and leaf litter and he fell forward, exhausted and in shock as his gasping breath blew small twigs and dust back into his face and eyes. He rolled onto his back, coughing. Waves of pain surged up from his leg.

He lay on his back, gasping, looking toward the clear blue sky through tree limbs with leaves in shades of yellow, red, brown, and green.

A sudden scythe of cannon-fire blasted and ripped through the canopy of trees. Iron shot shredded branches with the sound of a great cloth being torn. Leaves and twigs rained down in a bright confetti that covered him with flakes like warm, colorful snow.

Alex struggled up on one elbow. Blood dripped from the ragged hole behind his knee, bright red spidery drops that stained the leaf litter a shimmering crimson. The blunt club of trauma thudded in his leg, reverberating through his entire body, into his brain. He felt the world begin to whirl around him.

Pain slashed him awake. A ripping, lightning stroke that radiated up from his right knee. He lay on his back, breathing heavily, teeth clenched against a scream.

The sun was low on his left. Late afternoon. Hours had passed. He tried to move his mind from the pain to some way of alleviating it. What were his medical options? *Nothing. No antibiotics, no analgesics, only dirt, disease, and death. Severed arteries, massive blood loss. Smashed bones. Amputation, always the treatment of choice.*

As he lay staring up at the sky, trying to control his breathing, attempting to fight back the pain and the fear, the only thing he knew for sure was that he had not yet died, which in this case would have to be enough in the way of encouragement, at least for the moment. He pushed himself up on his elbow.

He could hear that the main battle had moved some distance away. He looked around and saw the trunk of a fair-sized tree several yards behind him. He dragged himself over to it, and pushing up until his shoulder leaned against the trunk, examined his leg.

It had stiffened into a slightly bent position. He could see that the blood was still leaking from behind the knee. His trouser leg was sopping wet with it. If the bleeding did not stop, life would leave him one drop at a time.

He was wearing a pair of brown, rough cotton trousers and a light shirt of the same material, though paler in color, woven far away in Japan by women who fashioned the same clothing for their fishermen husbands. It was clothing from another time, but the color had probably saved him from drawing more Confederate fire than he had. The Rebel soldiers would have thought he was one of their own, a skirmisher or picket placed high on the hill, when the battle began. The Union cavalry, on the other hand, probably thought him an enemy not worth bothering with.

He gently picked scraps of cloth from the edges of the wound. He knew that infection and blood poisoning from dirty clothing, greasy bullets, or filthy skin punched into wounds were the real killers on the nineteenth-century battlefield. Unless, in this case, he bled to death first. He pulled up the hem of his shirt and examined it. He picked apart the seam on the right side and tore the cloth up three inches. He put the shirt in his teeth and gnawed several threads loose until he could start tearing the fabric around his body. After several minutes of work, he had a three-foot length of cloth.

He looked into the tree that spread overhead, an evergreen, the bark rough against his back. But the ground he was sitting on was as soft as a down pillow. He felt it with his hand. He was on a bed of thick moss. Without thinking he pulled up a handful of the moss and examined it. Tiny bright green stems tangled together into a soft mass. It smelled clean.

He pushed the moss into the wound behind his knee, gathered another handful and pressed it into the blood and torn flesh on the front of his leg where the ball had entered. He wrapped the cloth torn from his shirt around the wound until he had just enough left to tuck under the winding. He straightened the leg as much as possible and leaned back and rested.

The world was slowly being imbued with an aura of light that seemed to amplify all his senses and accentuate the edges of objects, bringing everything into a startling equality. As if there were not near, nor far, only a single plane of shimmering clarity.

Nearby he heard the sound of horses pushing through underbrush, and for a moment instinct seized him and he almost shouted for help, but he stopped himself. He rolled under a nearby bush. From where he lay he could see the legs of three horses as they walked slowly through the underbrush.

What would a shout for help have brought him? He had seen enough to know where he was, or at least generally *when* he was: the American Civil War, sometime between 1861 and 1865. The turning leaves in the forest indicated that it was early fall, the warm weather and deciduous trees pointed to an eastern, mid-Atlantic location: Virginia, Maryland, perhaps Pennsylvania.

The horses moved on.

He had several problems. *Several?* he thought. He would have laughed, if he hadn't been so hurt. He was a civilian, dressed in clothing that would probably be seen as Confederate in origin.

Unknown civilians of any stripe found on battlefields were usually identified as spies, or at least the enemy. And dealt with accordingly. He could think of no credible explanation as to why he would be where he was. *I'm innocent. I come from the future.*

But the more immediate problem was his leg. If he were discovered, and not shot for being a spy, he would be given medical treatment–which would assure that his leg would be sawed off somewhere above the knee.

He would hide. At least until the battle was over. Then he would carefully seek help.

He dragged himself deeper into the forest.

The underbrush began to thin out, and the crawling, while still excruciating, became easier. Alex found himself among tall oaks and hickories with an understory of sassafras and delicate dogwoods covered with flame-red leaves and berries.

As he crawled he realized he was no longer alone. His peripheral vision expanded from the six square inches of ground directly in front of him to his immediate surroundings. There were other wounded, and dead, men scattered among the trees and bushes.

The others seemed to follow his own urge to walk, stumble, or crawl from the battlefield. They lay, or in some cases, sat, alone. They were from both armies, Union and Confederate.

A man, face blackened by gunpowder blasts from his rifle, waved one arm weakly in his direction. "Hey, Reb. You got any water?"

Alex crawled on. "No. No water." His voice was stiff and rough.

He found himself a thick oak tree and pulled himself up against the trunk. The shells of last year's acorns, split and plundered by hungry squirrels, littered the ground beneath him.

Water.

The thought of it began to consume him. As he sat he heard

from others, all around him, slumped against their own trees, or rocking back and forth, some facedown, clawing and kneading the earth like mewling kittens.

"For the love of God, give me water!"

"Mother!"

"I don't want to die."

"Goddamn, goddamn."

"Please."

"God."

"Water."

And as if their prayers had been heard, God sent rain. With it came a brisk wind from the north, and rolling thunder, and lightning, and the rain poured down and through the trees until the men, those that still lived, lay drenched and cold and shivering. Their calls weakened.

Night came and stretched on and on. Alex could no longer hold himself upright and slumped on his side and slept for a time. When he awoke, he listened to a strange new sound, wondering what monster could be snorting and rummaging among them, snuffling and rooting, until death itself came out of the dark night and touched his hand with a cold bristly snout. He screamed and struck out and knew then what the sound was. He tried to make himself small, hardly daring to breath as he listened to death in the shape of wild hogs foraging among them, feeding on the bodies of the dead and the living.

chapter two

HE COULD NOT hide. They found him again.

Alex shouted and cursed and beat the hogs with his fists and they moved on to more docile prey. At last he slept, or maybe fell unconscious. And now that he was awake, his leg throbbed, his heartbeat echoing in the infected tissue. He touched the wound lightly. The skin was hot and puffy. The moss mixed with blood had formed a hard scab, which at least had stopped the bleeding.

Twenty yards on his left Alex noticed two figures dressed in Union blue. They must have moved in sometime during the night. One of the men was sitting against a tree and the other was kneeling nearby. The man leaning against the tree was drinking from a dented tin cup.

"Water!" Alex croaked. "Please!" The kneeling man turned, searching, then saw him. After a moment he stood, took the cup from his friend, and walked to where Alex lay. He knelt down and handed him the cup. The water bearer was young, little more than a boy; thin with fair skin, blond hair, and startling blue eyes that held the haunted presence of fear suppressed, as if part of the fear was in the showing of it. The uniform on the boy's right arm was bloody from shoulder to cuff, and the arm inside hung slack and useless.

Alex looked into the cup. The water was rust colored. He didn't want to think why. He drank.

"Thank you," he said. "You saved my life." The boy nodded, turned, and went back to his friend.

Alex watched them. The wounded man beneath the tree was large and dark and rough-looking. He had a black beard and a hawk nose. His friend, the young water bearer, was so much smaller that he struggled as he kept the wounded man upright. The boy had a sparrow's build, thin across the chest with long arms. They spoke in tones too low for Alex to understand.

The second night of rain was better and worse than the first. Worse, because Alex was weaker and hope seemed only a distant sentiment, remembered rather than felt. Better, in that the fever continued to elevate, and he drifted off into a numb borderland between dream and nightmare, sleep and delirium, a place not so hurtful as being awake.

He lay on the wet ground and thought, or dreamed, of his past.

Molly. Images bathed in a red-gold light flickered through his mind. Molly when they were in college together. Then Molly older, when they had found each other once again.

She had shown up one day at his classroom at the New School, in New York, unannounced, after ten years. It was as if there had been no time lost between them.

But she had returned to him just when he found himself traveling back in history, back to Russia in the early days of the revolution.

When he had arrived back home there was Molly, and he had begun to understand that without her there was no home, no anchor, only loss, drifting, never to return.

When he floated back up into consciousness, it was still night, still raining, and the hogs had returned to graze among those too weak to resist and those who had faded and passed into death.

He tried to struggle into a sitting position as he smelled and heard a beast snuffle toward him. Slashing rain pelted through the leaves. Wind whipped away his cry as the hog loomed and butted dumbly against his shoulder and chest, sharp hooves trampling his wounded leg, testing to see what life remained.

No!

The brute strength was too much as he futilely punched the thick, muscled, bristled body and felt himself borne down beneath the heavy pushing insistent head, the stink of the animal filling him with fear and disgust.

And then the hog squealed and leapt to the side and squealed again as a streak of lightning illuminated above them the boy, the water carrier, thick tree branch raised high with his one good arm, then thudding down on the pig, slamming down and driving the animal off, disappearing into the brush—more lightning—as the boy stood, exhausted, dropped the branch, then turned and moved away back into the night.

Morning. The tenor of his dreams lifted and he floated nearer the surface of consciousness, toward the light.

He felt the water cup against his cracked lips, and opened his eyes. The water was dirty and warm, but he drank it all. The face before him was the boy with the frightened blue eyes, the boy who had risen above him in the night and saved him from the beast.

"Thank you. Again. For last night. For this," Alex said, aware that thanks were thin payment for his life. But he had nothing else to give. "What's your name?" he asked.

The boy hesitated. "Alister," he said.

Alex nodded. "I will repay you, Alister. I promise."

The boy nodded and moved away.

Alex lay against his tree, soaking wet, shivering, and dying. At some point he felt a coat being pulled on him, over his arms, and he was warmer then.

His periods of wakefulness and lucidity were few, until all his time was spent in some netherworld as the poisons of fever held him to the licking flames of bonfires, interspersed by intervals of teeth-chattering chill.

It was the crackling of the underbrush that woke him. He tried to sit upright, but a bolt of pain squeezed sudden tears and left him gasping for breath. He raised his head. This time it was not hogs.

He could see heavy black boots that crushed sticks and leaves underfoot, brush swishing; could smell sweat-stained wool, gun oil, black powder.

A man walked into the clearing on Alex's right. He was middle-aged, white, wearing a black suit and a flat-brim hat. *Looks like a preacher,* Alex thought.

Against the tree, the wounded man and the boy, Alister, peered up, startled from sleep.

The boy pulled himself to his feet. "No! What are *you* doing here?"

The man in the black suit stopped and smiled. He nudged the man on the ground with his foot.

Alex strained to hear, but only the shouted words came to him.

"Leave him alone!" the boy demanded. The smiling man pulled out a huge pistol. The boy climbed to his feet and threw himself forward. The gunman caught him and held him to the side as if he were a small child. The wounded man on the ground had heard enough. He'd lain still, playing dead, waiting. His hand crept behind his back and pulled out a Colt .45 pistol. He opened his eyes and aimed.

The gunman shot him before he could pull the trigger.

The report was loud in the hushed woods. The seated man was knocked to the side as if kicked. The boy screamed a man's name: "Solomon!"

The gunman pulled the trigger again; yellow flame jetted from the barrel. The big pistol spurted blue smoke. The prone, still body jumped from the bullet.

The gunman looked around at the woods, at the trees, searching for witnesses. Alex felt himself shrink away from the man's eyes, eyes a pale shade of gray that seemed washed and bleached by years of sun and enmity. The rest of the face was set and grim, weather-beaten, scarred and pockmarked, framed by a close-cropped black beard and the hat. He walked away, half carrying, half dragging the boy.

Alex stared at where the man had been, feeling his mind turning the vision this way and that, attempting to fit it into some sort of coherent framework.

Who could do such a thing? Thousands had died here in these fields, but not this way, not after the heat of battle had cooled. This was murder, death delivered with deliberate malevolence. Who was the enemy here? What could it mean? He felt the fever-mist rising to envelope him. He tried to sit up straighter, but it was no use. He fell back and lay, sick, with his face staring up into the trees.

Molly came to him then, in a dream, and placed her cool hand on his forehead. He slept.

chapter three

M OLLY GLENN PULLED the quilt up on the bed and folded the sheet over the edge. She straightened her pillow and lined up

Alex's pillow alongside. It had been two months since he had last slept in the bed, his pillow used now for her to clutch close as she slept. Or tried to sleep.

This time he had been gone so long. She sat down on the bed, feeling vaguely ill, wondering if she was coming down with something or if this was just one more manifestation of her worry.

It was not the first time Alex had gone away, *been taken away*, she corrected herself, but this time was the worst. This time she felt that something really bad had happened. Or was going to happen.

She touched the quilt again. It was a double-wedding-ring pattern in reds and blues, old and soft to the touch. They had found the quilt in a sweet-smelling old antique shop on a road trip to West Virginia. Which reminded her yet again of that last night before he disappeared, when he had asked her to marry him. And she had said no, for reasons that were probably logical at the time, but which now she deeply regretted. And then he was gone.

Yes. Let's get married. I say yes, she now thought.

She stood up, walked to her dresser, stopped in front of the mirror, and picked up her hairbrush. The bristles ruffled through her thick hair with a comforting sound. She looked at herself, seeing a thirty-year-old woman with pale skin and red hair. Alex liked to say she had the same beauty as a heroine in a Pre-Raphaelite painting. Only thinner, she would always add. She appreciated the compliment but thought the comparison far-fetched. She put the brush down and touched her eyes where the dark circles betrayed her lack of sleep.

In the kitchen, she boiled water for tea on the huge gas stove that Alex used to make their meals. She shook her head as she poured the water into her Fiestaware teapot over a bag of green tea. *This is not like you, Molly, straighten up. You are strong. He'll be back. He always comes back.*

She sat at the wooden counter, sipping from her favorite yellow cup, thinking about her life, their life, and wishing that they could simply live a normal existence. *If wishes were horses . . .* she thought. *And fairy tales don't come true. Will the lovely ballerina be rescued by the steadfast tin soldier? Again?*

Alex, where are you?

Molly walked down the sidewalk on the way to the subway. At the end of the block she glanced up at a new building where workmen scurried, guiding a long cable, attaching it to a huge sign that was about to be hoisted up to the roof by a giant crane. The Bender Building, Molly read as she crossed the street. Alex would be furious. The building had been con- structed on top of a small park where he loved to sit while he read his morning newspaper.

She was trying to work up a list of everything she should be doing to get ready for her upcoming trip to Japan, when a glint of sunlight caught her eye, a pinprick gleam from the other end of the block. She glanced back. Fifty yards away a man in a black suit was standing on the corner, and he was taking a picture of her.

No, he's photographing the new building, the raising of the sign. That must be it. Why would he be taking a picture of me? She thought for a minute about going back and asking him what he was doing, but rejected the idea. *What if he's crazy? What if he has a gun? Oh, bull- shit.* She turned back, determined to find out what was going on. She stopped.

The quiet street was empty. The man was gone. She walked back down to the other end of the block. There was no sign of him.

chapter four

Two Negroes assigned to a search for wounded Union soldiers found Alex beneath a tree. Lifting him as carefully as they could, they backed out of the underbrush and carried him along the edge of a small pond, across a sunken road still scattered with the many bodies of Union defenders, and up a hill to a makeshift hospital in an old log cabin. The stench of death and rotting flesh was almost unbearable even in the outdoors. Near the cabin a four-foot-high pile of amputated arms and legs, which no one had yet had time to bury, was baking in the sun. The injured lay in unmoving, white-faced rows, waiting to be seen by harried surgeons then carried away to hospitals in the North, where if they survived the journey they would either be nursed back to health or, most likely, die.

"What in God's name is this mess?" The surgeon touched the packed poultice behind Alex's knee. The right leg of his pants had been cut off at the crotch and the long cloth bandage unwound, displaying the wad of moss that had been pressed over the wound. The doctor and his assistant were kneeling near the leg.

The assistant peered close. "Well, sir, it looks as if he gathered some sort of vegetation and packed it into the wound to stop the bleeding. As he's still alive after three days on the battlefield, I'd have to say that his strategy was sound."

The surgeon grunted. "The leg should be taken off. The bone is broken, that's a certainty. The mess he's put on has retarded the formulation of pus. The leg must pustulate, otherwise he will die."

The surgeon stood and looked down along the long line of waiting, injured men. He'd been on duty for most of the last three days, stealing an hour or two of sleep when he became too tired to grip the amputation scalpels and saws. These men were the last of the wounded, those that had endured days on the battlefield after being hit because it was too dangerous to send out stretcher-bearers while the fight was on.

"He'll die, most likely," the surgeon said, looking down at Alex. "There needs to be an abundance of pus; it should have appeared by now. I'll not bother with the amputation. Wasted effort. We'll send him to Washington City. If the journey doesn't kill him, they can deal with him there. Mark him for Washington."

And so they loaded him into a boxcar and forgot him, one more wounded man who would probably die before the day was gone.

The train rattled north, boxcars of injured Federal soldiers and Rebel prisoners rocking back and forth, suffering alike the heat and stench and jolts and jerks as the train negotiated the rough track. At each stop for fuel and water and supplies, those who had died since the last stop were unloaded.

The train steamed into the station in Washington City and was met by a long line of horse-drawn ambulances. After being loaded into the ambulances they were transported to the Patent Office Building, a mercifully short ride from the train station. The roadway was rutted and chopped and the houses that lined the streets were dark. The Patent Office, a huge, white-columned building, a copy of the Parthenon, had been finished the year before. A row of torches were placed at the front so the stretcher-bearers could negotiate the broad front steps. Shadows flickered across the marble facade. From the beginning of the war this faux Greek temple had housed Colonel Ambrose Burnside and his First Rhode Island Regiment, as well as the patent clerks who attempted to get on with their work in spite of the distracting military presence. After the Second Battle of Bull Run, with casualties streaming into Washington, several of the building's great salons had been turned into hospital wards. The stretchers were carried up the entrance to cavernous third-floor galleries and placed in rows. This operation was supervised by a contingent of stern-faced women in religious habit.

The next morning a volunteer nurse removed the uniform jacket Alex had been wearing, washed his body with a sponge and a pail of water, and dressed him in a set of white cotton pajamas. She looked at the packet of letters that were in the breast pocket of the jacket and found that the wounded man's name was Lieutenant John Jordan. She recorded this on a card attached to the end of the cot and moved along to the next man.

She was followed by two more nurses and a surgeon, who removed the vestiges of dried vegetation from Alex's leg and cleaned the wound. While the infection was significant it was not as advanced as most of the cases that came into the hospital. One of the nurses contended, with humility, that the vegetation, whatever it was, had been medicinal and had retarded the normal poisons that were likely to carry a man off. The surgeon laughed at this ignorant supposition.

On the third day after his arrival, in the middle of a long, still, airless night, with a nurse sitting at the far end of the marble salon by a flickering lantern amid the breathing and quiet moans of the injured, Alex Balfour opened his eyes.

Night. He was alive and knew he was alive because of the pain. He remembered lying beneath a tree, shredded fall leaves drifting down like colorful snow. But here there was no snow. Only a dim yellow light glinting off . . . what?

He could see reflections, and behind the reflections shadowy forms, small and unmoving: a long row of large bulky objects that housed smaller spiky complicated objects like the hearts and brains of mechanical beasts set on display for the night to see.

He struggled to sit up. He could see a woman at a desk. "Water. Can you give me water?" His voice was thin and weak.

The woman, frowning, stood up. She was a volunteer, young and blonde, not one of the nuns. She smoothed the material of her loose, dark dress and walked toward him.

"Water," Alex said again.

"Praise God," the nurse said. "I'll get you some."

She walked to her station and returned carrying a bucket. She bent over him and touched his forehead, smoothing back his hair. Her hand was soft. Cool. She raised the dipper from the bucket and put it to his lips. The water slid down his throat and soothed him. "Thank you," Alex said. "Thank you."

For three more days he slept, waking only to eat and drink. Then he awoke one morning and ate and drank and did not fall back asleep.

In the next cot was a man with a head wound. Alex turned and saw the man watching him.

The young nurse, whose name was Leah, stopped at the end of Alex's cot. "Lieutenant Jordan, you're still awake," she said. "That's a very good sign."

"Yes," Alex said. He wasn't going to question the name confusion until he had figured out his circumstances. "I have decided to rejoin the living." He raised his hand and pointed at the glass cases in the aisle at the foot of his bed. "But I have one question. What the hell are those?" He remembered fever-clouded visions of light glinting off strange devices.

This ward of the hospital was housed in an echoing room of gray-veined white marble. The rows of white-sheeted cots ran the length of the entire ward on both sides. In the center, effectively screening one side from the other, was a long line of dark-stained wooden cases with glass fronts. Inside the cases were small replicas of various machines.

Leah laughed. She walked to the nearest case. "We're in the United States Patent Office, this part of which has been turned into a hospital. These are models of machines. This one"—she pointed to a small iron device made up of wheels and levers—"is a Type Recycling Cylinder Machine. At least that's what's written on the label. I have no idea what that is. There are all manner of devices. I'm so used to them I've forgotten they were here."

Alex nodded. "I have some other questions," he said. "I guess they're going to sound odd."

Leah looked very serious, as if readying herself for an ordeal.

"Where am I? What is the date? And exactly who am I?"

Leah frowned.

"Please, humor me," Alex said.

"I'd not thought that a knee wound would effect the head regions quite so thoroughly," Leah said. "I'll have to ask one of the surgeons if this is normal in a case like yours."

The man on the cot next to them, the man with the head wound, cleared his throat. They both looked at him.

"Pardon the intrusion, but I couldn't help overhearing your conversation." The man's voice was strong, clear, and young, startlingly so in its relationship to the large wad of bandage around his head and face. "It is my humble opinion that more than just the actual site of a wound is involved in these situations. I believe the blood becomes poisoned, and thus effects the entire body, including the brain. I have witnessed other cases in the field and here on this very ward. Total forgetfulness, which usually fades with time, is often the result. If it were me, I would humor him, as he suggests, Miss Leah."

The nurse looked at Alex, who shrugged. "Total forgetfulness," Alex said. "He's right. Can you tell me who I am?"

Leah bent and reached beneath the cot and pulled out a knapsack. She undid the front buckle, took out a uniform jacket, and removed a packet of letters.

"Your name is John Jordan," Leah said, "and these are letters from your family. I must beg your pardon for reading several of them, but I was told that we needed to know who you were." She handed Alex the letters. She was blushing. She leaned close. "You have money," she whispered. "Two hundred dollars, I believe, tucked into an envelope among the letters." She returned to the foot of the cot and went on as if she were reciting.

"You are from the state of Virginia, but the portion that is now known as either West Virginia, or Kanawha, no one is quite sure which yet. As for the date, it is October the twenty-fourth, 1864. You are presently housed in the new Patent Office Building in Washington City, the current capitol of the Union. And I would agree with the young man on the next cot that you are suffering from, as he calls it, 'a state of total forgetfulness,' which I believe is known, technically, as amnesia, though I am certainly not a surgeon."

There was a snort from the man with the head wound. "I knew the term," the man said. "I simply thought you would not and wanted to spare anyone among us from embarrassment. And now I shall invade your privacy no more."

Amnesia, Alex thought. *Yes, why not?*

He looked at the stack of letters and the uniform jacket that Leah had placed beside him. The jacket must have been put on him while he was lying in the forest. He remembered the feeling of his arms being pulled through the sleeves and the resulting warmth. It had been put on him, undoubtedly, by the boy who had given him water.

The jacket, Alex thought, *and the pack must belong to one John Jordan, a Union officer who is quite probably now buried in an unmarked grave on the battlefield. I have inherited his jacket, his possessions, and his name.*

"I need newspapers, magazines, anything I can get that will help me learn, help me bring back my memory." *No one can expect much from a man who has lost his memory.*

Leah nodded. "There's a gentleman who comes around the wards, a big man with a beard. He hands out food and writing materials, and postage stamps. He brings in newspapers and gives them to those who can read. Some say he's a poet. Most everyone thinks he's as crazy as a bug in a jar, but I think he is very nice. Sometimes he'll sit by a bed and read the newspapers to the injured. I'll find him for you."

Alex watched Leah fold his, *no, John Jordan's,* jacket and push it under the cot, and rise and walk away.

The ward was quietly buzzing with low talk. The same two nurses and the doctor who had seen to his leg earlier walked the rows of cots, examining men. All the wounded wore white cotton pajamas. Large floor-to-ceiling windows were partially open to lessen the stink of gangrenous flesh.

"A word to the wise," the man on the next cot said. "The big man the fair Leah is looking for is a bit stranger than a simple bug in a jar. His name is Whitman and he will indeed sit and read you the newspaper. As she said, he is a poet, but what she did not say is he is known for producing work that decent people cannot read without blushing."

"I found him," Leah announced, smiling and walking back to them. "But he says he's fresh out of papers, and he'll be gone for several days of travel to the battlefields beginning tomorrow. I'll try and find you newspapers myself in the morning."

Alex watched Leah walk away down the long aisle. The man on the next cot waved a hand in Alex's direction.

"The name's Bierce. Ambrose Bierce. I'd offer to shake your hand but I'm afraid I'd fall out of bed. What unit were you with, Lieutenant? And what battle has brought you here?" After a moment's silence from Alex, he went on. "Ah yes, your amnesia, I had almost forgotten."

chapter five

ALEX BALFOUR SAT by a large, open, third-floor window in a wooden chair. His leg had been strapped into a leather splint with stiff wooden braces. He looked out across the streets bounded by low wooden buildings. In the distance he could see the Capitol building and discerned tiny, insectile workers crawling over the dome.

Alex had been in the hospital for more than a week since he came to consciousness. The clean fall air moved through the open window and into the ward, diluting the ever-present stench of blood and wounds and sickness.

He allowed himself to think. Until now he had simply concentrated on existing, narrowing his focus to his wound and to the world of doctors and what was considered the practice of medicine of the time. He would overhear two doctors discussing a particular technique or medicine and pray that none of it would ever be used on him. He still shuddered every time he heard the words "laudable pus," the doctors' insistence that a wound must leak pus if it was ever to heal correctly. He, with Leah's help, washed the wound with strong soap and hot water two times a day. The doctors thought him insane, but Alex insisted, and Leah and the other nurses had begun to believe in the efficacy of this treatment as they watched the wound rapidly heal.

And now, when it was fairly clear that he wouldn't die, he had to decide how he was going to live.

He had traveled back into the past three times and he had learned many things, but the mysteries still far outweighed what he understood—the *Why* of it all.

He knew that the ability, possibly the curse, was inherited. His father, Charles Ames Balfour, a best-selling historical novelist, had the same gift. Charles Balfour had been at best a distant father, and cruel to both Alex and his mother when he wasn't distant. He would disappear for long periods of time, then reappear to hide himself away for months while he wrote what would become best-selling historical novels. Alex had not known of his father's ability until they shared the same time shift into the past, back to revolutionary Russia. By then Alex's mother was dead; and Alex hadn't seen his father since. He could only hope that his father was dead as well, as he always thought that the man had been responsible for his mother's death. And so he had mourned his mother, and hated his father. He had moved beyond the mourning, but not the hatred.

And now I must decide what it is I will do here, and who I will be. I am, for the moment, Lieutenant John Jordan. I will fight to stay alive.

I must change the events that led to Molly's death. I will return to her and to my own time.

He thought for a moment. *I will find the boy who saved my life. I promised I would repay him.*

Alex felt someone come up behind him. He twisted around and saw a boy named Harvey Porter, whose left arm sported a bright white bandage on the stump where it had been amputated a few inches above the elbow.

"Ambrose and the others will be along directly. They're rounding up lunch." Harvey dragged up a chair and sat down.

Ambrose Bierce, Alex's neighbor on the next cot, was now ambulatory. His head wound, confined to the area of his right ear, was on the mend and much more lightly wrapped. He and Alex had formed a friendship and aided each other in the everyday tasks that their injuries made more difficult.

Alex tried to remember what he could of Bierce. He had instantly recognized the young man's name and knew that Bierce would become a writer. He'd read at least one of his short stories, "An Occurrence at Owl Creek Bridge." It was one of those stories that he and every other kid read in school at some time or other. He also remembered laughing in college at the bitter humor of *The Devil's Dictionary,* Bierce's second most well-known work. Other than that he remembered little of what Bierce had written, though he knew his historical reputation was one of a cynical, caustic, uncompromising social and literary critic. A reputation that Alex found at odds with the uncomplaining young man who helped out around the ward and was well liked by everyone. Alex also knew that in 1913, at the age of seventy, Bierce disappeared, mysteriously, into the hills of Mexico and was never heard from again.

Bierce was known around the hospital as a mesmerizing storyteller.

The men always prodded him for a tale to take them away from their general misery.

The patients were a sad lot, almost all of them young men, some blind, many crippled and disfigured. Alex realized he had always unconsciously thought of Civil War veterans as old geezers with grizzled features and hillbilly accents. But it was obvious here in the hospital that most of the soldiers in this war, like most of the soldiers in all wars, were young men, some of them hardly more than boys. And while their wounds had changed their lives for the worse, they were alive and thousands of others weren't, which gave them a sort of rough cheer.

"What do you know of Bierce?" Alex asked Harvey. "Weren't you in his unit?"

Harvey nodded. The fingers of his right hand lightly stroked the bandages on his stump. "We both joined up with the Ninth Indiana Volunteers when we was nineteen. I stayed a private, but it was obvious right soon that Ambrose would move up the ranks. We was with General Morris at Laurel Hill when Ambrose first showed what he was made of." Harvey fell silent and looked around the room. "He wouldn't like to hear me tell it. He never boasts about his exploits."

Alex looked at the room behind them. "Well, I don't see him anywhere. Go ahead."

Harvey smiled. "It was something to see. We'd been taking potshots all day at a bunch of Rebs. They was dug in behind a breastworks of trees they'd cut down and piled up, so we wasn't havin' no effect. Ambrose and a few other boys had grown tired of it and organized themselves for a charge. All this was strictly on their own. They come out of the line and charged up the hill and made it to about fifteen paces from the Rebs when a boy named Dyson Boothroyd took a ball to the neck and went down.

Ambrose could see they was getting shot to pieces and wasn't going to accomplish much, so he stopped and collected poor Boothroyd. Still carrying his rifle, he threw that wounded boy over his shoulder and ran all the way back to our lines with the balls falling around him like hail from hell. We all held our breath a-watchin' it. He made it without a scratch. Later on, after we re-upped, they promoted him to sergeant major because of that charge. And that weren't all. At Missionary Ridge . . ." He stopped talking as Bierce came up.

Bierce stood behind them for a moment, looking out the window. He was tall and handsome with a ginger mustache and blue eyes that held a look of constant curiosity. There was an air of competence and organization about him, and Alex could see that even though Bierce was young, he had a natural gift for leadership. Bierce pointed at the Capitol building. "Did you know that they bake sixteen thousand loaves of bread a day down in the basement of the Capitol building? For the Army. A drover making a delivery just told me that." Outside, a very large pig snuffled by in the mud. Two geese followed the pig.

"We've brought lunch," Bierce added, nodding in the direction of several other wounded men who arrived carrying plates and pots. Alex and the other ambulatory patients gathered by the tall windows to eat their lunch whenever possible and thus escape the gloom and stench farther back in the dark, high-ceilinged marble rooms.

As they were setting up their chairs the tall bearded poet Whitman joined them. "I have oranges and tobacco, gentlemen," Whitman said. "And the latest papers from New York and the city."

"You're welcome to join us," Alex said. Whitman found a chair and pulled it up.

"How's the head today, Ambrose?" Harvey Porter asked.

"Not too bad. I've seen those with less die from it. And how's the arm?"

"Mostly missing," Harvey answered. "What's left of it commenced to itchin' something awful last night. I got me some coal oil that I poured on it. I caught hell from the Sister, but burnin' sure beats itchin'."

"Itchin' generally mean healin', though," another man offered. They all nodded. " 'Ceptin' in the form of skeeter and graybacks, a course." They all nodded again. Graybacks was the accepted term for body lice. The Rebels called them bluebacks.

One of the men pulled up a small table and put a pot of food and plates on it.

"Where'd you pick up that wound again, Ambrose?" The men had found that if they could get Bierce talking he would soon break off into a tale of some sort. Alex knew this would be a mainstay of Bierce's career, eventually writing hundreds of stories, ranging from Civil War memoirs to horror tales.

"Kennesaw Mountain," Bierce replied. "Sherman was fixing to outmaneuver old Joe Johnston and I was General William B. Hazen's topographical engineer. Sharpshooter got me. Never saw him, nor heard him, though others said they heard the shot. Dropped me like a hare. It's strange, but I don't remember a thing of it until I ended up here."

"Lots of strange on a battlefield," a blind man offered. "Ambrose, what is the dangdest thing you ever saw on a battlefield?"

"That's a difficult question. How about we have some of that stew while I think about it." The meat and potatoes were spooned onto plates and passed around. Whitman placed a plate and spoon into the blind man's hands. A loaf of bread was sliced and handed out.

"The dangdest thing I ever saw?" Bierce mused. "There are so many possible answers. Any man who's been on a battlefield has seen strangeness that can hardly be accounted for. Not ghosts, and haunts, though they are there as well, but the curious turns of events in life itself. Have I ever told you boys the story of Coulter's Ridge?" There was a silence as the men politely considered the question.

"I don't believe so," the blind man answered. The others shook their heads.

Ambrose sat quiet for a moment.

"It was down in Tennessee," he began. "I had been assigned temporary duty in my topographical capacity to a Colonel Henderson, who was part of a Federal unit chasing a large Rebel retreat through the hills. We were held up on the only road through the hills by several batteries of Rebel artillery. They had their guns set up beyond two creeks and in an orchard about a half-mile beyond the notch in the ridge where we were holding. This later became known as Coulter's Notch. There were eleven guns down there in the orchard, and one gun out in the open in the yard of a big plantation house. That one exposed gun in the yard seemed to be sort of thumbing its nose at us." He stopped and ate some of his stew, then continued.

"We were on the near side of the hill, before the crest, having found that if we showed ourselves at the top, the enemy artillery immediately opened up and cut any prolonged observation particularly short. The road was hardly more than a track, barely wide enough for one gun to set up. On either side of us for a mile to the right and a mile to the left were our troops, lying in wait for something to be done about that artillery." He broke off a piece of bread and dunked it into his bowl.

"Just then the general in charge of the division, a General Holt, rode up and asked a question of my colonel. 'Do you think,

Colonel, that your brave Captain Coulter would like to put one of his guns right here?' The way he said it made me think this was a continuance of a conversation they had begun some time earlier. The general said it with just a hint of a sneer in his voice.

" 'Only room for one gun here, General, against twelve down there.'

" 'But surely you can see that this is the only place to get at them. And you've told me before that your brave Coulter is worth a whole battery in himself.'

"Right about then a young artillery officer rode up. He was a smallish man with a little blond mustache and long blond hair. He had an intense expression and he was staring at the top of the hill. The colonel stopped him.

" 'Captain Coulter, the enemy has twelve pieces over there on the next ridge. If I rightly understand the general, he directs that you bring up a gun and engage them.'

" 'Are the guns near the house?' Coulter asked. 'And is it necessary to engage them?'

"I was surprised at the question, and the colonel looked downright mortified, as Coulter's face had gone pale as he asked it. With that, General Holt shook his head in disgust and rode away. Just as the colonel was about to order Coulter to do as he was told, Coulter leaned over to his aide and issued an order. The aide rode off down the hill, and Coulter turned around and rode right up in the notch and got out his field glasses. Then behind us a single gun with its caisson, drawn by six horses and with the full complement of gunners, came banging up the grade in a storm of dust. In no time at all they had that gun set up and sent the first charge down on the enemy. And so the affair at Coulter's Notch had begun."

Bierce ate several spoonfuls of his stew. "This stew is a good bit better than what we're used to out in the field, isn't it, boys?"

"A good stew can't never be allowed to rapid boil," the man with one arm said. "Just barely simmer. Otherwise the pores of the meat close up and harden. And you got to skim it. The whole time you're cookin'. But what about that cannon, Ambrose?"

Bierce set his now-empty plate on the marble window ledge.

"As soon as Coulter fired that first shot it was answered by all twelve cannons on the opposite ridge. We—the colonel, his immediate officers, and myself—had moved down a quarter mile on the left where we could observe in relative safety. We had a clear view of the enemy, or at least the main gun in the plantation yard. It was this gun Coulter concentrated on, firing every few seconds with good effect. We could see the shots arriving in the enemy's position, some in the house itself, but most amid the men and horses surrounding the gun.

"About this time an officer came up to us from the woods and announced that his infantrymen were now in position to fire on the enemy guns and wished permission to do so. The colonel refused him that permission. It seems the general had left specific orders that only Coulter's gun was to engage the enemy. I could see that it cost the colonel plenty to turn the offer of aid down, but he had his orders.

"I could also see that the colonel's aide wanted to say something so bad, he was about to bust. Then he just came out with it. Here's his story, which he swore he'd got from a source who he would trust with his life.

"It seems that General Holt had been down in this part of the country a year before. And it turns out that Coulter lived here before the war started. As chance would have it, the general stayed at Coulter's house—Coulter was serving elsewhere—and, well, there was some sort of trouble between the general and Coulter's wife. She made a complaint to army headquarters and the general was reassigned. To the division I was a member of. Shortly after that Coulter was assigned to this division as well."

"Be goddamned," one of Bierce's listeners said. "That's the Army for you. There'd be trouble coming from that."

Bierce resumed his tale. "After the colonel heard what the fellow said about the general, he turned around and started off at a run, and we followed. We got to the road and mounted up and turned the bend toward the cannon. What we saw there was as bad as anything I have seen in this war.

"There were the piled wrecks of four guns that had been brought up one by one and blown to pieces. It was like having a horse shot out from beneath you. As one gun was hit and destroyed, Coulter would order up the next. The fifth was still firing. The men, what there was left of them, resembled demons from the pit. They were stripped to the waist, their skin black with blotches of powder and spattered with gouts of blood. They had their swollen shoulders and bleeding hands to the wheel of the gun, heaving it back in place after every shot. The gun itself was horrible to look at. The man in charge of sponging down the barrel had run out of water at some point and taken to using pooled blood from those slain around him. The colonel strode into this hell, found Coulter, and bid him to cease fire. When he did so, the enemy's guns fell silent as well. The battle of Coulter's Ridge was finished."

All of the men had stopped eating during the story, some with spoons half raised to open mouths. The spoons were lowered.

"But the story is not quite finished," Bierce went on. "An hour later we moved forward. The colonel set up in the plantation house, which was somewhat shattered, but better than the open air.

"We were having supper when an orderly bent to me and asked

if he might disturb the colonel, saying there was something wrong in the cellar. I fetched the colonel and we all went down to see what was the matter.

"We had but one candle for light. There, leaning against the wall, was a man, crouched down over a woman. In the woman's arms was a babe. The colonel, holding the candle, stepped forward. There was a hole in the dirt floor that contained two objects. A chunk of iron from an exploding shell and an infant's severed foot. We could now see that the woman and the babe were dead, but the man crouching over them was not. He looked up at us. We did not know him. His face and clothes were filthy and he reeked of gunpowder and smoke.

" 'Who are you?' " the colonel demanded.

" 'This house belongs to me, sir,' the man said.

" 'To *you*? Ah, I see. And these others?'

"The man wiped at his face and sat up a little straighter into the candlelight. 'These two are my wife and child. It is me, sir,' " the man said. " 'Captain Coulter.' "

The men sat quietly for a minute, their bowls of stew forgotten.

"Sweet Jesus," the blind man said. "And may God damn that General Holt to eternal hellfire."

"My sentiments exactly," Bierce said. "At that moment, in that basement, I vowed if I ever saw the man again I would beat him within an inch of his life. And I still intend to do so someday."

chapter six

MOLLY WAS CAUGHT as she came up out of the subway by the man who was following her. She had glimpsed him several times over the past two days; tall and distinguished-looking, always dressed in a suit. He was an unthreatening figure, although his hovering presence was disturbing. She thought about calling the police, but she had lived in the city long enough to know that a New York cop was going to take a pretty dim view of the nature of the complaint: *I'm being stalked by a well-dressed gentleman who never bothers me.* Because she was leaving for Japan soon she put the man out of her mind. He would have to be one hell of a stalker to follow her halfway around the world.

"I need to speak to you, Miss Glenn," the man said. "It's a matter of some importance."

They were standing at the top of the subway entrance. She could smell the chestnuts and pretzels warming on an open cart down the street. A tall elegant blonde carrying a large portfolio case strode by, followed by a street guy with no shoes and purple feet with open sores. Not a likely spot for a killer to strike.

"And you are . . ."

The man handed her a card: Lambert, Rowland, and Scott. There was a Washington, D.C., address. "Andrew Lambert," the man said. She considered him. Her normal New Yorker's response would have been to tell him to leave her alone, but curiosity overrode that reaction.

"All right, you have some explaining to do. We'll have coffee." She led him around the corner to a coffee shop where she sometimes ate breakfast. It had taken a year of steady patronage but she was now "Hon" to the waitresses, who were more than willing, in fact eager, to insult anyone not considered a regular. They slid into a booth opposite each other and ordered coffee.

"You've been following me. Did you take my picture?"

Lambert looked embarrassed. "Yes, well, I'm sorry. This is something of an unusual situation and I needed to be absolutely certain of your identity." He keyed in a combination to a slim leather attaché case, opened it, and handed her a manila envelope.

She opened the envelope. Inside was another, smaller, envelope, made of thick, cream-colored paper browned around the edges with age. A wax seal held the flap closed.

"And inside here I'm going to find, what?" she asked, holding the envelope by one corner. "The keys to the kingdom? A fabulous inheritance from a long-lost relative? A summons?"

"Actually, I have no idea what you'll find. I must admit to a certain amount of curiosity as to the contents. Perhaps if I may give you a short history of how it came into my possession?"

Molly put the envelope on the table and picked up her coffee cup. "Go right ahead, Mr. Lambert."

Lambert folded his hands in front of him.

"The firm of Lambert, Rowland, and Scott is quite old. My ancestor, Reginald Lambert, founded it more than 130 years ago after leaving the employ of the Jay Cooke and Company bank after the Civil War ended. This envelope, which is known as the Balfour Bequest, passed to our firm when Reginald Lambert left Mr. Cooke and started his own concern. It has been passed along since then by every male Lambert who has gone into the family business. None of us has ever opened the envelope, or has any idea as to the contents. It is family lore that several of the old

Lambert gentlemen have on their deathbeds remarked on their sadness at departing life not knowing what was inside."

At the words "Balfour Bequest" Molly felt her hands tighten around her coffee cup.

"Balfour Bequest?"

"Yes, the name of the man who entrusted it into our care was said to be Balfour. First name not supplied. In-house legend has it that this man appeared at Cooke's bank and, speaking with my ancestor, had a rather unusual request: he would entrust this envelope into the bank's care to be delivered, to you, on precisely this date, 138 years in the future. He was quite specific. He supplied Reginald Lambert with your present home address, and, I must say, a surprisingly detailed and accurate description of you."

Lambert picked up his coffee and took the tiniest of sips. He looked mildly surprised and drank more.

"Excellent coffee."

"Try the bialys here sometime. I don't know where they get them, but they're the best in New York. The envelope?"

Lambert nodded and went on. "Our Mr. Balfour paid Jay Cooke no money for this service. Rumor, which has by now become folklore within the firm, has it that Cooke did this as some sort of favor for Abraham Lincoln. Several years went by, and in 1873 Mr. Cooke attempted a rather serious gambit to buy up all the railroads in the country, a plan that led to the demise of his company. Reginald Lambert left his employ at this time, and with Cooke's blessing, took on the Balfour Bequest to honor what he had begun to see as a personal obligation." Lambert leaned forward and spoke quietly. "But Mr. Balfour had done something very unusual. He left, along with the packet you have now received, a short list of companies and products that he felt would be excellent investments over the years, plus the advice that the attempt to buy all the railroads in 1873 was not a wise financial move. Mr. Cooke never paid serious attention to Mr. Balfour's valuable advice. Unfortunately for him. After leaving Cooke's bank, Reginald, more for amusement than any faith in the suggestions, actually put some money into the market on one of Mr. Balfour's proposals." Lambert spoke quietly. "After an immediate success, these suggestions have been followed religiously and have amounted to a considerable fortune. So substantial that the firm could exist very nicely doing no other work than simply waiting, year after year, to deliver this envelope." He leaned back again.

"And now, Miss Glenn, you have the envelope. You could take it away and open it later, in private, and that would probably be my professional suggestion to you. But I must say, I do not wish to be the last Lambert to go to his grave wondering just what could possibly be inside. The decision is yours."

Molly ran her finger beneath the lip, snapped the brittle wax seal, and opened the envelope. Inside was a small card, approximately 2 inches by 3 inches. A photograph. She picked it up and looked closely at it.

A woman, wearing a nineteenth-century hoop dress, stood beside a seated man. Molly touched the face of the woman in the photograph and felt the blood rise in her cheeks, as if she had been slapped.

That is me.

And the man in the photograph was almost as surprising.

Abraham Lincoln. In the photograph she was standing behind and to the side of Abraham Lincoln.

Below the picture, scrawled in what she instantly recognized as her own handwriting, was the sentence, *"Don't go to Japan."*

chapter seven

I N THE *New York Times* newsroom, Molly sat across the desk from Tommy Fellows, watching him polish off a jelly doughnut. Tommy was overweight, eccentric to the point of derangement, and easily the most brilliant person she had ever met. And she needed his help. She waited while he wiped his fingers on his handkerchief and brushed a light dusting of powdered sugar off his vest. Then she placed the manila envelope on his desk. He picked it up and turned it over, examining it.

"Looks old. I thought you were supposed to be off to Japan on that germ warfare story?"

"I'm scheduled to leave tomorrow. Would you take a look at this for me?"

He squinted closer, peering at the wax seal. "Been working the flea markets? Cleaning out the attic?" he asked, eyebrows raised.

"I was given this yesterday, in what, I think I can safely say, were extremely unusual circumstances. It seems to be a message from the past. I need to know what it is, and I guess more importantly, what it means." Responding to his still-raised eyebrows, she nodded. "You may open it." Tommy Fellows's general knowledge was known by all on the staff of the paper as encyclopedic, and because of this he was often used as one. "Take it to Tommy" was a phrase heard around the newsroom.

Tommy cleared a space and gently slid the contents of the envelope onto his desk. He hummed softly to himself as he studied the material.

"One carte-de-visite photograph, approximately 1860 to 1865, in pristine condition." He picked it up and looked at the back.

"Carte-de-visite?" Molly asked.

"A type of photograph extremely popular during the Civil War. People collected pictures of family, friends, and the famous, and stuck them in albums." He placed the picture on his desk. "Now, the interesting thing here is that one of the individuals is contemporaneous to the period, but the other is decidedly not. Very clever. Probably done by computer." He smiled at Molly. "Cute. Where did you have it done? Coney Island? The boardwalk in Atlantic City? There's a photographer in Gettysburg, Pennsylvania, who does excellent work of this type."

"I didn't have it done anywhere. It was delivered to me, just as you see it. I have been told by what seems to be an extremely reliable source that it is genuine."

"Molly"—Tommy smiled gently—"someone is pulling your leg. This is a picture of you. In period dress."

Molly shook her head in exasperation. "Believe me, Tommy, I never put on a hoop dress and had my picture taken with Abraham Lincoln."

"What's the joke?" He picked up the picture. "How about this? It says, 'Don't go to Japan.' Who wrote that? What does it mean?"

"Tommy, I don't know what the joke is. And I don't know what it means." She told him about being followed and her meeting with the lawyer and his story. Tommy leaned back in his chair doing his best Nero Wolfe imitation, eyes closed and hands folded over his chest. At the end of the tale his chair creaked forward and he stared at the picture.

"All right," he said. "I don't buy it, but let's send it down to the photo department. A couple of the guys there are history buffs, they'll be able to tell us if it's genuine. Meanwhile, there's one other curious thing about the picture that I noticed." He turned it around so she could see it. She leaned close. "Unless I'm mistaken, you're pregnant in this picture."

Molly sat across from Tommy in the *Times*'s lunchroom. They were waiting for one of Tommy's friends from the photo department to join them.

She picked at a ham sandwich that didn't really appeal to her, while Tommy plowed through a double order of fried catfish with collard greens and corn bread, the sight and smell of which made her vaguely nauseous. *Pregnant. No. No?*

Molly recognized the little man scurrying across the lunchroom toward them as Mike, one of Tommy's chess friends, the guy from the photo department Tommy had given the picture to. Mike was a wiry, bearded man who spent his weekends reenacting battles of the Civil War. He pulled out a chair at their table, sat down with a worried expression, and began speaking all in a rush.

"Unprecedented, in my experience. I'd have to say that this print hasn't seen the light of day until you handed it to me." He had wrapped the envelope in a torn page of the *Times* and secured it with a piece of tape. "The envelope paper is extremely brittle," he explained. "I'd keep it wrapped up when you aren't looking at it." He carefully unwrapped the envelope and took out the photograph. He handled it reverently. "Must have come from some relative of yours, huh, Miss Glenn? She's the spittin' image of you. Noticed it right off."

"Well, yes," Molly said. It seemed the easiest answer at the moment.

"Tommy, you were right, definitely Civil War era, though I think I can narrow it down for you." He put the envelope on the table and turned the picture so the image was facedown and they were looking at the back. "That imprint there, the cherub and the camera, dates it to 1864 and after. The thickness of the mount and the lines around the edges tell me it's 1864 or '65. The assassination precludes it being any later than that, of course."

"The stamp says Mathew Brady," Tommy said.

"That's right. Though Brady wasn't working much during this period, if it turns out to have been made when I think it was. He was still taking pictures of the president, but his commercial business had pretty much stopped while he worked on his war pictures. This is an albumen print. Albumen is made from egg whites. Photography studios used up millions of eggs during the period the carte-de-visite was in vogue. There weren't even enough left over for the soldiers."

"And this picture is authentic?" Molly asked. She didn't know what she wanted the answer to be.

"It sure is. I tested a tiny bit of the paper. Sometimes crooks will find a bunch of unused card stock of the period and put faked prints on 'em. This is original. You don't want to sell it, do you?"

Molly shook her head.

"I didn't think so, what with your relative being in it and all. It's valuable, sure enough. Is there anything else you want to know? I gotta get back upstairs."

Oh yes, Molly thought, *there is much much more that I would like to know.* She shook her head again. Mike carefully wrapped the envelope back in the piece of newsprint, taped it shut, and stood.

"Thanks, Mike," Tommy said. After he left, Tommy sighed. "Now what I thought was a joke has become a mystery. And I sense you know more than you are telling."

"You wouldn't believe me if I told you."

"Why don't you come by my place tonight. I'll cook dinner for us. You can tell me whatever it is you think I'm not going to believe. Meanwhile, how many people know you were planning a trip to Japan?"

She thought about it. "Three. You, my editor, and the guy in the travel department who makes the arrangements."

"You want my advice?"

"Sure."

"Like it says on the picture. Don't go."

chapter eight

THE SUNLIGHT SEEMED impossibly bright. Alex stood, blinking, leaning on a crutch, between two huge white marble columns outside the Patent Office hospital. Squinting, he looked down the wide steps to a row of wooden buildings. Beyond them were rough fields, a few shacks, and dirt roads. He took a deep breath.

The air smelled like shit. Literally.

He put his hand over his face. "Does it always smell this bad?"

Bierce laughed. He was standing, only slightly more steadily than Alex, on the other side of one of the columns. "I'm told that our present season, fall, is a great relief from the trials of summer. I have been to this city once as a boy and when I first joined up in sixty-one, so I know it tolerably well, but have never been here in that season. During especially hot days it is said that the air is near violet with stench. Tiber Creek, to our left, runs through and carries off the effluvia of Swampoodle into the City Canal, which in turn dumps it into the Potomac River. The citizens of Washington City eagerly await the first hard frost, which will kill much of the odor, as well as the multitudes of insects." He touched his hair, newly liberated from the large bandage that had covered his head for the last month.

"Does it hurt?" Alex asked.

"Not any more than you'd expect from having your head cracked open like a walnut." Bierce had been shot in the left temple and the bullet had come to rest behind his left ear. Most such wounds meant instant death, but Bierce had survived, much to everyone's, including his own, surprise. "We're a fine pair, aren't we?" he went on. "The lame and the halt. All we need is a blind man to lead us around. We could form a band, carry a flag, and beg for alms down on the avenue."

The two of them stood at the top of the steps and looked out over Washington City. Alex had lived in Washington, D.C., when he was fifteen years old. His father had accepted a job teaching at George Washington University and Alex had run wild over the city. His father soon grew tired of students who asked questions instead of listening in adoring silence, so they'd left after his one-year contract was over.

"Swampoodle? What the hell is Swampoodle?" Alex asked Bierce. "You said the creek took away the effluvia of Swampoodle."

Bierce gestured to their left to an area of ramshackle wooden houses. "It's where the soldiers go to be fleeced. There's gambling, saloons, and plenty of fallen women for entertainment. The city police stay clear of it most of the time. Personally, I'm drawn in that direction myself," Bierce said. He smiled at Alex. "A moth to the flame."

"I guess we'd better go in the other direction then," Alex

said. "You're not yet fit enough for such pleasures. Besides, our purpose is to look for a room to rent."

"All right. But once I regain my health," Bierce said, "it's Swampoodle for me. I never could resist the devil and his many interesting diversions. At least not for long."

Alex looked in the direction of Pennsylvania Avenue. Even though he had stood here as a young man, probably in this exact spot, more than a hundred years had changed the landscape until it was almost unrecognizable to him. In his time this building had become the National Portrait Gallery and was surrounded by other ornate government buildings, busy streets, and rows of businesses. Here, in this time, there was almost nothing that suggested what it would one day become.

On his left he could see the Capitol building with its just-completed dome gleaming in the bright sunlight. But it was a Capitol building oddly truncated compared with the one he was used to seeing, shorter on both sides. The grounds around the building were overgrown and scattered with workmen's sheds, piles of timber, and blocks of unused marble.

The only other structure of note was City Hall, another Greek revival building, looking just as it did in his own time. Except here it was surrounded by fields and scrub.

"If we're through being struck dumb by the scenery, I suggest we soldier on," Bierce said. They started down the steps. It was soon evident that Alex was going to need practice with his crutch before they could make much more than halting headway and that Bierce's sense of balance had been damaged by the invading bullet. They slowly reeled down the steps and reached the bottom, where they negotiated a ride in a horse-drawn ambulance that was headed back to the military camps across the river. It would haul them as far as Pennsylvania Avenue. Bierce looked at Alex with a critical eye.

"I believe we must relinquish our original mission. As much as I hate to defer to the wisdom of a woman, a woman nurse to boot, I fear that if our negotiation of the steps is any indicator, neither of us is up to moving to new quarters, at least not just yet. Perhaps we might consider this a reconnaissance mission to scout a new bivouac. With permanent relocation to come in the near future." Both of them had been told by the head nurse that it was too soon for the two of them to venture out on their own.

Alex's leg hurt with a deep, throbbing pain. He was sick of lying on his cot in the hospital, but he knew that Bierce was right. He nodded and set about trying to haul himself into the wagon.

Alex and Bierce sat in the back, hanging on to the sides, feet dangling as dust from the road powdered their legs.

The wagon made its way down Fifth Street, rattling along, jouncing from rut to rut. Flocks of geese waddled out of their way as pigs looked on from the sides of the road. Dirty children, some without shirts or shoes, played in dusty dooryards. The smell of rotting food and human waste grew worse, accompanied, and then overtaken, by the smell of manure. The streets became more populated as they moved south, and as the chief means of transportation was the horse, the sheer volume of horse waste rose to almost unbelievable proportions. The streets were paved with it, smashed flat and ground into the dirt. As the sun rose and heated the mess, the smell rose as well. Alex wondered when, or if, he would ever grow used to it. None of the people around them even seemed aware of this particular element in the overall stench.

It was a glorious fall day, the temperature rising easily into the low seventies. The two men felt the sun seeping into them, rejuvenating bodies grown pale and feeble after weeks spent lying indoors on cots. When they reached the intersection with

Pennsylvania Avenue the driver paused long enough for them to disembark.

They peered up the avenue. To their left was the stretch of land at the base of Capitol Hill, cluttered with builders' shacks and supplies, but to the right the avenue stretched westward toward, eventually, the White House, though it could not be seen from where they stood. The right-hand side of Pennsylvania Avenue was built up with three- or four-story buildings, many brick and in good shape, while the buildings on the left side were lower, mostly wooden, and run-down. They started off, up the avenue.

In the first block they passed a pie shop, a cracker shop, a drugstore, and a boardinghouse. As they went by the boardinghouse they heard a shouted "Hello!" from an upstairs window. They stopped, looking around to see who was being hailed.

The door to the house opened and Walt Whitman emerged, stuffing a large hat on his disheveled head.

"Uh-oh," Bierce whispered. "It's the poet. Anyone who sees us will think we're friends of his."

Whitman brought a newspaper to Alex every day at the hospital. For his part, Alex had endeared himself to Whitman by expressing his admiration for the man's poetry and being able to quote lines from *Leaves of Grass*. But the younger Bierce kept his distance from Whitman, still muttering on occasion about Whitman's indecency.

"Hello, hello," the poet said, hurrying up beside them. "What are you boys doing out? This is where I live." He gestured to the nondescript three-story boardinghouse.

"Actually, we're looking for a place ourselves, for when we get out of the hospital." Alex felt Bierce stiffen beside him.

"I wish I could recommend my house," Whitman said, "but the air here is much too pestiferous for convalescing boys."

"Absolutely," Bierce said. "Much too pestiferous. Why, I'd not make it through the first night in this despicable swamp."

"Farther up the avenue the air improves decidedly," Whitman said, gesturing up the street. "It's the canal down here and the creek that does the damage. I'll walk with you. I know all the boardinghouses and shopkeepers."

"I'm sure we can—" Bierce began.

"No, we'd be glad for your help," Alex interrupted. "Won't we, Ambrose?" Bierce managed a weak smile.

Whitman smiled in return and said, "Good, that's settled."

A hurrying man bumped into Alex, nearly knocking him off his crutch. "Check your pocketbook," Whitman advised. "That was probably a pocket artist." Alex didn't bother, as he didn't own a pocketbook. He kept his money, the few dollars he had removed from John Jordan's stash, rolled up in the front pocket of his pants.

They walked three abreast. "This is the St. Charles Hotel, very popular before the war with plantation owners and prosperous slave dealers," Whitman said, stopping in front of a hotel. "They were known for their slave pens in the basement." A doorman peered out at them suspiciously. "The owners are still waiting for the South to win. You boys couldn't afford it even if you could stomach their politics."

He moved on, pointing to a building on the next corner. "The National Hotel. That's a possibility. The rooms are small, but clean and reasonably priced. Also known for its Rebel sympathizers, but they're not as numerous as at the St. Charles." One-story white columns framed a small porch against the three-story brick building. They hobbled across the intersection under the wary eye of a dragoon in brilliant full-dress uniform atop a large bay horse. The dragoons were posted at almost every street corner. Their job was to arrest civilian speeders, usually hot-blooded young men on

high-strung horses, and direct traffic whenever an Army detachment marched through.

"Look there. We're in luck," Whitman whispered, gesturing at
the doorway of the National Hotel, where a well-dressed man
was standing, checking his pocket watch.

Alex felt a cold wash of fear flow over him. The man standing
on the doorstep was instantly recognizable, even at a distance.
John Wilkes Booth.

"It's the actor, Johnny Booth," Whitman said. "Though I'm told
he's called Wilkes by his friends. Many consider him the handsomest man in the entire city and maybe in all the Union. He lives
at the National when he's not onstage in some other city. I've seen
him on the streets quite a few times. I believe he enjoys going about
in public and creating a stir. Perhaps you could rent a room near his.
Wouldn't that be exciting?" Booth stepped off the hotel stoop and
turned toward them. Alex felt his heart thud in his chest.

Booth looked at Alex, who couldn't stop himself from staring at
the pale, Byronic actor. Booth nodded and walked on, used to the
stares of the crowd.

I could kill him right now, Alex thought. *Assassinate the assassin,
incapacitate him some way; I wouldn't even have to kill him, and it
would all be changed. Or would it?* He'd never answered the question. Whenever he'd tried to change events, the outcome always
seemed to remain the same.

Whitman turned back to them and pointed to a building in the
middle of the block.

"Brady's gallery," he said. "The finest portrait photographer in
the city. I've sat for him several times. Perhaps you gentlemen
would like to go in and schedule a portrait? Your loved ones at
home would certainly appreciate a photograph."

Bierce sneered. "My loved ones at home were perfectly satisfied to see the back of me. I have no doubt that any reminder of my existence would only pain them."

"Surely you can't mean your mother and father," Whitman said. "We always have the love of our parents."

Bierce looked even more disgusted. "Perhaps in your case," he said, "but not in mine. My whole town was glad to see me go. As I was to be gone." He shook his head and looked at the building in front of them. "But I do perceive that there is a perfectly fine saloon here on the ground floor of Brady's picture palace. I don't know about the rest of you, but this outing has engendered a powerful thirst in my person. I propose that we avail ourselves of beer and lunch."

A sign advertised Thompson's Saloon. Above it a mock-up of an oversized box camera built out of wood projected from the front of the second story of the building, announcing Brady's establishment.

"Surely you've a sweetheart somewhere, Lieutenant Jordan," Whitman went on. "Someone who would appreciate news of you in the form of a photograph."

"No," Alex said. "Not now." He looked at Whitman, who was watching him with interest. Alex could understand why the man was good at nursing the wounded, both mentally and physically. There was something in his sympathetic nature that called up confidences and confession. "There was someone," Alex said. "Her name was Molly Glenn. I've lost her for now, but I intend to find her again." He said Molly's name, aware of the pain it would cause him. The stab to his heart dwarfed the pain in his leg.

"Glenn. An Irish girl, from the sound of it," Whitman said. "Was she a seamstress? Or a schoolteacher? Many intelligent Irish girls are schoolteachers. And where is this fair lady now?"

Alex shook his head. "I don't know. The last time I saw her was in Japan. She was a journalist."

Whitman looked blankly at him.

"She wrote for newspapers. The *New York Times* in particular."

"I never heard of such a thing," Whitman said. "I myself write on occasion for that paper, though normally I appear in the *Brooklyn Eagle*. I never heard of a female doing so."

"Enough, enough," Bierce interrupted. "No more talk of sweethearts and family. At least on an empty stomach. I must have some of Mr. Thompson's viands. Those who wish to join me should stop their jabbering and follow along." Bierce pushed through the batwing doors of the saloon. Whitman and Alex followed.

They stopped in the dim interior, adjusting to the gloom and the cigar-smoke atmosphere. The restaurant was crowded, but they found a table in the back room.

"Oysters," Bierce said as they settled into their chairs. "And beer. That seems to be the specialty here. " A waiter with a dirty apron appeared at their side.

"We'll have beer," Bierce said, "and oysters, three dozen, and some of your lamb stew."

"Stew's gone," the waiter said. "I got oysters, bread, and cheese. Been soldiers in here since daybreak, drinking and driving everyone crazy. Supposed to be a rule against soldiers drinking, but you wouldn't know it."

"Bring us whatever you have," Whitman said. "Enough for our lunch." The waiter nodded and scribbled on a scrap of paper. Whitman placed a newspaper on the table. "This morning's *New York Times*."

Alex turned the paper around so it faced him. The paper was the size of a large tabloid of his time. The pages, eight of them, were thickly printed with differing sizes of type. There were no half-tone photographs or pictures.

The waiter set three mugs of beer on the table.

"Who's going to win the election? That's the question of the day," Whitman asked. "General McClellan or the president? The *Times* says it will be Lincoln. Who do you think will win, Mr. Bierce?"

Alex sipped at his beer. It was warm, but good. It had more body and flavor than most draft beers of his time.

"There was a day when Little Mac could have been the dictator of this country," Bierce said. "Three years ago, back when he was organizing the Army. But he never fought, never used the Army, frittered it all away while he waited for the odds always to be in his favor."

"I believe Lincoln characterized it as McClellan having the slows," Whitman said.

Bierce nodded. "Back then Lincoln was thought of as nothing much more than a cheap lawyer from the farm country. McClellan was a god. The savior of America. But not now."

"Are you interested in politics, Mr. Bierce? Most young men don't give it much thought," Whitman said.

Bierce drank his beer and appeared to think about the question. "I'm not sure 'interested' is exactly the right word. I usually think of politics as the conduct of public affairs for private profit. Though I suppose there are some in the profession who are not so dishonest."

While he was listening to Bierce and Whitman discussing politics, Alex was struck by a thought so obvious, but at the same time so encompassing, it almost took his breath away. These men did not *know* who would win the election. They didn't even know who would win the war. The newspapers didn't know; only he, Alex, knew. And he could use that knowledge for his own ends. This was not a new revelation, but thinking it now made him feel better. Maybe he could figure it out, given time, the *Why* and the *How*. Just maybe.

chapter nine

M OLLY SPENT THE afternoon canceling her travel plans and lying to her editor about her reasons for doing so. She was torn, first of all about the lying, but most importantly because she had no logical basis for the change, only the slim evidence of the strange photograph and the scrawled note.

On the way home from work she stopped at a drugstore and bought a pregnancy testing kit. She opened the box and read the instructions. Several times in her life she had resorted to one of these kits, and each of those times the results had been negative. Each of those times the results had brought intense relief. This time, she did not know what she wanted the test to tell her.

She put the mystery of the picture away for now and followed the test directions. Fifteen minutes later she knew she was pregnant.

She sat in Alex's chair in the living room, still holding the red-tipped test strip in her hand, and watched the late afternoon sunlight cut across the floor and move, imperceptibly, to the far wall and touch the baseboard before beginning to fade into evening. The light in the room became a soft, pearl gray. The furniture was reduced to dark bulky shadows before she stood up, threw the test strip away, changed out of her work clothes, and left the house.

Molly arrived at Tommy's apartment building, a tall, dirty, typical New York industrial structure on the edge of the Bowery, at seven o'clock. Inside, she rang the bell of his apartment and waited for him to eyeball her through the peephole, then snap open an array of locks.

Tommy popped the last lock and opened the dented heavy metal door, which appeared as if it had withstood a number of heavy assaults by thieves and drug addicts. He was wearing black pants, black shirt, and black sneakers. She had never seen him in clothing so informal, and realized, even accounting for the slimming effect of black, that Tommy wasn't so much fat as simply large, all over.

"Have any trouble on your way in?" he asked.

"You mean did any of the bums loitering on your stoop harass me? I told them I was here to see you and they parted like the Red Sea. Very impressive."

"They're not bad guys, they're just bums. We've coexisted for many years. Can I get you something to drink? I've got pretty much anything."

"Tanqueray martini with an olive," she said, then stopped herself. *You are pregnant.* "I just changed my mind. I'll have a glass of orange juice."

Tommy went behind the waist-high wall that divided the kitchen from the living area. The apartment was huge, a made-over industrial loft. The kitchen was partitioned off by a counter. Several barstools were on the living-room side. She watched him as he poured her orange juice and mixed himself a drink.

"What's for dinner?" she asked, aware that she was making small talk, knowing that soon enough they would be discussing matters large and probably difficult. She had made a decision on the way over in the cab: no more bullshit. She was going to tell Tommy the truth about Alex. About everything. If Tommy thought she was crazy, so be it.

"Tonight we will be having fresh soft-shelled crabs over crawfish étouffée, frozen French fries, fresh sugar snap peas, and a Romaine lettuce and hearts of palm salad with a Maytag blue cheese dressing."

"Yow. I haven't eaten like that since . . ."

"Alex left?"

She nodded as he came around the corner and handed her the orange juice.

Molly went to where Tommy was working and sat on one of the stools. He dusted the crabs with flour mixed with Old Bay Seasoning, then moved them off to the side. On the stove an old black cast-iron frying pan held sizzling onions.

"Do you want to talk about it?" he asked.

"It?"

"Alex. The picture. What it is that you said I wouldn't believe. I can think, talk, and cook all at the same time; I am a miracle man."

Molly sighed and sat up straighter, remembering her earlier decision: no bullshit. Tell him everything.

"Alex seems to be . . ." She stopped herself. "No. Alex *is*," she went on, her voice firm, "a time traveler. Literally. He has gone into, and returned from, the past, on three occasions that I know of. I have to assume that's where he is right now."

If Tommy hesitated, it was hard to tell. He turned to the refrigerator and retrieved a package of frozen French fries and a bowl of crawfish tails that he had already cleaned but not yet cooked. He turned the gas on under a skillet filmed with olive oil.

"This, obviously, is the part I'm supposed to have a hard time believing," he said, looking at her with a small smile. "I have to say, you were right about that. Tell me why you think Alex has this ability." He spread the French fries on a cookie sheet, put them in the oven, and gently placed the soft-shelled crabs in the hot oil in the skillet.

"Alex and I were a couple in college, then afterward we went our separate ways. I was married for a while, that didn't work out, and after my divorce I moved here to work at the *Times*. I

searched him out. Our original attraction was still there. If anything, the intervening years made it even stronger. I moved in
with him and not long after, he went back in time. He was gone
for a month, had traveled back to Russia, during the era of the
Russian Revolution."

"This is what he told you?"

"This is what I *saw!*" She put her hand to her forehead. "Sorry.
I didn't mean to shout. Here's what would happen: Alex would
literally disappear. Just sort of fade away. I saw it happen to him
on several occasions, though usually it occurred at night when
we were asleep. When he came back he would just appear,
though again it usually happened at night, and he'd be dressed in
other clothes, period clothing like in a play or movie. Sometimes
he was wounded, starving, or injured in other ways. Mentally as
well as physically. It took months for him to heal. Then when he
had, he would tell me about it. And as unbelievable as it sounded,
there was no other explanation that was as believable as the one
he gave. What's that Sherlock Holmes dictum about the solution
to a mystery?"

"You mean 'When you have eliminated the impossible, whatever remains, however improbable, must be the truth.' "

"That's the one. Can you give me a better explanation for what
I actually saw and what Alex told me?"

Tommy stirred the crawfish tails into the onions in the cast-
iron skillet while he thought. "Nope."

"I've never told anyone about this," she went on. "But now
with the picture, the story that the man who brought it to me told,
Alex being gone so long . . . I'm just not going to hide it anymore.
Not from you. I've got to tell someone. I need help. I'm . . ."

"You're what?"

"I'm pregnant. On top of everything else."

Tommy nodded and was quiet for a moment, not looking at her.

"Alex is the father," Molly added, giving Tommy a wry smile. "He hasn't been gone *that* long."

"I don't know what I can do to help you there, but I will if I can. Let's focus for now on the time travel. How many times has this happened?"

"Four times that I know of. Actually, he went to three historical periods and came back twice, though within each period he might come and go several times. Now he's gone again, so that makes it four."

"And what was his explanation?"

"Beyond just telling me what had happened? He didn't have one. I mean an explanation as in, 'Here's how this happens.' No science, no physics, not even magic. But he did say that his father could do it as well."

Tommy topped and tailed the fresh sugar snap peas and gave her a close look. "Well, if true, that would explain something about how the estimable Charles Ames Balfour achieved his precise historical detail in his novels, wouldn't it?" He dumped the snow peas into a pot of boiling water.

"Have you read his father's books?" Molly asked.

"Yes, I read them. The period detail was astounding. He deserved his success from that alone." He poured a cup of white wine into the crawfish mixture.

Molly inhaled as the fragrant wine steam wafted over her. "Alex always described his father as a real bastard. Alex said he met his father back in the past, in Russia, after his father was thought to be dead. And that he was an even bigger bastard than he had been when he was alive in this time. Their problems seemed to go beyond Alex simply being neglected. I believe he blamed his father for his mother's death."

Tommy turned the crabs over. They were a crisp, golden brown. "So Alex has no idea how or why this happens to him?"

"He has some ideas. What I said before was he had no *explanation*. As in a scientific explanation."

The timer on the stove dinged. "Why don't you sit down," Tommy said. "I'll bring the food."

Molly sat at the table. Tommy brought out the salad and the dressing and the bright green sugar snaps, then the French fries and the platter with the crawfish tails topped by the soft-shelled crabs. Molly inhaled the aromas from the food. Tommy sat down and poured himself a glass of wine. "I know, you're pregnant, you don't want any wine. I brought you a glass of water."

They ate and talked about food. When they had finished, Molly sat back and looked at the empty plates. "This was wonderful. Alex would have loved it."

Tommy got up and began removing plates. "Sit still," he said, "I'll get coffee. Continue your time travel story."

"There's not much more to say. The second time he went back it was to 1876. He ended up trying to stop George Armstrong Custer from fighting the battle of the Little Bighorn. I don't know where he is now. I'm afraid he's back there again. Stuck in the past."

Tommy was in the kitchen, pouring hot water through coffee in a Melitta filter. "What do you want me to do, Molly?" he asked quietly. He put the kettle of hot water back on the stove and leaned against the counter.

She looked down at her hands resting on the table. "I don't know." She looked back up at him. "No, that's not true. I do know. I want you to explain it to me. The whole *time* thing. I want you to tell me that everything will be all right, that Alex will come back, soon, that I'm not crazy. I want you to tell me what that picture means. I want to understand. I want knowledge, comfort, and reassuring words."

He put a coffeepot and two cups on the table. She gave him a half-smile.

"I'm not usually this needy," she said. "Do you believe me? About the time travel?" Tommy poured them each a cup of coffee.

"It's interesting," he began. "Time travel is suddenly quite a hot topic in the scientific community. For years no one would mention it for fear of sounding like a crank. That attitude changed a few years ago when Carl Sagan was writing his last book before he died, a science fiction novel that was made into the movie *Contact*. Sagan needed to have his female character travel a great distance across the universe. He was going to have her utilize a black hole for this, but he wasn't sure how to do it. So he asked his friend Kip Thorne, a physicist, for some help. Thorne thought about it, and said to send the character through a wormhole. But first you would have to *find* a wormhole, which can only exist on the quantum level, that is, the level of the very small. Then make it big enough to accommodate a person, which would require an incredible amount of energy, then you'd have to keep it open for a long enough time . . ." His voice trailed off as she shook her head.

"Sorry. I don't know what you're talking about," Molly said. She had decided to tell Tommy everything because he was the only person she knew whose general knowledge was so broad he might actually have some answers to the Why and How questions. And if she could answer those questions she could . . . what? She frowned, realizing she hadn't worked things out that far yet. *Try to summon Alex back from the past? Send out a search party?* She shook her head. "Anyway, Alex doesn't do any of that stuff. Doesn't sit in a weird chair with clocks on the arms, doesn't seal himself in a chamber and throw a big switch. No giant sparks of electricity. He just goes. Back."

Tommy pursed his lips and nodded. "All right, let's try it this way. There's another theory that posits an infinite series of parallel universes. If one could shift into another of these universes it would be possible to do so and find oneself in the past. Our past." He leaned forward. "Let me ask you a question: Does Alex change anything when he's back there?"

"That's the Grandfather Paradox, right? If I go back into the past and prevent my grandfather from marrying my grandmother, I will never be born, so how could I go back and keep him from marrying?

"Right."

"Alex says he's not sure. He thinks he may be able to change some things, but the outcome will always remain the same anyway." Tommy didn't say anything. Molly tried to figure out what Tommy was thinking. *He thinks I'm nuts, that's what he's thinking.*

"Maybe I should just go," she said, starting to stand up.

"No, no," he said, holding up his hand. "Allow me some time to get it all straight."

"But what do you really think? Is it all bullshit? Is there any indication that any of this is possible?"

"The truth is, I don't know. As far as the theoretical possibilities are concerned, they're certainly plausible."

"But do you believe *me*?"

"I know you, you wouldn't lie to me." He shrugged. "So there we are."

"Will you help me?"

"Of course I will. Let me think about what you've told me. I'd like to see the photograph again. I think we can get an even more precise answer as to its actual age. And I want a couple of researchers I know to look at the image of Lincoln to see if it's been taken from any other known photographs. Then there's the ink where someone has written 'Don't go to Japan.' Inks can reliably be typed as to age; the same lab that's testing the paper can do that as well. But mostly I need to think."

Molly stood up. "Good. Can you get me a cab?"

"Sure. I'll take you downstairs. That way I can formally introduce you to the guys who live in my vestibule. They're going to think you're my new girlfriend. Don't disabuse them of this notion; it's sure to increase my stock in the neighborhood."

Molly let herself into the house and turned on a floor lamp in the living room. She noticed the photograph, wrapped in newspaper, on the lamp table. She would take it to Tommy tomorrow. It wasn't even nine o'clock, but she was tired and sleepy. She lay down on the couch and closed her eyes. *Just for a moment,* she told herself.

She slept.

Alex Balfour lay in his hospital cot, sleeping. He was exhausted from his day of walking in the city, talking, eating, and drinking. He had fallen asleep within minutes of coming back to the hospital.

He awoke. His head was throbbing. He sat up. He recognized the feeling, he was going . . . somewhere. He looked at Bierce in the cot beside him. He thought that Bierce's eyes were open.

Then Alex was gone, away from the hospital.

He felt himself appear, in his living room in New York City.

Molly was asleep on the couch.

He was home.

. . .

The phone rang. The answering machine clicked on. Molly rolled over. Her eyes opened.

"Hello," Alex's recorded voice said. *"Neither Molly nor I are here. Please leave a message."*

At that exact moment, in another time, another universe, Molly Glenn was in Japan and died there. In this time, this universe, she did not die. She had not gone to Japan.

Alex took a step forward. Toward her. "Molly," he said. He felt his heart pounding. He could smell the scent of her, sleepy, sweet.

She looked at him, confused. She seemed to shimmer, for just a moment. She disappeared.

Alex stood, hand outstretched toward where she had just been sleeping.

No! Please.

He heard a voice on the telephone as it was being recorded by the answering machine.

"Molly, this is Tommy. It's just past eleven so you must be in bed. See me in the office first thing in the morning. I think I've figured part of it out. I think you're in danger. If the picture is real it means you are going to go back in time."

Alex turned toward the telephone. He felt the air tremble around him. He looked at a thin package wrapped in newsprint, lying on the lamp table. He picked it up. He was gone. The room was now empty.

The machine continued recording. *"It all has something to do with the trip to Japan, but I haven't figured that part out yet. See me in the morning! We've got to come up with some way to keep you from being taken back!"*

chapter ten

A LEX WOKE UP, saw the ornate metal-stamped ceiling of the hospital overhead, and felt an almost crushing sense of sadness. For a few minutes he had returned to his own time, had been about to wake Molly, then saw her vanish. Now he was back in the past again.

He remembered the thin package he had picked up in his living room. He sat up and found it lying near his feet. He glanced around the room and slipped the package under his bed and swung his legs over the edge of his cot.

Next to Alex, Bierce lay in his own cot, arms behind his head, gazing over at him with an expression of friendly interest. Reddish hair was beginning to grow back over his wound, hiding the pink puckered flesh at his temple.

Alex leaned forward slightly, not looking at Bierce, and tested his leg, putting weight on it. *Better. Time to leave here.* The leg test had become a habit, a morning ritual, performed every day after awakening.

"You know," Bierce said. "Last night. You disappeared. Where'd you go?"

Alex looked around. No one was paying any attention to them. He wanted to get the package out and open it, but he couldn't. Bierce would want to see what it was.

"What do you mean, disappeared?" He knew what Bierce meant, but he wanted to buy a moment's time.

"My mother, who imparted very little to me of sound advice, did say that a man who answers a question with another question was usually a man with something to hide." He waited a moment, then went on. "I was just lying here last night. I couldn't sleep. You sat up. You were looking down the room. I turned to see what you were looking at, saw nothing, looked back, and you were gone. Quiet, and as quick as a cat. I got up, walked to the end of the room, asked the nurse if she'd seen you, she said no, I came back, and there you were, lying in your bed. Seemingly asleep. The whole business couldn't have taken more than three or four minutes. Five at the most."

Alex stood up. "Maybe you were dreaming."

Bierce shook his head. "No."

"I can't explain it," Alex said, giving him a half-smile and shrugging.

Bierce stood. "I didn't imagine you would. Someday perhaps."

Alex didn't answer. Bierce seemed to accept that they weren't going to settle the question that stood between them, at least not this day. He looked around the room at the soldiers who were rising, those that could, and those that simply stirred in their cots. Someone down the row moaned.

"Are we leaving this place?" Bierce asked. "I believe the surgeons would be happy to see us go."

"Don't you have to go back to your division?"

"Eventually. I've been invalided home. Except that's the last place I wish to go. I had an understanding with a girl there, but that has turned out the way those things always turn out. Not that I've had much experience. A good, if simple, lesson: Never trust a female. Besides, no one expected me to live in the first place. The doctors say I'm not fit for combat, but I say I'm not fit to lie around in a bed that could be used more profitably by someone else. I can take as much time as I want. One of those rooms at the National Hotel looks good to me as a base for convalescence. But don't you have to report back yourself?"

Alex pulled his meager possessions from beneath the bed. They weren't even his; they belonged to a dead man. "I'm in pretty much the same position you are. Not fit to fight, too fit to lie around in bed. Washington City seems a good place to observe this war. And the National seems better than . . ." The moan from down the row came again, louder.

"Better than a hospital," Bierce said, finishing Alex's sentence. "Better than a tent. Better than a hole in the ground with rain pouring on your head."

Alex nodded. "For the moment at any rate. There's another thing. I have something I need to do, a debt to pay. A mystery to solve."

"It doesn't surprise me. You've got the smell of a mystery about you almost as noticeable as that coming up out of the canal." Alex frowned. "Sorry," Bierce laughed. "Bad example. Anyway, I'd be glad to go along, if you could stand the company. Most men bore me. There are enough questions swirling around you to keep what's left of my brain occupied. And there's the matter of money. I've sufficient to keep me, but a sharing of expenses will make it last even longer. I'll chance it if you will; we may be of some help to each other." He held out his hand. Alex shook it.

"I'm going to visit the jakes," Bierce said. "Then let's clean up and furlough out of here." He turned and walked away.

Alex waited till he saw the other man go through the huge doorway at the end of the room. Then he was on his hands and knees, searching for the package. He retrieved it and sat back on the cot, taking another look around, feeling guilty, nervous, and afraid. He pulled the tape loose and unwrapped the package. He opened the envelope and slid out the contents.

One small picture, mounted on stiff cardboard. A picture of Molly. With Abraham Lincoln.

He felt the room turn around him, shift, spin, lurch. He looked away from the image. The world stopped, and held. He looked back. There were words written across the picture: *Don't go to Japan.* He stared at the words and recognized Molly's handwriting.

She was alive. She had been here. Or maybe she was going to be here in this time. Or she might be here now.

A nurse walked by and smiled at him. She probably assumed that the wounded man was looking at a photograph of a loved one. She was right.

Alex turned the photograph over. The lettering was ornate: *Mathew Brady.* Walt Whitman had shown them Brady's studio. It was hard to miss with the giant camera as his sign. That was where he would begin his search.

Alex put the photograph back into the envelope, then thought for a moment. This was valuable, too valuable to leave where it could easily be found. He picked up his standard U.S. Army–issue knapsack. Bierce carried one just like it. He examined one of the seams, found a loose thread, and pulled the double layer of canvas apart. He picked at the strings and got the opening between the two layers wide enough, then slid the picture inside.

"What are you doing?" Bierce asked, coming up behind him.

Alex felt his heart pounding. He hadn't heard Bierce come back. "Uh, just fixing my knapsack. Do you have a needle and thread?"

"Yes. I'll get it. You wouldn't want your pack to fall apart. You might lose something valuable." Bierce went to his cot and pulled out his pack from underneath. Alex quickly folded the newspaper that the picture had been wrapped in and stuck it under his pillow. As soon as he was dressed he would transfer it to his pants pocket.

By midafternoon they had taken a room at the National Hotel. It was approximately ten feet by twelve feet and held two single beds with horsehair mattresses, a washstand, and a wardrobe for them to share. At Thompson's Saloon they ate corned beef, which Bierce said was probably horse, and a vegetable called cabbage, which it undoubtedly was as the establishment positively reeked of it. Both men drank beer. The two rooms of the tavern were crowded.

Alex told Bierce the story of his wounding, the mystery of the boy who saved him at least twice, and the murder of the boy's friend.

"Could you not go to your unit and see if anyone among them had seen anything that would help?"

No, I could not. I have no unit. "I saw no one I recognized after I was wounded. I had only recently transferred, and knew almost none of the men."

"You need to find what other elements were on the field that day. You could begin in the office of some clerk or paymaster and dig that particular mine until you were lucky or went insane. Or you might go to the top man and enlist his aid. That would be my preference, were it me who was set on this particular mission."

"And who would be the top man, in your opinion? And why would he consent to meet with . . . a lowly lieutenant?"

"I'd go to the president of the United States. He's the commander in chief of the Army, isn't he?"

Alex laughed. "Yes, I suppose he is, but he wasn't anywhere around when I got shot." He noticed Bierce wasn't smiling.

"Of course he wasn't. But he'll know where to send you to find your answer." Bierce still wasn't smiling.

"Are you serious? Why would the president deign to see a lowly soldier like me?" Alex asked. The thought of meeting Lincoln thrilled and frightened him at the same time. Of all the men in history, Alex felt that Lincoln was the most important. His original mind, courage, intellect, and humor made him a man for not just this age, but all ages.

"It's well known Lincoln makes himself available to the general public, of which you are one, for an hour or so every day. Why shouldn't he? He's a public official. I would suggest that this is simply the price of democracy. These people, even the president, are hardly royalty. Just walk up the street past Jay Cooke's new bank and you're at the President's House."

Alex mopped up the last of his corned beef in the cabbage juice and considered Bierce's suggestion. *Was it really possible to just walk in and ask to see Abraham Lincoln?* "You said Jay Cooke's bank. You mean, of course, the financier."

"That's right. Jay's sold more than five hundred million dollars' worth of war bonds, or so it says in the papers. This country ran out of war money years ago. They say if it wasn't for Cooke, we'd have gone under by now."

"I wonder if it's as easy to get in to see Jay Cooke as it is to see the president?"

"I wouldn't guess so. The president serves the people, or at least that's how I understand the theory. Jay Cooke serves no one, except perhaps his god, if he has one."

Their waiter scrawled a number on their bill and tossed the torn paper on their table. Alex looked at it and saw that they'd drunk and eaten a twenty-five-dollar lunch and here it had cost them each a bit more than fifty cents. But even at these prices he would eventually run out of the dead lieutenant's money. *Time to go see Jay Cooke?*

Outside the restaurant, Alex walked next door to the entrance to Mathew Brady's walk-up studio. The first place to start looking for Molly was in the studio of the man who had taken the picture of her with Lincoln. Of course, it was certainly possible that Brady hadn't taken the picture yet. As long as Lincoln was alive this would be a possibility. There was a handwritten notice tacked to the door: *OUT OF TOWN*. It was signed by Brady. Bierce walked up beside Alex.

"Going to have a photograph made?" Bierce asked.

"Um . . . no, yes, well, possibly."

Bierce laughed at Alex. "He may have returned from out of town by the time you make up your mind. You might try Alexander Gardner, I've read he's good. I'm not sure I'd trust Brady."

"What's trust got to do with it?"

"I saw him at work on the battlefield several times. After the fighting was over. He and his assistants were arranging the dead."

Bierce tried the door to Brady's. It was locked. He bent close and examined Brady's handwritten note as he continued speaking. "One day the burial crews were out, with Brady right in front. I saw him set up his camera over a dead Rebel sharpshooter. He moved the man's arms and legs around until he had what he must have considered a pleasing composition. Brady put the musket he had brought with him on the man's breast as if it had belonged to the sharpshooter. Then he produced a severed hand—God knows where he'd picked it up—and laid it beside the body. For visual interest, I suppose." Bierce turned to Alex with a broad smile.

"There's an idea," he went on. "If you have him make your photograph, ask if he still has the hand. Might make a very interesting composition."

chapter eleven

N IGHT. MOLLY HIT the ground from about two feet up, just the height of the couch she had fallen asleep on. She landed not on the oak floor or Oriental carpet of Alex's living room, but on hard dirt that knocked her awake. For a moment she stared, uncomprehending, into the packed earth and dry grass beneath her face. She rolled over.

She shivered, looked up and saw stars, and heard a stream of water. A mosquito whined in her ear.

"By Jesus," a rough voice growled from somewhere behind her. "Who's down there? Can't a man piss without someone pesterin' him?"

Molly sat up. A full moon washed the night with a thin pale light. She was on the bank of a small, foul-smelling stream, no more than five feet wide. A dirt path ran beside the water. The voice came from a man standing on a wooden bridge no more than three feet above her. Looking under the bridge and behind the man she could make out lights burning on a street, and low houses. Men and horses seemed to be moving on the street. *Horses?* She could hear shouting in the distance. Laughter.

Horses?

"Who the hell are you and where in hell did you come from!" the man demanded. "I've got a mind to come down there and dust you good if you don't give out an answer. By God." He fumbled with the buttons on the fly of his trousers.

Molly stood up, unsteadily, and wondered if she should run. The man stomped off the bridge and down the bank toward her.

He stopped and peered down at her. She backed up. He stank of dirt, sweat, and whiskey.

"Be goddamned. What the hell are you?" He reached out and pinched her arm, hard. "Be damned. You a woman? Dressed up in britches?"

"Keep your hands off me."

He stood up straight. "Well, I'll be. It talks. Talks sass, too." He appraised her. He was tall and gaunt with a sharp, hawklike face with biblical-length whiskers. He was wearing a straw hat and a long overcoat. "I get you in the light, I figure you're goin' turn out lookin' fine. I don't give a damn what you're wearin'. Maybe won't be wearin' it long anyway. What manner of soiled dove are you?"

"Touch me again and I'll break your arm."

He laughed, stepped down the bank, and reached for her. "Godamighty. Come here, sweetpie."

Molly grabbed his outstretched hand, whirled, and threw him over her back and into the creek. The man landed with a splash. He sat for a minute and said again, quieter this time, "Godamighty. Gonna fuck you good for that one." He started to stand, was halfway up, when she kicked him with the side of her sneakered foot just under the chin. His head snapped back and slammed into a brace that tied the bridge to a short piling. Slowly he slumped forward into the shallow water.

Molly stood, breathing heavily, more from fear than exertion, and watched for movement, ready to kick him again. When he didn't move she bent down. His face was underwater. Bubbles trickled from his nose. She could smell the sewer odor that came from the creek. She slapped at a mosquito that bit her on the neck. She considered the situation for a moment, then reached down and grabbed the man by the collar and pulled him out of the water.

Her heart was pounding. *Two long years in a self-defense class at the YWCA just paid off,* she thought. *I should let him drown.* She dragged him farther up the bank and rolled him on his back so she could get a better look. She glanced around to see if anyone was watching, but they seemed to be completely alone, hidden from the movement and noise on the street.

The man's straw hat had come off and was lying beside him. His hair was tangled and matched the generally filthy condition of his wet beard. He was wearing thick denim pants with suspenders, an old work shirt, and square-toed boots.

Molly breathed deeply, trying to slow her heart and the fluttery feeling of fear in her stomach. She walked quickly up the dirt path toward the street and moved into the shadow beside a rough-hewn, one-story wooden house. She inched to the end of the building, staying in deep shadow, and looked out.

It's a dream. A nightmare, she thought. But she knew it wasn't. She knew what had happened.

To her left the road meandered off through dark fields of low scrub. To her right it was flanked by other rough houses like the one she was pressed against. The scene resembled an old engraving, one found perhaps in a book warning of the perils of evil. Large iron drums blazed with leaping flames as men, the majority in uniform, walked and staggered along the wayside, shouting and laughing. Women stood on the porches of the houses and called to the men, many of whom were drinking from bottles. Horses tied to hitching posts stood patiently. The sound of breaking glass punctuated a dribble of music from an out-of-tune piano that floated in the still air—which smelled of smoke, dust, horse manure, and sewage. She leaned back against the house and felt the splintery boards against her back.

She hurried back to the man on the stream bank, now snoring, having passed seamlessly from unconsciousness into sleep, and forced herself to go through the pockets of his filthy pants. There were two dollars in paper money, a button, and a plug of tobacco. She put the money in her pocket, threw down the tobacco and the button, and picked up his hat. With a feeling of revulsion she tucked her hair up into the sweaty hat and pulled it far down on her head. The man rolled back and forth as she pulled the overcoat off him. It was wet, but it would dry. "You deserve worse," she said quietly to the downed man.

She went back to the shadow beside the house and looked out onto the street. All the action was to her right, the road to her left, empty. Stepping out onto the dirt track, she walked quickly away from the scene behind her.

Lights twinkled in the distance. Her mind went back to the moment at home when the phone had awakened her, when for just a second she had seen Alex, or thought she had seen Alex. He had long tangled hair and was dressed all in white, some sort of pajamas. He had stood silent, spiritlike, then had spoken her name. She would have thought it was a vision, a trick of her mind and desire, except that she had seen in his eyes the same longing that she felt within herself. He had reached for her. *It was no vision. It was real. He is alive. I will find him.*

The night, once away from the scene behind her, was silent. No sounds of traffic, no jetliners traversing the sky overhead, only the slight pad of her Nikes on the dirt road.

chapter twelve

MOLLY TRIED TO guess what time it must be. The moon was high in the sky, which meant nothing to her. If it was the sun, it would have been around one o'clock, she thought, but she had no idea if the moon followed the same general rules as the sun.

She stopped walking. In the distance she heard hoofbeats. She jumped over a low ditch at the side of the road and crouched down behind a row of bushes. Mosquitoes whined around her face.

Two horsemen trotted by, soldiers wearing long overcoats. As soon as they had disappeared into the dark she was back on the road, slapping at the mosquitoes. She could feel the bites on her hands and face itching and beginning to swell. She moved on toward the flickering lights, which she now saw were widely spaced rows of gas streetlights.

She understood she was in the past, and there was nothing she could do about it but try to stay alive.

Horses. No electricity. Urban gaslight. Before the late 1870s, but probably later than 1850. Soldiers. Lots of soldiers. She thought of the men she had seen in the street. *Blue uniforms. Civil War, 1861 to 1865. Temperature too cool for the Deep South, which means I'm in the Mideast or the North. A city. Small towns wouldn't yet have extensive lighting systems.*

She was passing a row of wooden houses with no lights showing in the windows.

A dog rushed her, a medium-sized, light-coated, barking, frenzied dog. She had time to turn to the side as it leapt. It hit the heavy overcoat. She felt the jaws searching for purchase as it clawed from her hip down her leg. She turned and kicked out, knocking it away from her. She tried to run but the coat slowed her, and she felt teeth sink deep into her ankle. She fell down, rolled and kicked again, heard a yelp and felt the jaws open, releasing her. She stumbled to her feet and ran, hearing the dog panting behind as he chased her. A light came on in a house, and a man called out the front door. The dog stopped. She ran on.

She ran until a stitch in her side slowed her to a walk. She found she was crying, and made herself stop. She wiped her nose on her sleeve. Her ankle hurt. She could feel that it was wet, stopped to look, and saw dark blood running down into her sneaker. She touched her cheek and found more blood from a scrape incurred when she fell down. She walked on, limping.

The houses were bigger now, some three stories high, and solidly built. She was obviously in a more affluent part of town. In the dim light from the moon and a nearby gaslight she saw a narrow street sign on the side of a building. She crept close until she could read it, afraid to get too close for fear of another dog. The sign read: C STREET. She walked around the corner and looked at the other side of the building. N. CAPITOL STREET.

I know where I am.

She turned to her left and saw it, dimly, the white dome of the Capitol, right where she knew it would be, three blocks away. *Washington, D.C., 1861 to 1865 or 1866. There could still be soldiers even if the war is over.* She thought furiously, wishing she had paid more attention in any one of a number of American history classes she had taken over the years from grade school to college. She had been in Washington recently to interview a congressman and had probably driven past where she was standing at this moment.

A light on the street was moving toward her. She shrank behind a small tree in a dark front yard. The light came closer and she could see it was a man on foot, carrying a lantern. She moved far-ther back into the shadow of the house. Another light came from the opposite direction. Molly watched while the two men with lanterns stood on the corner, talking.

Policemen. A double row of shiny buttons on their long coats winked in the light. She sank down and sat in the wet grass and leaned against the building, tired, afraid, and hurt. A longing rose in her to go to the policemen and simply ask for help. To be taken someplace dry, and warm, where she could eat and sleep. *Jail,* she thought. *That's where they'll take me.*

She had no identification and was dressed, to these people, like a man. There was a war on. Telling the truth was out; if she did they'd put her in an asylum, which would be far worse than being put in jail. There may be a time to ask for help from the authori-ties, but this was not yet it. *What would Alex do?* A moment's insane laughter bubbled up as she thought about T-shirts from her own time, emblazoned with the letters WWJD—What Would Jesus Do? She didn't have the slightest idea what either Jesus or Alex would do. What she did know was that she was too tired to go any farther this night. She got to her feet and slipped along beside the house toward the rear. In the backyard there was a small building that seemed in the dark to be shaped like a Japanese pavilion. She took a deep breath, quietly tried the door, and stepped inside.

A trickle of starlight from the outside came in through two small windows and revealed a single room with a bed. There was an unlit lamp on a small table, and a series of empty shelves on one wall. She went to the bed and sat. A thick mattress rustled and sank beneath her.

She put her feet up and gathered the old coat around her. The bed smelled of perfume, the coat stank of sweat. She slept.

·　·　·

The voice was shrill, frightened. "Carter! Carter! Come quick! Someone in the teahouse!"

Molly sat up. The door was open. Light streamed in through the two windows. She had slept the night through.

"Now he sittin' up!"

Molly could see the face of a young black woman who was standing back from the now open door, but peering in at her. Molly, still half asleep, swung her feet over the side of the bed. She felt guilty that she had put her dirty shoes on the bedcover. A door outside slammed.

A tall black man carrying an ax handle sidled into the room. "All right, get on up. What you got to say for yourself? Breaking and entering, that's what. Dixie, tell Miss Ann to call out for the marshals. I'll hold this man right here."

"No, wait. I didn't break anything. The door was open."

The man was staring at her thick red hair. "Dixie, tell Miss Ann she'd better come out here herself. You're not going anywhere, mister. Miss."

Molly stayed on the bed and Carter waited by the door until Miss Ann, a tall, dark-haired woman dressed in a formal green silk dress with bustle and wide hoops made her appearance. She had to maneuver the bottom of the dress to fit through the door. Molly stood up.

"Well, what have we here?" Miss Ann asked.

"I'm sorry," Molly answered. "The door wasn't locked, and I was tired. I hurt my foot." She shrugged. "I'm sorry. I'll go."

Miss Ann looked at Carter, then Dixie, standing outside the door. "You two may leave. I think I can handle . . . What is your name, child?"

"Molly."

"Molly and I will talk. Everything is fine. Tell Angie to put out something for breakfast." She looked down at Molly's shoe, brown with dried blood from the dog bite, at her scraped face, and the red mosquito welts. "Put water on to heat for a bath and get out the muslin bandages."

Breakfast was bread toasted over an open fire in the kitchen, with marmalade, and hot coffee. After which Molly was led to a sumptuous bedroom in the back of the house, where she bathed in a large ornately stamped tin bathtub that had been filled with hot water by Carter. She was attended throughout by Dixie, the young black woman who discovered her. The house itself seemed to go on and on around them, decorated in what Molly assumed was a heavy Victorian style, everything cloth-covered with ruffles, the walls painted deep reds and greens, gilt-framed pictures of landscapes hung to the ceiling, all of it creating a plush, muffled atmosphere that seemed to be waiting for something to come in and shake it awake. The contrasting odors of stale cigar smoke and perfume hovered everywhere.

The tub was emptied and removed, and she was given a dressing gown and slippers to wear while her clothes were taken away to be cleaned. She was sitting on a velvet claw-footed love seat, when Miss Ann appeared, carrying a roll of white cloth and a pair of scissors.

"I hope you didn't mind my suggestion of a bath."

"It was wonderful."

"I insist on a weekly bath, though some of the girls resist. Several of them had never had a bath in their lives before they began working here. My mother was no different, discoursing to the end of her life on the unhealthful properties of bathing. She and my father had never bathed, and were quite proud of it. Now let me see your foot."

"It's all right. There's no bleeding. I hope I didn't get blood on your bed last night."

"Don't worry yourself. It wouldn't be the first time." She drew up an ottoman and sat at Molly's feet. She gently picked up her right foot and inspected the two small puncture wounds. "I'll just wrap it." She began gently wrapping the white muslin around the ankle and under the arch of the foot. "My name is Ann Benton," she said. "Perhaps you've heard of me. If you wished an appointment, you could have simply rung the bell."

Molly had no idea who the woman was. Or why she might have wanted an appointment with her. Or why she, Ann, was being so nice to her. "I'm Molly Glenn, and I'm from out of town," she said. It sounded weak, but at least was the truth. *Very far out of town.*

"I assumed as much from your outfit. Can you tell me why you were dressed as a man? Are you one of those ladies who dresses as a soldier to follow the troops? We hear of them from time to time." She finished the bandage by tucking the loose end in at the top.

"Thank you. For fixing my foot." Molly gestured at the dressing gown. "And for the breakfast and the bath. All of it. I've come down from New York. I felt that it would be less dangerous if I were dressed the way I was. A woman traveling alone, you know."

"Was there trouble in Baltimore? There's always trouble there. No matter how many troops are stationed in that city, travelers are always harassed by the toughs."

"I don't know how I can repay you, I don't have much money."

"Don't worry about that; we'll think of something."

"Oh, excuse me." A pretty blonde woman with tousled hair looked in on them. "I didn't know we had visitors."

"It's quite all right, Clara. This is Molly. She arrived late last night. You probably want your bath?"

Clara nodded at Molly, who smiled back. "Yes, ma'am," Clara said.

"I'll tell Carter to take the bath to the upstairs back bedroom. The other girls can use it there as well, when they arise. Will you excuse me for a moment," she said as she swept out of the room. Clara stepped in and smiled at Molly.

"Are you one of the new girls? I know Miss Benton said she had been looking since Martha had to leave us. You're sure pretty."

"Well . . ."

"We could have used you last night. I swear I was worn to a frazzle. Miss Benton says that election times are always that way, all the men so excited about what the results are gonna be. Of course I want Lincoln to win, but General McClellan is so handsome, don't you agree?"

"Well . . ."

"We used to see him everywhere, dashing hither and yon on that great brute of a horse, in his resplendent uniform with his boots so shiny." She pretended to fan herself. "It was all quite too much. Any man would have been proud to serve under him, and any girl as well, I might add." She giggled. "Not that he would ever have taken his pleasures in that manner, not one with half so pretty a wife. Have you ever seen her?"

"No . . ."

"Pity, such a tiny woman. He's referred to as our Napoleon, you know, and quite an apt description it is, I might add. . . ."

Ann Benton came back into the room. "I see Clara has been keeping you entertained. She's quite the talker, very much in demand with our gentlemen. Carter is seeing to your bath, dear; you can go right on up."

"So nice talking to you," Clara said, extending her hand to Molly. "I'm sure you're going to be very happy here." She and Molly shook fingers and Clara left. Miss Benton regarded Molly with a small smile.

"You two seemed to be getting along famously. And Clara seems to think you are joining us. I hadn't yet broached the subject, but I think it's a splendid idea."

Molly felt herself blushing. She felt like a dolt, should have seen it coming. Perhaps not. She hadn't had much experience with nineteenth-century bordellos. She didn't even know how to react to the offer.

"By your quite charming blush and your silence I presume the idea does not meet with your approval."

Molly studied her hands. "Actually, I'm quite flattered. The possibility hadn't occurred to me."

"Do you disapprove, Miss Glenn? Many find our occupation, and even our presence, odious. At least in public they do. In private, it can be quite another matter."

"No, I don't disapprove. It really has nothing to do with how I feel. I can certainly see it as a reasonable opportunity. Not for me, but for other women."

Ann Benton sighed and sat down. She arranged her dress around her. "I wish everyone had your enlightened attitude. There are hundreds, and I am not exaggerating, of sporting establishments in this town, hundreds, of every stripe imaginable. We fancy ourselves a cut above here, but still, many, if not most, are respectable houses. The town is filled with men from all over the country, not only judges, legislators, and soldiers, but honest businessmen as well. And where are they to go for relaxation? Where are they to find the pleasures of hearth and home? In their mean little bed-sitting-rooms? In the public rooms at Willard's Hotel? No, of course not. They come here, and happy they are to find us, and happy they are when they leave. I feel we provide not just a necessary service but a patriotic one as well." She stopped and looked at Molly. "Oh my, that was a speech, wasn't it?"

Molly laughed. "I like a woman who's passionate about her work." Ann laughed along with her.

"Oh my, Molly, I like you. We must find something for you to do around here. Perhaps you will warm to the idea of joining the rest of the girls in earning a very comfortable living. One thing that I have learned in this business is to never predict the future."

Carter, the tall black man, entered, carrying a small pile of clothes. "Excuse me, Miss Ann, but Miss Molly's clothes have been washed and dried. Where shall I put them?"

"Anywhere is fine. Thank you, Carter." He nodded, put the clothes on a side table, and withdrew.

"And now, Molly, what are we to do about your clothing? Surely you don't intend to continue going about dressed as a man."

"Don't *any* women wear men's clothing, as you refer to it? Pants? Bloomers? Pantaloons? Whatever they would be called?"

"You really are quite amusing, Molly. The idea of wearing pantaloons in public. It's all much too scandalous. And I haven't heard of anyone wearing bloomers in ten years or more. Even Mrs. Bloomer has renounced them."

"But pants *are* more comfortable."

"They well might be. And just between the two of us, I have worn men's clothing. Briefly. In my earlier years, before I rose to become the proprietor of an establishment, certain men would require their partners to don men's clothing. Not often, but occasionally. I can assure you I was more than happy to get back to feminine attire." She smiled. "Or out of it, as the case may be. But none of this answers the original question: What are you going to wear? You cannot wear men's clothes; it is impossible."

Molly knew she was correct. It wasn't simply a matter of women's rights, the option did not exist in the 1860s.

"I guess I'll wear a dress. Can I borrow one? Something not so fancy? Just one or two layers?"

Ann Benton stood up. "Good. I have just the thing. This will be fun."

chapter thirteen

M OLLY, WEARING THE robe she had been given, stood in a circle of five giggling girls. Ann Benton watched from a love seat to the side. Clara, whom Molly had already met, had been joined by Alice, Blanche, Marie and Grace.

Ann Benton prided herself on a wide selection of girls. The talkative Clara was blonde, busty, and Nordic, while Alice was a thin, no-nonsense, midwestern type. Blanche offered plain-spoken farm girl solace, in contrast with Marie, an exotic octoroon from New Orleans. Grace was just that—willowy and intelligent, with long silky hair and a honeyed voice. All five wore silk robes in different colors. Blanche had brought one of her dresses, a light green off-the-shoulder low-neckline gown, with a wide hoop at the bottom, for Molly to try on.

"I've been searching for an Irish lass to round out our little coterie," Ann said. "Are you sure you won't change your mind, Molly?"

"I know *I* once said I'd never be a sporting girl," Grace said, studying Molly's full red hair, "but circumstances have a way of altering the best-laid plans. So to speak."

"I don't think anyone plans on this life," Blanche said matter-of-factly. "But I've seen a lot worse. Miss Ann looks after me better than my momma ever did."

Marie went to a pile of clothing. Her skin was the color of honey and she moved with a slow elegance. "I see we are dressing Miss Glenn from the skin out." Her words were slow and inflected with the South. "Let us begin."

Clara, standing behind her, lifted the robe off Molly's shoulders and pulled it away. Molly stood in her bra and panties.

I don't believe this, she thought.

"Oooo," Blanche said. "What in the world is that?" She stretched out a tentative finger and touched Molly's bra strap.

Ann stood up and came over for a closer look. "And what manner of drawers are these? Are they French?"

Molly felt herself blushing. "They are perfectly ordinary," she said. Ann walked around her, appraising.

"Not in my establishment they're not. My dear girl, please explain your perfectly beautiful self and these wonderful undergarments. It's a sort of corset, isn't it?"

"It's an inexpensive white Bali brassiere that I bought at a two-for-one sale. The panties came in a plastic three-pack tube."

"Panties," Grace said. "A diminutive of pantaloons, I would say. Brassiere. You were right, Miss Ann, they are definitely French. But what on earth is a . . . what did you say? . . . something tube?"

Molly realized that she was going to have to be more careful with her off-hand remarks. "It's just a polite phrase for undergarments where I come from."

Marie held up a chemise and a corset. "You're going to have to

take off your top, your *brassiere*"—she gave it a French inflection—
"if we're going to get these on you."

When Molly hesitated, Ann said, "Don't be shy, my dear, you
are in the company of professionals."

Molly unsnapped the bra and dropped it. A blush spread across
her face.

"I know five members of the Lincoln Administration who
would pay a hundred dollars each to see that blush," Ann said. She
took the chemise from Marie and held it up. "I think we'll do
away with the chemise for now. The neckline on the dress is too
low, the lace will show, and really, why cover up such a charming
display? The corset, please." The corset hooked up the front and
laced in the back. Ann held it in place while Blanche gathered up
the laces and began to tighten them.

"How do you ever get dressed without help?" Molly asked.

"We don't." They maneuvered the corset just beneath Molly's
nipples and began pulling it tight. It took three full minutes to get
it tied up.

"How can you stand it? I can't breathe!"

"Loosen it a bit, Blanche. For now."

"I spent several years hauling a plow on my daddy's farm after the
mule died," Blanche said. "Not being able to breathe seemed like a
pretty fair exchange to me the first time I put one of these on."

"Step over here, Molly," Ann said. "I've laid out your hoops."
Blanche led her to where Ann stood before five concentric iron
rings, each smaller than the other. The largest was five feet in
diameter, the smallest two feet. They were connected by pink
silk ribbons. Molly stepped into the circle.

"You'll want to take off those little drawers while you can,"
Clara said. "My goodness, they're not even open at the seam.
How do you manage?"

"Wait a minute," Molly said. "You mean you're naked underneath these things?" The girls all looked at each other.

"Of course. Why on earth wouldn't you be?" Marie asked.

"Is everybody?" Molly asked. "I mean, not just, not just . . ."

"Fancy girls?" Ann asked.

"Soiled doves?" Marie drawled.

"Sportin' women?" Blanche asked.

"Fallen ladies?" Clara trilled, pretending to faint onto the love seat. They all laughed at Molly's embarrassment.

"For someone who wears men's clothing you certainly are possessed of delicate sensibilities," Ann said. "We wear drawers only in the coldest of circumstances, and certainly nothing like yours. How do you relieve yourself with the center closed? Our drawers go on one leg at a time and tie around the waist, and are quite open. Once inside the hoops, you cannot lift your dress to pull down anything you are wearing underneath. Yes, you are as naked as when you were born, beneath the hoop. Which is why a woman who slips and falls becomes a serious social disaster. First, it is almost impossible to get back up unaided, and more importantly because of the hoops you are completely exposed for every man to observe. And rest assured there will be no averting of eyes, no matter what a gentleman may profess." She lifted the top hoop by a pair of shoulder straps and slipped them over Molly's arms. The other hoops followed, forming a bell shape. "You may retain your little drawers if you like. We certainly have no wish to embarrass you further."

Marie brought two petticoats and slipped them over Molly's head. They tied at the waist and swept the ground. Then the heavy silk dress was drawn on and situated correctly after many minute adjustments. They led her to a full-length mirror.

Molly gasped. Even as a young girl she had never played dress-up.

She had disdained high school dances and proms in favor of foreign films and intellectual discussions. In college she was strictly a jeans and late-night bull sessions student. Later, when she'd gone out into the real world, she would dress up when she had to, but power suits and a simple black cocktail dress on occasion were what she considered her style, when she even stopped to consider it at all.

This, though, was on a whole new level.

"Very, very, nice," Ann said. "We'll have Dixie do your hair, and then I think we'll have just the sort of effect we were looking for. Our gentlemen are in for quite a pleasant surprise this evening."

Molly didn't hear her. Her entire attention was focused on the green-silk-wrapped person before her in the mirror. Her waist was pinched into an hourglass shape that thrust her bared breasts up above the neckline of the gown. The corset and dress-top neckline allowed just a hint of nipple. She turned to the side and the movement sent the belled hoops in a graceful turn.

"What did you say?" she asked. She couldn't take her eyes off the image in the mirror.

"We'll discuss it later, dear," Ann said, with a small smile.

The men smelled of cigars, perfume, hair pomade, sweat, and whiskey. It was a curious mixture, the offensive attempting to hide beneath the pleasant. And failing. Molly wondered if she was the only one who noticed the odors.

Why did I let them talk me into this?

Actually, she knew why. She possessed nothing of any value, knew no one, and had no way, at least not yet, of staying alive economically in this time. These people, especially Ann Benton, had been gracious and generous to her. She understood that much of

Ann's motivation was based on her wish to have her join the ranks of her girls and actively participate in the business of prostitution. Since she certainly wasn't going to do that, she had to offer something else in return.

The least I can do is sit here and look like a porcelain doll, smile, and make pleasant conversation.

That had been the deal: Wear the dress, smile, and make conversation. Nothing more. Ann had agreed, with her knowing smile. Molly wondered just how many girls had begun this life with exactly the same intentions.

All the girls were present, dressed in full hoops, but subtly different, as if to illustrate each girl's personality: languid, exotic Marie; wholesome, milkmaid Clara.

There were ten men in the room, though the number seemed to fluctuate as couples discreetly removed themselves and others rejoined the room. It was all quietly and ably managed by Ann Benton, who moved easily among them, directing the participants as if conducting a small chamber orchestra through a pleasant evening's performance.

"Molly," Ann Benton said as she steered an elderly gentleman toward her, "I'd like you to meet Judge Stanford Haywood, one of our city's ablest jurists. Judge Haywood takes it as his particular responsibility to protect us from seditionist elements, and we all thank him for it. Judge, this is Molly Glenn, who is visiting us from out of town. Perhaps you can convince her to join us here in Washington City on a permanent basis."

"Molly, you appear quite delicious to these old eyes. If anyone can convince a beautiful lady to join us in our efforts here it will be Miss Ann."

"Why, thank you, Judge," Molly said, as the old man eased himself into a chair. She had to stop herself from speaking with a put-on, Southern belle accent. The judge was prototypical: stout, white haired, florid faced, and wearing a three piece, black wool suit. "Now why don't you tell me all about your interesting work," Molly went on. "I'm from out of town and know nothing of such important matters."

Oh Lord, how easily such drivel trips from my tongue. Maybe it's the corset cutting off the oxygen to my brain.

The judge settled himself in his chair. "Why, certainly, my dear. As you know, or possibly not, since I'm sure a woman of your beauty does not involve herself in these sordid matters, our young city is positively acrawl with secessionist spies and Southern sympathizers, any one of which would be happy to aid in a plot to bring down the Union. And I believe I'm divulging no secrets to your pretty little ears when I say that these plots are legion. My job, simply, is to imprison any man or woman whom I, or rather we, deem suspect to any degree of such crimes. If I catch even the slightest whiff of the stench of Rebellion in my courtroom, I will act to the furthest limit of the law. And I'm pleased to say that our city prisons and even our prisoner-of-war camps are positively filled with miscreants of this nature, sent there by yours truly. But does not all this talk of legal matters tire your lovely head?"

Molly had the urge to plunge the heel of her shoe into the judge's instep.

"Well, Judge, I'm sure all that is beyond my reckoning, but it seems to me that I once heard of a little old thing called 'habeas corpus.' I guess I just never understood that concept."

The Judge chuckled. "Why, aren't you the sweetest thing? Habeas corpus. You even pronounced it correctly. But let me explain. Habeas corpus is an old Latin term that means 'find the body.' The legal concept is that if one is suspected of having committed a murder, the prosecution is legally obliged to produce the body in question. And while the term originally was restricted to that particular crime, in these modern times we extend it to other legal areas as well." He took a puff on his cigar. The ash fell onto his vest, where he brushed at it indifferently.

"It seems to my poor mind to be a most admirable notion," Molly said. "And does a 'whiff' of sedition qualify as enough evidence to lay such an important concept aside?" She knew she should shut up, but she couldn't stop herself.

"There's your mistake, though one could never blame such a pretty head. Our President Lincoln himself has rescinded the writ of habeas for the duration of the war. It's all perfectly legal."

"I was under the impression that habeas could not be rescinded without the consent of Congress."

The judge removed his cigar from his mouth and regarded her coldly. "Lincoln declared the country under martial law once hostilities began. A sitting president does not need the authorization of Congress under martial law."

She knew she should just fan herself and shut her mouth, but she couldn't stop. "And are you sure that was legal? That President Lincoln wasn't just using it as an excuse to exercise a right that he had no legal basis to exercise?"

The judge had finally had enough. He stood up. "Of this I am sure, young miss. I will excuse your misunderstanding of legal matters as a function of your sex. You of the fairer nature cannot comprehend what God did not give you the ability to comprehend. And so you must not be held responsible. If I were you, though, I would carefully rein in my intemperate observations. Please inform Miss Ann that I have been called away on a rather urgent matter." He bowed deeply.

Molly watched him go. She fanned herself, trying to cool down her anger, at herself as much as at the judge.

"Well, look at this," a man at her elbow said. He was dressed in an officer's uniform and was holding a glass of whiskey. His face was red and leering. "You are by far the prettiest dove in the room."

Molly stood up. "I'm sorry. I'm not for sale." She swept the hoops around her and left the room.

Ann Benton found her in the upstairs back bedroom where she had dressed earlier in the day.

"Well," Ann said, "you made quite an impression on the judge. By the color of his face as he retired you left him near apoplexy. Was this from unrequited desire?"

Molly looked at Ann. "I'm afraid not. The judge and I had a difference of opinion on a political matter." Ann sat beside her on the love seat.

"It is not wise to discuss politics in a brothel. Particularly with one who has such firm opinions as the judge. He has filled the Old Capitol Prison with those who disagree with him."

"I'm sure he wasn't that upset."

"Let us fervently hope so."

chapter fourteen

ALEX WATCHED BIERCE smear butter on a piece of roll, dip it into his coffee, and put it into his mouth and begin to chew. Bierce frowned at him.

"What's the matter," Bierce asked, around his mouthful of roll, "haven't you ever seen anyone eat breakfast?" He continued to chew.

They were in a room, not really a restaurant, close to the hotel. The woman who lived in this small house, a Mrs. Duggan, made hot rolls every morning and served them in her living room to customers who washed them down with strong black coffee. There were three rickety tables with two chairs at each. The bill of fare was limited to the rolls, a bit of honey, butter, and coffee. In the week Alex and Bierce had been in their hotel room it had become their custom to start each day at the Widow Duggan's Coffee House.

"I'm just not used to seeing a man enjoy his breakfast quite as much as you do," Alex said, tearing off a piece of roll and eating it. He didn't use any butter, it was rancid, but this didn't seem to bother Bierce.

Bierce slurped his coffee. "I guess not. And why shouldn't I enjoy it? My usual breakfast for the last several years has consisted of one hardtack cracker mashed up in coffee, complete with all the weevils I either did or did not bother to skim off the top, depending on whether anyone was firing guns in my direction. Standard soldier's fare. Has yours been so different, John?"

Alex looked over at two drovers occupying one of the other tables as they scraped back their chairs and stood. They were dressed in rough canvas pants and homespun shirts, and hadn't bothered to remove their sweat-stained felt hats while they ate. Their heavy boots were caked with mud and horse droppings. After a few minutes of banter with the Widow Duggan, they stomped out of the house leaving Alex and Bierce as the only customers. Alex wondered if the widow, a pretty, plump woman of about forty years who didn't seem to mind the affectionate pat on the rump one of the drovers had bestowed on her, had a side business she ran in the house at night.

"Are we having a conversation here?" Bierce asked.

"Sorry," Alex said. "My mind was wandering. What did you say?"

"I was wondering how you and your messmates dealt with the hardtack cracker for breakfast. There seemed to have been untold recipes and stratagems."

Alex knew what a hardtack cracker was, but he had never eaten one. His military life had been limited to coming under fire and getting shot in the leg. "You know, the usual," he said.

Bierce raised his eyebrows. "More amnesia, I suppose," he said. He didn't bother to conceal the sarcasm in his voice.

"Yes, that's it," Alex replied. He knew Bierce was as tired of hearing this excuse as he was of trotting it out every time he was asked a question that he should know the answer to.

"And still you have no memory of your time in the field?" Bierce asked. "Perhaps nothing so simple as a piece of hardtack or a cup of coffee, but no battle, no moment of doomed heroism?" He waited. Alex shook his head.

Bierce sighed. "Memory is a funny thing," he said, finishing off his roll and carefully wiping his mustache. "I don't profess to your years and wisdom, of course, but I've seen things in the war that have become a permanent part of my being. As has every other man I've known who has served in battle. Many of us refrain from discussing these events with civilians, but with other soldiers these memories pour forth of their own volition." He drank the last of his coffee.

"For example," he went on, "I was unfortunate enough to have participated in the great battle at Shiloh Church. You've heard of that one, of course." Alex nodded.

"We had to fight our way ashore from our transport through a mob of demoralized soldiery, all of whom had run off from the battle and taken shelter beneath the bluffs there at the shoreline." Bierce smiled. "It's interesting that the greatest cowards in an

Army are its bravest men. You could have put a gun to the head of any one of those soldiers and threatened him with instant death if he did not return to battle, and yet he would look you in the eye and refuse to budge without the slightest hesitation. Once the rest of us coming ashore reached the battle we learned why those men had turned tail and fled. It was horrible, a monstrosity of death.

"Midway through the next afternoon we were resting after fighting all morning. Behind our lines was a ravine where the day before the Fifty-fifth Illinois had been caught and butchered by Rebel marksmen. A fire had subsequently sprung up and immolated all therein, both living and dead. I walked down into the ravine to satisfy my rather reprehensible curiosity."

"Ambrose," Alex began, "you don't really need to do this, I understand . . ."

Bierce waved him into silence. "Allow me to make my point. I walked through the ankle-deep ashes. There were burned bodies aplenty. Some of them had fallen in attitudes denoting sudden death by bullet, but far more were in positions of agony that told of the tormenting flames. Some were swollen to double girth, some were shriveled to manikins. Contraction of the muscles had given them claws for hands and cursed each countenance with a hideous grin." Bierce looked away from Alex, staring at the wall, seeing again the cindered men. "And now I have arrived at my point.

"This sight, which in my memory I see still, could no more be dashed from my mind by a simple wound than by death itself. It is a part of me as much as my hand, or my leg. I could no more forget it than I could forget my hand or my leg. And yet you have nothing of a like nature to remind you of hell?"

Alex shook his head. "No, nothing."

Bierce laughed, bitterly, and looked Alex in the eye. "Then you, my friend, are the most fortunate of men."

Outside they stood for a moment, blinking in the bright sun. It was cold and Alex shivered. On most days they split up after breakfast, Bierce to the hospital to see his friends, and Alex to walk the city exercising and stretching his leg, which every day grew stronger and less painful.

"I've decided to take your advice," Alex said. "I'm going to go see Lincoln. Tomorrow morning."

"I wondered if you had given up your hunt for the young man who saved you." Bierce shaded his eyes and looked down the avenue. "Strange how you remember *that* particular incident with such clarity."

"It wasn't long ago that I heard you remark that there were many strange occurrences on a battlefield."

Bierce nodded. "Yes, I did say that, didn't I? I guess we can enlarge that comment to include most of life itself. I'll see you back at the room tonight." Bierce turned and walked down the avenue, toward the Capitol building.

Molly looked out the window and pulled a shawl tighter around her shoulders. All the windows in the house were hung with three separate layers of curtains, but even that blanket of insulation couldn't keep out the cold. Outside, the leaves fluttered down and scattered about in a fall wind. In the house, islands of heat radiated from fireplaces and coal stoves, but the in-betweens—the hallways, the outer edges of almost every room, and especially the trip outdoors to the privy—left her longing for the homey comforts of a more efficient method of central heating. There was a crude furnace in the basement, she had been told, but the pipes extended only to the first floor and the delivery of heat was leaky and weak.

More than a week had passed and Molly's initial fear had gradually melted away under the weight of boredom. She was grateful to Ann Benton for providing her with food and shelter. She was amused by the girls, Clara, Alice, Blanche, Marie, and Grace, of whom she had begun thinking as a small tight family of loyal sisters, almost a single entity to be pronounced in one long rush: ClaraAliceBlancheMarieGrace.

Molly had reached a sort of middle ground with Ann Benton in matters of apparel. When not actually engaged in her own special brand of entertaining, she wasn't required to wear the full hoopskirt regalia. They had worked up several dresses that were far simpler, even though all of them still involved crinolines. Now she could maneuver without the cumbersome cloth bell sweeping the floor around her and the suffocating embrace of the corset. The evenings, though, were different. Then she was squeezed back into the corset and hoop, powdered and painted, wound up, and put on display. Her job was to entertain, but solely socially. Intellectually. Ann Benton had found that the men who came to the house were attracted to Molly at first by her beauty, but then to her intelligence, as if brains and a quick wit were a new, interesting type of deviancy. They gathered around her like cigar-smoking, liquor-drinking schoolboys with a crush on the new schoolmarm. Ann Benton's house was getting the reputation as being *the* place to go for a new sort of gentlemen's entertainment, and all because of Molly.

"Come away from the window, child, it's cold there," Ann said, entering the room. Molly turned to her. She was always amazed at the ease with which Ann maneuvered her clumsy dresses as she negotiated the house. Unconsciously, she tipped the bottom edge of her dress when she walked into a room so the hoop fit through the doorway without a hitch in her gliding gait. Small tables with knickknacks remained undisturbed. She sat in chairs with the grace of a nesting bird, unobtrusively smoothing and arranging her skirts to gracefully alight looking like a perfectly composed, expensive confection. Ann patted the sofa. Molly walked across the room, surprised as she always was by the feeling of the soft floor that rustled gently beneath her feet. Dixie had told her that straw was strewn beneath all the carpets in the house to soften the step. In the spring the servants took the rugs outside to beat them clean, and swept out the old straw and laid down new. Molly sat beside Ann.

"I've had several messengers today," Ann said. "We'll be having new visitors this evening. We should be quite busy."

"Busy on a Thursday?" Molly asked. "What do they tell their wives?"

"Most of our gentlemen's wives are hundreds of miles away in their real homes. As you know, we cater to politicians. I've often thought that in an emergency on a busy weekend night we could raise a congressional quorum and pass legislation here. As to why we will be busy on a Thursday, rather than the usual weekend, it is the upcoming election, of course. Politics enflame men in more than one way.

"Which brings me to this evening," she went on. "We're to be hosting a number of journalists, including the editors of the *Tribune, Evening Star,* and the *Capitol Constitution.* So you must be very careful."

Molly looked up from her study of the fire. "Me?"

"Yes, my dear, you. You have drawn these gentlemen to us. Word has circulated among them that we have here in our possession a woman not often found in sporting establishments: one of unusual intellectual powers. A beautiful woman who is not, in our sense, for sale. A woman who simply talks to men, and on their own level of discourse. Men, you see, are drawn to oddities.

Though I have never done so, there are many houses in the city who offer such attractions—women with scars, lost limbs, or other unusual qualities."

"I'm not sure I like being lumped in with that company, as an oddity. I feel sorry for those poor women."

Ann's voice had just a hint of sharpness as she replied. "Without such employment those unfortunate women's lives would be far harder than they are now. Do not be so quick to judge."

"I'm sorry," Molly said. "It's just that I don't exactly enjoy being thought of as an object of curiosity."

"As I was saying, you must be careful this evening. You must show yourself as interesting and able to joust with these gentlemen on their own terms—but you must not show them up or ridicule them in any way, even though many of them deserve ridicule. Men have a power that women will never be afforded. Which is not to say we don't have our own strengths, equal, and superior in some ways, to theirs."

Molly felt herself walking the thin line she had still not grown accustomed to: being honest but still being careful not to give offense. "You know, those powers you ascribe to men are not necessarily God-given. Don't you ever imagine a future where men and women are equals intellectually and professionally?"

"Oh, I hear this sort of talk from the lady suffragists who come to town to lecture. They say someday we will vote and walk the streets with men as our equals. It's not a particularly pleasant vision, at least to me. I wouldn't know whom to vote for even if I were allowed."

"That's only because you've never been exposed to the information that would inform you to make such a decision. Or even if you have been exposed to it, you don't assimilate it because you have no practical use for it. I'm sure, given the chance, you are just as able as any man who comes here to make an informed and intelligent decision on most political matters. You are no less intelligent than any of them. In fact you are far more intelligent than most of the ones I've talked to."

Ann frowned. "And this is where I must caution you. It is one thing to discuss equality as a casual matter of interest, it is another to promote our sex as greater than theirs. Men do not take well to being told they are inferior, either in the bedrooms upstairs or down in the drawing room. You must be careful. You could ruin us all."

"All right," Molly said. "I'll be careful."

Alex sat alone on the steps of City Hall, a new building built in the same grand manner as the Patent Office hospital. The gleaming marble edifice was surrounded by flat brushy fields and a few ramshackle houses.

Alex unfolded the half-sheet of torn newspaper that had been the wrapping around the photograph of Molly and Lincoln he had impulsively picked up in his brief reemergence in the future. He had read the fragment so many times he had most of it memorized. He usually left it back in the hotel room, afraid that something might happen to it if he continued to carry it in his pocket. It wasn't necessary for him to actually see it to know what it said, it was more that the paper had become a talisman of hope for his return to his own time.

Half of one side was taken up by a striking picture of a model, nude from the waist up except for voluminous strands of beads that covered her breasts. Barely. It was an advertisement for the jewelry department of Barney's of New York. If you looked closely you could almost see her nipples. Or at least imagine them. Which was another reason he usually left the newspaper at the hotel. He had no idea what the penalties for pornography were in this time, if any, and he didn't want to find out. He folded the paper so the advertisement didn't show and studied the articles beside the picture. There was a long piece about President Bush's problems appointing federal judges and other appointee difficulties. What he once would have skimmed over if he had looked at it at all now had attained the qualities of an archeological discovery of importance. He weighed every word, searching for signs and portents of his own world, greedy for any news of that coming time, even the most mundane. A boxed roundup of short national news items told him that a gunman had gone berserk in Texas and shot up a fast food restaurant, that a group of students had discovered a new species of butterfly while on a class field trip, a homeless man had been found dead in Los Angeles with a hundred thousand dollars in large bills stuffed into his sleeping bag, and that Ford's Theater in Washington, D.C., had been reopened after undergoing a yearlong renovation. He reread the Ford's piece and decided to attend a performance there. He had visited the theater when he briefly lived in Washington as a teenager. He and his mother had attended a performance of Dickens's *A Christmas Carol.*

The other side of the paper had a large photograph of a stealth bomber coming in for a landing at Andrews Air Force Base in Maryland, and an accompanying story about the escalating costs of building this airplane. Beneath the bomber story was an analysis that speculated on the effects a dock strike would have on the nation's stumbling economy. Alex wasn't aware that the economy was in trouble.

One thing that confused him, and it turned up in several of the stories, was the term "9/11." This number was almost always used in the phrase, "Since the events of 9/11 . . ." and would go on to compare some coming circumstance in the light of the 9/11 event. He knew of course that 911 was the number you dialed in an emergency, so perhaps this was a variation on that information. Or it was shorthand for the date of an event. Certainly the stories indicated that whatever the 9/11 event was, it had been a great emergency.

A gust of cold wind plucked at the newsprint, almost tearing it from his numb fingers. He carefully folded the paper and put it back into his pocket. He stood and started up the steps. He would loiter in City Hall until he'd warmed up enough to head out to continue his walk. He wondered if Bierce would still be impatient with him for his continued inability to remember his soldier past, when they met for dinner that night. *Probably not. A day spent swapping stories with the soldiers at the hospital will relieve him of that need.*

Bierce unpacked his writing materials and lined up the paper, pen, and ink on the desk. He had been coming not to the hospital but to the Soldiers' Aid Society for a week, and the young lady volunteers all recognized him and left him alone as he worked. Which was fine with him. He wasn't sure why he seemed to have this compulsion to set his thoughts down on paper, and he certainly didn't want to discuss it. He unstopped his ink bottle, dipped in his pen, and began to write at the top of a fresh page: *What I Saw of Shiloh.*

chapter fifteen

MOLLY STOOD IN the small, hidden antechamber that looked out onto the main drawing room through a cleverly concealed window. In the house's original plan the area had been a cloakroom but Ann Benton had modified the room to fit her own special needs. Casual observers would be unaware of its existence unless they knew where to look for the concealed door. Inside, Ann could assess the evening's crowd without showing herself and identify potential problem clients before they became disruptive.

Molly, wearing an elaborate hoopskirt of deep ruby silk, barely fit into the small room. Ann Benton told her there were seventy-five yards of material in the incredibly heavy dress and warned her to stay far away from the fireplace and to avoid candle flames.

The house was crowded, the air thick and blue with smoke from cigars and the wood-burning fireplace. The men lounged in chairs, while the girls glided around the room in dresses revealing pushed-up bosoms with peeping rouged nipples.

Molly sighed. *Showtime.*

She quietly exited the back of the chamber, walked through the dark hallways and dining room on the first floor, and into the brightly gas-lit drawing room opposite where she had just been watching.

Ann saw her and immediately rose and took her arm. "Don't you look lovely tonight," she said, steering her around the room.

"Thank you," Molly said, nodding at the few men that she

recognized from other evenings. Several of them lifted their glasses to her. Off to the side she heard a small shriek of laughter from Clara, whose pink silk dress swirled around her as she twisted away from her partner. The man had been attempting to drink out of a shot glass and lick Clara's pert left nipple at the same time. Clara pulled the fellow by the arm and the two of them made their way to the stairs.

Ann waited until the couple had ascended and then guided Molly up the stairs. "I've put our new friends into the back drawing room. There are five of them. One of the group is a high government official, so I had them use the side stairs and bypass our regular customers. Carter has mixed their drinks, but if they need something else—anything—pull the bell cord and Dixie will come up."

They swept into the room, Ann Benton a good bit more gracefully than Molly.

Ann stopped in front of the five men, who rose to their feet. They had been seated in stuffed chairs drawn up to the fireplace. There was another chair for Molly, this one with open sides. She had learned that there were two types of chairs in the house, known as male and female chairs. The female version was open so the great dresses could fit without bunching.

"Gentlemen," Ann Benton said, "I'd like to introduce you to my friend, Molly Glenn."

Molly smiled at this small crowd of black wool and unruly hair. She still hadn't gotten used to the fact that many men of this time seemed not to notice, or perhaps just not care, what the hair on their heads looked like. They were vain and particular with their beards. Most of them wore great flowing splendors of facial hair, but on their heads, everything was permitted to sprout in any direction.

"Charles Dana," one of the men said, stepping forward. He took her hand, not in a handshake, but just a small grip of her fingers for a brief moment.

"Mr. Dana is the Assistant Secretary of War," Ann Benton said. "And we are honored to have him with us tonight."

"And as far from that official capacity as it is possible to get, I hope. I am here this evening with these disreputable characters"— he gestured at the other smiling men—"as a compatriot spirit from my days toiling behind pen and desk."

"You never toiled, Charles, you were always the head man. It is we humble scribblers who got the job done." The next man advanced and took Molly's hand in the same manner as Dana had done. "Bradley Osbon," he said. He nodded at the others. "And these gentlemen are Sam Wilkeson, late of the *New York Times* and now bureau chief of the *Tribune,* John Rawlings, editor of the *Evening Star,* and J. Noble Firth, editor and correspondent for the *Capitol Constitution.*" All of the men gave her the same handshake except Firth, a short, florid-faced Irishman, who bent slightly as if to kiss her hand but stopped short of it.

Molly nodded and smiled at the group. "Well, gentlemen, I feel a little like some piece of prize livestock just gone on display. Should I sing and dance?" she asked.

"I'm sure nothing would be lovelier," Wilkeson said. He was a tall, clean-shaven man, the only one without facial hair, with a hawk face and high forehead.

"I could hardly compete with the other girls here. You really must get to know them," she replied. "They are much more talented than I am."

"And," Ann Benton said, "I must go back downstairs and see to my talented ladies. I second Molly's recommendation. I'm sure you would find any of them a gifted companion. If you gentlemen should want anything at all, Molly will send for our maid. If you will excuse me?"

They all stood until Ann left the room. The men stared silently at Molly until she realized that they would never sit down before she did, so she settled into her chair with as much grace as she could summon. The acres of burgundy silk rose around her like the petals of a deep red rose. Which was probably the idea, she supposed.

She watched the men as they went back to their chairs and busied themselves with cigars and glasses. She found that she was slightly nervous, particularly since she was facing Charles A. Dana, newspaper legend and subject of an entire journalism class she had taken in college.

"I'm surprised that so many eminent journalists would have any desire to come talk to me."

"Which of the papers do you read, Miss Glenn?" Osbon asked.

"I have only had the pleasure of reading the *Evening Star* because I arrived in town just recently, Mr. Osbon."

"I pride myself on identifying regional speech," Rawlings said. "I would say you are from the midwestern section of the country."

"And you would be completely wrong. I'm from New York by way of China," she replied, feeling as if she were in a small leaky boat that had just pushed off from shore. Over the past few days she had conceived and discarded several stories that she could use to explain herself. She'd settled on the China explanation in the hopes it was so foreign and inaccessible that people would simply believe what she was saying. "My parents were, are, missionaries, and we left New York for that country when I was just a teenager."

"Teenager?" Dana said, quietly, to himself, looking thoughtful.

"Interesting," Osbon said. "I spent some time in China myself. I was there in 1840. I fought with a sort of coastal guard backed by the British against pirates. Those were rough-and-tumble days."

"Oh no," Wilkeson said, with a theatrical groan. "First it's the Chinese pirates, next will be his days with the Argentine navy. Mr. Osbon has many stories, Miss Glenn, and he is only too eager to share them with you."

"I'd like to hear them."

"Well, the rest of us already have. We're more interested in listening to you."

"And why would that be?" Molly asked, giving them a brilliant smile.

The men were quiet for a moment until Dana broke the silence. "To be honest, several people overheard your conversation here with Judge Haywood the other evening. Few persons in this city have the nerve to engage the judge in any sort of debate, especially in public, so your brief skirmish was gossiped about over the bar at Willard's, which is where we heard the story. And so we decided to come see for ourselves this paragon of beauty who dares to enter the arena of political intrigue and speculation."

Oh, what bullshit, Molly thought, *and how they love to sling it.* She wondered if they spoke so ornately among themselves, or if this was just a style used to flatter women.

"I'm not sure I like being an object of gossip," Molly said. She was positive the standards of the time required a lady to be offended at such a disclosure.

"Let me hasten to assure you," Osbon said, "that you are the hero, or rather heroine, of the tale. No stain is attached to your name."

"Tell me about the judge," Molly asked. "His fame is not so great that we have heard of him in China."

"The judge is a powerful man," Sam Wilkeson said. "He has sent quite a few newspapermen in this city and elsewhere to the Old Capitol Prison. If he suspects you of treason, or if he simply takes a disliking to you for something you have written, you are swept up and taken away, without redress to the courts. He is Lincoln's long arm of the law, at least in matters of loyalty to the Union and the president."

"I would say," Rawlings interrupted, "he is more Stanton's man than Lincoln's."

"It amounts to the same thing," Wilkeson said.

"Allow me to defend, if not the judge, Secretary of War Stanton and the president," Dana said. "I will admit the judge is overzealous, but these are extraordinary times, which demand extraordinary measures. The Union deserves no less."

"That sounds like something men have always said when attempting to justify illegal means in defense of political goals," Molly said. " 'The last refuge of the scoundrel being patriotism,' I believe the saying goes."

Dana looked at his friends. "And now I am a scoundrel?" he said. "I feel the sting of the lash and begin to sympathize with the judge."

"You know, you men are awfully sensitive," Molly said. "I didn't mean you personally. I believe this is the same problem I had with the judge. He and I seemed to be unable to discuss politics without his thinking I was attacking him. Can't we discuss ideas without sinking to the personal? If a *man* had said the same thing to you, would you have been so quick to take offense?"

Dana looked bemused. "I take your point, Miss Glenn. Perhaps we aren't used to discussing such matters with those of your sex, and are thus unable to separate our minds from our feelings; feelings being those subjects we are generally used to dealing with in regard to females. You are correct. If a man had said the same thing I would have simply allowed him a debater's point. I must say, it's disconcerting to talk this way with—"

"What about the lady suffragists?" Molly interrupted. "And the lady abolitionists? They have a political agenda that they put forward and defend. They're taken seriously."

Several of the men laughed.

"What's so funny?" she asked. They looked startled.

"We meant no offense, once again," Firth said. "But, good Lord, have you not seen those creatures? They are mannishly stern, singularly unhumorous, and decidedly unattractive. Even when their points are well taken, and I say this in the case of the abolitionists, they force them down one's throat like some terrible medicine. Surely you, sitting there in all your loveliness, sitting *here*," he gestured vaguely, indicating the house around them, "are not allying yourself with *them*."

"If you mean do I ally myself with those who believe in equal rights for women and the abolition of slavery, then yes, I certainly do. And what has one's attractiveness, or lack of it, to do with anything? Since when is beauty an indicator of intelligence? You would never apply those standards if you were assessing the intelligence of a man. Mr. Firth, would you care to discuss the capabilities of your friends here in reference to their physical characteristics? Is Mr. Osbon a better or worse writer because he is more or less handsome?" Firth flushed red with embarrassment, and the others laughed at him.

"Less, I'm afraid," Osbon said. "Though perhaps Firth would like to take you up on your proposition to discuss my physiognomy."

"A gentleman does not discuss the physical characteristics of another gentleman," Firth said.

"I believe I remember your newspaper referring to President Lincoln as 'The Original Ape' in appearance," Osbon went on.

"We were hardly alone in doing so at the time," Firth answered. "And that was one of the least pejorative of the assessments. And really, is it so far off the mark?"

"Firth here is a McClellan man, Miss Glenn," Osbon said. "His newspaper has always taken a rather dim view of Lincoln's policies. In fact I rather wonder that the judge hasn't scooped him up and removed him to prison."

"I won't have to worry about that soon, my friends. In a matter of days Little Mac will be in control of the government, and it is you gentlemen who will have to curb your tongues for fear of prison. What do you think, Miss Glenn, how bad will be Lincoln's defeat?"

Molly laughed. "How on earth could anyone defeat Abraham Lincoln for the office of president? Surely you can't believe that."

Firth sat up straighter. "I do believe it. With all of my being. The nation is sick of this interminable war. Little Mac will be elected president and will craft a just peace and we can all, North and South alike, go back to our former lives."

"And what of the Negro?" Wilkeson asked. "Will he willingly go back to his life as slave? Will we allow the slave owners to come into our city and reclaim what they feel is their stolen property? There are ten thousand former slaves who have escaped from the bloody South to come and live amongst us in this city alone. Where do you propose they go?"

Firth's blood was up, his voice climbing into higher-than-normal registers. "They can go where your sainted Father Abraham has suggested they go: to colonies in Africa or South America. He has made it clear that he would pay every slave owner for every slave the Union has stolen from them."

Wilkeson was on his feet. "The Union has stolen nothing. These men, women, and children have fled their insufferable bondage into the grace of—"

"Gentlemen! Gentlemen!" Molly lifted her hands. "Please!" She made placating motions. "Please." She lowered her voice. "Let me tell you what is going to happen." Wilkeson looked at her as if he'd forgotten she was in the room. He lowered himself back into his chair. Firth unlocked his hands from the arms of his chair and sat back.

Molly looked at all of them. *I don't care,* she thought. *It doesn't depend on me. History. Whatever happens is going to happen.* She began.

"Abraham Lincoln is going to be reelected president by a huge margin. The North will win the war in the next six months. The slaves will be freed forever. The black man will go to the polls and vote like any of you. Eventually women will go to the polls and vote as well. Women will abandon hoops and crinolines. A new international order will be born and the United States of America will be the leader of that free world."

Colonel Lafayette C. Baker squatted in the rain against the ram-shackle exterior of a small two-story square whorehouse located in the Murder Row district of Washington City. The colonel had risen from obscurity as a San Francisco vigilante through the opportunities of the present war to arrive at his current position as chief of detectives for the War Department and head of the secret service.

And now, Baker thought, *I am about to break down yet one more door on yet one more cheap nigger whorehouse and see what shit will be dredged up inside.*

Baker stood, motioned with the barrel of his Colt to the three other men with him, then trotted around the corner of the shack. He lifted one leg and kicked in the flimsy front door.

Screams. Slurred shouts of confusion from several low-ranking soldiers drinking poor quality whiskey and waiting their turn. Supplications from the fat Negro woman who ran the establishment. Baker strode through it all, Moses parting the sea, knowing the men behind him would collect and subdue the rabble while he hunted more interesting game.

He kicked open a door and found a skinny bare-assed white soldier, still wearing his hat, on the cot with a mulatto; another soldier behind the second door, this time with a woman so dark Baker could barely make her out in the dim candlelight. He had better luck with a sergeant in the third crib, then struck gold in the last and meanest of the rooms, behind not even a door but a cheap, ragged bedspread curtain. Baker could not suppress a small smile of satisfaction as he looked down on the fat, bewhiskered white man who blinked up at him with a nearsighted expression of surprise that, Baker knew, would soon harden into self-important, self-righteous outrage.

"Hello, judge," Baker said. "Best get your pants on."

chapter sixteen

Alex was thrown out of Jay Cooke's bank not more than five minutes after he asked one of the clerks there if he could have a few moments of the financier's time.

The man laughed. "I'm afraid Mr. Cooke is not available. Sir." The "sir" was added with the not-so-subtle nuance of a man addressing the town idiot. Alex looked around the huge white-marble room of the bank. The architecture was Greco-Roman pretentious, an imitation of Washington's official buildings, but with just enough extra opulence to reflect the status and importance of the owners.

"If you have no other business, sir . . ."

"I'm sure Mr. Cooke will want to see me. I have information for him that will prove to be valuable."

The teller smirked. "You and a hundred other schemers with important information. Mr. Cooke does not see anyone who is not referred. Unless you have legitimate bank business, you'll have to leave."

"I'm telling you . . ." Alex saw the clerk nod to the bank's guard.

"All right, all right," Alex said. "I get the point. But I'll be back."

"Sure you will," the clerk said, going back to the papers on his desk.

Outside, Alex stood waiting for a railed horsecar full of passengers to roll by, then limped quickly across the wide street, dodging several mounted soldiers and a dray wagon.

So much for trading valuable insider information to Jay Cooke.

Alex stopped to look at the White House, known in this time as the President's House. There was a large red barn behind it, along with a scattering of other outbuildings. The house itself was a good deal shabbier than it would later be, needing a new coat of paint to make it actually white.

He had told Bierce he was going to see Lincoln about his search for the boy who had saved his life. Which was true, but he'd left out that he was also seeing Lincoln to ask him about the photograph of Molly with the president. *He knows where she is.*

Alex walked up the circular driveway, unchallenged. Several soldiers lounged on the front porch watching him with little interest.

No real guards, no Secret Service, no fence, no guard box, no cement walls to keep out truck bombs, no gunmen on the roof. Amazing.

He stepped up on the porch, stopped, and looked from the front door to one of the soldiers.

"Hafta knock before they gonna let you in, pilgrim," the man said. His friend laughed.

Alex knocked. An elderly black man dressed in knee breeches opened the door.

"Yes?"

"Well, uh, I'd like to see the president," Alex stammered.

"Upstairs to the left," the man said, stepping back with a curt nod.

Alex mounted the stairs, noticing the carpet was frayed and stained where tobacco juice had been spat on it. The wallpaper was marked by greasy hands and had small bits torn away. At the top he proceeded down a hallway until he came to a low balustrade. A young black man sat in a chair on the other side of the railing.

"I'm here to see the president," Alex said. The man simply nodded, opened a small gate, and pointed him farther down the hall.

Alex walked into a room where several men sat stiffly in wooden chairs. They looked at him, curious. A young white man, Lincoln's secretary, stood up from a desk and Alex told him that he was Lieutenant John Jordan and he would like to see the president. Alex was astounded that this simple phrase had gotten him this far. Evidently Bierce had been correct: In this time the president really did meet with the people. A nearby door opened and

Alex almost gasped as Abraham Lincoln strode out, followed by a smaller man in a bowler hat.

"John," Lincoln said to his secretary, "we're off to the beef depot. Professor Agar has cordially invited us to a demonstration of his new rapid-fire gun. He promises it will be quite exciting." Lincoln's voice was high pitched and heavily accented with a Kentucky twang.

Lincoln's secretary said, "These men are waiting to see you, as well as this lieutenant." Lincoln glanced at the two men in the chairs who rose and nodded hopefully in the president's direction. "Haven't I already talked to you gentlemen earlier this week?"

"Well, sir, we thought you might have changed your mind."

Lincoln looked thoughtful. "No, I don't believe I have." He turned to Alex. "Know anything about weaponry, Lieutenant?" he asked.

"Well, uh . . ." Alex stammered.

"Fine," Lincoln replied, "neither do I. And I'm the commander in chief. Come along, you can talk to me in the carriage." With a gallop of footsteps, a small boy charged into the room. Alex recognized Tad, the president's son, mostly from a famous picture taken of the two of them looking at a book.

"Me wanna come, me wanna come!" the boy shouted. The words were garbled, almost incomprehensible. Tad capered around the adults, making faces at each of them. Lincoln smiled at him.

"Of course you can come, Tad. Just don't tell Mother that we'll be shooting guns." He rested his hand on the boy's shoulder. Tad ducked away and ran out of the room. The boy seemed to Alex to be at least twelve, far too old for baby talk.

Lincoln followed and the rest of them fell in like a small marching band behind a towering drum major. Outside, they sorted themselves out among several carriages that were brought up the gravel driveway. As they waited to climb in, Alex heard a plaintive moo. At the side of the White House a cow peered out at them from a small fenced-in enclosure. Lincoln saw him looking at the cow.

"That's my wife's cow," Lincoln said. "She bought it when we moved in so we would have fresh milk every day. She can be quite thrifty in some ways." He shook his head. "Would it were all ways."

"Cow!" Tad shouted. "Moo!"

Lincoln patted the boy on the head.

The elderly black man in knee breeches pointed each to where he was supposed to ride. Alex found himself inside a carriage facing Lincoln, now wearing his familiar top hat. Tad rode up top with the driver.

As they jolted out of the driveway and onto the cobblestones, Lincoln held on to his hat to keep it firmly on his head. "Speak," Lincoln said, having to shout over the sound of the horses' hooves and the carriage wheels grinding on the irregularly spaced cobblestones.

"I know this is an unusual question," Alex began, "but have you ever been photographed with a woman named Molly Glenn? A pretty woman with red hair?"

Lincoln sat back, looking astonished. He did not speak for a full thirty seconds. "I have no idea what you are talking about," he finally said.

Either Lincoln was lying or it meant that the picture had not yet been taken. Alex could not bring himself to believe that Abraham Lincoln would lie. He was disappointed, but decided to move ahead. He told Lincoln the story of his wound, the boy who had saved him, the pigs, all of it. They had plenty of time—at the corner of Pennsylvania Avenue and Fifteenth Street an entire regiment of soldiers marching past stopped the carriage. Traffic around them waited patiently. Lincoln smiled and waved at the soldiers.

"A mystery," Lincoln said. "I've always liked a good mystery. I even solved a few in my early days. And you intend to follow through with this. Find the man who saved your life, solve this thing? You're determined?"

"Yes, sir."

"Laudable." The last of the soldiers marched by and the carriage began to move again. "If I didn't have more important tasks to deal with, I'd help you myself. But seeing as I have a war on my hands, I believe I'll send you to Colonel Baker, the head of my secret service." Lincoln took a small pad of paper and the stub of a yellow pencil out of his coat pocket. He laboriously wrote a short note, fighting the rocking carriage to keep the pencil on the paper. They stopped at a wooden gate, waited until it had been opened, then pulled inside to a stop.

Lincoln handed Alex the note, opened the door of the carriage, and climbed out. "Now let's see Professor Agar's new method of dispatching insurrectionists." Alex tucked the note into his pocket and watched Lincoln negotiate the carriage step. The president moved with the sort of gawky grace that Alex had seen only on giraffes at the zoo.

Alex stepped out of the carriage into a surreal version of the landscape that he had known well in his own time. The focal point was the stump of the Washington Monument. It sat on a small rise, 156 feet tall, or short, with rickety scaffolding crowning the truncated top. Lincoln saw him staring at it.

"Yes, well," he said, "we intend to do something about that. Someday. They ran out of money. We use it as a watchtower now, looking over into Virginia to see if Bobby Lee has come to invade us."

The wind shifted in their direction. "My God," Alex said, "what's that stink?" He did not think it possible that any new smell could be worse than what was present every day.

"What stink?" Lincoln asked. "The mountain of cow flop or the slaughterhouse? We've got ten thousand beeves on the hoof grazing here. It takes a lot of cows to feed an army. Also might be the dead ones rotting in the canal. Every night a few fall in and drown." Lincoln stopped talking as he watched Tad chasing a very live cow.

"John," Lincoln said to his secretary, who was standing nearby. "Would you send one of the soldiers to corral that little cow-poke?" Lincoln laughed as Tad, clutching a cow's tail, was dragged along the ground. A soldier chased the cow and the boy. Alex and Lincoln approached a group of men, who turned to greet the president.

"Professor Agar," Lincoln said, shaking hands with the same man in a bowler hat who had been in his office earlier. "General Smith, Captain Rolfe," he said, greeting several of the Union officers. He nodded at Agar's assistants. "Let's see what she can do, Professor." He turned to Alex. "The professor has declared that this weapon will win the war for the Union."

"Unna run cow! Unna run cow!" Tad said, dashing up. Lincoln seemed to understand the boy's speech without any trouble. "Not now, Tad. Come see the new gun the professor has developed." Tad pushed his way into the circle.

Alex was surprised to see that this gun had a single barrel, rather than the numerous rotating barrels of the Gatling. Its chief feature was a hopper with a large crank at the top of the stock end. Tad reached for the crank.

"Stop!" the professor shouted. "Good Lord!"

Lincoln pulled Tad away. "Coffee! Coffee!" the boy yelled.

"It does resemble a coffee grinder, doesn't it?" Lincoln said, eyeing the handle. "But I think the result would be a bit more exciting than ground beans if you give that crank a good turn. Right, Professor?"

"To say the least, Mr. President." Even though the day was cool the man took off his bowler and mopped his brow with a handkerchief. Tad twisted out of the president's grasp again. "If we might begin the demonstration?" Agar asked. Lincoln nodded. Agar turned and pointed over the grounds. "We've set up two paper targets about two hundred yards away. You can see them at the base of the small rise that the monument is being built upon. We'll fire at those. If everyone could assemble here behind the gun where it's safe, we'll get started. Jenkins here is the sharp-shooter, he'll be operating the weapon." A man with a cigar stub in his mouth raised his derby hat and nodded.

Lincoln was frowning at the monument. "Mr. Agar," he said, "might we reconsider before we begin? A paper target is all fine and dandy for a demonstration of marksmanship, but will do little to record the strength of the hits, the power of the weapon itself. Perhaps we might change the target?"

"What did you have in mind, sir?" Agar was frowning.

"Lieutenant," Lincoln said to Alex, "run up to the monument and cut two cows out of the herd. They're destined to become U.S. Army rations anyway; why might they not serve their country in a more meaningful way? Herd them over to the area of the paper targets. Then step back out of the line of fire."

"Me go!" Tad shouted.

"Certainly, son, I'm sure the lieutenant would appreciate your help."

Tad scampered off. Alex hesitated, never having been near a cow without a fence intervening in his life. "That was your commander in chief speaking, son," Lincoln said quietly. Alex jogged off after the boy.

He stood at the base of the monument, looking back at the group of men who now seemed very far away. Tad galloped up, pulling a cow along by its ear. "You hold," he commanded Alex, who did as he was told, holding the cow in place by one of its sharp horns. He felt stupid holding the cow, but he knew that the boy was a lot better at snagging the animals than he would be. There were thousands of cows in the herd, most of them lying in the grass, chewing their cud. The cow he was holding looked up at him with soft brown eyes. Tad dragged up another, this one more resistant, as if having some premonition of what was to come.

"Chase the others away," Alex said, pointing at the herd. Tad ran off laughing, whooping and waving his arms until the herd climbed to its feet and shuffled farther away. Both of the target cows settled down and began to munch grass. Alex walked quietly away, careful not to disturb them. "Come on," he whispered to Tad. They circled away from the targets to the far side of the herd.

Before they were a third of the way back to the group, the gun started firing. "Jesus Christ," Alex said, alarmed. He looked back at the target cows. One of them was down, legs up in the air. The other, bellowing in fear, raced toward the safety of the herd. Bullets kicked up dirt behind her hooves, and the herd began to move nervously toward Alex and Tad. The boy glanced up at him. He wasn't laughing now.

"Let's go," Alex said, limping into a trot.

The gun caught up with the second target cow, which went

down in an explosion of blood and entrails. The herd, a thousand head of now-terrified beef, began to trot.

"Come on!" Alex shouted, grabbing Tad by the hand.

They ran together, Alex glancing back. The herd spread out, wide-eyed, galloping faster. Every step radiated pain up his leg straight into his brain. All he could really see were a thousand pairs of bobbing horns, heading right toward them. Their only choice was to get over the fence that enclosed the stockyard. They had a hundred yards to go, and Alex figured they would make it with seconds to spare, when Tad tripped and went down. "Leg! Leg! Leg!" the boy shouted. Alex had Tad up in a matter of seconds, but it was clear the boy had hurt something. Alex picked him up and slung him over his shoulder and started to run again.

He hadn't gone fifteen yards before he was gasping for breath. He was using his good leg to propel them forward and hopping off the bad one. Slowing, he looked back, and saw the herd not twenty feet behind. He lowered his head and ran, the boy bouncing painfully on his shoulder, the extra weight translating into extra pain in his leg.

He reached the four-foot fence, threw the boy over it, and clambered over it himself just as the first cow smashed into the rough wooden boards and went down. On the other side, Alex grabbed Tad by the arm and staggered away as more cows hit the fence with great thuds and bellows. The fence shook and began to tilt toward them. Lincoln and his secretary dashed up in one of the carriages. Lincoln jumped down, ran to them, picked up Tad, and held him close. "Cows, Papa!" Tad shouted. "Run! Run!"

"Yes," Lincoln answered, patting the boy. "I saw them. Many cows." He looked at Alex, who was sitting on the ground, breathing heavily, holding his leg.

"Thank you," Lincoln said. "If anything had happened to him

Mother would have gone insane. She's not been right since Willie died. Nor have I." He turned to John Hay, his secretary, who was holding the bridle of the carriage horse.

"Mary must never hear of this. Talk to the others; tell them that no one is to know what has happened here. Tell the professor the War Department will contact him." He looked back at Alex. "The professor will give you a ride back to town."

"All right. Thanks."

Lincoln nodded. "If you ever need anything, come to see me again."

Alex smiled. Lincoln helped Tad up onto the driver's seat of the carriage, climbed up after him, and took the reins. Alex had a thought.

"Excuse me, sir, but do you know Jay Cooke? The financier?

Lincoln nodded. "Well, I guess I do. We've had dealings, as we used to say back in Springfield."

"I tried to see him today, and was unable to get past the clerk at the front desk of the bank. I wonder, could you recommend me? That's what it seems to take."

Lincoln smiled. "Why, yes, Lieutenant, I believe I could recommend you. I'll send word over. I'm sure Mr. Cooke will see you whenever you like. Yes indeed." He clucked at the horse and drove off in the direction of the White House.

Alex stood with General J. P. Smith and looked down at one of the target cows. The first to be shot, the cow lay stiffly on its side, tongue lolling from its half-open mouth. A series of bullets had stitched a row of ragged holes down the cow's side.

"Terrible waste of money," General Smith said. He looked at the captain who stood at his elbow. "Right, General," the captain agreed.

"It will never stand," the general went on. "Ammunition costs money. That's something that the professor doesn't seem to realize. We send each soldier out with forty cartridges and if he returns from battle with at least twenty of them he receives an oral commendation. Here we have"—he stopped to count—"sixteen . . . seventeen . . . eighteen bullets simply to dispatch one cow. Lord in heaven, think of the waste. No, my recommendation to the War Department will be to dispense with such foolishness. No gun needs to throw 120 bullets in a minute, when one, properly aimed and fired, will do the job. What was the man thinking about when he invented this nonsense?" The general and his aide turned and marched away, back to where the professor was packing his machine gun onto a wagon. Alex watched them go.

He limped up the small rise to the base of the truncated monument. He had been afraid that his run with Tad would have torn open his wound, but it all seemed to have held together.

He had his introduction to Colonel Lafayette Baker, Lincoln's head of secret service. And the promise of a recommendation to Jay Cooke. It had been quite a productive day, even if he had risked the ignominious death of being run down by a herd of stampeding cows.

He stood and looked out over the Potomac River. He watched a large, dead pig, all four legs raised to the sky, float by.

chapter seventeen

W HEN BIERCE AROSE he had enough time to notice that his roommate John Jordan was not in the room before a lancing pain knifed into his head, driving him to his knees, then facedown onto the wooden floor.

He was in a woods. It was night and he had been sleeping, leaning against the rough bark of a great elm tree. He awoke, not to sound, but to a feeling of men around him. There was a round dinner-plate moon casting a hard clear candescent light strong enough to throw shadows from the trees, and the men.

Most were on hands and knees, crawling, dragging useless limbs, missing limbs, spilled entrails tugging through the dirt and litter, eyeballs gone, jaws shot away, tongues wagging, heads split open, all of them smeared and splattered with blood shining wet and black in the pale light. The woods, the underbrush, the ground, pulsed and undulated with their movement.

He joined a group of men who were ambulatory in that they were upright, staggering, some falling to the earth but rising again slowly, painfully. They were headed to the east toward a red glow in the sky as if drawn inexorably to light or heat or solace.

After a march that seemed to take hours they emerged from the woods and onto a field, the mass of them creeping toward a house that stood silently engulfed in a great tangle of licking orange flame, the men like an army of black-backed beetles humping through tall grass. Bierce moved to the fore of the crawlers and stood looking at the house, sparks flinging toward the black sky, but felt no heat, smelled no smoke, heard no crackle and rush of flame. He recognized the house as the one he had grown up in.

Bierce moved to the two figures lying in the dooryard of the house. The first was a woman, his mother, the front of her dress twisted and sodden with blood, her eyes open, the pupils rolled up in her head. The second figure was his father, a tall gangly man with his shirt torn open as if he had been searching for the wound that killed him shortly before it did so. There was one more man lying in the flickering red light of the flames.

He knew who it would be, of course. But still he walked to the body. It was himself, his head riven as by an ax and his brain spilling from his skull, leaking creamily to the corners of his mouth which bubbled words that he could not hear. He bent to listen and felt himself fall to the ground.

"Bierce!" Alex rolled the man over, searching for blood. The unconscious man seemed to be breathing normally. Alex felt the dull thud of Bierce's pulse at the side of his neck. He dragged him to the bed and got him up on the mattress. Bierce snorted and opened his eyes. As he looked up at Alex, recognition appeared, as the smoky tatters of his dream dissipated.

"My head . . . is . . . splitting," Bierce said. "Again." He managed a faint smile. Alex looked at Bierce's right temple where the scar from the bullet wound curled pink in front of his ear.

"You look in one piece to me," Alex said. He wondered what he should do. "Do you want to go back to the hospital?"

"Good God, no." Bierce rubbed his head. "Holy Mary sweet Mother of God. What time is it anyway?"

"Not long after noon. Since you're still in your nightshirt I'd guess you've been lying on the floor for a number of hours."

"I guess I have. I also guess this sort of thing is part and parcel of surviving a serious head wound. They told me that there were likely pieces of minié ball still nesting in my brain and that they might speak up and cause me unknown troubles in the future. Well, they were right. Where have you been all day anyway?" Alex sat down in the hardback desk chair that was their sole amenity other than the beds, the dresser, and the washstand.

"I've been thrown out of a bank, met the president, and been chased by cows. All before lunchtime."

Bierce nodded and winced. He paused for a minute before going on. "Do you suppose you could take that towel off the dresser and pour some water from the jug on it?" Alex wet the towel and handed it to Bierce, who wrapped it around his head. "All right," he said. "I believe I'm prepared. Tell me about it."

"I'm not supposed to tell the tale. President Lincoln told me to keep it to myself."

"And why was that?"

"As near as I could tell, he seemed to be afraid his wife would find out that the boy had a close call. That she would be mad at him for endangering her child."

"I can understand," Bierce said. "They've lost two of their boys. She's said to be quite insane because of grief. I promise not to divulge the story. Tell me."

And so he did. Bierce lay silently on the bed, eyes closed, taking it all in. Several times Alex wondered if his friend had fallen asleep, slipped into unconsciousness, or died.

"And just what was it you wanted with Jay Cooke?" Bierce asked, opening his eyes.

"I've had experience in financial matters. Some of that is coming back to me," Alex answered. "I'm beginning to remember at least that part of my past. I was going to ask him for a job." Alex was aware that he sounded extremely naïve, that he expected to walk in off the street, chat up the leading financier of the time, and land a job. But he couldn't tell Bierce the truth, that he wanted to sell Cooke advance information on the outcome of battles. He had some reservations about doing this, but his compunctions were moral rather than time-related. He didn't think information of this nature would cause any serious shift in the course of events. He wasn't trying to stop those events, just profit from them. He was becoming less and less concerned with those time theories that suggested that stepping on a butterfly in the Amazon rain forest would result in massive historical change a thousand years later. And as far as the morality of foretelling battle outcomes for profit, well, sometimes personal interest took precedence.

He knew that the public wasn't aware of it, but this practice was a common occurrence. Newspaper correspondents made deals with stockbrokers, telegraph operators earned extra money informing bankers rather than the government who had won battles, even Secretary of the Treasury Salmon Chase kept Jay Cooke not only abreast but ahead of the news, fattening the accounts and ledgers of both men.

"I guess you failed in that particular mission, but what about this man Baker that Lincoln is sending you to. His name is sometimes in the papers, but what do you know about him?" Bierce asked.

"I'm going to his office as soon as I've had lunch," Alex answered. He shrugged. "The only thing I really know is that he's the chief of detectives and has an office in the War Department. The president seemed to think he's the one who could help me find the boy. Do we have any paper and a pen? I'm going to write a letter to Cooke telling him that the president is sending him a recommendation that he see me and asking for an appointment."

Bierce started to get up off the bed then thought better of it. "There's a portfolio and a pen in my bag. It's under the bed."

Alex got down on his hands and knees and looked under the bed, where the floor was surprisingly clean. The floor in the rest of the room, like the floors in most of the buildings he had been in, was covered and stained with old tobacco juice. Sometimes while crossing the lobby downstairs the marble floor was so slick with spit he had to be careful that he didn't skid in it and fall down. He pulled Bierce's carpetbag out. Bierce had thrown away his soldier's knapsack and bought the bag after they had moved into the hotel.

Alex sat back in the chair and pulled the bag onto his lap and opened it. He found a leather portfolio case that contained a thick ream of paper, ink, and a pen.

Alex pulled out the paper, which he was surprised to find was covered with writing in a small, tight hand. He looked at Bierce.

"There're some unused sheets on the bottom of the pile," Bierce said. Alex shuffled the paper and found several clean sheets.

"There's at least a hundred pages of written material here," Alex said. He carefully put the manuscript pages back in the bag.

"Yes, well, I've been at it for some time. At first it just seemed to me that it would be a good idea to take notes, that someday I might want to write up my war experiences. Then I decided to try my hand at a story or two, just to while away some camp time. Now it's become a daily activity. Nothing serious, mind you."

"You don't consider yourself a writer?" Alex asked. "As your profession?"

"When I was a boy my mother said my favorite toy was a dictionary. I would make up fanciful definitions of words." He pressed a hand to his head. "A is for Awful, which is the pain in my brain." He laughed. "Before I took to soldiering my only literary position had been as a printer's devil, a job at which I was mostly a failure. I've spent the war in service as a topographical engineer, scouting ahead, noting the lay of the land and drawing up maps. I've been successful, so I guess that's what I am."

"And is that what you'll do after the war?" Alex asked. He didn't know enough detail about Bierce's life to know when or how the man became a professional writer. But he did remember reading that Bierce had been not only a short story writer but an editor of newspapers and a columnist as well.

"After the war," Bierce said. "My, that has a nice ring to it. Sometimes it feels to me like this war will go on forever. Though I suppose my part in it is over." Bierce winced, leaned back on his pillow, and closed his eyes.

"Is it bad?" Alex asked.

"Oh yes," Bierce said. "Oh yes."

Alex waited until Bierce's breathing was slow and even. After he was sure that Bierce was asleep, he took the fragment of *New York Times* out of the top drawer of the dresser where he had hidden it after coming home last evening. He was surprised at how frightened he had been on finding Bierce facedown on the floor today. His immediate thought had been that Bierce was dead. His second thought was that he was now alone.

The touch of the newsprint was reassuring. The paper had become a talisman, evidence that it was possible to leave this time, to go back home. He sat on his bed and held the paper so that it caught the light from the window. He read a story that was headlined: SAFETY OF SMALLPOX VACCINE QUESTIONED. The story indicated that millions of doses of smallpox vaccine were being readied to inoculate Americans, and that recent tests had shown that there had been a high number of side effects, some serious. He had read the article several times and still didn't understand why smallpox, which had been declared eradicated when he was a small boy, was suddenly again a concern.

He refolded the newspaper. Once the morning sun no longer cut in through the small window there wasn't enough light to read without turning on the gaslight. He didn't want to wake Bierce, and he still intended to go see Baker. He went to the dresser, opened the top drawer, and tucked the newspaper beneath his extra socks and spare shirt.

Molly spread the morning newspaper out on the table in the kitchen. The cook, a black woman named Angie, brought her a steaming cup of tea. She and Angie were alone, the other girls not yet up. Molly liked Angie and she liked being in the warm kitchen with the smells of food cooking rather than the upstairs odors of perfume, whiskey, and stale cigar smoke. She felt mildly guilty that her usual time for rising had begun to slip, later and later. *I'm keeping whore's hours,* she thought.

The newspaper, the *Evening Star,* was only four pages long, so it didn't take much time to browse through the latest war news, local and national politics, and notices of plays and amusements. She read about a piano recital of the night before, and an upcoming lecture by Julia Ward Howe to be held that evening. And then she came across the article she had been looking for.

•   •   •

An Interesting Time
She Knows All
She Sees All

A pleasant evening was spent last night by your correspondent and several other members of the scribbling fraternity. Spirits, cigars, and lively conversation were found late in the evening at the home of one of the city's most gracious gentlemen's gathering places. This elegant establishment, in one of our city's finer neighborhoods, is widely known for the beauty and refinement of its feminine habitués, but a new addition proved delightful to all and a considerable surprise to some. There are those who feel that a woman's place is in the home, where her remarkable God-given characteristics are so eloquently displayed in the arrangement and running of the house with all the intricate and delicate managements that must be seen to in the course of a single day. We are among these thinkers, of course, but imagine our surprise to find a specimen of the fairer sex who is not only comely to the eye, but possessed of considerable intelligence, the ability and, dare we say it, the temerity, to express herself on a wide variety of subjects, particularly those long considered to be the provenance of the male tribe. In a word, dear reader, politics.

No sooner had the fair maiden begun her discourse and pronouncements than she was dubbed the Seer by the gathered scribes. She graciously accepted the appellation, though explaining she had no connection with other ladies and gentlemen who have appeared in our city as practitioners of the ancient arts of divination and prestidigitation. Our Seer claims no special powers other than native intelligence, common sense, and the possession of facts known to all the population. When asked by her smitten and humble audience, the Seer made the following predictions:

Abraham Lincoln will be reelected president by a huge margin.
The North will win the war within the next six months.
The slaves will be freed forever throughout our states.
All black men will go to the polls and vote.
Women of all colors will go to the polls and vote.
Women will abandon the hoop skirt and crinolines and wear pants, just like men.

To say we were no little astounded at these portentous pronouncements is no small understatement. And to say we viewed a few of these predictions with some apprehension is also true. Perhaps we will leave it to the reader, and to the Seer, to guess which of these predictions your humble scrivener would just as soon never come to pass.

After this dramatic announcement, our brother journalists and myself bid our adieus to the lovely Seer and made our way home to our own abodes and our own feminine helpmeets, whose views are always listened to with great respect and sometimes amusement, but are far less radical and unsettling to the nerves.

While the Seer made no timetable for her predictions, we might just note that the veracity of the first, the election of a president, will become clear in just a day or so. Good luck, fair Seer, we shall be watching.

—Blackestone

. . .

Molly put the paper down on the table. *Fair Seer? Where did they get that one?* Reading this smug male condescension made her seethe. She wondered which of them used the nom de plume Blackestone? Did they draw lots to see who would get to make their jolly fun of her? Perhaps they had all retired to the *Star's* offices and sat around drinking while each contributed their share to the drollery.

Molly looked up as Ann Benton came through the doorway.

"Good morning, Molly. I see you've found the paper. I sent Carter out for it first thing this morning. Quite amusing, isn't it? You were absolutely the hit, as I knew you would be. We'll be crowded all next week because of it. Congratulations."

"Thanks." Her tone of sarcasm was ignored.

"I would recommend you stay a bit further away from the more inflammatory predictions, but that whole Seer skit was very amusing."

"That wasn't my idea. They made that up."

"Oh, really? Well, never mind. Now that it's been in the newspaper, I'm afraid you're stuck with it. You can look forward to many repeat performances."

chapter eighteen

M OLLY COULDN'T DECIDE if she was excited or not. Ann told her to get dressed; they were going shopping for new material for another gown. Going shopping didn't excite her, and looking at material held little allure; but getting out and seeing downtown Washington interested her. She felt that if she saw more of her environment, she might come up with a plan for finding Alex. She thought that he must be in this time: Why else would she have been drawn here? But if she simply sat around Ann Benton's, she was never going to find him.

Ann sent Carter off to make the arrangements while she and Molly prepared for the expedition. Ann loaned her another dress from her seemingly inexhaustible collection. It was explained to her that this was a carriage dress: more formal than a morning dress but less formal than a walking dress; but still bulky, uncomfortable, and a pain as far as Molly was concerned. It featured crinolines rather than a hoop, which she supposed was because there wouldn't be room in the carriage for both of them rigged out in full-hoop fashion. After Dixie had trussed her into the dress, she was given a hat and a coat and a muff to ward off the cold November day. She and Ann waited at the front of the house while the coach was brought around. Ann was carrying an umbrella, though there was no hint of rain that Molly could see.

Carter clambered down and helped the two ladies up the step into the interior.

"I believe we're ready, Carter," Ann said.

He nodded and closed the door.

"You're lucky to have Carter," Molly said, as the carriage began to move. "It seems that he can do just about anything."

"Yes," Ann said. "I came across him some years ago, before the war. I was traveling through the South looking for some special girls for my house." She stopped for a moment and her expression seemed to harden. "When I first saw Carter he was tied to a stake in the slave quarters of a plantation. An overseer was beating him with a whip. I had of course heard of such behavior, but I had never seen such a thing. The man I was visiting, a planter, told me such beatings were necessary. I knew they were not. They are an abomination against man and God. I bought Carter off that stake, set him free, and brought him here where the girls and I nursed him back to health and gave him the position he occupies today. He has fulfilled all my expectations, and more. We are lucky to have him, and he is lucky to have us." The carriage swayed as a wheel slipped into a muddy rut. They drove by a large old building of whitewashed stone that was guarded by several soldiers at either end.

"Old Capitol Prison," Ann said. "At one time the Congress met there, after the British burned the original Capitol. It has housed several hundred Southern sympathizers, spies, disgraced Union officers, and captured Confederate soldiers. And for some time a bushel of newspaper editors from around the country, and the mayors of both Washington and Baltimore. Though the mayors and most of the editors have been set free by now."

The carriage rolled over a wooden bridge that spanned a small creek, about the same size and smell as the one Molly had ended up beside when she first came to this time. Then they were on "the Avenue," as Ann called it, and the carriage slowed as they became involved in more traffic.

"We'll stop at Harper and Mitchell first to see if they have anything decent, but I fear we'll have to buy material and have Dixie run something up. Green is your color; it sets off your lovely red hair," Ann said.

The carriage pulled up in front of a store. Carter swung down and paused at the carriage window, which Ann opened. She told him to go fetch Mr. Harper or Mr. Mitchell. Molly looked out the window and down the block of buildings, each with a sign over the entrance: NEW YORK HERALD, NEW YORK TRIBUNE, EVENING STAR, NEW YORK TIMES, CAPITOL CONSTITUTION. Ann Benton noticed her looking across the street.

"Newspaper Row," she said. "All of your admirers will be over there. Except for Mr. Dana, who is probably at the War Department, just up the street. Ah, here's Mr. Harper." She opened her window. "We'll remain in the carriage, Mr. Harper. I believe you have some dresses to show us?" Harper was a bald man with chin whiskers and big ears. He was smiling unctuously.

"Indeed I do, Miss Benton. I'll send them right out. If you see anything you like, come inside and we'll have tea and fit the dress." He bowed and went back in his store.

"We're not going in?" Molly asked.

"No, my dear, I have no wish to ruin my outfit dragging it through the mud. He'll bring us the dresses. We'll be quite comfortable where we are." Molly thought for a minute about how they had gotten so dressed up to simply sit inside a coach where no one could even see them. She pushed the thought away, as she had been making an effort to banish her constant annoyance over matters of dress.

She looked back across the street at the row of newspaper bureaus.

Alex walked up Pennsylvania Avenue. He had eaten several dozen oysters and drank a beer and was on his way to take his note from Lincoln and go see General Lafayette Baker, Washington's chief detective.

He stopped as a small parade of three women exited a clothing shop carrying bright silk dresses that seemed to gleam like colorful burnished metal in the sun. He waited while they crossed the sidewalk to a carriage, then walked on.

. . .

The seed of an idea that had planted itself in Molly's mind the night before, as she talked to the newsmen, began to grow as she looked out the window at Newspaper Row.

"Molly?" Ann said, touching her elbow. Outside Ann's window were three women in a semicircle, each holding a billowing dress. The wind caught and pulled at the fabric. Molly half expected the women to fly up into the sky as if carried away by three colorful balloons.

"What do you think?" Ann asked.

Molly didn't think anything—at least about the dresses. "The center one," she said, just to be done with it. "I like it the best. Could you go inside and see about it for me?" Ann frowned. "Well," she said, "we'll have to have it fitted. . . ."

"Ann," Molly said, rising and beginning to inch past the other woman, "please do this for me. You go inside and wait. I'll be a few minutes, but there's something I really must do." She had the door open and was stepping down out of the coach. Carter looked down at her from his perch. She turned back to Ann.

"But where are you going?" Ann asked. Molly could see she didn't like this one bit.

"Just across the street. Talk to Mr. Harris about the dress. I'm going to need shoes and accessories—you pick them out for me, my feet are the same size as yours."

"Well, I suppose . . ."

"Trust me. I'll be back soon, I promise."

chapter nineteen

MOLLY STOOD ON the corner of Pennsylvania Avenue and Eleventh Street. With no center pedestrian islands, stoplights, signs, or painted lines, the avenue appeared to be a mile wide and paved with several feet of mud and wet horse dung. She lifted her skirts and waded across the street with as much aplomb as she could manage.

She stood on the sidewalk on the far side, looking up at the *Evening Star* building, wondering if this was where she should start.

"Excuse me?" a voice said at her elbow. She turned. Beside her was the short, florid editor she had met the night before. *J. Noble Firth. The* Capitol Constitution.

"Mr. Firth," she said coldly, extending her hand.

He took it and bowed slightly. "By your tone of voice I suspect you've read the piece in this morning's *Star.*"

"Yes, I have. Which of you made up that Seer nonsense?"

"Well, I'm afraid that was a group invention. We could hardly have mentioned your pronouncements in any other way."

"I'm sure you found it quite amusing," Molly said.

"I'd have to say that some of us found it less amusing than others. That's the reason you saw it in the *Star* rather than in the *Constitution.*"

She felt her anger trailing away. She was too well acquainted with newspapers and journalists to hold a grudge when it came to embellishing a story. Even when the story was about herself.

"Your offices are near here, aren't they?" she asked. Firth pointed down the block.

"Just down the avenue. Our building is not so grand as the Star's, but you can't miss it. The name's over the door. I was just going there."

"May I walk with you? I have a few questions I'd like to ask."

Firth gave her a broad smile. "I'd be honored."

They turned and began to slowly stroll. "Tell me, Mr. Firth," Molly began, "do you have many women writers on your staff?"

Firth laughed. "Well, Miss Glenn, I can't say as we have any at all. And I've never heard of any at the other papers either. Are you asking me for a position?" He was still smiling, and Molly could see that he was making a joke.

"Yes," she said seriously. "That's exactly what I'm doing. I have a number of years of experience as a writer. I understand you couldn't hire me without some sort of a tryout, so what I'm proposing is this: I see that Julia Ward Howe is speaking this evening at the Smithsonian building. What if I write an account of her talk and submit it to you for publication. At no expense to you, unless you use it in your paper. What do you think?"

They were halfway down the block and several men had greeted Firth by name and doffed their hats to Molly. Firth was now frowning.

"It's completely irregular," he said. "There are a few lady novelists, of course, and then there are those who write for the domestic magazines, *Godey's,* and others, but for a respectable newspaper? I would be the laughingstock of the journalistic fraternity. It's just not possible."

Molly, resolving to remain calm, waited a moment before going on. "What if I wrote under another name? A man's name?"

"I really don't . . ."

"Look," Molly said, stopping and turning to face Firth. "You treated me as an object of amusement in the *Star,* if not you personally then you did along with your friends. I understand your hesitancy and I'm not asking you to lead a revolt and batter down any barriers, no matter how ridiculous they may be. No one will know that the article is anything other than what it seems to be; written by a man. I believe you owe it to me to at least see what I can do and consider what I have to offer."

Firth glanced around at the others passing by them on the sidewalk, as if he were checking to see if anyone was listening to him about to commit a terrible sin.

"All right, he said. "As long as you use a nom de plume." Then, as if making a joke out of his embarrassment, he held out his hand and asked, "And to whom do I have the honor of addressing?"

"Glenn Balfour," she answered, letting him take the fingers of her hand. "At your service." *And if Alex sees that byline he'll know, without a doubt, I am here.*

Alex walked into the War Department. The front hall was filled with loungers, soldiers smoking cigars, officers carrying sheaves of papers, and civilians bent on selling the Army various goods. Alex stopped one of the cigar smokers and asked, "Do you know where I can find Mr. Lafayette Baker?"

The man looked him up and down and said, "It's *Colonel* Baker, and I'd be real careful to remember that if I were you. He's downstairs."

Alex nodded, found the stairs, and descended.

The downstairs hallway was the opposite of the busy scene above. There were no loungers here, just one rough-looking sergeant with spiky hair and a week's growth of beard who sat, feet up, at an old scarred wooden desk. The man looked at him with a suspicious, bellicose expression.

"I'd like to see Colonel Baker," Alex said.

"You got a reason?" The man's voice was flat and angry.

"If you don't mind, I'd prefer to tell my reasons to Colonel Baker."

"Well, maybe I do mind." He took his boots off the desk and sat up. "We don't get many visitors here. Most folks seem to understand that if you come down, you just might never go back up." His thin smile had no humor in it. "Specially if you got a smart mouth on you." He stood.

Alex handed him the note from Lincoln. The man held it up to the gaslight and read it, or at least pretended to read it.

"It says that Abraham Lincoln recommends me to Colonel Baker and asks him to assist me if he can," Alex said. He was trying to keep his temper but he was running out of patience.

"I know what it says," the man said, eyeing the paper some more. "Well, maybe it's okay. I'll show it to the boss. You stay here," he ordered. He walked to the end of the hall, opened a door, looked back at Alex to make sure he hadn't trespassed beyond where he was supposed to be, and went into another room.

After several minutes the sergeant sauntered back. "He'll see you." He jerked his thumb in the direction he had just come. "But don't take up a lot of his time."

"Can I have my note back?" Alex asked.

"Hell, no, I tore it up and threw it away after the colonel saw it. What you want it for? You're gonna see him. That's enough." He pulled his chair out and sank into it. "Get on with you."

Colonel Lafayette C. Baker did not stand. He was writing, dipping his pen into a bottle of black ink. He didn't look up until he'd added his signature with a flourish to the paper he was working on. He rocked a blotter back and forth over the signature and looked at Alex under his brows without raising his head. "Yes?"

Baker was an older man, in his late fifties, with piercing John Brown–type eyes and a full black beard. His hair, fastidiously combed, swept straight back from his forehead. He was wearing a high-collared blue uniform coat that seemed to hover halfway between a military and a civilian look. "You've been sent by the president. How can I help you, Lieutenant Jordan? Please sit down." He gestured at the wooden chair in front of his desk.

Alex sat down. He told his battlefield murder story once again. Partway through, Baker got out fresh paper and began to take notes. Alex could hear the gold-nibbed pen scratching as he talked.

After Alex finished his story, he answered questions about where it had all taken place, what hospital he had been sent to here in Washington, and whom he had spoken to about the case. Alex tried to keep everything general so he would have to lie as little as possible, but as he answered he found the lies coming no matter how he tried to avoid them. He could see that he had made a mistake coming here and would have to abandon his Lieutenant Jordan persona sooner than he had thought. Baker was relentless with his questions, his face set in a grim, thin-lipped aspect. Finally he seemed to come to some conclusion, folded the paper he was writing on and asked, coldly, if there was anything else he could do.

"Anything that might help me find the boy who saved my life will be greatly appreciated," Alex responded.

Baker stood up. "I will look into the matter. You are correct; war is no excuse for murder. Though it would be difficult to explain the difference to the average man. Where can I get in touch with you, Lieutenant?"

"Willard's Hotel," Alex lied, without knowing exactly why he did so. "I've taken a room there. But I will check back with you on this matter." He stood up and shook Baker's hand. On his way out he noticed that the sergeant was not at his post.

As Alex closed the front door of Baker's office, a back door opened and the sergeant entered.

"Quickly, get Preacher," Baker ordered. "He's right down the hall. Have him follow the man who just left. He says he has a room at the Willard. When he's not there, search the room. Tell Preacher to take all the help he needs. He is not to lose this man."

Alex walked past the White House and thought of going into Jay Cooke's bank to see if the president had sent over a recommendation for him yet, then decided to wait. He should get back to the room and check on Bierce's condition.

He would see Cooke tomorrow. He had to get money. His meeting with Baker reinforced his opinion that keeping John Jordan's persona would lead to trouble. It was only a matter of time before he was found out. *Only a matter of time*, he thought. His brief appearance in his house in his own time, his momentary passing of Molly as she faded away to wherever she had gone had shown him that the forces that pushed and pulled him were at work, that he was part of a process that was ongoing. This stirred hope within him. *She is not dead.* It reawakened the possibilities that he had walled away over the past months: that he was not trapped forever in the past, and that Molly might even be somewhere in this time.

He would get money. He would search for her and he would hire others to help him in his search.

Now that he had gone to Baker, the need to chase down the boy who had saved him, to solve that particular mystery, seemed, if not less important, at least under control. As if the act of turning the problem over to someone else, an authority, partially released him from his debt. *How quickly all my notions of moral imperatives fade. I'll do both. Find Molly and the boy. I promise.* But he wasn't sure he believed himself.

Alex pushed through the knot of men who were standing outside the National Hotel, reading the latest news tacked up on the news-board there. The lobby had the usual contingent of tobacco-spitting loungers. The desk clerk hailed him and when he approached handed him a handwritten note, which Alex read.

Would you care to attend a lecture this evening to hear Julia Ward Howe speak on Moral Trigonometry? *I have two extra tickets, one for your friend Bierce as well.*

It was signed by Walt Whitman.

He stuffed Whitman's note into his pocket and hurried up the steps to his room, which was empty. On the dresser he found another note:

Gone to Willard's bar to drink. Join me.

Bierce

He would go to the Willard and meet Bierce. And later they might attend that lecture on Moral Trigonometry. He had no idea what that was, but instinctively knew that he would have to have a couple of drinks beforehand to get him through it.

chapter twenty

THE BAR AT the Willard was half-filled with drinkers. Alex entered on the Pennsylvania Avenue entrance and walked through a small hallway up a flight of six steps to the ornate main lobby. The bar and restaurant were off the hall to the right. He found Bierce in the bar eating a bowl of turtle soup. He sat down at the small table and ordered the same from the Negro waiter. He found it excellent—thick with chunks of tender turtle meat in a velvety sherry-infused sauce. He had eaten turtle soup only a few times in his life, though Bierce said it was common enough here to be served to soldiers in the field.

He and Bierce were both drinking Old Crow whiskey in honor, Bierce said, of General Grant. "It's the great man's favorite brand," Bierce said, holding his shot glass up in salute. "The general is a credit to drunkards everywhere."

"Are you sure you should be drinking so soon after your . . . whatever it was."

"My fit?" Bierce asked. "My seizure?" Bierce eyed the whiskey, holding it so it caught the gaslight and glowed a deep brown. "The odd thing is," he went on, "that I wake up curiously refreshed after these episodes. Reinvigorated, but, I have to admit, with a touch of bitterness. Well, more than a touch. As if I've been seized by a malign spirit that bids me down a corridor of, if not evil, at least mischief." He smiled briefly. "When I woke up, I saw you reading your, I don't know what to call it, your newspaper?"

Alex felt a shock. He remembered thinking Bierce was still

asleep. Remembered sitting on the bed and reading the piece of newspaper that had wrapped the photograph of Molly and Abraham Lincoln. He didn't respond.

"When I awoke from my . . ." Bierce went on, " 'stupor' I guess would be the correct word, 'sleep' being much too mild a term, you were engrossed in your reading. You got up, put the paper in your dresser drawer, and left."

"I went to see Colonel Baker at the War Department."

"Ah." Bierce nodded. "You must tell me about that meeting. But first, I have a confession. Perhaps I could blame that imp that possesses me after my attacks, or perhaps it's merely my bad nature that leads me astray, but I looked in the drawer and I read your paper."

Alex tried to remember the articles Bierce would have read, tried to come up with the lies that he would now have to tell.

Bierce took out a piece of writing paper from his pocket and unfolded it. "I must say, I found it most perplexing. I consider myself a well-read man, but puzzling out your, whatever it is, was like trying to decipher a foreign language. Some of it I could understand, and we'll get to those parts in a moment, but let's begin here." He turned the paper around so Alex could see. Bierce had sketched out a picture of the stealth bomber coming in for a landing. He had written words beneath the drawing.

"I copied this from . . . what?" Bierce asked, turning the paper back around so he could look at it. "I made my drawing from a picture, of course, but what sort? It is either a photograph or the most remarkably rendered drawing I have ever seen. But it is on a paper that I consider quite like that on which our newspapers are printed. Underneath were the words, I copied these as well, 'Rising labor expenses boost overall costs of stealth bomber.' I could read the words, but I am at a loss as to what they mean. And

I have no earthly idea as to what the object in the picture is. I don't even understand how the picture is applied to the paper." He held his hands palms up and shrugged. "I apologize for invading your privacy, but I believe I deserve an explanation."

Various phrases ran through Alex's mind: *tissue of lies, house of cards, web of deceit.* . . . Lying to Bierce wasn't going to work. The man was too smart, too curious, and the evidence was too unusual to be easily explained away. Besides, he had already decided that it was time to give up the John Jordan fiction, time to move on. And perhaps most of all, he was tired of lying to a man he considered a friend.

"What you saw," he began, "is part of a page of a newspaper."

"But . . ." Bierce began. Alex held up his hand.

"Please. You asked for an explanation. I'm going to give it to you, even though it will sound unbelievable. But there is the newspaper—you have seen it, you know it exists. That will be the proof. Hear me out, then ask your questions. Most of all, you are going to have to trust me."

Bierce looked at him and nodded. "Say your piece."

"My name is Alex Balfour, and I am from the future." He stopped and ran his hands over his face. "It sounds so stupid when I say it. Like a line from a science fiction B movie."

"A what?"

"Never mind. I live in New York City. That partial sheet of newspaper is from my time."

"Your time?"

"Approximately one hundred fifty years in the future."

Bierce sat back in his chair. "And you came here from the future in what manner? On the train?" Alex ignored Bierce's smirk.

"I don't know how it happens. It just takes me."

"How convenient," Bierce said.

"Look, you can mock me all you want; keep it up, and you'll piss me off and I won't explain *this* to you." He tapped the drawing Bierce had made.

" 'Piss me off'? I take your point. Yes, there is this, isn't there. What exactly is it anyway?"

Alex turned the picture so it was right side up to Bierce. It really was remarkably well drawn. "What you copied is a photograph. In my time the newspapers can print photographs in color. The object in the photograph is an airplane."

Bierce burst into laughter. Alex watched the other man for a moment and he too began to laugh. They laughed together until tears started in Alex's eyes. Some of the other drinkers in the bar were staring at them. Bierce calmed down and wiped his eyes.

"An air train?" he asked. "That thing is the size of a train?"

"An air *plane*," Alex explained. "And it's bigger than a train car. It's a stealth bomber, which means it can't be detected, it's practically invisible and it drops bombs on enemy soldiers."

Bierce stared at him and shook his head. "You're insane."

Alex understood that he must sound crazy to Bierce. "If I'm insane, how do you explain the newspaper and the photograph and the articles?"

Bierce shook his head again. "I can't explain it. But that doesn't mean I believe what you say. Forget the air carriage for a moment. There was another item that bothers me even more than that impossibility. There was a small piece of writing about Mr. Ford's theater. If this artifact is from some far time, why does it refer to our time? And more importantly, and this is most troubling, this writing says that President Lincoln was assassinated at the theater. How can this be?"

Alex remembered the article. It was a small piece announcing that the United States Park Service had reopened Ford's Theater after a yearlong renovation. "Because it will happen," Alex said. "It will be a great tragedy."

"It will be a great tragedy to you personally if someone besides me sees this writing. And even I am torn about my part in seeing it and not turning you in to the authorities. I am an officer in the United States Army. I feel that it is my duty to report you. You have knowledge of a plan to assassinate the president and you feel no guilt?"

"I certainly had nothing to do with Lincoln's assassination. I didn't write that article."

"How do I know that? How would anyone know that? This seems to me to be evidence of a plot. And it will seem to be so by anyone else who sees it."

Alex tried to remember. Was there a byline on any of the articles? He thought that the Ford's piece was taken from a wire service. "It's a newspaper. The pieces are written by reporters. Look, here's what is going to happen. Lincoln will win the election, Lee will surrender to Grant at Appomattox Court House on April the ninth, and Lincoln will be assassinated and die on April the fifteenth. The entire war will end shortly thereafter. To me this is history. I guarantee it will happen just as I said."

Bierce frowned. "I guess it's better that you're insane, you can use it at your trial in your own defense. It's a new tactic, did you know that? It was invented by Secretary of War Stanton at a rather famous trial a few years ago. But of course you knew, you're the man from the future, you know everything." He looked at Alex, who said nothing. A long silence passed between them.

"You're serious, aren't you?" Bierce asked.

Alex nodded.

"Are you crazy?"

Alex shook his head.

"If you have nothing to do with it, who will murder the president?"

"John Wilkes Booth. Who will himself be killed several days later. In a barn in Virginia."

"Booth?" Bierce looked incredulous. "In a barn in Virginia? The man is one of the greatest actors in the country. He has everything to live for. Women prostrate themselves before him; he has the pick of any of them. I don't believe it."

"It's true."

Bierce shook his head. "Prove it to me. Let me see you do it. Whatever it is you do. Travel to the past, or the future."

"It doesn't work that way, I can't just make it happen. I told you, it takes me. I don't control it. Besides, you've already seen me do it. The other night when I disappeared." Alex thought for a moment. "All right," he went on, "I've already told you Lincoln will be reelected—"

"I could say the same thing, be right, and it would prove nothing," Bierce interrupted.

Alex thought harder. *This is my field. I know this stuff.* "Lincoln will not only win, he will get over fifty-five percent of the vote." Bierce still looked skeptical. "Okay, Lincoln will get 212 electoral votes and McClellan will get 21. New York will go for Lincoln. But it will be close."

"No!" Bierce interjected. "McClellan will surely make a stronger showing. Even the president says that the election will be very close, that he might lose in the end."

Alex shrugged. "Nonetheless, it's true. You can verify it after the fact in the newspapers. If the numbers come out the way I said they would, will you believe me?"

"It will take several days after the election to get a complete account," Bierce said. He looked away, then back to Alex. "But yes, if you're accurate, I would have to believe. Believe something, I'm not sure what. There's no way you could know those numbers beforehand, or ever guess them so closely. Unless you have some sort of secret dealings with the election officials?" Bierce asked, eyebrows raised.

Alex laughed. "And when would I have established such a connection? And besides, there is the evidence of the newspaper. We'll go over it together and I will explain everything. We'll read each article and I will tell you what it refers to, what it means. You'll believe me then."

"All right. But it's damn hard to swallow. I guess I'll go along with it for now." He frowned. "So what am I supposed to call you?" he asked. "Swami? What's your name again?"

"Alex. And stop looking at me that way, I'm the same person."

Bierce nodded. "It *would* explain some oddities in your character." He held up a hand. "Not that I believe you. Yet. How *can* I believe you?" His voice was almost plaintive.

"I know it's hard," Alex answered. "If it didn't happen to me, I'm not sure I would believe it myself. Let it go for now. We'll talk about it after you see the paper and the Lincoln election numbers. All right?"

Bierce was staring into his whiskey glass. He pursed his lips, then nodded. "All right. But if it's true, I have a long list of questions I want answered." He drank the last of his whiskey.

"Why didn't you bring the newspaper with you?" Alex asked, gesturing to the waiter for another round.

"First of all," Bierce answered, "while it is true that I am a snoop, I am not a thief. I do not take another man's belongings, even if they do seem to be seditious. And there is something else." Bierce leaned forward and spoke in a lower voice. "There is the matter of the French picture." He stopped talking as the waiter filled their glasses again.

"What French picture?" Alex asked. "What's a French picture?"

Bierce gave him a sly smile. "On the back of the flying thing there is a large picture of a naked woman. How could you forget such a thing? I had no idea you were interested in matters of that sort."

Alex remembered the jewelry advertisement for Barney's. Bierce was right, the model was naked from the waist up, even though you couldn't see much of anything besides beads. "In my time, that's not considered particularly risqué. Do you understand the word?"

"Of course. I'm not some Hottentot in the jungle. In your time it may not be risqué, but here it is illegal. You could be arrested for possessing such materials, which is another reason I did not carry the paper away from where you had hidden it. But your interest in such things has given me an idea for this evening."

"I almost forgot," Alex said. "Whitman has invited us to attend a lecture on Moral Trigonometry given by Julia Ward Howe this evening. It might be interesting."

"No, it won't," Bierce said. "Be interesting. It will be very boring, and I'm not going to a lecture from any female poetess." Bierce smiled at him. "We're going to a bawdy house. I've not had a woman for much too long, so tonight I will buy myself one. I know a very respectable establishment where we can enjoy ourselves to the fullest."

"But . . ."

Bierce held up his hand again. "No arguments. You will be perfectly comfortable there, I promise. If you've no interest in a real woman, you can buy yourself some more pictures for your collection. You're going with me, and that's the end of it." He signaled the bartender. "Two more, bartender. My friend is in the need of some Dutch courage."

· · ·

Colonel Lafayette Baker waited for Preacher outside Nellie Starr's house of prostitution on Ohio Avenue. This was Hooker's Division, home of gamblers, prostitutes, pickpockets, con men, deserters, and Confederate sympathizers and parolees. It bounded Murder Row on the east and had the unwholesome distinction of being larger and even more varied in its criminal amusements. It catered, generally, to whites rather than to the black inhabitants of the Row. The name came from the camp followers of General "Fighting Joe" Hooker, one-time commander of the Army of the Potomac, who abandoned his stragglers and sutlers here when he shipped south to fight in the spring of 1862. The camp followers, unable to book passage on the steamships needed to follow Hooker, stayed in town and thrived.

A man leading a horse approached Baker in the dark. The man was of medium height but strong build. He wore a black suit and black, flat-brim hat. His pockmarked face was edged by a short black beard. He stopped and stared into the shadows of the house. "Colonel," he said. Baker stepped out of the shadows.

"Preacher." Baker nodded. "You got a report for me?"

Preacher smiled at the note of impatience in Baker's voice. Baker could go sit on a damn tack. Preacher had the man's tit in a wringer for past favors and both of them knew it. "I followed that Lieutenant Jordan to his room at the National."

"He said he was at Willard's."

"Then he lied. He's got a room with another man who's on the register as one A. Bierce. He then went and met some fellow, maybe Bierce, for dinner and whiskey at Willard's. Looks like they're having a big night, they've just arrived at Ann Benton's establishment for some horizontal refreshment. I left a man there to watch him. You want us to break them up and bring him in?"

"No. Not yet. We can catch him at his room. You just make sure you don't lose him in case he goes somewhere else for the night. This is damn important, Preacher. Important to both of us."

Preacher narrowed his eyes. "The hell's that supposed to mean?"

"You remember that job you did for me down near Winchester? This man just might know something about that. So don't lose him. I'll wait for you back at his room at the National. I want to be there to take him, but I've got some business here first."

Preacher nodded. "No hurry," he said. "Those two will be a while." He mounted his horse and trotted off.

Baker walked around the front of the house and up the steps. His knock was answered, and the door was opened quickly when the man inside saw who had come to call. Baker handed his hat to the doorman and entered the brightly lit, noisy front room. A half-dozen men in varying stages of drunkenness stood and sat surrounded by the same number of women in varying stages of undress. The women wore loose shifts that exposed bouncing breasts and plump thighs when they were pulled squealing onto the laps of the men. No one paid much attention to Baker; he was a regular, like the others, even though he never paid for his custom.

The proprietress, Nellie, stood next to a piano where an old Negro played. Nellie was dressed in a sedate hooped skirt, as was her sister Ella who sat near her. Baker might have Nellie tonight, if he desired, or any of the other girls. Anyone except Ella. Ella, who was pale, blonde, and beautiful, was the mistress of the actor, Wilkes Booth. No one touched Ella but Booth. This rankled the colonel, but Nellie had made it clear that if he were to continue his status as favored customer, he would have to abide by that one rule. Even the threat of jail wouldn't sway her. Ella was the most beautiful woman Baker had ever seen; he hated the actor for his outspoken secessionist views, but he would abide by the rule. For now. There was time to come up with something that would remove Booth from the picture and open up the way for Baker to take his place with Ella.

The doorman who had admitted Baker came into the room and whispered in Ella's ear. She nodded, stood up, said something to her sister, and left. Baker glanced back down the hallway and saw Ella putting on a coat.

He looked back, hooked a finger, and beckoned to Nellie across the room. She put her fan on a small table and stood. She smiled faintly and walked across the room to the colonel. She didn't like Baker, found his self-importance personally repugnant, but she knew that he could bring untold amounts of trouble down on her and her house if she did not do what he wanted. The one saving element, though, was that it would be over quickly. The colonel was as fast at his business as he was in his moral condemnations of others.

"I don't have much time," Baker said.

"My, how romantic," Nellie answered. "Let's go."

Molly entered the auditorium and stood at the back of the room, looking over the rows of well-dressed men and women. They were in the Smithsonian Castle, the lone public building on a swath of land that someday would be the Washington Mall, but now was a large, rough field bordered by the stinking Potomac River on one side and the pestiferous canal on the other. At one end was the unfinished Washington monument, currently a stockyard and butcher shop, and at the other the Capitol building. Tonight the carriages of the upper classes waited patiently outside while their passengers waited patiently inside. In a matter of moments the well-known poetess and author of the "Battle Hymn of the Republic" was about to appear and lecture them on the subject of Moral Trigonometry.

Molly was dressed in a variation of the carriage outfit she had worn earlier. The salient characteristic of this fawn-colored dress was that it had no hoop, so she could more easily fit into the seats of the auditorium. She was glad to be spared the hoop, but she was still strapped into a breath-threatening corset and draped with annoying crinolines. She stood inside the door and scanned the crowd. A man in the audience turned and looked back in her direction. With a mild shock of recognition she realized she was looking at Walt Whitman. *Poetry. Of course he would be here. What is he looking for?*

She noticed there were two empty seats beside Whitman and wondered if she had the nerve to go and sit beside him. And decided she did. She walked down the aisle to where Whitman was still twisted around, craning toward the back of the room. "Is this seat taken?" she asked.

Whitman looked at her and frowned.

"If it is, I can sit elsewhere," she added, flustered by his frown.

"No, no, my dear lady. It's just that I was expecting two friends, but I see now that they won't be joining me tonight. They must have had a more pressing engagement. But I really thought one of them at least would have come. No matter. Please, sit." There was a rustle and murmur from the crowd around them. Molly sat down. On the stage a man and a woman had entered and walked to two chairs positioned at center-stage next to a podium. The woman was tall and attractive, hair done in a tight bun. She was wearing an elaborate hoopskirt with a tightly tailored, vaguely military jacket.

"I'm hoping we get more poetry than trigonometry this evening," Whitman said, speaking in a low voice. Molly positioned her skirts and laid her gloves and her small purse on the empty seat between them.

"If one of your friends comes, I'll hold my things," she said. She held out her hand. "My name is Molly Glenn."

Whitman took her hand and pressed it lightly. "Walt Whitman," he said.

"I know your work, Mr. Whitman," Molly said quietly, almost positive that *Leaves of Grass* had been published years before the Civil War. "*Leaves of Grass* is one of my favorite works of poetry."

He looked at her appraisingly. "You're one of the few women to have read it. Or at least one of the few to admit it. What did you say your name was again?"

"Molly Glenn."

Whitman frowned, thinking. "I'm sure my friend won't be coming," Whitman said, as the man on the stage approached the podium. "Too bad," he added, "I think he would have enjoyed this." He looked at Molly closely. "You know, I think I've heard your name before, but for the life of me I can't remember where."

The man onstage introduced Julia Ward Howe, stressing her many accomplishments as an author, abolitionist, moral crusader, women's rights activist, poet, and last but probably foremost in the public's mind, author of the "Battle Hymn of the Republic."

Julia Ward Howe, who was always addressed using all three names, was a pleasant-faced, forty-ish woman, with a strong speaking voice. She began her speech. After ten minutes Molly felt herself beginning to nod off. Howe's lecture seemed incredibly dense and convoluted to Molly, but the rest of the audience appeared to be entranced by it.

"There are many," Howe was saying, "who will tell you, from the pulpit and through published tracts, that it is not till the calling of Abraham and the establishment of a sure line through which *her seed* should be manifested, that *woman's destiny* as the moral helper of man . . ."

"I've remembered," Whitman whispered into Molly's ear. She looked at him quizzically. *"Where I've heard your name."* They both looked back at Howe for a moment.

". . . when he is overborne by sin and the punishments of sin, and doomed, apparently . . ."

"Do you know a man named Jordan?" Whitman whispered. *"He's around five feet, ten inches in height. He has slightly curly blondish hair. A handsome man. No beard."*

". . . to utter destruction, is brought out and clearly established. We might cite many Bible proofs . . ."

Molly felt a small shiver. *"What color are this man's eyes?"* she whispered back.

". . . of her spiritual insight in . . ."

"Blue. An unusual color, a very attractive light blue. He said this woman he knew was a female journalist, if you can believe that. He's kind of an odd fellow in some indefinable way. He said his Molly Glenn worked for the New York Times. *He's the one I was waiting for tonight. You're sitting in what would have been his seat."*

Molly felt the outer world recede. Howe's words faded into the distance.

". . . discerning the true way, and her aid in helping men to keep the true faith . . ."

A roaring seemed to encompass her, as if her blood could be heard rushing through her veins. She was hot, flushed, light-headed, and thought she might faint. Whitman was looking at her with concern, his brow furrowed. His image seemed to recede as well, as if she were looking down a long tunnel.

She closed her eyes and clenched her hands, determined not to pass out.

"Are you all right?" Whitman whispered.

A man in the row in front of them turned and glared at them. She shook her head. *"I don't know."*

chapter twenty-one

THE HIRED CAB deposited Alex and Bierce in front of a three-story Victorian house, a far more elegant and respectful destination than Alex had imagined.

"You don't think I'd take you to one of those disreputable cribs that the soldiers favor, do you?" Bierce asked. He rapped lightly on the front door, which was opened by a tall, stately black man who ushered them in. A graceful woman in an elaborate hoop skirt approached.

"I'm Ann Benton," she said. "Welcome to my house." She gestured them into the parlor.

There were a half-dozen men scattered around the room, seated in deep chairs. Each was accompanied by an attractive woman dressed in simpler, hoopless, looser versions of what the lady of the house was wearing. All the dresses were extremely low-cut, exposing breasts and nipples and yet maintaining a certain level of decency. The men, who were smoking cigars and drinking, glanced at Alex and Bierce, but the rule seemed to be to show no interest in who was in attendance. Ann Benton seated them in two chairs that faced each other. They gave drink orders to the black man who had let them in. A young lady carrying a half-filled champagne glass appeared at Bierce's side. "Good evening, gentlemen, my name is Marie. May I join you?" She had lovely brown skin and a French accent.

"Of course," Bierce said.

"A moment, please," Alex said to Marie. "I'd like to speak to my friend for just a minute, then I'm sure we'd love to have you join us." Marie nodded, touching the tip of her tongue to the rim of her glass. She smiled, walked away, and sat at a piano where she began to play.

"Please, what are we about to discuss now?" Bierce said in a tone of mock agony. "No more lunatic notions."

"I'm perfectly happy to have a drink here." Alex laughed. "I have no qualms whatsoever about your indulging yourself in the pleasures provided. But I'm not going to avail myself of any of the ladies. It's not a matter of morality, it's simply that I have someone I am remaining true to. Someone at . . . home."

"At your home in the land of flying railroad trains?" Bierce asked.

"Very funny. In the future. Your future. My past."

"I'm sorry for amusing myself at your expense," Bierce said. "If what you say is true, about your situation in general, not about your true love . . ." He paused.

"Molly. Her name is Molly," Alex said.

Bierce smiled.

"And now what is so amusing?" Alex asked.

"The song that Marie is playing on the piano. It's titled 'Molly, Do You Love Me?' by Stephen Foster. At any rate, if what you say about this Molly is true, that she pines for you in some far-away time, then you are to be pitied, and if it isn't true and you are insane, you are to be pitied as well. In either event, not something to be amused by, I suppose. All right. Save your manhood for the fair Molly, wherever she may be. Now, may we recall Marie?

Alex nodded. "Of course. But didn't you mention an association with a young woman as well?"

Bierce frowned. Alex could see the man's mood darken. "I guess you don't remember, I said that my association had been broken off. I did not find the lady's affection for me to be sufficiently strong. She continued to attend evenings out after I had gone to war."

"That doesn't sound like much of a sign of unfaithfulness."

"It was enough for me. After a bond of affection is formed it is the duty of the female to withdraw from her former life and amusements."

"That seems a little harsh," Alex said mildly.

"You are a man, if you are to be believed, who lives in a land where pictures of nearly naked women grace the pages of public newspapers. I'm not sure your opinions on the morality of others can be counted as irreproachable," Bierce said stiffly.

They drank in silence for several minutes. "Of course you're right," Alex said. "It's not my part to tell you how to conduct your relations with women." He could see Bierce soften. Bierce was a man whose contradictions seemed to hover always just below the surface of his personality. It didn't take much to push any one facet out into the open.

Soon enough Marie convinced Bierce that they should repair to the upstairs, not that he took much convincing. Alex watched the two of them walking up the stairs and felt a pang of . . . something . . . he wasn't sure what. Jealousy? The need to touch another human being in at least the semblance of love. He shook it off and said his good-byes to the mistress of the house. She directed him to one of the carriages for hire that waited outside.

He stepped down from the carriage at the National Hotel and paid the driver. The man would return to Ann Benton's house and wait for the next gentleman who needed to be ferried home.

He walked through the lobby, up the stairs, and opened the door to his room; surprised to find it unlocked and then surprised to see the gas lamps already lit.

Lafayette Baker stepped out and said, "Seize him!" A soldier came from behind the door, grabbed Alex, and held his arms.

"I arrest you for plotting the assassination of the President of the United States." He held up the fragment of newspaper. Alex could see the picture of the bomber. "We're taking this as evidence." He stuffed it into Alex's knapsack. "Take him to Old Capitol Prison."

If the lecture had seemed interminable before, now it afflicted Molly with the agony of the damned. She would have walked out but she was so weak after Whitman's bombshell she was afraid she might faint. Better to wait until she gathered her strength.

It could only be Alex. Whatever name he was going by, only Alex would have used her name and said she was a reporter. He was here, in Washington. She felt the blood leaving her head again and fought against the cold vortex, willing herself inch by inch back from the brink.

She realized the roar she heard was not the blood pounding through her veins, but the audience around her applauding the end of Julia Ward Howe's lecture. "Meet me outside," she said to Whitman. She took three deep breaths and stood up. Whitman was looking worriedly at her. "I'm fine, I'm fine," she said. "Outside."

They stood in the long lines of carriages waiting for the lecture-goers. The breath from the gray carriage horse steamed in the cool air. Carter was up top, waiting for Whitman to help her into the carriage.

"Do you know where he is, this? . . ."

"Lieutenant Jordan. Yes, of course, he's at the National Hotel."

IN TIME OF WAR *163*

Molly called up to Carter. "Take me to the National Hotel." She opened the carriage door. Whitman put his hand on her arm. "Allow me to escort you."

"Get in," she commanded. She rapped on the ceiling of the carriage. Carter opened a small door in the roof and peered in at her. "Go," she said. "Now!"

"I'm sorry, madam," the clerk was saying, "but neither of the gentlemen is at home." The lobby of the National was mostly empty, though several men sat in the lobby chairs, smoking cigars and smirking at Molly. There was only one reason a woman would appear at a hotel this late at night, and this particular woman seemed highly incensed that her gentleman friend was not where he was supposed to be.

"I want to go to his room," Molly said firmly. "I'll wait for him there."

"Really, madam . . ." the clerk began.

"Really, Molly . . ." Whitman began.

"Really," a voice said behind them. They all turned. "Molly?" Bierce asked. "Your name is Molly? That's a name I just heard this very evening. Not two hours ago. May I be of some assistance? I'm Ambrose Bierce."

"She wants to see Lieutenant Jordan," Whitman said. "I've been trying to convince her that she should wait until tomorrow to call."

"No, I think I know why the lady is so insistent. Perhaps we should all go upstairs and wait for . . . Lieutenant Jordan. He should have been here before this. Perhaps he stopped somewhere for a drink."

The door to the room was half-open. Bierce stepped inside.

"Mother of God," he said. The drawers of the dresser had been pulled out and dumped on the floor. His carpetbag had been emptied and all his manuscript pages were scattered around the room. Whitman and Molly came in behind him.

"What happened?" Whitman asked.

Bierce looked at him like he was an idiot. "I don't have the slightest idea," he said. "I've just arrived myself."

"It appears you've been robbed," Molly said. "Does this have anything to do with Alex?"

"Who?" Whitman asked.

Bierce and Molly ignored him. "There wasn't anything much to rob," Bierce said.

"Mr. Bierce, you said you were with"—she looked at Whitman, trying to remember the name he had used—"the lieutenant tonight. Where were you?"

"We were at a . . . gentlemen's sporting house. Run by a Miss Ann Benton. It's possible that he's still there, maybe with one of . . ."

Molly blanched and Bierce and Whitman started toward her. She held up her hand. "I'm all right!" She gave herself a moment to recoup.

"I knew I shouldn't have told you where he was."

"No, no, that's all right. My sense of propriety is still intact." She thought for a moment. "Did the lieutenant go anywhere today that might have some bearing on this?" She gestured around them.

"He went to see Colonel Lafayette Baker," Bierce said. "About something he had seen when he was wounded."

"Wounded? How badly was he wounded!" Molly asked.

"He's all right now," Whitman said.

"We need to go see this Baker," Molly said.

"We can't go tonight," Bierce said. "It's past eleven, he won't be at his office, and it would be a mistake to seek him out at home. It will have to wait for morning."

"It can't wait for morning," Molly insisted.

"I'm afraid it must," Whitman said. "It's much too late for any sort of business. You should go home and sort it all out in the light of day."

Molly fought against it, then gave up and nodded. "Mr. Whitman, thank you for all your help. I won't be needing you any more this evening. My carriage is still waiting downstairs. I'd like a minute to speak with Mr. Bierce." Whitman gave a small bow and left.

Bierce sat on the edge of the bed.

"Did he tell you," Molly asked him, "about himself?"

Bierce knew what she was talking about. "Yes. His name is Alex Balfour. And though I still feel the fool for saying it, he has come here from the future."

Molly lifted her head and looked at him. "As have I, Mr. Bierce."

Colonel Lafayette Baker had been up much of the night and was feeling the effects. When he had arrived at his office in the basement of the War Department at eight A.M., late for him, he had found Judge Stanford Haywood waiting. The judge, even though Baker himself had rousted him out of bed at 2:00 A.M. the night before to sign an arrest order, looked remarkably rested. He was dressed in a black suit with matching silk waistcoat, the thick gold chain of a pocket watch stretched across his ample stomach, and a snow-white shirt, with freshly combed silver hair.

"Good morning, Colonel," the judge said. "I have come on the matter of that man we remanded to Old Capitol Prison last night, or rather this morning. The one we charged with plotting to assassinate the president."

"Don't worry about him. He'll be shipped out to Point Lookout, or Elmira or perhaps the Tortugas. I can personally guarantee that he will never be heard from again."

The judge nodded. "You see, there is the matter of his impersonation of a Union officer that we did not address at the time, his use of an officer's identity . . ."

"I believe the charge of planned assassination takes precedence," Baker said.

"Yes, of course, I mention it only in reference to the whole matter coming under military jurisdiction. I did a little further investigation this morning. I checked the War Records department upstairs and found that on the official rolls Lieutenant John Jordan was reported killed in the Battle of Cedar Creek. The man we arrested is guilty of the crime of impersonating an officer. In this case a dead officer. Which will make him of especial interest to the military authorities, who as you know take a particular delight in prosecuting such cases. Were he taken into custody by them, there would indeed be a very comprehensive investigation. Which, I fear, might bring on a great deal of trouble. Especially for you, sir."

Baker's eyes narrowed. "Explain yourself, sir."

The judge smiled. "While you were occupied with your men, the fellow, I guess his real name is Balfour, told me the reason he first came to see you. The matter of the murder of the soldier at Cedar Creek. I paid it little mind last night, but when I awoke several connections were made and I came to a rather tentative conclusion."

He knows, Baker thought.

"His description of the perpetrator was quite detailed, as was his description of the victims. I believe I can be of assistance to you in this matter, in finding the man who committed the crime.

In fact, I don't believe we'll have to stray very far from home at all in our search." He ostentatiously looked around the room.

"What do you want?" Baker asked. His voice was flat and hard.

The judge smiled at him. "There's the little matter of your interrupting my entertainment the other evening. I know you keep records on your arrests and the activities of the citizenry who cross your path." He gestured at Baker's massive wooden cabinets. "It's well known that you have files concerning almost everyone in this godforsaken town. I don't wish to be among them."

Without saying a word, Baker rose and went to one of the cabinets. He opened a drawer, searched for a moment, then came up with a file. He laid it on the desk and sat back down again. The judge picked up the file, glanced at it, and closed it. "Fine. This will do nicely."

He stood, began to say something, and stopped. There was a commotion in the hall.

"I don't give a damn what he's doing," Molly said as she swept by the startled sergeant.

The door to the office burst open and Molly piled in, skirts swarming. "Which one of you is Colonel Baker?" she demanded. She stopped and looked at the judge, recognizing him as the man she had argued with at Ann Benton's. "I guess that answers my question," she said. She turned to Baker. "Colonel, I'm looking for a friend of mine. A Lieutenant Jordan, I'm told he came to see you yesterday."

The sergeant pushed through the door, followed by Bierce. "Sorry, Colonel, she got by me before I could stop her."

Baker held up his hand. "Quiet! All of you." He lowered his hand. "It's all right, Sergeant, I can handle this. You may go back to your post." He looked at Bierce. "And who are you?"

"Captain Ambrose Bierce. On medical leave. I'm with her." He gestured toward Molly.

"Not right now, you're not, Captain. You'll wait with the sergeant." Bierce looked at Molly. She nodded to him and he turned and went out, followed by the sergeant.

"Now," Baker said to Molly. "Yes, I did meet with a Lieutenant Jordan yesterday. But why are you seeking him here? I have no idea where he is."

"I think you do," Molly said. She had talked to Bierce at length last night and he had told her Alex's whole story: his wounding, their stay in the hospital, moving to the National, and his meeting with Baker to relate the story of his witnessing the murder. "He was here because he saw one man murdered and another abducted. Now he himself has disappeared. I've heard of your methods, about the people who are thrown into the jails without due process."

"Colonel," the judge said, "I am acquainted with this woman. She lives at a well-known bawdy house in the city. No one knows a thing about her history, and as for what I've heard from her very mouth she is at least a Southern sympathizer, at worst a spy. She had nothing but derogatory pronouncements about President Lincoln and his conduct of the war."

"That's not true. I was commenting on the methods of silencing the press and the renunciation of a citizen's basic civil rights."

"Not according to the president," Baker said. "He's the one who instituted the process of putting dissenters in jail. And I agree with him. In the performance of my duty I have incarcerated more troublemakers than you could ever imagine."

"And it's my honor to have assisted him," the judge added.

"And was Alex Balfour, or rather John Jordan, one of them?" Molly asked.

"Miss Glenn, where are you from and when did you arrive in the city?" Baker asked. He got out a clean sheet of paper and took the cork out of his inkbottle.

"I've been in Washington more than a month. I'm originally from New York."

"And what was your address there? And rest assured I will be checking your answer through my staff in that city. You admit knowing this Alex Balfour, also known as Lieutenant John Jordan, Miss Glenn. And you admit to questioning the legitimate actions of the War Department police and the policies of the Union government as instrumented by the president, Abraham Lincoln?"

Molly was angry, but she wasn't stupid. She was now making an effort to speak calmly. "I told you I knew Lieutenant Jordan, that's why I'm here, to try and find him. As for the other, that's a matter of opinion."

Baker handed the paper he was writing on to the judge. "And it is our opinion that you are a dangerous operative, and until we have a chance to interrogate you and verify your past you will be living not in your brothel, but at our expense at the Old Capitol Prison. We have just found out this morning that your friend, whatever his real name might be, was impersonating a deceased officer in the Union Army, besides plotting to assassinate the president. Judge Haywood has already attested to your antipathy toward President Lincoln. Judge, do you find the remand paper in order?" Judge Haywood got out his pince-nez and put them on and studied the paper Baker had been writing on.

Molly was staring wide-eyed at Baker. "You can't do this. I'll go to President Lincoln. He'll help me. He knows John Jordan."

He smiled a stony smile at her. "I can't do it? I just have." He handed the pen to the judge, who dipped it into the ink and signed it. Baker blotted it with a roller. "And I might add, if I ever hear of you going to the president of the United States with any of this matter you shall never see daylight again. You will grow very old, in a very harsh prison. And Jordan or Balfour will be summarily dealt with as a traitor and an imposter. Is that clear enough for you?" He stood up and walked around the desk, opened the door, and called to the sergeant, who came immediately, followed by Bierce.

"Sergeant," Baker said, stepping aside, "take this woman immediately to the Old Capitol Prison." He picked the paper up off his desk and handed it to the sergeant. "Tell our people there that she will be held indefinitely, until such time as the Federal authorities see fit to release her. She is to be held with the other women spies and under no circumstances is she to communicate with any male prisoners." The sergeant saluted and took Molly's arm.

"Wait a minute . . ." Bierce said, pushing into the room.

"No!" Molly said to him. The soldier was beginning to pull her out into the hall. She knew Bierce was her only link to the outside. If they threw him into prison, no one would ever know where she was. She stumbled as the sergeant pulled her along. "Tell Ann Benton!" she shouted. "Tell Ann!"

Alex rolled over on the hard planks, trying to find some position that was comfortable. He was on a straw-strewn table in the center of a small, stinking cell with no windows. There were two bunks, but his cellmate told him the straw on them was infested with lice. Better to sleep on the hard table.

Alex had been in the room since he'd been seized the night before. His cellmate, on the other hand, had inhabited this six-foot by ten-foot wooden-walled room for two months. Alex couldn't tell if the man had been driven insane from the incarceration, or if he'd been that way when they put him in here. He declared that his name was Whinny, because people thought he laughed like a horse. Alex had to agree.

Whinny giggled. "Hey there," he said. Alex rolled over and sat up, looking at the man. Whinny was dressed in dirty wool pants, lace-up boots with no socks, and a tan shirt that appeared to have been made out of a feed sack.

"You wanna see somethin'?" Whinny asked.

"What?" Alex answered.

"Somethin' good. Cost you a quarter."

"I don't have a quarter. They took all my money."

Whinny shrugged. "Too bad, it's real good."

Alex waited. Evidently Whinny wasn't going to change his mind. "What is it?" Alex asked.

Whinny looked around the room, as if checking for anyone listening in on their conversation.

Insane, Alex thought. *Completely gone.*

"I made me a hole," Whinny said. He gestured at the wall behind him. "I keep a stick in it so nobody knows. The cell next to ours, they's got women in it." He looked around again and lowered his voice. "Sometimes they's take a bath in there. Out of a bucket, like. With a sponge." He giggled. "You can see titties. Had you a quarter I'd let you look."

Alex shook his head.

"See, they's got a new one over there. Just came in this morning. I heard 'em puttin' her in. I took a look. She's real purty. About the purtiest I seen so far."

"No thanks," Alex said.

"Could be she's takin' a bath, like."

Alex shook his head again, and lay back down on the table.

"Not interested," he said.

Whinny looked disappointed. "You a married man or somethin'?"

"Yeah, sort of."

"Where's your wife at anyway?"

Alex shook his head and looked at the wooden beams of the ceiling. "I don't know," he said.

BOOK TWO

chapter twenty-two

MOLLY STOOD IN line. When she reached the front she said, "Number 421."

"Sorry, ma'am, nothing today." The counterman in the advertising section of the *Capitol Constitution,* a one-armed veteran, looked past her to the next customer. The man in line behind Molly, a dapper, silver-haired gentleman, smiled faintly and waited patiently as Molly stood for a moment at the counter. Nothing today and nothing any of the days in the last several months she had been out of prison and placing her advertisement in the paper. She wondered if Alex were really in this time. *If he had seen the ad, he would have come. If he was able.* There were only two possibilities: either he was here, somewhere, or he had shifted to yet another time.

She walked by the line of customers. She had to pee. She always had to pee these days. The weight of the baby pressed upon her bladder, pressed upon her back when she tried to sleep, slowed her down during the day and kept her up at night. Although she had never been pregnant before, she knew her lack of mobility and her conspicuousness was only going to get worse.

But the pregnancy had served her well in at least one way: It had gotten her out of the Old Capitol Prison. After a month inside, her condition was obvious enough that she was released on grounds of compassion, although she was sure that Ann Benton's continued pressure had more influence than the official reason given. After enough prison time for official face-saving, she was released with a strong warning to keep her nose out of places it didn't belong. But by then any trail that might have led to Alex had disappeared.

The advertising desk of the newspaper was situated in the front of the reporters' area, where the public could come in and line up to place their advertisements for lost cows, help wanted, positions desired, and all the other small pieces of business the commercial ads allowed. Each advertiser was issued a number for their advertisement, and by checking in they would be given any results that the ad had engendered. Molly was number 421 and so far there had been no response.

She walked through the swinging gate in a low railing and continued on back through the main office of the *Capitol Constitution*. Behind her the silver-haired man stood for a moment and watched her work her way through the room of cigar-smoking, ink-scribbling men.

There was no real door on J. Noble Firth's office, so she knocked on the door frame. He looked up from a stack of papers and smiled at her.

After Molly brought Firth several of the pieces she had written—an article based on an interview with Walt Whitman, and a think piece on the wounded soldiers who were in the dozens of hospitals in the capital—his view began to change. When her prediction of Lincoln's re-election by a wide margin came true, he gave her more respect, not for her ability as a Seer, but as an astute political analyst.

Lately she had been trying to sell him a Q & A interview with Julia Ward Howe, the poetess. After Molly had been released from jail she contacted Howe, who was again in the city lecturing, and convinced her to grant an interview. Firth considered the Q & A format, as described by Molly, bizarre, never having heard of anything like it. This sort of article had yet to be invented and Firth questioned the interest readers would have on learning about various celebrities without the intervening reporter chiming in to explain things to them. He had rejected her hospital piece because he said it showed equal concern for the Confederate wounded as well as the Union's. Such a position could be considered seditious. But he recognized talent when he read it, so he encouraged her by assigning her reviews of light amusements.

They had several sessions where they discussed writing and style. He wanted to know where she had learned to write. She had fallen back on her "in China" assertion so many times it had become a joke between them. But as she learned to tailor her writing to the style of the times, he became more receptive to what she brought him and had begun to publish the pieces under the name of Glenn Balfour.

Her first published articles were reviews of plays and stage entertainments. She was surprised to find these shows slight, pallid, racist, and usually stupid. She seldom even smiled, though everyone else around her in the audience seemed to think them exceedingly amusing. It was only after she began using phrases like "exceedingly amusing" and words like "pallid" that she began to get the right slant to her writing. Firth had pointed out the mistakes in her first efforts.

"You write so plainly," he told her, holding up the sheets she had written. "People like a bit of style in their reading. Why use the word 'audience' when you can say something more interesting like 'habitué of the theater'? Why refer to something as 'good' when you might say 'singularly meritorious'?"

"Well, basically," she said, "because I was taught that simple clear writing is superior to grandiose, florid, hothouse prose."

"Hothouse prose?" He looked puzzled. "And where were you taught such a thing?" He held up his hand. "Stop! Let me guess. In China, am I right?"

"Absolutely," she said, still smiling. "My writing tutors were Mr. Strunk and Mr. White."

"I fear Mr. Strunk and Mr. White would fail quite miserably as writers at this newspaper. Take this back and work on it again. I want to see some flash, some verve, some intellect."

And so she had learned to stilt her writing, to go back over everything and rework it into the language of the newspaper. She was quite proud when she pronounced an evening's performance ". . . piquant and picturesque, precisely the kind of perform-ance that the habitués of the Olympia Theater expect, desire, and require." She worked hard on the alliteration and rhyme. Mr. Firth admired the turns of phrase as well and published the entire review.

She was grateful for the exposure in the paper and the small amount of money Firth paid her. She knew if Alex were in this time he would read the papers—he was always an avid newspaper consumer—and eventually he'd see the Glenn Balfour pen name and make the connection. He might not read the personal ads, but he'd read the news portion of the paper and if he saw her pen name he would understand and investigate. And then he would find her.

"Noble," Molly said to Firth—they'd moved to first names after several of her articles had been published—"I have an idea for a story I want to do."

Firth moved his chair back a few inches and frowned. He almost always found her ideas somewhat disturbing. A bit like she wrote, or at least used to write, as if English were a second, or even third language, squeezed through a filter that extracted the more eloquent and descriptive words available to a seasoned professional.

"I want to do an interview," Molly said.

"An interview? For what purpose?"

She stopped herself from rolling her eyes. "With the purpose of writing an article about that person. Here's the way it works: I go and talk with them, ask them questions, write down the answers, and then put it all together. Not into a straight news article, but a piece about the person themselves." She could see he was still puzzled. "Like a small biography. That's it, a short biography that would be published in the newspaper."

Firth's frown deepened as he thought. "And you think readers would be interested in such a piece?"

"If the subject was interesting."

"And who, pray tell, would you subject to this interview?"

"Abraham Lincoln. The newly elected, second-term president of the United States."

Firth rubbed his hand over his face. She knew this was what he did when he was thinking. In this case he seemed to be wiping away his frown, which he replaced with a small smile. "I have it," he said. "Instead of interviewing Abraham Lincoln, you'll talk to Mary Todd Lincoln. The article will be pointed out to female readers by their husbands, and the *Constitution* will gain a wider readership. The only section of the paper women now read is the advertisements. Perhaps we can lead them to the news articles as well. Or at least to those articles that would be of interest to their sensibilities." Now he was beaming. "I like this idea. Perhaps we could eventually devote an entire section to the ladies."

She had to admit, the man was smart. He had just invented the newspaper Women's Pages. "It's a good idea," she agreed, "but I really think a presidential interview would be more important."

He waved away her comment. "No, no, this is good, this is excellent, I know it. Mary Lincoln has been at odds with the society of Washington City ever since she arrived. There is great interest in the dress she wore to the inauguration. You must ask her about the dress, and give our lady readers a minute description using all your finest prose. She spends a fortune on clothing; you know, rumor has it she's crippled both the President's House and her own family with debt because of it. I'll make the arrangements; there should be no problem. She'll leap at the opportunity to show herself in a positive light and to best her critics. I'll let you know when and where this will all occur. I should have all the details by this afternoon. Go home, rest. You shouldn't be out on the streets in your condition anyway." He stood up.

"Are you sure I can't..." she began, but he was shaking his head.

He came around the desk and took her arm as she stood up. "No, leave everything to me. I insist." He steered her out the door, still talking. "Maybe later you can do Mr. Lincoln. We've plenty of time for that. He'll be around for another four years."

chapter twenty-three

ALEX HURRIED DOWN the sand road that led past the idle cannons of the Second Wisconsin Artillery toward the southern end of the peninsula and the star-shaped complex of hospital buildings. The few guards who noticed him paid little mind; he was a familiar sight. After four months in the Point Lookout prison camp he was known to pose no threat.

The morning was cool but not cold. He had endured the previous winter months packed into a ragged tent with eleven other men, each with one thin blanket, but no fire or any other way to keep warm. Out of the original twelve men in his tent four were now dead, carried away and buried. New prisoners had quickly replaced them.

Alex approached the Hospital Supplies building and saw that he was in for trouble. Lounging on a folding wooden campstool by the door was the guard, Chaney King, a private in the Third Maryland Negro Regiment. A soldier who loathed all Confederates, even though Alex had explained a number of times he was not one of them.

"Where you goin', Picture Boy?" King drawled.

Picture Boy was one of the few benign nicknames King had for him. It referred to his job in the camp photography studio. "The same place I usually go," Alex answered. "I'm here to get some chemicals for Mr. Spaulding."

King stood, straightened his uniform, and picked up his rifle from where it was leaning against the door frame.

"You got a pass?"

Alex dug the tattered piece of paper from the pocket of his canvas pants. Another prisoner had made the pants for him out of a discarded tent. He had paid two greenback dollars for them. He handed the smudged paper to the guard, who pretended to read it. King had seen the pass a hundred times.

King handed the pass back. "Now sing me the song."

This was one of King's jokes. Alex didn't mind much; many of the other jokes were far more painful. He began to sing. " 'Mine eyes have seen the glory of the coming of the Lord, he has trampled down . . ."

"Okay, okay, tha's enough, now what you got to say 'bout the whole situation?" Several smirking soldiers stood nearby watching this familiar ritual.

"Bottom rail on top now, Boss," Alex said. "Bottom rail on top."

"Good. Very good. Now go on an' get what you come for, Picture Boy." King leaned the rifle back on the door frame and sat back down. He nodded and smiled at the nearby soldiers, both Negro and white, who gave him a laugh in return.

Inside, a private in shirtsleeves stood behind a counter. He was chewing on a twig. His name was Ardel and Alex had dealt with him many times. " 'Day, Alex," Ardel said. "Brother King out there giving you a hard time again?" He put his chewed twig on the countertop.

"He doesn't bother me," Alex said. The commissary smelled faintly of ether and strongly of a multitude of bitter medicines.

"I got to say, you take his guff pretty darn easy for a Reb. Must rankle."

"I've told you before, Ardel, I'm not a Reb."

"I guess someone thought you were, otherwise you wouldn't be here. Anyway, what does Mr. Spaulding need today?"

"A five-gallon jug of collodion and the usual bottle of potassium cyanide."

Ardel nodded as he dragged out a large maroon-colored ledger and turned to a blank page. He dipped a pen into a bottle of ink and wrote Alex's order along the top line. "I'll just go and fetch it," he said.

Ardel came back in and hoisted the jug and the bottle onto the countertop. "Haven't seen Mr. Spaulding in some time," he said.

"Neither have I. He pretty much leaves the business in my hands these days." Alex picked up the cyanide and put it into his coat pocket. The collodion was another matter. The gray clay jug was heavy itself and with the five gallons of collodion it was all Alex could do to pick it up. He realized how weak he'd become from the meager prison food and living conditions. He turned to leave.

"Remember," Ardel said. "You be careful of that collodion. It'll blow you ass over hinder-post you get it near a fire."

Outside, King was ten yards away laughing with a group of other guards. Alex briefly considered picking up the man's untended rifle from where it was leaning against the door frame and throwing it at him, just to make a point, but let it go.

The hospital itself was sixteen long buildings that resembled sixteen railroad boxcars formed up into a starburst pattern with a courtyard at the inner ends of the cars. Around the outer edge was a sort of covered-deck walkway. Alex went up the two steps onto the boardwalk and headed three buildings around the circle to the cookhouse, where he picked up a small bag of used coffee grounds from a cook who owed him for photographs. He then resumed his walk back to the photography studio.

Point Lookout Prison was situated on a narrow spit of land that projected out into the Chesapeake Bay from the shores of southern Maryland. Alex had spent his first several weeks, day and night, in a thirty-acre walled enclosure where most of the prisoners were housed, and where he was still locked up every night. After being let out during the day to cut brush and work on maintaining the roads, he had secured himself a position with the camp photographer, a Mr. Spaulding. He now spent his days working as a photographer and at night would go back to his twelve-man tent in the enclosed stockade. Alex knew if he kept a low profile and held out a bit longer the war would end and he would eventually be released with the rest of the prisoners. Or at least he hoped he would be released. He wasn't sure what

Lafayette Baker had in store for him. The fact that he had not brought him up on formal charges of plotting an assassination, but had rather had him whisked away to this prison camp, made Alex wonder just what the man's motives were.

The small brick building that housed the photography studio was a ten-minute walk from the hospital. The studio measured twelve feet by fourteen feet, had a wooden floor, and was filled with shelves and counters. Photographic equipment and chemicals were stocked on the shelves and under the counters. A canvas tent where the actual photographs were taken was fixed to the back of the building. The top of the tent rolled back so that the maximum amount of light was admitted.

Alex took off his coat, hung it on a nail on the back of the door, and stowed the chemicals on a shelf.

A bout of shivering convinced him to use up a little of his precious stock of firewood. He opened the door of the cast-iron stove, struck one of his precious lucifers, or wooden matches, and started a fire with a few twigs and a piece of old newspaper that he had read a hundred times. He lifted a battered pan off a shelf and poured in water from a jug. He shook in a scant handful of used coffee grounds from his bag and put the pan on the stove.

On another shelf was an old tin can that had once contained oysters and now held a bouquet of green leaves in rusty water. He picked three stems of sour leaves out of the can and chewed them. An older prisoner had pointed the plant out to him, growing near the woods where they exercised. The grizzled veteran told him that the heart-shaped leaves would prevent scurvy and showed him his own brown-stained but intact choppers to prove it. So Alex ate three or four leaves several times a day and so far the man had been proven right.

The coffee was boiling, sending up some lovely scented steam. Alex took a tin cup off a nail in the wall and carefully poured the liquid through a once-white rag into the cup. He would dry the grounds again and save them. They were good for at least two more cups. He wrapped his hands around the hot cup, sipping and savoring the warmth.

The knock on the door startled him so much he almost dropped his cup. He opened the door.

"You the one they call Picture Man?" a young soldier asked. He looked at a piece of paper in his hand. "Balfour?"

"Yes, that's me."

The soldier handed him the paper. "This is from General Barnes. I was told to deliver it to you." Alex took the paper. The soldier was looking behind him into the room. "Can I come in? It's cold out here."

Alex stepped aside for the soldier to come in, closed the door and read the note:

MR. BALFOUR,

ON FRIDAY THIS WEEK WE WILL BE HOSTING A CIVILIAN INSPECTOR WHO HAS EXPRESSED A DESIRE TO VIEW YOUR FACILITIES. IT IS POSSIBLE THAT HE WILL WANT TO HAVE HIS PHOTOGRAPH MADE. PLEASE BE IN READINESS FOR HIS ARRIVAL AND MAKE YOURSELF AVAILABLE TO HIM.

BRIGADIER GENERAL JAMES BARNES

Alex folded the note and put it into his pocket.

The notice that Alex might have to make a photograph of the visitor was not unusual. The fact that he was being informed of this beforehand by the camp commandant was.

"Do you have any idea who's coming to the camp for inspection tomorrow?" Alex asked.

"They didn't say nothin' to me about it. Just handed me the message and said to give it to you."

Alex thanked the soldier and closed the door behind him.

At five o'clock Alex entered the thirty-acre stockade-fenced enclosure where thousands of Confederate prisoners lived and died. If he had not come back he supposed he might have gone unnoticed till the next morning, giving him a twelve-hour head start on an escape, but he had long ago given up on any thoughts of breaking out. Point Lookout itself was a natural enclosure, surrounded by water on three sides and almost completely on the fourth. Some men escaped by going out to use the jakes, long boards with toilet-seat holes that extended over the waters of the bay, and then dropping off and swimming to the Maryland shore. But the patrols were many, and although there was almost complete sympathy for the Southern cause in the Maryland countryside it was still Union and tightly controlled as such.

The air in the compound was full of the smell of cooking food, smoke, dust, mildewed tents, and the cries of prisoner-merchants hawking goods to the thousands of prisoner-buyers milling through the sand streets between the once-white, now ragged bell-shaped Sibley tents and houses built of discarded cracker boxes. Everyone who could scrape up a few coins attempted some sort of scheme to increase his stake.

"Vegetables, here's your vegetables . . ."

"Apples, apples . . . potatoes . . . onions . . ."

"Rings, braided rings, bone rings, carved to your liking . . ."

"Get your 'baccy, chews just a nickel, hardtack for sale or trade."

"Bread, bread, clean and pure."

"Here's your coffee, coffee."

The vegetables were rejects bought from the cooks or rescued from the garbage, the rings and jewelry were meticulously carved from beef bones, the bread was corn bread made mostly from the ground-up cob, the tobacco came from the sutler outside who was happy to sell it to one and all, and the coffee was made from burnt bread crusts.

Alex threaded his way through the masses of men. Dinner would be served soon, but until then there was nothing to do but roam the compound, haggle with the vendors, and talk. The sound of musical instruments, banjos, fiddles, harmonicas, twined with men talking, shouting, singing, and arguing.

Above it all, looking down on the scene, were the guards, most of them drawn from the two regiments of United States Colored troopers assigned to the prison. They marched along a parapet outside the wall, three feet down from the top of the palings. There were no guards inside on the ground. Several times Alex had witnessed wrenching scenes where Negro guards recognized former owners among the Rebel prisoners.

As he approached his tent, number 228, two incongruous sounds came to him, as if out of some other place and time: the silvery notes of a flute, and the cries of a baby.

He entered the tent. There were four men out of the twelve who shared the space inside, the others were probably waiting near the cook tent for their dinner. The four inside were on the pallets they had fashioned from pine needles and moss and whatever scraps of cloth they could scavenge.

A young man sat playing a flute. He played it extremely well, a classical composition. He was sitting on a pallet next to where Alex slept. He stopped when Alex ducked into the tent.

"Where's Shattuck?" Alex asked. Barkley Shattuck had slept beside him for the last month. The man had been sick almost the entire time, and while Alex had never got to know him well, he had grown used to the sound of his labored breathing in the night.

"I fear he's dead," the flute player said. "I'm sorry." He put the flute down and stood up.

"Well, he was sick. I tried to get him to go to the hospital but most of the men feel that once you go there the only way out is through the Dead House."

The flute player gave him a slight smile. "And is it?" he asked.

"I'm afraid so," Alex answered. "At least most of the time it seems like it."

"I'll remember that," the flute player said. He held out his hand. "I'm Sidney Lanier. Late of the Macon Volunteers of the Second Georgia Battalion."

"Alex Balfour." He shook Lanier's hand. "I'm a civilian prisoner. From Washington City."

The sound of the crying baby came from outside. Lanier looked at Alex with raised eyebrows. "They say that Lincoln is a demon," he said, "but has he stooped to imprisoning babies?"

A man lying on the ground at the back of the tent pushed himself up on one elbow and shouted. "Quiet! Quiet out there! Shut that baby up. Can't you see a sick man is trying to sleep here? Nurse! Nurse! I fear I am dying!"

"You be quiet, Jesse," Alex called. He motioned to Lanier to follow him. The two of them stepped outside. Lanier was taller than Alex by several inches. He had brown hair pushed straight back and the standard long unruly beard that most of the Southerners wore.

"Should we get that fellow back in the tent some help?" Lanier asked.

Alex laughed. "Jesse Hudson? He's not sick, he's drunk. Come on."

They walked around the tent. "And how does one accomplish getting drunk in a prison camp? I didn't know it was allowed," Lanier asked.

"It's not allowed, but it's possible. Anything is possible in here. The men who go out on wood-clearing detail are paid off in whiskey. They get one swig at the end of each day's work. Some of them hold it in their mouths till they get back here, then they collect it and sell it. It's called spit whiskey. If you don't want that, you can get beer made from fermented potato peelings that the boys steal from the garbage." They crossed the street behind their tent and stopped where a clot of men stood in front of a closed tent. The baby's cries came from inside.

"When did she have it?" Alex asked one of the men. The man, grizzled and wrinkled from a lifetime of working the fields, smiled, showing very few teeth, and said, " 'Bout midmorning. Baby Perkins they call it. Come real quick once she commenced. They say it's a big fine-looking boy."

Alex nodded. "Mrs. Perkins, the mother, has been here about a month," he explained to Lanier. "Brought in with the rest of her artillery unit. They say she joined up with her husband and fought alongside him since the beginning of the war. The husband was killed in the battle where she was captured. She'll be sent home soon." The baby cried again and the crowd of men shifted and looked at each other and grinned. "Damned if that don't remind me of my babies," one of them said, and the rest of them nodded.

"Let's go get in line for dinner," Alex said.

Alex knew that it was going to sound like an odd question, but he decided to ask it anyway. He wanted to know if he had the right

Sidney Lanier. "Are you a writer?" he asked. Lanier was staring forlornly into his tin bowl of soup, which was made up of a watery broth, a chunk of pickled pork that was almost entirely gristle, and a pale onion that bobbed near the meat. "Eat it all," Alex said. "Eat everything they give you. It's only enough to sustain life."

Lanier looked up. "Yes. I mean yes, I write poems. I guess that makes me a writer, though I've not made a living at it. How did you know?"

Well, Alex thought, *we studied you, briefly, in an English class I took in college. Sidney Lanier: Minor Southern poet, musician, and consumptive.* That was about all Alex could dredge up at the moment. He remembered finding, as a college student, the man's poetry slightly mawkish and fairly impenetrable. "Save the bread," Alex advised, not answering Lanier's question. "We only get two meals a day, so you'll be hungry by midday tomorrow." He tucked the three slices of bread he'd been issued into his pants pocket. He'd found that the bread was so tough and stale it kept its shape even when carried all day.

"Do you have any money?" Alex asked. Lanier shook his head.

"You need at least a little money so you can buy some extra vegetables. Lemons if you can find them. Otherwise you'll get scurvy. I can show you a plant that will help, but it grows outside the compound. Maybe you can play your flute and earn a little money. I'll loan you some, you can buy paper and make up some flyers."

"You mean give a concert? Here?"

"Yes. We have all sorts of entertainment. The charge is usually only a few pennies, but it helps. You need to do everything possible to stay alive. Eat everything you can, bathe whenever you have the opportunity, exercise, get your vitamin C."

"And what, pray tell, is that last? Some sort of prison jargon?"

"Sorry. Just a word I made up." *Vitamin. A word that wouldn't exist until 1911,* he thought. "Eat citrus fruit if you can get it. They give out vinegar to treat the scurvy but it's hard to get enough of it down to do any good. The guys that eat the rats are okay, but I can't bring myself to do it." Alex knew that rats synthesized and stored vitamin C and that rat meat could stave off scurvy. Several prisoners specialized in catching and cooking rats for general consumption. He was told that the results weren't bad at all, far better than that offered by the fellow who caught and cooked seagulls.

That night in the tent, Lanier played his flute again. He gave them "Annie Laurie" and other popular tunes and also classical pieces. The other ten men in the tent lay on their pallets, fully dressed and in coats, if they had them, each struggling to keep warm beneath his one blanket. Listening. And, Alex knew, many of them weeping as the pearl-like music curled and floated and reminded them of other lives, theirs and those they loved, better times, the past, and the possibility of a future.

In the morning Alex showed Lanier where the jakes stretched out over the waters of the bay. They joined the line of men waiting their turn. Later he gave him one of the licorice-root sticks he collected and used to clean his teeth. They washed in a communal barrel of water and dried with their blanket, which would in turn dry during the day. From the time they got up until they ate their breakfast of bread and molasses Alex listened to Lanier cough and hack and knew the man was consumptive. And that this stay in a prison camp would most likely kill him, if not immediately then eventually.

"I'll loan you this until you get some of your own," Alex said, handing the man two one-dollar bills. "Look around and buy yourself some paper and make up a few flyers. After last night I'm sure you can sell plenty of tickets to a concert. There's a guy selling some pretty decent apples up on the north side of the camp. Buy some and eat them with your bread for lunch. Get some for me as well. I've got to go to work."

As he hurried through the gate and down the road toward the photography gallery he thought out his plan for the day. He had no idea when the personage he had been told to ready himself for would arrive, but he would gather the paper and chemicals needed for the job so there was as little delay as possible. If everything proceeded smoothly the man might give him a tip, which would buy more scraps of garbage to help sustain him.

The weather was still cool, but it would warm up again as it had yesterday. Spring was on its way. Alex thought about spending another several months here. In the preceding five months he had been seriously ill twice, though with what he had no idea. Bad food, random bacteria, or any stray disease carried by thousands of men who had never had a vaccination against anything. Viral strains were different from those in his time and against which he had no immunity. There were no antibiotics, and short of growing bread mold and eating it on the off chance that he'd ingest some penicillin, there was nothing he could think of to save himself if the worst came.

He entered the small brick gallery. It was Friday and Mr. Spaulding would be coming by tomorrow to collect what money he had taken in from the week before. Alex would be given a few dollars, and was grateful for it. Spaulding didn't have to pay him, had only to pay the officers who looked the other way as a prisoner ran the man's profitable business. Alex felt it was probably the few dollars he received and the vegetables that he could buy with those dollars that had spared him the misery most of the other men faced.

He struck a lucifer and started a fire in the cold stove. As the small branches crackled and smoked and caught fire, he held his hands to the warmth. He went to his shelves and equipment, finding ease in the familiarity of the job. He organized his supplies. When the knock on the door came he was ready. He looked around, making sure everything was in order, walked to the door, and opened it.

There was a moment when his brain refused his eyes, refused to make the connection. But only a moment. There were two men waiting. One was the young soldier who had delivered the note yesterday. The other was his father.

chapter twenty-four

B IERCE RAN HIS hand lightly through Marie's thick, jet-black hair as she slept lightly, her head on his chest. It was time for him to go, dawn near enough that he would have light as he walked back to his room at the National. He rested his hand on Marie's warm back. Around him Ann Benton's house slept the sleep of, if not the just, at least the sleep of the exhausted. More and more he had been coming to Marie's room after she finished her work, bringing himself to her bed not just because she was beautiful and she seemed to like him, but because he had found her to be quick and intelligent. And she filled a space in not only his mind and his interests, but in his heart. *No*, he thought. *Don't let this happen. Not the heart.*

He was, he had to admit, lonely. Alex had been gone now for long enough to convince Bierce that he probably was not coming back. Lafayette Baker had done something with his friend, or perhaps Alex had gone back to his own home and was now flying around the sky in his airborne train.

Where was home for Ambrose Bierce? It would soon be time for him to go . . . somewhere. Not back to the town where his mother and father still lived, locked in their bitter, angry marriage. The town where he had once been engaged to a woman who had not the decency to wait patiently for him. Nor here, in this bed with this woman who had far too much past to be forgotten by any man who felt seriously about her. *It will not do.*

He thought about the woman, Molly, sleeping in a bedroom on the floor above, and how she, at least, had returned. How she and Alex had searched for each other over a disconnection that he still did not understand. He had not gone to see her since she came back, didn't have the nerve quite yet to face her loss. He would come in the day and talk to her and ask what he could do to help. He owed that much to his friend Alex.

Marie stirred on his chest. He would go. He lifted her head and placed her gently on her own pillow. She opened her eyes, briefly, smiled at him, and fell back asleep.

No, he thought again, *not the heart. Please.*

It took Firth two days to set up the meeting. Molly was nervous. She buttoned up the dark green dress that Dixie, the housemaid, had let out and resewn to fit over her rapidly expanding pregnancy and looked at herself in the mirror. After getting out of Old Capitol Prison she had come back into the embrace of Ann Benton and her household. Being pampered and fed well had lifted away most of the effects of being held in the prison.

The day was gloomy, with alternating periods of rain and thin sunlight. Molly was to meet Mrs. Lincoln at Brady's studio, where the First Lady was going to be photographed in her inauguration outfit. It seems there was a great demand for photographs of Mrs. Lincoln in her elegant dress. Molly would be allowed to speak with her while the photographic session was in progress.

Carter drove her to Brady's studio and waited outside. Molly walked up the wide staircase into the main area of the salon. The room was wide, high, and extremely long, with photographs covering the walls, leaned up against the stair's balustrade, and exhibited in glass cases. The air had a thick, dusty feel, underneath which was the sharp bite of photographic chemicals. Molly stood alone in the long room. Hundreds and hundreds of photographed faces gazed out at her. There wasn't a smile among them.

"Hello!" a voice called from the far end of the room. A man in a black suit gave her a small wave. "We'll just be a moment. We're back here in the laboratory attending to a few last-minute details." Molly smiled and waved back as the man disappeared through a doorway.

She walked down the long room, looking at the faces of history. Civil War generals: Grant, Sherman, Meade, George Custer in all his finery, and dozens of other military men she didn't recognize. Writers and other notables, Lincoln, her friend Walt Whitman, and portrait after portrait of women who she supposed were luminaries, or wives of luminaries.

There was a bustling on the staircase and two women, one short, pudgy, and out of breath, and the other tall, Negro, and aristocratic-looking. Molly recognized the pudgy woman as Mary Todd Lincoln.

"Oh my," Mary Lincoln said, stopping at the top of the stairs with a hand on her chest. "Three flights is simply too much to demand of a person," she complained. "Had I remembered this terrible climb I would have insisted that Mr. Brady attend us at the President's House." She was dressed in an elegant white gown. Her attendant carried a basket of white flowers.

"Mrs. Lincoln," Molly said, "I'm Molly Glenn. From the *Constitution*."

Mary Lincoln gave her a long look down her nose. She reluctantly extended her hand and let Molly clasp the very tips of her limp fingers. "Oh yes," Mary said, "the lady journalist. If there can, or should, be such a thing. You've come to talk with me. I guess it can't be helped. Father said I must do so, though I expect all that will come of it is inaccuracies, or worse, lies."

Molly's eyes narrowed. "I try to be as accurate as possible, and I never lie, Mrs. Lincoln."

"Then you are assuredly not a journalist. Which is probably a very good thing."

"Ladies, ladies, Mrs. Lincoln, how wonderful to see you in your magnificent gown." The man who approached them, hand outstretched, was a bit taller than Molly and wore a black suit with an artistic silk tie around his neck. He had a large nose and a salt-and-pepper goatee and mustache.

"Mr. Brady," Mary Lincoln acknowledged.

"And Mrs. Keckley," Brady said to the tall Negro. "So good to see you again." He turned to Molly. "And you must be Miss Glenn. Mr. Firth said you would be attending our session."

"Surely not *Miss* Glenn," Mrs. Lincoln said. She was staring at Molly's obvious pregnancy. Brady blushed. "Please, ladies, I beg your pardon."

"It's quite all right," Molly said. "Actually, it's Mrs. Balfour." She tasted the words as she said them and found them quite odd.

"Glenn is my maiden name. The name I will be using in writing this article is Glenn Balfour." The others looked confused. There were a number of untruths in these statements, but under the circumstances Molly felt they were called for.

"I hadn't noticed that you were with child when we came in," Mrs. Lincoln said. Her manner had softened. "And I believe I neglected to introduce you to Mrs. Elizabeth Keckley, my friend and the lady who made the dress I am wearing." Elizabeth Keckley and Molly smiled and nodded to each other. "Now, Mr. Brady, Lizzy needs to do the flowers for my hair."

Brady bowed and showed them to the back of the salon. There were two rooms, a wide-open one with a skylight where a large view-camera was set up, and a smaller one with chairs and a settee. The ladies went into the smaller room and Mrs. Lincoln sat while Mrs. Keckley arranged her flowers. Mrs. Lincoln dabbed at her eyes. "Now, Mrs. Lincoln," Elizabeth said, "please don't start. You know it will lead to a headache."

Mrs. Lincoln looked at Molly, who was sitting to her left. "Your condition has brought me memories of my poor Willie who died last year. The day of Father's inauguration was my first day out of mourning. And when I think of Willie, I think of little Eddie, dead these many years. It is all too sad." She sniffed and touched her eyes with her handkerchief.

"Perhaps we could talk, Mrs. Lincoln," Molly suggested, hoping to nudge the lady away from her painful memories, "about how you feel about another four years in Washington?" Molly felt herself blush with the stupidity of the remark. Then realized that no one else knew that Mary Todd Lincoln's time in the city was a matter of months.

"Grateful!" Mrs. Lincoln snapped. "That's how I feel. Grateful, not for myself—I hate this city—but grateful for my country that will have my dear husband at the helm once again. Had that monster McClellan won, he would have signed a peace treaty with the South that would have left us in the same situation we were in four years ago. Abraham Lincoln is this country's savior, though most politicians and journalists are too blind to see it. They revile him on the floor of the House and the Senate and they screech and vilify his name from the pages of their scurrilous rags. They picture him in their cartoons as an ape and a dictator and yet it is he who has saved their lives, he—"

"Mrs. Lincoln," Brady said from the doorway. "If you're ready, we could begin."

Mrs. Lincoln looked blank for a moment, as if she had forgotten why she was where she was. "Yes, of course," she said. She stood up and they all went to the other room. Brady introduced them to his assistant, Mr. O'Sullivan, and led Mrs. Lincoln to a spot next to a desk and began to situate her.

"Your gown is spectacular," Brady said. "I'm sure you were the belle of the inauguration."

"I would be the nation's doormat if the ladies of Washington City had anything to do with it. They have conspired against me from the beginning. It is there that these lies of treason and Southern sympathies began. These harpies are led by Miss Kate Chase, said to be the most beautiful woman in the country, whom I must pronounce the most horrid and most manipulative in all the world. Thank the Lord that Mr. Lincoln has seen fit to take her father out of the Cabinet and install him on the Court, where he can do little harm. Miss Chase and the other young ladies have tried to seduce my husband, have tried to take him from my side, but I have beaten them every one." She turned her head to Molly. "They are whores, Mrs. Balfour, and I will fight them to my last breath."

"Now, now, Mother," a high-pitched voice said from the

stairway. "No need of that sort of talk. It's Tad and I, come to see your picture made."

Abraham Lincoln strode toward them, twelve-year-old Tad bounding in front of him.

"Muffa! Muffa!" Tad shouted, "Papa said I can take you picure!" Molly heard Brady's assistant, from underneath the focusing cloth, groan. She had heard Tad described as mildly retarded and completely undisciplined.

"Mr. President," Brady said effusively, "Master Tad. So good that you could come. We are about to make the exposure. Mrs. Lincoln!" he clapped his hands. Mary Lincoln turned toward him, a tiny smile for her son still lingering.

"Hold just there!" Brady sang out. "Now, Mr. O'Sullivan!" They all froze for five seconds, as if the picture were being taken of everyone in the room, then there was the sound of the shutter closing.

"No, me!" Tad shouted. "No, me!"

"You can make the next exposure, young man," Brady said in a cheerful voice. He turned to his assistant and spoke quietly but audibly enough for Molly to hear from where she sat. "Take the plate and develop it so we can be sure that it is acceptable. I'll occupy the little beggar until we're sure we don't have to make another." Brady led the child across the room to another camera that seemed to be simply a prop. There he had the boy click the shutter on the lens over and over.

"Father," Mrs. Lincoln said, "I'd like you to make the acquaintance of Mrs. Molly Balfour. Or maybe Mrs. Glenn. Or something."

Lincoln moved to Molly. "I'm pleased to make your acquaintance," he said, taking her hand. "It is seldom that I am privileged to meet a young lady with several names."

"I can explain . . ."

"Call her Mrs. Balfour," Mrs. Lincoln said. "It's what she prefers. At least for the moment. I confess, I don't understand at all."

Lincoln nodded, still holding Molly's hand. She was amazed at the size of his huge knobby hand and how it engulfed her own. And Lincoln, close up, was also an amazement. The skin on his face was furrowed like a just-plowed field, rough and dotted with several large moles. Stiff black hairs projected from his brow and his beard was black with patches of gray. His hair was cut in a wire brush manner that would be quite at home in her own time. Lincoln was overwhelmingly tall; his face and hands an unusual color of brown. But his eyes were riveting in their depth and their intelligence. He seemed to be, at the same time, mildly amused and terribly sad. She couldn't tell if this effect was a combination of physical factors, or some indication of his spirit that was expressed through his arresting eyes. The combination of the separate parts left her with a feeling of awe even though she considered herself a woman who was not easily affected by surface characteristics or of celebrity.

"And you are the lady writer from the *Constitution,* I assume?" Lincoln said, bending over her.

"I am the *writer,* yes."

Lincoln stood upright and smiled. "Point well made," he said. "And it sounds as if Mother is giving you grist for your mill. I hope she was not being too harsh on our stay in this city. It has not been an easy time."

"Hands in th' air!" Tad demanded at her elbow. He was holding a shiny revolver and it was pointed at her head.

"Now, Taddy," Lincoln said, gently pushing the barrel of the revolver away from Molly's vicinity. "It's impolite to point a pistol at anyone, particularly a lady. Even if she is a journalist."

"I'm a Rebel!" the boy shouted.

"Of course you are," Lincoln said. He patted the boy on his head. "For some reason," he said to Molly, "my son has decided that he is a soldier in the Army of Secession. He's taken to waving the Rebel flag from the roof of the President's House on rather inopportune occasions." He turned back to his son. "Please holster your sidearm. We don't want anyone shot at Mr. Brady's. It would be embarrassing at the very least, and politically, as well as physically, damaging."

Tad climbed to the top of the camera and saddled it like he was riding a horse. From this perch he reached up and patted Lincoln on the top of his head. "Good, Papa," he said. Lincoln laughed, plucked the boy from the camera, and set him on the ground. Tad whooped and pulled out his pistol and began galloping down toward the other end of the hall. "That's a good boy," Lincoln said. "Head down that direction and see what you can do. I believe General Lee is on the wall somewhere, take a shot at him."

"Father," Mrs. Lincoln said, "we really must be going. The air in here is positively deadening and you know how exhausted dressing and posing makes me. I fear a headache will be the result."

Lincoln's brow furrowed into a frown at the word "headache." And Mrs. Keckley seemed to stiffen.

"Please sit down, Mary," she said. "You mustn't overtire yourself."

"Yes, Elizabeth is right," Lincoln said. "It would be best if you went home to lie down."

"But I haven't . . ." Molly began.

"You must come and visit us," Lincoln said to her. "Anytime. Mother will talk to you and you'll get enough material for your purposes. Besides, I have the distinct impression I know you from somewhere, or at least I know your name. One of your names. It will come to me eventually. I'm often not first when it comes to thinking, but I always finish the race."

"Mr. Lincoln," Brady said, "do you suppose we might make a few exposures since you are here?" Mrs. Lincoln frowned at Brady. "We could perhaps mount them with the one we have made of Mrs. Lincoln in her beautiful gown." She smiled and made a small curtsey at the compliment.

"Not today, Mr. Brady, I need to see that Mrs. Lincoln—"

There was a sudden *bang!* from the front of the room and everyone stopped talking. They could see Tad walk to the wall and stare at it curiously.

"Good Lord," Brady's assistant, O'Sullivan, said, and hurried down the room.

"It would . . . be a great . . . favor to me . . . personally," Brady stammered, still watching Tad as he peered closer at the wall. "The photograph of yourself?" he added.

"Yes, well," Lincoln said, contemplating Tad and the possible damage he had inflicted. "You've been very patient with us. Mother, perhaps it's best if you take Tad home. I'm sure he needs to reload, if nothing else. Mr. Brady has been very kind; I think we can do him this small favor." Brady's assistant led the boy back to them.

"I foun' Gen'ral Lee, Papa," Tad said. "But I missed him."

"No harm done," O'Sullivan announced. "Just a small hole in the wall."

"Good," Lincoln said. "Bobby Lee is a great general. Though I would stop him any way I could, I draw the line at cold-blooded murder. Go on, Mother, I'll be along directly."

Mrs. Lincoln hesitated, looking pointedly at Molly, who in

turn looked at the floor in modesty and placed her hand on her pregnant belly.

"All right," Mary said, patting Tad's jacket, making sure he was all right. "You come to the President's House, Mrs. Balfour, and we'll talk. I believe I can give you some good sound advice on child rearing to write about for your newspaper."

They all murmured their good-byes as Mrs. Lincoln, Mrs. Keckley, and Tad walked down the length of the room to the stairway. As the two ladies started down the stairs, Tad stopped, raised his pistol, and pointed it in their direction.

"Good God!" Brady said.

Lincoln raised a hand and waved good-bye to Tad. "No worry, Mr. Brady, it's a single shot pistol. I would never give a repeater to a child."

Brady seated Lincoln in a hard-backed chair in front of the camera. As Lincoln sat down, Molly realized that his slow movements and sad eyes were products of exhaustion as much physical as spiritual. It was as if Mary Lincoln and Tad had taken with them some internal reserve of resources he used when they were with him. Now, as he settled into the chair, he seemed tired almost to the point of incapacitation. As if once seated, he might never rise again. With a sudden start, Molly realized that this was the pose in the picture of Lincoln she had been given in her own time. She thought about that picture, remembering that she had left it on the lamp table beside the couch where she had fallen asleep before being brought here to this time. Then she realized that the Molly in that picture was wearing the dress she had on at this moment.

Brady took the photograph. "I can always count on you, Mr. President," Brady said. "You're the most photographed man in Washington City."

"As I have always said, your early pictures made my appearance well-enough known to the public to encourage them to vote for me. I believe they felt that a man as homely as I am had to be honest. I certainly have no lofty visible characteristics to recommend me. But wait a moment, how about we take one more photograph, with Mrs. Balfour. Would you like that?" he asked Molly.

Molly stood. "Yes, I would like that very much." She looked at Brady, who nodded and indicated where she was to stand. She walked behind Lincoln's chair and stood where she remembered she had been in the original photograph.

Brady made the exposure.

"There, Mrs. Balfour. Perhaps someday in the future you will look at that photograph and remember me with some small fondness."

"I'm sure I will, Mr. President." She hesitated, then decided she had to try. The opportunity was too great to pass up. "Mr. President, if I were searching for someone, a man, to whom do you think I could go for help?"

"Is this person in the Army?" Lincoln asked. She had come around to stand in front of him. "Yes," she said. "I think so. But possibly not." He looked at her sharply, the tiredness leaving his eyes.

"I would send you to Colonel Lafayette Baker in the War Department. He will find your man for you, if he is alive. Should I have an appointment made for you with Colonel Baker?"

"No," Molly said quickly. Too quickly. Lincoln frowned. "I mean, not yet," she added. "Perhaps when I've exhausted normal channels."

Lincoln nodded. "Normal channels," he said. "Interesting way of putting it. You must have seafaring experience."

She smiled at him, with difficulty, remembering Lafayette

Baker's words the last time they had met: *". . . if I ever hear of you going to the president of the United States with any of this matter you shall never see daylight again. You will grow very old, in a very harsh prison."*

Lincoln looked at her with tilted head, as if he had just remembered something. "I believe it's coming back to me. Having my picture made with a red-haired girl. I've almost got it."

Molly's cry burst out before she could stop it. The pain came out of nowhere, coursing through her. She pressed a hand to her abdomen. Lincoln stood up, frowning, and guided her into the chair.

"Go for a surgeon," he said to Brady. "Quickly."

chapter twenty-five

THE LAST TIME Alex had seen his father was on a train manned by Cossacks in the wilds of Russia in 1917. His father was dying and Alex had not cared. A lifetime of hatred for his father had brought him to that point, and nothing had happened since then to change his mind. Now the man was standing in front of him outside the photographic studio.

"Yes, I didn't die. Obviously," his father said, paying no attention to what the soldier beside him might think.

"This here's the visitor I brought you the message about yesterday," the soldier said, indicating Alex's father. "This is Mr. Balfour, he's inspecting for the Sanitary Commission. The general said to bring him on over here and get him anything he needs. Are y'all related? Havin' the same name and all."

Alex and his father looked at each other. "No," Alex said. "Just a coincidence."

"Thank you, Private," his father said. "I won't be needing your services any longer. You're dismissed."

His father was much as Alex remembered him, not from Russia but from when he had last seen him in New York. The only concession to age was the ivory-headed walking stick he carried.

The guard didn't move. "I understood my orders as to stay by your side, to be of service. Besides"—he glanced at Alex—"That'n there is . . ."

"A prisoner, yes, I am aware of that."

"Don't worry," Alex said, "I'm not going to hurt him. Mr. Balfour and I go back a long ways. You can keep guard out here if you like."

The guard frowned but nodded his head. Alex's father took off his top hat and Alex stepped to the side for him to enter. His heart was pounding and he wasn't sure from what emotion: anger, fear, astonishment, curiosity, hate. It could have been any or all of them at once.

He closed the door behind them. His father stepped to the stove as if interested in it. Alex noticed that he limped badly. The man looked around, found a peg on the wall, and hung up his hat. He held his hands out to the stove, warming them.

"I'm not sure what to ask first," Alex said to his father's back. The man turned to him. His smile was more of a smirk than a manifestation of humor or goodwill.

"You left me for dead back there in that train. Maybe you should say you're sorry."

Alex thought for a moment and found no regret, thinking only of his father lying in a tangle of sheets on a sweat-stained, bloody bed. Of having to watch as the Cossacks who guarded the train killed innocent men and women. "I left you to whatever would happen. To fate, I guess. And I'm not sorry, at least about what I did. God only knows what you did. You were in the process of trying to seize your own Russian fiefdom and you didn't seem to care how many people died in the process. Besides, you lived."

"I damned near didn't. I lost a leg. As for the fiefdom, you know I choose to live well, no matter what time or place I am in. You, though, are consumed by your silly moral questions and conundrums. I seize whatever opportunities present themselves."

Alex shrugged. "And now you're here, as a member of, what was it?"

"The Sanitary Commission. It would equate to the Red Cross of your time. It allows a certain freedom of travel and access, and there are other opportunities I won't bore you with. May I sit down?" He tapped his trousers. "The leg," he added. Alex nudged the stool toward him. His father leaned heavily on his stick and sat clumsily, his right leg stretched out in front of him. Alex realized there was a certain irony in both of them being wounded in like places.

"Why are you here?" Alex asked.

"What do you mean by 'here'?"

"In this place where you are sitting. Point Lookout prison camp. In my presence. Have you come to gloat? To poke the caged animal with your stick? Is this revenge?"

His father struggled to his feet. His complexion was ruddy. Alex couldn't tell if it was that way because of the exertion of standing, heat from the stove, or anger.

"I've come to have my photograph made. Otherwise I'd have no explanation for the general as to why I'm talking with you.

My reasons are much too complex to be discussed in these few minutes. I'd like you to come to the residence they have made available to me here. I'm told it's where all important visitors stay. Do you know it?"

Alex nodded. Point Lookout was once a vacation destination, designed for wealthy families from Washington City. The beach on the east side of the peninsula held a number of fine homes. The commandant of the prison had his residence there.

"Good," his father said. "You can bring my photograph there this evening and we will have dinner. Now let us get on with it. I have my inspection duties to perform."

Alex moved through all the steps, performing the requisite tasks before making the photograph: readying the plates, sensitizing the paper, and setting up the camera. This would be no cheap tintype, but a full-blown paper photograph that he would affix to a stiff cardboard mount with Spaulding's special imprint on the reverse side. The details of the process occupied his mind just enough to keep him from dwelling either on the past or on the future, both long- and short-term. After he had taken the picture his father nodded and began walking away. "Why don't you bring those to the house this evening, as we discussed," he said.

"You'll have to clear it with the general," Alex said.

"I've already done so. And now, I'm due at the hospital." Alex watched as his father limped away, and wondered what trouble he had brought with him this time.

Alex was seated on an empty cracker-box as Virgil Needen-bocker sharpened his razor on a square of leather. Virgil, before he became a soldier, had been a barber in a small river town in Mississippi. Somewhere here in the camp he had acquired a large piece of sheet that he kept reasonably clean. This was now tied around Alex's neck. Most of the men let their hair and beards grow without a thought to personal appearance, but a few, enough to make it a going concern, came to Virgil for haircuts and beard trims.

Sidney Lanier stood beside Alex, holding out a piece of paper. "That was fast," Alex said, taking the paper and reading it.

GRAND CONCERT THIS EVENING
FLUTE RENDITIONS OF YOUR FAVORITE MUSIC.
OLD FAVORITES. CLASSICAL SELECTIONS.
Requests accepted.
SIDNEY LANIER, ESQ. LATE OF MACON, GEORGIA.

Alex admired the calligraphy. The script was probably done with ink made of bone ashes, penned with a goose quill. There was a man for every purpose here in the camp.

"Some of the men heard me playing last night and wanted me to do it right away. I couldn't see any reason not to. I got the paper from the Bible thumpers and paid a man the next street over to write me up five copies. This is the last one. I've posted the others. I thought I'd put this one on our tent." He handed Alex a dollar. "Thanks for the loan. I'll pay you back the rest out of what I make tonight."

"Let's quit jawboning and get to it," Virgil said, eyeing Alex. His equipment consisted of a pair of long scissors, a straight razor, and a tin cup of hot water with a sliver of soap floating in it.

A collection of spectators began to form.

"You ought to sell tickets to these haircuts, Virgil." Alex said.

"Don't talk," Virgil said. "I don't want to cut you with these rusty old shears. Down in Biloxi I got me some English scissors as sharp as cut glass. Razors that can split a single hair. All in a wonderful leather case that smells of bay rum. Pomades from Arabia. Macassar oils from the Levant. When this damn war is over I'm hightailing it back home and never stepping foot out of town again."

"Hey, Balfour," one of the onlookers said, a man with a thick black beard and a slouch hat that appeared to be permanently molded to his greasy head. His name was Sherod Overton, and Alex knew him by sight and reputation. "That's your name, ain't it?" Sherod jeered. "Alex . . . no . . . Alice Balfour, I believe I heered that's what you're called. You steppin' out with a Yankee tonight? Or just cleanin' up for one of your tent-mates?" The small crowd laughed. Alex ignored them.

"Ain't you boys got nuthin' better to do, Sherod?" Virgil asked as he chopped off handfuls of whiskers.

"As a matter of fact," Sherod said, "we ain't got one goddamn thing better to do."

"Don't pay them no mind," Virgil said to Alex, clipping close to the skin. Alex felt air on his cheeks and face where the beard was disappearing.

Sherod made kissing noises, which drew another laugh. "He is sweet-looking, ain't he? Or should I say she?" Sherod said.

A gang of thieves had been going around camp at night, slitting tents from the back and stealing what few miserable valuables the men had. The suspicion was that Sherod and his gang were the thieves, but no one had yet caught them at it.

Virgil worked the sliver of soap with a brush made of pig hair into a thin lather and spread it on Alex's cheeks. He tilted Alex's head up. The dull razor scratched painfully along the blond stubble, making Alex wince.

"What's the matter, Alice?" Sherod asked. "Virgil give you a nick? Want me to slap him down for you?"

Virgil finished the cheeks and chin and tilted Alex's head farther back. He applied more lather to skin and drew the razor upward in long, sure strokes.

"I believe I'm going to have to give Alice a kiss, she's so sweet smellin' now."

Virgil stepped back, eyeing his handiwork. "Ain't got no mirror but you look pretty good if I do say so myself."

Alex stood up and wiped his face with the sheet.

Sherod stepped close. "Lemme see here, Alice . . ."

Alex threw the sheet over Sherod's head and kicked him in the crotch. When the man bent double he kneed him under the chin, which brought his head up. Alex punched him full in the face, snapping the man's head back and knocking him down. It was over in less than three seconds, over before anyone in the man's gang had had a chance to react.

Alex yanked the sheet off Sherod, who sat dazed in the dirt. A small red spot of blood showed on the sheet where his nose had begun to bleed. "I got your sheet messed up," Alex said. "I'll wash it for you."

"Ah, hell, that's all right," Virgil said. "Any decent barber expects a little blood in the line of duty. I'll take care of it. You go on." Two of Sherod's men were helping the downed man to his feet.

Alex and Lanier walked away, slowly enough to show that they were leaving because they wished to and not because they were afraid.

"That was an impressive piece of work," Lanier said.

Alex rubbed his hand. "I've been here four months, been in several fights and watched at least twenty of them. Most of them spring up out of boredom. Some of the men are like that one, though, just plain mean. But they're pretty much like schoolyard bullies from when you were a kid. I've found that the man who lands the first punch is the winner in ninety-five percent of the fights. And that the first punch is usually the only punch thrown. You just have to be willing to throw it." He looked at his hand, which was beginning to swell. "You never want to hit with your hand if you can help it. Pick up a stick, a brick, anything. Hand bones break too easily. Teeth'll cut you up and get infected, then you're really in trouble. I just got carried away back there." They turned down the street toward their tent.

"Think he'll be trouble?"

Alex shrugged. "There's no way of knowing. There's always trouble of one kind or another here. Keep your eye out for him, though. He saw you with me so he might get in your face."

"Get in my face? Hmm, that's an unattractive image." They had come to their tent. "Are you coming to the concert tonight?" Lanier asked as he fixed the notice to the tent.

"I'm not sure. I'm eating outside the compound this evening. It depends on when I get back. I'll bring you some food." Alex stepped to a nearby barrel of water and stripped off his shirt. This was salt water from the bay; regular drinking water was far too valuable to use for washing. The few fresh-water pumps in the compound were always surrounded by men with tin cups, fighting their way to the spouts for a drink.

"I have some soap, if you want it," Lanier offered.

"I'd appreciate it." Alex had used the last of his homemade soap the day before and hadn't been able to get to the prisoner who specialized in crafting soap and potions used to combat the ever-present lice. Lanier fetched the soap from the tent and gave it to Alex, who held it to his nose.

"God," he said. "Real soap. It smells so clean. Sure you want me to use it?" Lanier waved a hand in dismissal. Alex washed himself, splashing the cold water on his upper body and in his hair.

"A real meal," Lanier said. They were sitting on their blankets. "You're a lucky man."

"Oh yes," Alex said. "I'm a lucky man."

At five-thirty he checked out with the guards at the front gate of the compound. He was reasonably clean and well groomed, at least by prison standards, and carrying his father's photograph wrapped in a rag. Hundreds of lounging prisoners watched with undisguised jealousy as he walked through the open gate. Alex knew that he was considered a traitor by many of the men, as he had never disclosed any particular loyalty to the Southern cause. But the undeniable fact was and continued to be that he was locked up in the compound just like the rest of them, so what were usually just grumbles and stares remained just that.

As the gate swung shut behind him, Alex realized that any trouble he was facing in his upcoming meeting with his father was going to be delayed at least slightly by the trouble that faced him right here. Chaney King, the Union private, prison guard, and his personal tormentor, stood fifteen feet away from the front gate with a group of soldiers. All of them turned to see who had just come out.

"Well now, see here," King drawled. "Look what de cat drug in." He sauntered up to Alex. "Ooee. And don't he look fine? Ain't he a superior specimen of the Southern race?" He bent close. Alex could smell the sweat on him. "And don't he smell purty?"

"Private King, I have an appointment," Alex said reasonably. "Can we do this another day?" He knew it was probably the wrong thing to say, but he said it anyway. What else was there to do, or say, that would keep the man from doing what he was about to do? Most of the Negro guards were decent to the prisoners, or at least did their duty without particular cruelty.

"Can we do it another day?" King mimicked, his eyes wide with fake incredulity. "Oh yes, Master, we just skip the lessons for today, you just go ahead and amble on wherever it is you be goin'. Where you goin' anyway? You got a pass?"

As a matter of fact he did have a pass. He had picked it up at the provost guard's office at the front gate. He handed it to King, who studied it carefully.

"I'm going to the guest house. I have an appointment there," Alex said.

"Oh I see, yes indeed, very important." He handed Alex back the pass. "That pass look okay to me. You know it just so happen I be goin' that way myself." He looked over at his friends. "Boys, I got to go, my ride is here and I got to be gettin' on." He gave them a wave and turned back to Alex.

"And here is my own personal mule. Bend down, mule, I'm climbin' on."

Alex felt a flush of anger rush over him. "Look, I'm not–"

King stepped up until he was in Alex's face. "Yes you are. You hear me now, turn around and bend over. I'm riding you, or you gonna get a barrel put on you right now, and you won't be goin' to no appointment like you the president. Hear?"

Alex turned around and bent over. King laughed and jumped on his back. Alex felt his knees give as he pushed up and steadied himself. "Get up, mule," King rasped. "Get movin'."

chapter twenty-six

MOLLY FELT THE pain grow and recede as she lay on the plush velvet sofa in Brady's studio. She tried to remember everything she had ever read about being pregnant but couldn't recall much. The term "false labor" floated around in her head and she clung to it, hoping for the *false* part because if it was *true* labor, she knew she was in serious trouble. It was too soon. She had put off making any decision about how and where she would birth this baby, hoping instead that she would return to her own time before it happened.

"Mrs. Balfour," Brady said, panting slightly from his dash up the stairs. "This is Dr. Armand Winston. His office is just next door." Lincoln had waited until the doctor had arrived and then left after repeating his invitation for her to come to the President's House and talk further with Mary.

Winston, the doctor, was tall with long sideburn whiskers, rumpled dark hair, and a peevish frown. He was wearing a wrinkled suit and had a needle and thread stuck in the lapel where a flower might usually be pinned. "What seems to be the problem?" he asked brusquely.

"I'm having what feel like labor pains," Molly said. Brady brought her a cushion and placed it under her head.

"And how far advanced is your condition?"

"About seven months. Maybe more. I'm not sure."

The frown deepened. "What are you doing out of bed? It's not only unseemly but also dangerous for you to be away from home. Give me your hand."

She started to hold her hand out until she looked at his. His fingernails were rimmed with black and she thought she could smell whiskey on him.

"Would you please wash your hands before examining me?" she asked.

He stepped back. "I have no earthly intention of examining you. What do you take me for? I was merely going to read your pulse. And what do the condition of my hands have to do with anything?"

"If your hands are dirty, you can give me a disease. I won't be touched with dirty hands."

He shook his head. "What nonsense." He bent close and peered at her face. Now she was sure she could smell whiskey. "Your color appears normal. I don't believe there's anything wrong with you. Your temperament seems disposed to hysteria, which can cause flights of weakness. It's the female imagination at work. You don't need me; you need to go home and get into your bed where you belong. A double dose of calomel will set you right and teach you a lesson as well. Then perhaps you might take some Blue Mass to calm yourself. You must inform your husband that you have been dangerously active. You're an invalid, and you should act like one." He looked at Brady. "I'll be going. Put this woman into a carriage and send her home." He shook his head irritably. "Wash my hands, indeed." He nodded to Molly and strode away. They could hear the heavy clump of his boots as he stomped downstairs.

Molly pushed herself up. The pain seemed to have receded, though she could still feel it lurking not far away.

"My carriage is outside," she said. "Please ask Carter to come up and help me downstairs. I'm grateful for your assistance, Mr. Brady." Brady bobbed his head. He was almost, but not quite, wringing his hands. He hurried away. "And please send me my photograph as soon as possible," she called to his back. "I'll pay whatever's necessary." Brady stopped and turned around.

"One does not need to pay when one has had his, or in this case, her, picture taken with the president of the United States. It is always an honor to have made such a photograph. The pleasure, Mrs. Balfour, is all mine."

Ann Benton insisted that Molly see a doctor, and so she acquiesced. Ann sent for her friend, Mary Walker.

"Mary," Ann said, sitting on Molly's bed, "besides being an old friend of mine from my college days, is the only female surgeon in the Union Army. You will undoubtedly find her eccentric, everyone does, but I trust her implicitly. Whenever she is in town I have her come and see to all of my girls." They both looked up as the door of the bedroom was thrown open by a small figure dressed in a man's uniform.

"Mary," Ann said, "how good of you to come."

Mary Walker was a short plain woman with an unlined face and curly black hair.

"Ann"—Mary Walker nodded in greeting—"I assume this is the patient."

"I'm not sure 'patient' is exactly the right word," Molly said. "I'm pregnant, and today I experienced what felt like contractions for around ten minutes. I rested, and they now seem to have gone away."

"Have you been seeing a surgeon?"

"No."

"Excellent. They'll do you more harm than good. Pregnancy is not a sickness, nor should it be treated as such. It is a purely natural condition. May I examine you?" Molly looked at the woman's hands. They were spotless, with the nails trimmed close and clean. She nodded.

"I'll just be leaving–" Ann began, before Mary Walker interrupted her.

"Just sit right where you are," she said, "I'm not going to do anything to interfere with this lady. I'm sure?. . ." She raised her eyebrows at Molly.

"Molly Glenn," Molly said.

"I'm sure that Molly won't mind if we prattle a bit while I'm looking things over." Mary Walker pulled down the blanket and looked at Molly's midsection. Molly was wearing one of Ann's high-necked cotton nightdresses. The doctor ran her hands lightly over Molly's abdomen.

"Will you be in town long?" Ann asked her. "I'd like you to look at the girls if you've time."

"Get 'em up. I'll see them today." She moved Molly's belly around and gently probed. "I'm leaving for Louisville tomorrow; they're sending me to be the surgeon at the women's prison down there. Nobody wants to deal with me, so they order me hither and yon, hoping I'll get lost along the way. Not even the South wants me. Sit up."

Molly pushed herself up in the bed. Mary Walker lifted her midsection, as if weighing it. "I stumbled into Rebel lines down in Georgia last year and got captured. They shipped me off to Castle Thunder Prison in Richmond and kept me for ninety days until I drove them crazy. They traded me for a couple of officers, and here I am, ready to head out once again. Stand up."

Molly stood up. Mary Walker looked her up and down. She leaned close and looked at Molly's eyes and skin.

"Why do you put up with it?" Molly asked. "Their telling you what to do and sending you away." Ann excused herself from the room.

"You can lie back down again," Mary Walker said. "Why do I

put up with it? Because I have skills, and I want to use them. The preservation of the Union is a great cause, and I can best aid it through the use of my training. If I can make my way onto the battlefield, I can not only save lives, I can save arms and legs. I was in the field at Fredericksburg and saw the piles of limbs lopped off because my medical brothers feel that expediency is more important than therapy. They won't work with me, though, the men surgeons. They fear me." She patted Molly on the arm. "I think you'll be fine. I believe you were only experiencing the symptoms of false labor, but to be on the safe side I'm recommending two weeks of absolute bed rest. Then if you continue to feel well, you can resume your regular duties, whatever those may be. Take no medicines, whatever any other surgeon may tell you. They'll dose you with laudanum and it is my contention that this is injurious to the baby. They use it to make women more tractable, not because it is beneficial."

"Actually, I was seen by another doctor. Briefly. He said I was weak in the head and needed calomel and Blue Mass. I don't know what those are."

Mary nodded. "Standard medical prescriptions, used for everything from war wounds to the complaints of small children. Calomel is a purgative, extremely harsh and debilitating."

"This doctor said it would teach me a lesson."

"Indeed it would, and the lesson is to not listen to fools such as he. Blue Mass is made with opium, which will make you feel wonderful but will be of no real use and quite probably will harm your unborn child. Another danger is bloodletting. Some few of us believe that bleeding a patient is not only ineffective but harmful. It is still standard practice in pregnancies. You must not let them do it to you. Nor should you let them apply leeches."

"I have no intention of letting anyone bleed me. Or put a leech anywhere near me."

"Good. You must be quite firm on this point. Placing leeches on your vagina is a treatment used if a birth becomes difficult. I have seen cases where they crawl up inside the woman and attach themselves. It causes excruciating pain. My dear, you look a little pale." She frowned at Molly.

"I just . . . it's just . . ."

"We'll talk no more of it. I believe you'll be fine. You're a sturdy lass, and remarkably fit."

Ann Benton came back into the room. "I've told Dixie to get the ladies out of bed and assembled in the upstairs drawing room," she said.

Mary Walker nodded. "I'll just go and set out my things," she said, turning to Molly. "I believe you're further along than you seem to think. Do you have a husband?"

Molly felt herself blush, and was surprised. "Not exactly. It's complicated."

"It's always complicated," Mary Walker said. "I shed mine in Iowa several years ago, and I've not regretted it one moment."

"I'll be seeing to her care," Ann Benton said. "She's not one of our ladies, but she is a friend."

"Good. Now I'll go see to these ladies as soon as I wash my hands." She nodded, and left the room.

"Well," Molly said, pulling the covers back up over her. "She's a real force of nature, isn't she?"

Ann laughed. "Yes, she is. Before the Rebels caught her, she announced that she had devised a plan to raise a battalion of hardened criminals who she would then tame, train, and send into battle. They were to be called 'Walker's U.S. Patriots.' Secretary of War Stanton sent her to Tennessee before she could implement that idea. The newspapers loved it."

"I'm sure they did," Molly said.

"Are you all right now?" Ann asked, smoothing the blankets around Molly. "If you are, you have a visitor. Mr. Bierce is here. Mr. Bierce is often here these days, as he has taken quite a fancy to our Marie."

"I'm fine. Have him come in. And thank you for everything you've done for me."

"You are quite welcome. I'll send Mr. Bierce in."

Bierce entered hesitantly. Molly smiled at him. "I hear you've been hanging around here a good deal these days."

Bierce laughed. "I'm not sure what you mean by hanging, but I have been much in evidence on the premises, at least in the evenings. Marie and I have formed a special friendship."

Molly refrained from pointing out the obvious dangers of forming special friendships with prostitutes.

"I know you want to talk about Alex," Bierce said. "I'm sorry I haven't come to you before."

Molly smiled. "I understand. I do want to talk about Alex. I want to know everything you know. And I need you to do something else for me. I've been placing an advertisement in the newspaper attempting to locate Alex. I need someone to check the responses every day and to pay the fee once a week. Can you do this for me? The doctor says I have to stay in bed for a couple of weeks."

"Yes, if you will do something for me in turn. I know you have been writing articles for the *Constitution*. I would like to learn to write for the newspapers, and I could use some help with the stories I am laboring with."

Molly thought about it. In her own time she'd read, as an undergraduate in journalism class, a few Bierce stories and columns. Bierce would become a journalist best known for his cutting wit and cruel invective. This Bierce, the young man standing before her, had a ways to go before he assumed his mantle of great cynicism. She wondered how this perfectly friendly, helpful man would turn into the writer known as Bitter Bierce. Meanwhile, he wanted her help in learning his craft. It was a curious conundrum: here she would teach a man to write the work she had already studied, that he had, at least to her, already written.

"Well," she said, turning on her side so she could face him more easily, "it doesn't look as if I'm going anywhere anytime soon. I'll be glad to look at your writing. And if I can give you some advice to aim you at journalism, I'd be happy to."

"It's a deal, then," he said, holding out his hand. They shook on it. Bierce felt something lift from him, a sort of darkness that had settled in since the night before, when he had lain in Marie's room and thought about what he had to do. He would not leave. Not yet. He would stay here and help, and learn.

chapter twenty-seven

THE GUEST HOUSES were a quarter of a mile from the stockade. Several lives ago in New York, in his own time, Alex had exercised every day. *That* Alex could have carried King, who was a thin, not overly tall man of around a hundred thirty pounds, to his destination without breaking much of a sweat. But *this* Alex had been without decent food for months. He had been wounded, consistently starved, without adequate medical care, driven to despair and debilitation.

He almost made it. A hundred yards from the house he began to laugh. He could feel King sit up higher on his back.

"What you find so dang funny?" King demanded.

Alex began to stagger. He stumbled to his knees, careful to keep the photograph out of the dirt. As he fell, King stepped off his back. Alex lay in the dirt, sending up little geysers of dust as he gasped. He quieted his breathing and rolled over on his back. He looked up at King.

"All right," Alex said. "I'll tell you what's so funny. To start off with, I marched to make it a holiday." He could see King frowning down at him, backlit by the sky now deepening toward evening.

"What in hell are you talkin' about?"

"When I was a kid in Washington, I was part of the great march, a demonstration to convince Congress to make Martin Luther King's birthday a national holiday." A thought suddenly occurred to him. He sat up and rubbed his face. "My God, you don't suppose you're one of Martin Luther King's forebears?" He started laughing again.

Private King was now furious. "Are you laughin' at me? Are you makin' fun a me? Callin' me a bear?"

Alex shook his head as he hauled himself to his feet. "No, I'm not making fun of you. It's just that it's so ironic. I've always seen myself as a staunch defender of civil rights, a man who challenges racists, who won't abide a bigot. I send the NAACP a donation every year. I'm a damn near-perfect example of a prejudice-free man. And here you've got the pick of thousands and thousands of Southern Confederate soldiers who probably actually *deserve* your hatred, and you choose me to be your whipping boy. You are so mistaken that it's actually humorous." He wondered if King was going to hit him. "That's why I was laughing. It was the irony."

King looked around but there was no one watching them. He seemed to lose a little of his anger, or at least realize it wasn't worth the effort without an audience. "Iron, huh," King said, shaking his head. "Maybe I'll just find me a piece of iron and hit you square between the eyes. Say you was fixin' to escape. Then they'll make me a colonel. I swear you white people ain't got the sense God gave a goose. You git the hell on to where you're goin' before I get really mad." He turned and walked off.

Alex brushed the dirt off his clothes and turned to the guest house.

Inside the house, Charles Ames Balfour stood at the front window watching his son brush the dirt off his clothing. Alex was a pathetic figure, wearing a ragged shirt and odd canvas pants tied with a rope around a too-thin waist, hair that looked as if it had recently been cut with a lawn mower, sunken cheeks, and eyes that were raw and rimmed with red, the whites veined and watery. Scabbed insect bites spotted his face and arms.

Alex began to walk toward the house. Charles turned from the window and limped into the next room.

He poured whiskey from a heavy cut-glass decanter. The whiskey eased the pain in his leg, and the arthritis in his joints, a disease that was becoming more and more debilitating every day. He allowed himself to think for a moment on what medicines they must have by now back in Alex's world. *Perhaps they've cured arthritis. Perhaps they've cured cancer. Maybe even old age. I need him. I have to get back.*

Age. He wasn't even sure how old he was anymore. He'd been in the past for thirty years. He'd cast away the yardsticks by which normal people measure time. But he felt old, felt whatever age he must be, felt it in his joints, his wounds, and all the small and large annoyances and discomforts that accrued into a rock of debility that he was forced to shoulder as he climbed the mountain of whatever present moment he was faced with. He was sick of it. He would ride the back of his son to the future, just as that black soldier had ridden him to this house. He heard Alex knock at the door.

He put his whiskey glass next to his place setting on the table and went to open the front door.

"You're late," Charles Balfour said.

"It took me longer to get here than I thought it would," Alex said. He entered the house and handed his father the photograph. It was the first time he had been in an enclosed wooden house in months, and the polished floors and darkness of the hallway felt odd, almost as if he had entered a cave.

Alex noticed that his father was frowning at him. Charles Balfour had always been a fine-looking man, one of those whose hair had gone silver early but which in no way suggested age, only elegance. He had always been tall and fit with ruddy skin that went well with the hair, worn a little too long, shading toward the artistic. Photographers and reviewers, especially lady reviewers, had always loved that hair.

"Perhaps we could go right to the table," Charles said. "Dinner is almost ready and I believe the cook would like to leave as soon as it's served." He walked down the hallway to the lighted dining room. The gaslights glowed from several wall sconces and an elaborate chandelier.

"Can I get you a whiskey?" his father asked. Alex nodded. His father went to a sideboard and poured the drink. The thick chunky glass was heavy and clumsy in Alex's hand. He was used to drinking brackish water out of a battered tin cup. The first sip burned his lips and the sharp bite of the alcohol caught in his throat and threatened to choke him. For a few seconds of burning pain he wondered why he ever used to drink, and then the soft warmth of the whiskey suffused his chest and he remembered very well.

His father raised his glass to him. "Truce," Charles Ames Balfour offered.

"Why?" Alex asked, not lifting his own glass. "Why now?"

"Because," his father said, his voice catching a ragged edge. He waited a moment. "Because I've become an old man. Because I'm sick and tired." He rubbed his arm. "Because I've always been allergic to wool and these damn suits are driving me crazy." He allowed himself a small smile. "Because I want to go home and I don't think I can do it without you." Mrs. Ludding, the cook, appeared at the door carrying a large bowl. She looked at the elder Balfour.

"All right, Mrs. Ludding, I think we can begin." She nodded and set the bowl on the table. "We can serve ourselves." He sat in a straight-backed chair at the head of the mahogany table and nodded to the place setting halfway down the table on his right. Alex went to the indicated chair and sat down. His father lifted a pair of serving forks from the bowl and Alex held out his plate while his father placed a mound of delicate spring greens on it. Alex recognized the long green leaves of poke weed, pointy wild arugula, and the thick juicy stems of purslane. Before they began to eat, the woman was back with a large covered tureen. "Just put it anywhere," his father said. "We'll have it when we've finished our salad."

Alex tasted the salad, marveling at the fresh peppery bite of the greens. He ate slowly and carefully and finished the salad. He gently pushed the plate to the side, each move precise and controlled. He looked up to see his father staring at him.

"Has it been that bad?" his father asked.

Alex folded his hands on the table in front of him, carefully, as if they might leap out and snatch more food if he did not consciously restrain them.

"It hasn't been"—he hesitated—"easy." He didn't want his father's sympathy. The balance of power between them was still unknown. "I've had it better than most. My job at the photography gallery gives me a little bit of money. I use it to stave off the worst effects of malnutrition. And I know that the ordeal will end, I know *when* it will end, and the others don't. It's mostly a matter of holding on till it's over."

His father nodded and uncovered the tureen. He ladled thick soup into two bowls and pushed one toward Alex, who pulled it to him with both hands. He bent his head over the bowl and closed his eyes and inhaled for just a moment, as if praying. He picked up a spoon and dipped it into the soup. He held it, letting it cool slightly. It was beef, onions, potatoes, and carrots in a milk broth. He ate it, chewing slowly, not used to so much food, different food, being on his spoon at one time. His father, who seemed only vaguely interested in eating, let him consume the whole bowl without asking him to talk.

Alex moved his empty soup bowl to the side, joining the empty salad plate.

Mrs. Ludding, the cook, appeared at his side and picked up the empty soup bowl. She disappeared into the kitchen and was back in a moment with a platter of fried chicken, a bowl of collard greens, and another of boiled potatoes. Alex could see a large pat of butter melting on the potatoes. He had not seen butter in months. She left again, and he sat, hands in his lap, afraid to move lest the spell be broken, until she came back, this time with a pie. "I'll put this on the sideboard," she said. "You can cut it when you're ready." She took off her apron. "Just leave all these things when you're done. The boy will be in come morning, and he'll clean up."

Alex's father nodded and half stood. "My thanks, Mrs. Ludding. You've done a marvelous job. The food is excellent. I'll be sure to mention it to the commandant tomorrow."

Alex finished the chicken breast he was eating and reluctantly pushed the plate away.

"You can take the leftovers with you when you go," his father said. Alex eyed the remaining mound of chicken, the pot of greens, and the pie on the sideboard. This was a fortune in food.

He put his hands in his lap and looked at his father. The two of them sat in silence.

"You proposed a truce," Alex said. "Why are you interested in making peace? It must be painful to you. The last time I saw you, you were contemplating killing me. Fortunately you were wounded badly enough so you weren't able to carry out the threat. Don't you remember?"

His father frowned. "Please, no more about Russia and that damned train. We discussed this earlier and came to no conclusions. Maybe I was a different person then. You know, I can't really remember. I must have been out of my head."

"You weren't that far out of your head. Your behavior was pretty much like it always was when I was growing up, only more so. Just a matter of degree. Why the sudden conversion?" Alex stood up and went to the sideboard and cut himself a large slice of pecan pie.

"Have you ever noticed," his father began, his voice low and controlled, "what a prissy, smug, sanctimonious *ass* you can be? How you act as if your opinions, your life, your choices are the only correct ones? How easily you rise to spit on me and what I have done, when you have only the barest knowledge of what I've gone through?"

Charles Balfour removed a thick cigar from his pocket, carefully cut the end with a small penknife, and lit it with a kitchen match. Alex's prison mentality overtook him for a second as he wondered if he could get some of the matches. Each one was worth a cup of coffee in the camp.

"Let's do this," his father said, blowing a stream of smoke toward the chandelier. "I'll talk, then you can ask questions. I'm sure you have many of them. But why don't you try to set aside your litany of boyhood complaints for at least a while? I can't change your past today."

He stopped. And smiled crookedly. "Actually, that's probably not true. That's one of the things I need to tell you." He was no longer smiling. "Listen carefully." His voice had taken on a neutral, slightly pedantic tone. "The past," his father said slowly, carefully, "is not fixed. It is not immutable. The past can be changed. And that is what I suggest we, you and I, are going to do."

"I—" Alex began, but his father's upraised hand stopped him.

"I talk," his father said, standing. "Then you ask questions."

He began to pace back and forth.

"I went back for the first time when I was twenty-seven years old. Looking back, I guess there were a few times before that when I dreamed I was in the past, but I never thought it was real. History, as you well know, is the family occupation, and I was surrounded by it growing up, just as you were. The library of my father's books, and his father's books, the university towns where he taught, his colleagues, all of it. So we Balfours dream about the past. Nothing unusual there.

"We were living in upstate New York and I was teaching at Gailard, that small liberal arts college in the mountains. You were just born, so you wouldn't remember. I was doing research for what I was planning as a nonfiction book on women and the California Gold Rush. We were between semesters and I had taken the time to go out West to do some on-site research. So when I 'disappeared,' your mother wasn't overly worried. I tended to keep in rather loose contact when I was absorbed in a project, and I didn't call in much anyway. She expected me back for the next semester, but beyond that we didn't have any set timetable. Besides, she was busy with you.

"I was in a seedy motel in the mountains of California when I shifted back. Sitting on the edge of the bed one minute, the next I'm picking myself up off the forest floor, looking out over a little town where a sawmill was under construction. I knew where I was right away. There was a sign on the sawmill that read Sutter's Mill. Did you ever read the book that came out of all of this, *The Golden Land*?"

Alex wondered if he was allowed to talk and decided he was. "Yes, when I was twelve years old."

His father nodded. "Fascinating time and place. I walked down out of the forest and right up to the men who were working. They didn't seem particularly surprised. I was dressed in jeans, a flannel shirt, and work boots, so I didn't look all that strange. I told them my horse had thrown me some miles back, that I'd heard there might be a job helping build the mill. Jim Marshall, he was the foreman, told me they'd be glad to give me a job, so I hired on right there. Even though I didn't have any idea how I had gone back, it was perfectly obvious that it was real. This was no dream.

"The next day Marshall found the first chunk of gold that would lead to the California Gold Rush. I was standing right behind him when he picked the nugget out of the river. He asked me what I thought it was. I told him it looked like gold, and he laughed at me and said it was fool's gold. I convinced him to keep it, take it to his boss and test it. The rest, as they say . . ." He walked over to the side board.

"Is history," Alex finished for him.

"You want a drink?" his father asked. Alex nodded, and he poured them both the same whiskey he'd given him before.

"I spent three months in the camp. I saw it all; the beginnings of the great Rush. Then one night I went back, home, to my own time. I'd been gone two weeks there."

"Is that the way it works?" Alex asked. "Is there some formula to figure out how long you've been gone in reality?"

"Reality?" His father laughed. "Not that I know of. Sometimes it was longer, sometimes it was shorter. Once I was gone for a week, and when I got home I found I'd been missing for a total of about five minutes. It's almost like dream time, where you can feel you've been asleep for days and in reality it's just seconds."

"Did Mother know?"

"Oh yes, I told her. When I came back that first time I had a satchel with a hundred thousand dollars' worth of gold in it. It's kind of hard to hide that sort of newfound wealth from your wife. Especially when it's in the form of raw ore. Yes, she knew. Though at the time I didn't suspect how important she was to the whole process. Later I understood: you only get back as long as there's someone in the present to be your anchor. But then it was too late." He carefully poured more whiskey into his glass. He warmed it with both hands.

"It was wonderful that first time. I saw things that no one had ever written about until then. As historians we get so much wrong. I saw the open prairie lined from one horizon to the other with wagons heading west. The popular schoolbook image was

always one of loneliness—tiny solitary bands of men dragging themselves and their belongings across an empty landscape. That was
wrong. I traveled in one of those wagon trains. Every night the
camps were surrounded by the stink of open latrines where thousands of others had dug their waste pits. There was no grass or
forage for miles—it had been eaten off like a great plague of locusts by
the horses and oxen that had gone before. I saw men sell other men a
glass of water for a hundred dollars. And I saw men die who didn't
have the cash to buy that glass of water. In the camps I saw men pay
five dollars just to *look* at a woman, an ordinary woman, they were so
rare. I witnessed acts of incredible kindness and unspeakable cruelty. And I wove it all together into *The Golden Land,* and I made so
much money on that book it made the hundred thousand in gold
seem like spare change. 'Marvelous fiction,' the critics said. I knew
better. It was nonfiction; I'd *seen* those stories. I didn't make them
up, I recorded them." He drank. Alex watched him.

"I met men who would later become well known. I knew Henry
Wells and William Fargo. I watched John Studebaker building
wagons by hand. I knew Philip Armour when he ran a one-man
butcher shop. I shopped in Levi Strauss's dry goods store. I drank
whiskey with Mark Twain."

Alex smiled to himself. *So did I. But that was another time,
another story.*

His father seemed to rouse himself from a trance. "My other
books were all born in the same manner. Some experiences
were not as pleasant. And now I have been back here for so
many years I've lost track. And what was once a marvelous
adventure has become torture." He looked at Alex. "And now
it's your turn. To talk."

"Why are we here?" Alex asked. "Not just here, in this room,
but here, in the past. Why does it happen?"

His father smiled briefly and sat down. "That's the big question, isn't it?" He leaned forward, placing his elbows on the table. "I've come to believe that our general conception of time is wrong. Or at least the popular conception. Most people think of time as a river that flows in one direction, and that we're all on this river, floating along together, moving from the past toward the future. But I believe that time is more like a huge fabric, woven together of strands, events, that intersect and create patterns.

"The fabric is reality." His father stopped and pushed the plate in front of him to the middle of the table. He ran his hand along the bright white linen tablecloth, his fingers tracing patterns where the threads had been woven to create a maze of curlicues and graceful shapes that twisted and joined together. "There are certain events where history can make a turn, a change, where the threads are so incredibly complicated and the design so intricate it is impossible to decipher, at least in human terms. Our lives are much too short to make sense of life while we live it. We, all humans, are the threads, interacting, weaving our lives into a particular history." He frowned. "Sometimes, though, the threads are misdirected and mistakes appear, knots form and the fabric is flawed, ugly. It can begin to unravel. These mistakes must be repaired. I believe we are the weavers, you and I, sent back to correct the mistakes."

"Mistakes? By whose reckoning are they mistakes? And who is sending us?" Alex interjected. "God? I would never have expected you to come up with so religious a theory."

His father shrugged. "Perhaps Time is God. You asked me what I thought, not what I know."

Alex shook his head. "It's not an inelegant theory," he said. "I believe some cultures think much the same thing, at least in their creation stories. I doubt they include the time elements. Your idea is based, though, on the idea that the past *can be changed.*

Repaired. I don't believe that. My experience has shown me that at most, if it *is* changed, the results always remain the same. Why are you so sure the opposite is true?"

"Because I've seen it. I've caused it. I told you that I knew Levi Strauss. After I appeared at Sutter's Mill I took a trip to San Francisco to help Jim Marshall bring some of the gold there to be assayed. While he was doing that, I went to Strauss's store to buy supplies that we needed. I didn't make the connection about whose store I was in until I was putting my purchases on the counter and the owner, who turned out to be Strauss, came around and looked at my jeans. They were old ones, from our time, and the leather tag on the back was too worn to read, but Strauss was interested in . . . what? Care to guess?"

"The zipper?" Alex guessed.

"No, they were button fly. It was the rivets. He got down and stared at them. Then he asked me to sell him the pants. I refused. At the time I was still laboring under the notion that you couldn't do anything to change the past under the threat of unknown consequences to the future. I was afraid he'd copy the design and, I don't know, cause World War Three or something. But he stole the idea of the rivets and put them in his own line of pants and invented blue jeans as we know them."

"You're saying he saw the rivets on your pants, invented rivets in pants, then you come back more than one hundred fifty years later wearing pants with rivets and he steals the idea from himself? One big enclosed circle?"

His father stopped behind his chair, putting both hands on the top. "Exactly. The woven cloth that circles around and joins in upon itself."

"And if you hadn't come back and gone to his store? . . ."

"We'd be wearing pants without rivets."

Alex put his hand over his face and rubbed his eyes. "Well, that wouldn't exactly be a tragedy."

"No, it wouldn't, and in some other time I imagine that's the reality."

"Some other time?"

"Yes, I think that as we change events we change times, change to a new fabric with different patterns. A new universe, a new reality. And that those of us capable of change are the only ones who will ever notice that things are not the same as they once were. And even *we* may not notice these changes."

"Rivets or lack of rivets seems a pretty small matter to influence a universe shift," Alex said.

"A small matter, yes. This is where you can find differences in fact that indicate a shift has taken place. Researchers come up with them all the time, but they generally don't make the news. You have to search in small, out-of-the-way places: old diaries, letters, advertising copy. Past events suddenly don't connect with present realities. I don't know what the mechanism is, how we slip from one layer of the fabric to another, and how people don't remember the last world they inhabited, but we remember it. Or at least I do now. In the beginning, maybe not, but now I know what's coming. I know what's coming is a matter of great concern." He stopped.

"I'm not sure I want to hear the answer, but what matter of concern would that be?"

"The assassination of Abraham Lincoln. And the future of the world."

chapter twenty-eight

A FTER HE AND HIS father had moved into the sitting room, Alex sank back into the enveloping burgundy plush of a heavy wingback chair. The room had the slightly musty smell of a house that sits empty much of the time. His father lit the fire that had been laid in the fireplace. The crackling flames quickly warmed the room. Cigars and a bottle of brandy were on a table between the two matched chairs that faced the fireplace.

He felt, for the first time in months, warm, satiated, and unwilling to question, or even think. And this was a mistake. He knew it. He had to pay attention to what his father was saying. He had to stay alert.

"The death of Lincoln," Alex said. "One of the knots in your fabric of history?"

"One of the knots? Yes. A tangle, a complexity, certainly," his father said. "To pretend otherwise is foolish. The death of any powerful man can influence events—when the death is premature, the events are influenced to a greater degree. By premature I mean death by unnatural causes. And when the death is caused by murder, as it is in this case, events are extremely fluid and run in any number of directions until they solidify. But it's not the death of Lincoln that's so important. History turns on the manner of his dying."

"Explain," he said.

His father lit another cigar. He and Alex were both staring into the fire.

"Because it's an assassination, there are further effects all down the timeline. The model for public assassination in

236

America is established right here. Without this first model, Garfield and McKinley are not shot, Kennedy does not die. Reagan isn't wounded nor are there attempts on the lives of Harry Truman or Gerald Ford. This extends further to non-presidents—men like John Lennon, Bobby Kennedy, and Martin Luther King, Jr., don't die." He rose and stood next to the fire, looking at Alex. "History is changed. For the better."

"How do you know?" Alex's tone was incredulous.

"Some of it I've seen. My position on the timeline is more fluid than yours. I believe this is because I no longer have an anchor in your time. I have moved through some of future history. If I am to be here, or any other time from now to the present, I prefer to exist in as much comfort as I am able to manage. And comfort extends beyond simple concerns of personal luxury. Public anxiety can be trying in its own way. I would just as soon do without national strife. Tell me, what is your time like? Has the country or the world renounced assassination as a political method? Is your time, your present, free of anxiety, personal as well as political?"

Alex wondered what acts of terrorism had been visited on the world since he left his present era. Could his father be right about this? Could history be changed? For the better? And could he be the instrument for such change?

"Your silence seems to indicate that the world I left years ago has not made much progress toward enlightenment. As I intend to go back to the present, if possible, I'd like to arrive in a peaceful country."

"What's your plan? What exactly would I do?" Alex asked. "Not that I'm agreeing to anything."

"It's quite simple. All that has to be done is to deflect Booth for a matter of seconds and the nation will be spared that tragedy."

"Why can't you do it? Deflect Booth."

"It's possible I could, but I can't take the chance." He tapped his leg. "I'm an old man with a wooden leg and serious arthritis. If any swift action is called for, even the smallest, I couldn't supply it. Besides, I'm going to save Secretary of State Seward. Lincoln wasn't the only man attacked that night. It is important that Seward not be killed by Lewis Paine, his intended assassin. I propose to do nothing more than show up at the Seward residence. I believe my presence will be enough to deflect Paine."

"Why not just tell the authorities to stop Booth? Or warn the president?"

Alex's father threw the cigar into the fire and sat down. He poured himself several inches of the brandy.

"I have connections in Washington," he said. "My position with the Sanitary Commission is one of responsibility. When I became aware that you were in this time, I nosed around looking for you. There is no actual record of your arrest or sentencing to this prison camp, but I was told that a man answering your general description had been seized for having materials indicating a threat on the president's life. I knew then it had to be you. Knowing what happened to you, do you really suppose I would go back and make the same prediction? That I would go to the authorities and tell them exactly what has caused you to be imprisoned? Especially when the prediction will come tragically true? And as far as warning Lincoln, he has been warned any number of times already. It does no good." He took a sip of his brandy and looked at Alex. "You'll have to escape if you are going to get out in time to help me."

Alex had seen men try to escape, and die in the attempt. Had seen the detachment of Negro troops whose specialty was chasing down anyone who somehow got themselves out of the camp into the countryside. His nemesis King was often a member of this detachment.

"I can't take a chance like that. If I sit it out in here a few more weeks, the war will be over, and I'll eventually go free like everyone else. You'll just have to do it yourself, or hire someone to deflect Booth. I'd be crazy to try an escape. No, it's off as far as I'm concerned."

"I wouldn't be quite so hasty," his father said. "I'll make arrangements to come by the photographic studio in the morning. I have some money that I'll give you. I know that men can buy their way out of prisons like this one. Others have done so before you. Enough money will assure you a guard's turned back, a special pass beyond the camp on some trumped-up errand. You've been here long enough to know the possibilities."

"I said I'd be crazy to try it. Get someone else."

His father stood. "I'll be back in a moment. I want to show you something." He left the room. Alex poured himself some of the brandy. *Screw it; I might as well enjoy myself for a few more minutes. I'll be back in my tent in no time.*

His father came back into the room. He handed Alex a newspaper. "Read the small advertisement that I've circled."

Alex checked the masthead of the paper: *The Capitol Constitution.* He knew it was one of the daily Washington papers. He turned the sheet toward the fire for more light. The type was small and difficult to read. He bent close. The circled box was the size of a typical personal ad.

ALEX. IF YOU ARE HERE PLEASE COME. I NEED YOU. MOLLY

He felt his heart leap and stutter. He closed his eyes. *No.* He looked at his father. Was it a joke? A trick?

His father was smiling. "She's run that advertisement every

day for a month, since I first noticed it. That's what tipped me off for sure that you were here." He waited, enjoying the look of astonishment on Alex's face.

"Do you know that you are going to be a father?" he went on. "And quite soon, from the looks of her."

Alex sat perfectly still. He felt his breath catch, heard a rushing of blood in his ears, swallowed against a lump that filled his throat, closed his eyes against the tilt and whirl that threatened for just a moment to blacken and actually plunge him into unconsciousness.

He turned to his father. "Explain. Everything."

"There's really not much to explain. And if you continue to use that tone of voice on me I'll tell you nothing. I need you, yes, but you need me perhaps even more. I can give you money you can use to get out of here. I can tell you where your—what do you call her?—your girlfriend, your enamorata, can be found. I know you're not married."

"How do you know that?"

"Because I've talked with her. With Molly. Oh, yes, we had quite a nice little chat. I had some luck in the matter of finding her, but mostly it was a matter of putting several disparate events together. There was a small humorous article in one of the papers about a woman who made fanciful predictions, then there were articles written by a writer named Glenn Balfour. The same last name caught my eye, and then I noticed little stylistic tics that indicated a writer not from this time. Nothing really overt. Then there came the advertisement, the phrase 'Alex . . . I need you.' I went to the newspaper office and bribed the counterman into telling me who had placed the ad. Then I waited for her, and followed her. I know where she lives. I'm going to go to her and tell her I've found you. That you are going to help me stop Booth. After that we will figure out how we can all get back to the future."

Alex felt his hands tighten on the arms of his chair. He could stop this all right now, if he had the nerve.

"So you see, you'll have to escape if you want to get back to her now. Otherwise you'll have to wait for the war to end, but even then I don't believe they are going to let you out. I'm not sure why you are here, but I don't think the reason is what the authorities are saying. I believe you are in great danger. You have to get to Washington to help. If not for me, at least for Molly. I'll come by in the morning and give you the money to bribe your way out."

"Why not just give me the money now?" Alex asked. His father was right. Baker had him in prison for his own reasons, even though Alex didn't know what those reasons were.

"I don't have the money here," his father said. "All my cash has been placed in the commandant's safe. It's some sort of prison regulation."

Alex hardly heard him. The idea of getting out had seized him. The idea of seeing Molly. He would do it. He would deal with his father later.

"I'm so glad you've come around to my way of thinking," his father said. "It will all work out best this way for us all."

chapter twenty-nine

ALEX WALKED BACK to the compound with only a sliver of moon and a wide swath of stars to light the way. The sand trail, surrounded by the skeletal black trunks and limbs of the sparse pine trees, was a steely gray path through the darker ground cover of pine needles.

He tried to sort out the information his father had given him, tried to separate the truths from the self-serving distortions and straight-out lies. But the most important revelation was Molly. She was here, now he knew that for sure. She was pregnant, and she needed him. He would use his father, even with his lies and distortions, to find her.

He had laughed when his father proposed that he escape. But that was before he knew about Molly. He would take his father's money the next morning and try to buy his way out. He no longer had the luxury of waiting out the war.

He left the copse of trees and joined the larger road that led to the prison compound. There were smoking torches inside the gate of the compound. He could smell the burning pitch and see the glow in the rising smoke. He stepped forward, announced himself, and heard the wooden bar that secured the door being scraped back. While he waited he realized that he had forgotten to bring the valuable leftover food from dinner. The knowledge that Molly was alive had driven everything else out of his mind.

The soldiers on the walkway high on the sides of the compound wall carried their rifles casually but watched him carefully as he stood waiting. A cloud of mosquitoes whined around his face. He walked through the doorway and nodded at the soldier who held open the heavy wooden door. "Sign in at the gatehouse," the guard said.

The man in the gatehouse was squinting over a newspaper by the light of an oil lamp as Alex walked in. He looked up irritably and said nothing as Alex handed over his pass. "Could you tell those boys up on the walkway not to shoot me on my way back to my tent?" Alex asked.

The man shrugged. "Maybe they will, maybe they won't. Don't make no never-mind to me."

The night was particularly dark. If he was careful, he could slip into the shadows behind the tents and make his way to his own pallet, where he would find little comfort but at least he could sleep. He waited for a moment, hearing in the distance the silvery tones of a flute. He was back in time for the concert.

He made it three rows down before they came at him out of the dark.

The first one was on him before he knew what was happening, stepping out of deep shadow and slamming him in the stomach with a bony fist. Alex twisted to the side, gasping for breath. He began to fall and saw another shadow-man step up and pull back a leg to deliver a kick. Alex caught himself on one hand and went into a roll. The foot missed his head by an inch.

"Goddamn it, hold still, you Union-lovin' son of a bitch," a man muttered as several hands reached for him. There seemed to be at least three of them. Maybe more.

"I got him, Sherod," another man said in a low voice. Alex could feel the man's hands clawing at his shirt as he twisted away. Fabric tore. Alex kicked out and felt his shoe catch a kneecap. One of the men went down with a yelp.

Sherod. He pushed another man away and got to his feet.

"Keep it quiet," the one Alex thought was Sherod whispered. "Them niggers'l shoot at anything they hear."

Alex stood, trying to catch his breath, as the men circled around him.

"You boys grab him. I'm gonna gut him like a hog," Sherod said.

"You mind that knife," one of the men said as they began to draw closer.

The knife changed the odds. Better to take a chance on getting shot from long range than getting stabbed up close. He spun around and pushed one of the men backward. The man stumbled into the side of a tent, which collapsed onto its inhabitants. Shouts and curses came from under the canvas.

"Fight!" Alex shouted. "Thieves! Help! I've got 'em, boys!" Men began to crawl out of tents. A guard on the wall shouted something unintelligible and raised his rifle.

"These men are robbing tents!" Alex shouted. Twenty prisoners piled out of nearby tents and cracker-box cabins.

"That there is bullshit," Sherod said in an aggrieved voice, as he and his men stood back to back, now surrounded by a growing mass of prisoners.

"No, it ain't," a man said. "We know'd you was a dog from day one." He stepped forward and swung a stick at Sherod's head. This set off a general melee as more than fifty men soon joined in combat, most of them unclear on exactly who or why they were fighting, but glad to be engaged as a release of the hatred and anger that constantly boiled in all of them.

Alex slunk away from the fight, back toward the gatehouse. On the walkway the guards were jogging toward the area closest to the fight. There were more shouts from outside as the front gate swung open. A squad of ten troopers mounted on horses trotted into the compound. The two lead riders leaned over and pulled the torches in front of the gatehouse from the ground. They spurred their horses toward the fighting men. Alex rounded the opposite, back corner of the gatehouse.

Now that the torches were gone, the house and the gate itself were in darkness. The soldier who had opened the gate minutes earlier stood watching the mounted men ride into the mass of fighters.

Alex looked around and realized no one had seen him, and that Sherod and his diversion had given him an opportunity he was now about to seize. A simple plan blossomed in his mind. *Run. Hide near the road. Wait for his father to drive out of the camp in the morning and ride with him back to Washington.*

He ran through the gate.

He sorted through an array of options as he ran. *Go to the studio to get supplies. No. The fight will draw the guards. Go, now.*

Behind him the sounds of what seemed to be developing into a riot faded. Gunshots popped as the guards began firing. He ran faster. North, then angling into the pine forest off the path. Soon he could hear nothing from the compound, only his own harsh, ragged breathing and the swish and slap of tree branches as he pushed them out of the way.

And, behind him, the swish and slap of tree branches as someone else pushed them away.

He stopped and turned.

A man slammed into him and knocked him to the ground. Alex felt the sharp bite of a knife dig into the skin at his throat. The man lay on top of him, his face inches from Alex's. "You so much as twitch," the man said, in a low voice between gasps for air, "and I'll slit your goddamn throat."

Sherod.

chapter thirty

SHEROD STANK OF sweat and dirt. Alex could see the silhouette of his face and straggly hair against the starry sky.

ALLEN APPEL

"You gon' give me any trouble?" Sherod asked.

"No," Alex said.

Sherod sat up. "I trust that about as much as I trust any other Yankee lie. What else you gon' say with a knife stuck in your neck?"

"What do you want with me?" Alex asked.

"I saw you duck out back there when the fracas commenced. I followed, figurin' you was just trying to get out of the fight. You been a burr in my boot ever since I first come across you. Then I saw your plan and decided I might as well skedaddle. What I want with you? It'll be easier for two to break out than one. It's like we got a common cause. Least for a while." He stood up. "You got any problem with that?"

Alex pushed to his feet. "No." *Like he says, what else am I going to say while he's got the knife?*

Sherod waited a minute. "Talkative sumbitch, ain't you?" He looked around. "You got a plan or are we just two mules on the loose?"

"There's only two ways off this spit of land," Alex said. "Neither of them are good, but we have to choose one. There's the road, which takes us through a detachment of soldiers on guard where this spit of land meets the mainland, or in the water, where we can be seen by anyone looking out at the bay."

"I cain't swim," Sherrod said, "so I just made the decision for us. Maybe all them that's guarding is back at the camp by now. Maybe we can just stroll right on out of here."

"No, there are more of them there than that. I've been up to the guard-post to pick up supplies. There's a whole barracks there. They wouldn't ever leave it completely unguarded."

"So what you're saying is we're done for."

"Maybe not," Alex said, thinking. "But before we do anything we've got to go back to the photography studio."

Twice they had to duck off the road as small detachments of

soldiers rode by. Evidently the riot in the compound continued to rage, drawing soldiers in from all over. Even so, they made it to the small brick studio within ten minutes.

Inside the studio, Alex pushed Sherod to the side. "Stand over there and keep quiet. Don't get in my way."

Sherod knocked Alex's hand off his shoulder. "What are we gonna do in here anyhow? I can't see a damn thing; it's as black as the inside of a cat's ass."

Alex went behind the counter and felt his way along the shelves. The heavy stone jugs of collodion were on the floor.

"What the hell are you doin'?" Sherod asked.

Alex was crouched down over the jugs and for a minute he contemplated several options: throw a glass of cyanide in Sherod's face, hit him with a tripod, smack him in the head with a jug. Then he decided that he needed the man's help for at least a while longer.

Alex stood up. "You want to try and get out of this camp by yourself, go ahead. Otherwise, open the door and make sure there's no one around."

Sherod, muttering to himself, went to the door and opened it a crack, then all the way. By the faint light, Alex lifted three jugs to the countertop. For a moment he contemplated pouring the two half-full jugs together, but he knew it would be too hard to do in the dark. He picked up two jugs and went to the door. "There's one more on the counter. Get it and follow me."

"You want to tell me what you got in mind?"

"I'll show you in a while. What I have in mind is getting us out of here." He pushed by Sherod and went outside. In a minute the other man joined him.

It took them half an hour to walk to the end of the camp. They stood in a sparse copse of pine trees, looking out at the guard's area fifty yards in front of them.

Their eyes had grown so accustomed to the dark, they could make out four sentries standing at either side of the road where the camp met the mainland on a narrow neck of land. The bay was to the right of them. Alex could hear water lapping at the small sandy beach. To the left was a saltwater swamp that was impassable. The road was their only way out. And there was no way to sneak by the four men on duty there.

To the left, seventy-five yards from the guards, was a barracks. Inside there would be soldiers sleeping, those who had not been called to help quell the riot at the compound. "There's where we want to go," Alex said, pointing at the barracks.

"What about them four by the road?"

"If we stick to the woods, we can get almost that far. As long as we keep the building between them and us they won't see us."

Alex felt Sherod's clawlike hand on his arm. "Wait a damn minute. What are we going to do when we get there?"

"This stuff's flammable," Alex said, lifting one of the jugs. "We'll set the building on fire. Hopefully that will draw the guards away from their post. In the confusion we just take off down the road." Even in the dim light he could see Sherod's look of disgust. "You have a better plan?" Alex asked him.

Sherod glared at him. "No, but I'll tell you what. This don't work and they grab us, I'm gon' kill you first. That's a promise."

"Let's go," Alex said.

They moved quietly down the long row of trees, crossed the road, and slipped into the trees on the other side.

The barracks looked as if it had been hastily built. There were no windows, and the only exit was in the front. Alex worried for a moment about the troopers inside and could only hope they would make it out before the building burned down.

"Give me the full bottle," he whispered. Sherod handed him the bottle of collodion. "We're going to start near the front. I'll pour the liquid along this side, and then you give me one of the half bottles. I'll pour it around the back. The other side will be in deep shadow; you pour what's left along that side, but only for fifteen feet or so. If you go too far forward the guards might see you. Then put the jug down and come back. I'll light it off, we'll get back to the trees and wait for the guards to come over to sound the alarm and get the soldiers out. While they're doing that, we'll run back to the road and just keep on going."

Alex trotted out from the line of trees to the side of the barracks. Sherod followed. Alex knelt beside the building and picked at the stopper in the jug. He'd forgotten the cork was sealed with wax.

"Give me the knife!" he whispered. Sherod hesitated.

"Give me the knife, you cretin!"

Sherod smiled. An evil, lopsided smile. He held up his left hand, index finger upraised, and slowly pulled out the knife. He took the jug from Alex and with a quick twist cut the seal off the cork. "Don't never call me no names," he hissed. He lifted the knife and with a swift motion cut Alex's cheek. Alex jerked back from the cold slash of pain. He felt blood drip down his chin. For a second a veil of fury almost blinded him. He forced himself to ignore the pain and the blood.

Alex stood up, bent into a crouch, and began pouring the collodion along the frame of the barracks. The smell was instant, a sharp odor of ether, unlike anything in nature. He reached the end of the building, emptied the last drops, and put the jug down. Sherod handed him one of the half-jugs. Alex poured the liquid along the back. He finished at the corner and placed the empty jug on the grass.

"Go ahead," he whispered to Sherod.

Sherod peered around the side of the building, waited a moment, then began pouring. As soon as he turned the corner,

Alex reached into his pocket, pulled out a wooden match, struck it on the side of the building, touched it to the wet collodion, and turned and ran.

A wall of flame burst upward and along the bottom of the building and raced around both corners. As Alex hit the line of trees he heard an explosion from the far wall as Sherod's jug caught fire and went off like a small bomb. Sherod screamed. Alex glanced back and saw the man, engulfed in flames, stagger around the corner of the barracks and fall to the ground.

Alex ran down the length of the trees, across the road, and into the stand on the other side. He slid to a stop at the point where he and Sherod had looked out at the four guards. They were now running toward the conflagration, shouting at the top of their lungs. He glanced back; the building was a mass of flames. The front door burst open and the first trooper crashed out, followed by others.

Alex broke from the trees onto the road.

chapter thirty-one

MOLLY TURNED FROM her position on the love seat and looked back at Bierce, who was at his writing table. His pen was lying on the desk, and he was holding his head with both hands.

"What is it?" she asked. "Are you all right?"

He didn't move for several seconds, then looked up at her. "Sometimes my head feels like there's a large stone embedded in my brain. I guess I'm lucky they didn't decide to amputate." He looked down at the small stack of paper in front of him. "And this doesn't help. This story has all the vitality of a sick fish."

Molly hauled herself out of the love seat. It had been more than a month since she'd been told by Mary Walker, the lady surgeon, to go to bed for two weeks. Those weeks had passed uneventfully. She was now so large she felt as if she were lugging around a full-grown watermelon under her skin. Bierce, on the other hand, had fainted twice in recent days, each time after bouts with a terrible migraine. There seemed to be nothing anyone could do about these "fits," as the doctors called them. But the usually placid Bierce had begun to give way to periods where he was angry and depressed. Convinced that Lafayette Baker had men watching the hotel room he had shared with Alex, Bierce had moved from there to the small teahouse behind Anne Benton's establishment. His forays into Marie's bedroom had grown fewer, subsiding from the heat of passion into the cooler waters of friendship.

Molly did little except lodge in the sitting room and help Bierce with his writing, read the newspapers, and talk to her visitors. Every afternoon Bierce went to the newspaper office and checked to see if Alex had answered Molly's advertisement. He had not.

She lumbered around the love seat and over to Bierce's desk. Brady had sent over her picture with the president, and they had propped it up next to the inkstand. She looked down at Bierce's stack of papers. The top one was titled "A Strange and Improbable Occurrence at Owl Creek Bridge."

"What's the problem?" she asked. *Besides the title,* she thought.

"It's this story," Bierce said, frowning. "It just lays on the page, flat and dead." He shook his head and sat back in his chair.

"Tell me about it," she said.

"We were in Alabama. Our lines were drawn up at a place called Owl Creek. We had been there for several days when they caught a man, a local planter, who had sneaked in during the night and tried to set fire to the bridge there. He was summarily tried and sentenced to death."

Molly picked up the first page and read: *A man perched precariously upon a railroad bridge in northern Alabama, staring morosely down between the ties to the swift, swirling, pounding curls and eddies of the water twenty long, long, feet below his booted feet.* "Give me the pen," she said. Bierce handed her the pen. She started at the top, marking on the manuscript, crossing out words. She handed it back to him.

Bierce read the new title, "An Occurrence at Owl Creek Bridge," and the first sentence: *A man stood upon a railroad bridge in Northern Alabama, looking down into the swift waters twenty feet below.*

"Kind of plain, isn't it?"

"We've talked about this before. You have a story to tell, so tell the damn story. Don't be a victim of your age's Victorian style."

"So what age should I be a victim of?"

She ignored his supercilious tone of voice. "None. Writers should never be victims. And don't spill the beans in your title. Don't tell the reader this is going to be a strange and troubling story, let them find that out for themselves. And the 'feet' confusion at the end of the sentence is terrible."

"I know," he said, pressing his hand against his temple. "I wish I'd been shot to rags back at Kennesaw Mountain. Is writing always this difficult?"

"Yes. Anyone who tells you differently is either a liar or a bad writer. The secret, and it's not much of a secret, to good writing is rewriting."

"But if you change one word, you have to copy the whole page out over again! It takes forever!"

She patted him on the shoulder. "I understand, but it has to be done. If it's any consolation, in the future there will be writing machines that will make it possible so you don't have to copy out the whole page again. Not in your time, though."

"Then it's no consolation at all."

"It's time to go check the advertisement," she said. "There's money in the desk."

Bierce snorted. "There'll be nothing for us. I've checked every day for more than a month and every day there's been nothing."

"Well, we're not giving up. Go. When you get back we'll move on with the rewrites."

Bierce gave her a disgusted look.

"All right, when you're done I'll help you copy everything over." He smiled.

chapter thirty-two

THE ROAD TO AND from the prison camp ran through Maryland in a northwest direction, crossing open fields of small and large farms with long stretches of mixed-wood forest. The forest itself was thick and silent, just beginning to bud into spring. It was the open stretches of farmland, the clear-cuts, that made Alex nervous. As long as his eventual pursuers had no dogs to track him, he could always travel deeper into the forest and hide, if he had enough warning of their coming. But a lone man on foot, particularly a ragged stranger, was uncommon enough to raise the interest of anyone who saw him.

He had been on the road for four hours, by his estimation, and he was exhausted. He would probably have another four hours, at least, before it was discovered that he was missing from the camp. The officer of the gate had checked him in and there would be no indication that he had gone out, until the regular morning roll call. And the riot, and later the fire, of the night before probably had caused great confusion with men hurt, maybe even killed. The official count would be late and as men turned up missing the count would have to be redone until an official tally was approved. It might even take all day, and even then any sort of pursuit would have to be organized and outfitted. And the confusion of the burned barracks would only add to the delay. All of this might buy him an extra day.

One thing he knew for sure. A few hours after daylight his father would load his bags into his buggy and trot out of the camp on his way back to Washington. He would first go to the studio, as he said he would, to give Alex the money to buy his way out of prison. When he didn't find him there perhaps he would suspect the fire had given cover for his escape and would move on alone. And Alex was determined to flag him down and ride north in the buggy with him. Otherwise, he would have to make his own way to the city through hostile territory—most of Maryland was and had always been for secession—expecting to hear the hoofbeats of Union troops bent on capturing him coming up behind.

He stood inside a line of trees, looking apprehensively out over a long expanse of wide-open country. The sky had that indefinite look that was not quite night and not yet dawn. He had no idea how far he would have to walk before he could find cover. He had to make a decision. He stood in the center of the road and shivered. Going on would probably offer no distinct advantage. If he missed his father's buggy, he was in trouble no matter where he was, here or five miles up the road. He would wait here.

He left the road and pushed into the brush at the side. The mountain laurel was thick, with long flat leaves covering spindly branches that shaded open areas floored with last fall's leaf-drop from the hardwoods overhead. He found the thick trunk of a walnut tree and sat down, leaning against the trunk. From this vantage point, he could hear anything coming up the road in enough time to either hide from it or hail it, depending whether it was friend or foe.

Not that he knew which his father was.

He crossed his hands in his lap and leaned his head back against the tree. He had to be careful not to fall asleep. Missing his father could be disastrous. He was asleep within sixty seconds.

He slept, and then awoke to the clip-clop of hooves, the jangle of harness, and the creak of a buggy as it passed him on the road. He jumped up, pushing aside the laurel branches as they clutched at him, crashing through the brush until he stumbled out onto the road and fell down. He could see the back of an open two-wheeled buggy as it went around a curve in the distance. He started to run.

His movements were clumsy, his body stiff and sore from sleeping underneath a tree, his old leg wound hurting, his breath coming in gasps after only a few-score yards of run.

"Hey!" he shouted. He would never have caught the buggy otherwise. It kept going, and he kept going, but he was losing ground.

"Stop! Stop!" He staggered as his ankle turned in a deep muddy rut. The buggy pulled up. Alex stopped running, and walked, hands on hips, breathing hard. He came around the side. "Jesus," he said, "I didn't think you would stop."

The woman in the buggy was wearing a farm-woman's bonnet, coat, and dress, and she was carrying a large pistol which was pointed at Alex's head. Her hand was steady, her gaze as sharp and as pointed as her thin nose.

"And who might you be?" she asked.

Alex stopped. He hadn't considered the buggy would not be his father's, and so had no lie ready. His brain seemed still half-asleep and he could only stand and try to catch his breath.

"I know what you are," the woman said. "I come across a bunch a them nigger soldiers back a-ways. Said they was lookin' for an escaped prisoner. That's what you are, ain't it? An escaped prisoner, by God."

Alex shook his head, both at the woman and the fact that the prison camp had soldiers out on the road looking for him already. "I'm not a Rebel," he said. "I was in there by mistake."

She smirked at him. "Mistake, huh? I'm sorry to hear that, as I am a Rebel and damn proud of it. You get on up in this buggy and be careful you don't try to pull nothin'. I'd just as soon shoot you as not. I'd probably even get a reward for your hide."

"Are you going to take me back to the prison?" he asked. If she said yes, and he had every reason to think she would, he was going to turn and run. He was not going back.

She shook her head. "Oh, no, sonny, them niggers'd just take you away from me and say they'd done the catchin'. I'm gonna take you home. My Hiram will decide what's to be done with you. You'll be safe enough with us. Or I could just shoot you if you try to run off. That'd probably be the easiest thing to do. What's it going to be?"

He weighed his options and found them all sorely lacking. He could run—he might make it away from her without her shooting him. Then he'd have to evade the soldiers she would undoubtedly put on his trail. She might hit him, wound him, or even kill him. She seemed remarkably at ease with the pistol. *What options?*

She scooted over on the seat. "Slow," she said. "You come on up nice and slow." He pulled himself up into the buggy. Up close he could see that it was in shabby condition. The leather was cracked and dirty. The horse itself, now that he looked at it, was sway-backed and painfully thin. She saw him examining the horse. "Damn soldiers took every decent animal anyone around here owns. Left us with this trash." She clucked her tongue, and the horse trudged into motion. The woman held the pistol in one hand, steady on Alex's midsection, and handled the reins with the other.

They rode in silence for ten or fifteen minutes. "How far are we going?" Alex asked.

"A ways," she answered, without looking at him. He didn't ask any more questions.

The sun had crossed over into the afternoon sky when the woman turned the buggy off the main road onto a dirt track that ran directly through the forest with brush coming close enough on both sides to tangle in the wheels. The trees canopied over the muddy track, and the sun dappled the low understory of budding dogwood and mountain laurel with spots of bright sunlight. There were no signs of habitation in the glimpses of small clearings off to either side of the road. The woman hadn't said a word in four hours and still kept the pistol trained on Alex.

When they clattered out of the forest into a clearing set between two low hills, Alex was almost relieved. He was, at least, not back at the prison camp, and it seemed to him he was far enough off the beaten track that the soldiers would not cast their net this far away. They would be searching for a man on foot, not a man who had ridden for half a day in a buggy.

A tall man as gaunt as the woman stepped off the porch of a log house into a bare dirt front yard. He was filthy, barefoot, greasy-haired, and his clothing was as least as scabrous as Alex's.

"What you got there, Marta?" the man said. He squinted at them, as if nearsighted. He reached automatically for the reins as the horse clopped to a halt in front of him.

"I caught this boy running off from the camp," she said, almost shouting. "I think he thought I was someone else. Decided I'd bring him along."

The man nodded. "Get on down here," he ordered Alex. "You keep that hog-leg on him, Marta."

Alex climbed down. The man approached him and peered close. "What's your name, boy?"

Alex stepped back. The fellow smelled like a hog. "Alex," he said.

"Speak up when you're talkin' to a man," Hiram shouted.

"Alex!"

"That's better. All right, Alex, you got any fambly?"

"Yes. I do now." A fleeting image of Molly flashed through his head. All that was standing between him and Molly was this fool, sixty or so miles of traveling, and the Union Army.

"They got any money?"

"I don't have any idea."

Hiram looked puzzled. Marta handed him down the pistol and got out of the buggy. "I'm thinkin'," she said, coming up beside them, still speaking in loud tones, "we ought to just shoot this one right now."

Hiram moved close to Alex again. Alex realized that besides

being unable to hear, the man couldn't see much that was more than a foot away from his face. "Naw," Hiram said. "Everybody's family got at least a little money. Can you write?" he asked. Alex nodded. "Write out the name of your family and where they live. Marta, get us a scrap of paper and the pencil."

"I don't know where they live," Alex said. The man squinted at him. "It's complicated," Alex added, louder. The man looked in Marta's direction.

" 'It's complicated,' " he mimicked, stretching the word out for comic effect. "The man says he don't know where his own kin live." He raised the pistol and pointed it at Alex. "How 'bout this?" he asked. "Is this complicated?"

Alex understood he was about two seconds from being shot, but he still didn't have a better answer. "I wish I could give you some money, or had someone to give you some money, but I don't," he said.

Hiram stepped back. "Let's put him in the cellar," he said. "Maybe a few days down there and he'll come up with somethin' more useful." Marta nodded. "You follow me," she said, and turned.

They marched their odd parade; Marta, Alex, Hiram, around the side of the log house and behind. They walked by a hog pen where two spavined pigs stared out at them, by several falling-down outbuildings, and farther, to a raised hill with a heavy plank door set hurricane-cellar style at a low angle into the hill. Alex recognized it as a root cellar.

The door was made up of two rough-hewn, bark-on plank panels that opened from the center. They were locked in place by a heavy beam slid through two handles. Hiram handed the pistol to Marta, then knelt down and dragged the beam out of the handles. "When I open this up you gonna get on down there. Otherwise I'm gonna take her suggestion and just shoot you and be done with the whole business. Understand?" Alex nodded. Hiram looked at Marta. "He don't get down there quick enough, just shoot him. You got my permission." He bent down, seized one of the handles, and hauled the door open.

At the same time Marta jabbed the pistol into his back, put a foot on his butt, and kicked him forward. He had a glimpse of dirt floor as he tumbled down into the hole. He landed hard as the door slammed shut, then he was surrounded by absolute darkness.

He struggled up on his hands and knees, gasping for breath. The air was full of dirt and dust kicked up by the slamming door. He coughed and blinked trying to clear his eyes. He sat back on his heels, still unable to see anything at all.

"Who are you?" a voice asked, somewhere in the dark.

chapter thirty-three

I ASKED WHO you are." The voice came from Alex's left. Then a different voice came from his right. "You just stay right where's you at." Alex had no intention of moving. He coughed. He kept waiting for his eyes to adjust to the dark, but it wasn't happening.

"Who are you?" Alex asked, his voice rough from the dust and fright.

"Believe I asked you the question first," the voice said.

Alex considered his deck of lies, wondering which one to deal.

From the sound of these men's voices, both were black, so neither was probably a friend to Southern sympathies—or escaped Southern prisoners. "My name is Alex. I'm a Union man. I'm just trying to get to Washington. I got caught on the road by that woman and thrown in here."

"She's somethin', that woman. That makes three of us now, don't it?" the first man said. There was a sound of scraping and movement. "Well, Rafe," the man went on, "I guess he's been tossed into the same boat that we're in."

After a minute the other man said, "I guess you're right. My name's Rafe, that other'n's Walter. We're pretty much the same as you, just on the road headed north when she got us. We been traveling for weeks, got out of Richmond and through the Yankee lines, made it to the coast, where we found an old boat that finally give out down-aways from here. Some soldiers we met on the road said to keep on going north and then west and we'd be in Washington City, where Father Abraham would give us a place to live and somethin' to eat. You got anything to eat on you?"

Alex sat down in the dirt. From the sound of the voices, Rafe and Walter were about three or four feet away from him on either side. He hadn't seen them when he was thrown in, both because he hadn't been looking and because they had been too far back to the sides of the doorway. Neither of them sounded dangerous.

"No, nothing to eat," Alex said. "How long have you been in here?"

"It's hard to say," Rafe said, "but I think this is the third day. We been fed twice. The door's got some cracks in it so you can tell when it's light outside."

Now that he mentioned it, Alex noticed that when he turned around and faced the slanted doorway he could see faint lines of light. The darkness in general was not quite so stygian as he had thought it to be. By using his light-sensitive peripheral vision he could just make out the form of a man on his right as long as he didn't look directly at him.

"What's the drill?" Alex asked. "How do they work things? Do they let you out to walk around? To go to the bathroom?" As soon as he asked that he knew the answer. There was the sharp tang of urine in the air.

"They ain't got no bath down here. Don't let us out at all," Walter said. "If you got to do your necessaries, we got a bucket down here for that. We got two buckets: one for that, and one with a little river water in it to drink. You don't want to go about getting the two mixed up. Once a day, usually in the late afternoon or early evening, the two of them come over and open the door. She holds a pistol on us while he hands down a bucket with some cooked beans in it and we hand up the bucket's got the necessaries in it, which he dumps to the side and hands back. And that's been the extent of our dealings with them two."

Alex moved over to the door and put his eye against one of the cracks and got an eyeful of dirt for his trouble. He rubbed at the eye, trying to clear the dirt out. "Why are they keeping you in here anyway?" he asked. He suddenly had a vision of Hansel and Gretel being fattened up by the evil witch.

"If you listen hard at the door, you can hear them talkin'," Rafe said. "She got to shout, as that man is as deaf as a post. That first day they put us in here I heard her tell him that we was probably run off and there'd be a reward for our return. They don't seem to understand that the war's about over and the side they're on's gonna lose. I seen some dumb white people in my time, black people too, but them two take the cake. She's the brains of the outfit, but that ain't saying much. What they throw you in here for? You got any idea?"

"They seem to think they can ransom me to my family."

"Can they?" Walter asked.

"No." He wasn't going to try to explain. "Have you thought about escaping?"

"Course we thought about it. So far the chance ain't arrived. Though we stay down here much longer we ain't gon' be fit enough to climb out this hole, much less do any serious runnin'. You think of anything?"

Alex shook his head. "No. Not yet." He put one hand on the inside of the door and pushed, but it didn't budge. He'd seen enough of the heavy beam holding it shut on the outside to know it wouldn't. Root cellars were built to withstand the depredations of large animals trying to get in. They were dug deep enough into the ground so that the temperature inside was always cool—which meant digging out without tools would be a matter of weeks, if it could be done at all. And he didn't have weeks.

"The only way we're gettin' out of here," Walter said, "is if they let us out. That's what we got to figure on."

Alex thought the man was right. Either their captors or someone else on the outside was going to have to open the door for them. He'd just have to wait awhile to see how he could arrange for that to happen, or take advantage of it when it did.

For a man who had been forced by circumstances to be so aware of time, Alex found he was a poor judge of it when left in almost total darkness. He sat right next to the door, and when he heard movement outside he couldn't have said if ten minutes had passed or two hours, though he was sure he had not been locked in longer than that.

Finally he heard their two captors approaching the root cellar. She was shouting so Hiram could hear her. From inside the cellar her voice was muffled, but when they were close it was distinct enough to make out her words. Alex looked through a crack, but could see nothing.

"Just do it like usual," he heard Marta say. "I got the gun, you got your axe. They ain't going to give us any trouble." There was an indistinct grunt from the man. The heavy beam began to drag back. Alex twisted his head away as dust and wood bits shook loose and fell on him.

The door swung open. Alex looked up and was immediately blinded by the light. He put his hand up to shade his eyes as he blinked rapidly.

"Get on back there now!" Marta shouted. "Hand up that waste bucket. Move quick, and you'll get yourself something to eat. Otherwise you'll go hungry plus you'll have a bullet hole to worry about." Alex looked away from the light. Beside him the man he knew was Walter crawled over, dragging a wooden bucket. Walter seemed to be in his early twenties. He was dressed in a homespun shirt and pants, was barefoot and covered with dust and dirt from head to toe. His curly hair seemed almost frosted, like powder on an old-fashioned wig. Alex glanced to his left and saw Rafe, about the same age, similarly dressed and dirtied.

"You there, white man," Hiram shouted, "get on back, or I'll split your head with this here axe and dump this bucket of shit on ye!" He reached down and grabbed the handle of the bucket and hauled it out. Alex could hear the splash as he dumped it off to the side. The bucket came flying back at him and thumped heavily off his arm, which he had drawn up to shield his face. Everything was moving too quickly. The only thing he could see was that Hiram and Marta had performed this act enough times to have it down to the level of art. He wondered briefly how many other men had graced the inside of the root cellar. And what had happened to them.

"Here's your food and be grateful for it," Hiram said, handing down the bucket that was received by Rafe. In another second the heavy door was heaved over and slammed down upon them while all three inside crouched low to avoid being hit by it. The beam slid through the handles and everything was again as quiet as a grave.

Alex lay back in the dirt, stunned by the suddenness and the violence of it all. He pushed himself up. He was completely blind again.

"Don't knock over the bucket," Rafe warned. Alex felt around. His hand found the wooden bucket. "Which one is it?" he asked.

"I got the necessaries," Walter, on his right, said. "You must got the food."

"Jesus, that was fast," Alex said.

"No need to take the Lord's name in vain," Rafe said. "And yes, it was fast. Been that way ever' other time they did it. It's too damn bright to see half a what's goin' on before it's all over. You try to come up out of here and that witch'd shoot you dead in your tracks."

Alex could smell the beans over the odors of dirt and mold. He heard a stomach growl, but in the dark he couldn't tell whose it was.

"Let's eat," Rafe said. "We'll think on it later. Only thing my brain knows right now is that my stomach's empty. Each take a handful and pass the bucket. You start, Alex."

Alex fumbled the bucket around until it was between his legs. He reached inside and felt a lukewarm mass of hard objects in liquid. He assumed these were beans. He thought that if he were ever delivered from this time he would never eat another bean again. He dipped up a handful and shoved them into his mouth. They had been cooked in nothing but water and tasted only of plain bean. He crunched down on a pebble that had been mixed up with the beans. His tongue probed to see if he'd broken a tooth. He heard Rafe passing the bucket to Walter.

It went around once again before it was empty.

"That's it?" Alex said. "That's all they've been feeding you?" There was a long silence,

"Yes," Rafe said. "Course, there was more for us before you came along. No offense."

"None taken," Alex said. He heard a stomach growl again and realized that this time it was his. He had last eaten, . . . when? He tried to add up the days, realizing suddenly that it was only a day ago that he had dinner with his father. Rafe and Walter had been living on a couple of handfuls of beans for days, and probably not much more than that before. They had to be weak from hunger, and so would he be in a matter of a few short days. He had to figure out how to get them out of here, or they would all soon be too weak to make any attempt at all.

They sat and talked, but none of them could come up with any plan beyond all three rushing Hiram and Marta at the same time, hoping that at least one of them would make it. But Alex realized that was almost no plan at all, that the woman seemed more familiar with the weapon than she was with a stove and a pot, at least judging from her beans. She would plug at least one of them and Hiram would do the others in with his axe before they could clear the door.

After a bit Alex realized he was exhausted. He'd had only a few hours' sleep the night before. The talk stopped and he heard Walter begin to snore. Then he slept, too.

"Sweet Jesus."

Alex opened his eyes. For a moment he was confused, unable to remember where he was, why it was so dark, what he was doing on the ground. Then he remembered.

"Sweet Jesus."

It was Walter, and his voice was low and shaky with fear.

"What's wrong?" Rafe asked. They were sleeping side by side, Alex in the middle. The temperature had grown colder, and they had moved together for warmth.

"Somethin's crawlin on me," Walter said.

Alex felt Rafe sit up.

"It's a snake," Walter said. "A big snake. I cain't stand this." They waited, straining to hear, afraid to move.

Alex felt the snake softly press against his chest as it moved onto him. "Just try to . . ." he began.

Walter screamed and rolled away from Alex to the side. Rafe scrabbled back toward the wall of the cellar. Alex sat up and grabbed the body of the snake, as thick as a weasel, and felt the head smash onto his left forearm and bite down. The pain lanced up his arm like a jolt of electricity. "Jesus!" he shouted.

He grabbed at the snake and tried to pull it off, but the reptile bit down even harder. The rest of the snake whipped up and slapped across his face. He grabbed the body of the snake with his right hand and it voided its bowels in a slimy mess. The thick body skidded out of his grasp and lashed against him again, twisting and curling. He was peripherally aware of Rafe and Walter scrambling out of the way and shouting as he rolled on the ground trying to pin down the lashing body of the snake.

Gasping for breath, he got the body more or less underneath him and immobile, though he could still feel the thick muscular length of it trying to squirm free. He slid his right hand down the length of the body until he came to the neck just behind the rocky head where it was fastened onto his arm. He pinched hard on the neck, trying to throttle the reptile and make it release its grip. This seemed to anger the snake and increase the thrashing. For a moment the only sound was his own harsh breathing.

"Somebody say somethin'!" Rafe said.

"Alex?" Walter asked.

"I've got the snake," Alex said between breaths. The worst part was that it was all happening in total darkness like some horrible nightmare. "Or I guess he's got me. He's bit me on my left arm. I can't get him off."

"How big a snake is it?" Rafe asked. His voice was rough with revulsion.

Alex thought about it. He could feel the length of the snake under him. "It must be six feet long. It's as thick around in the middle as your arm. Or at least my arm. I haven't touched the head directly, but it feels as big as an apple where it joins the neck. That stink you smell is where he shit all over me."

"Oh, my living Lord," Walter said. "What are we going to do?"

The snake seemed to have quieted down and was no longer struggling. Alex waited and felt the grip loosen for just a half-second, then crunch down again twice as hard. "Damn!"

"What? What?" Walter shouted. Alex could hear the man pushing back into the farthest reaches of the cellar.

"He seemed to be letting go. Then he bit down harder," Alex said.

"That's what them big black snakes do," Rafe said. "I was poking one down out of the barn rafters once with a rake, and it slid right down the handle and fastened onto my thumb. What they do is they hold on for a while, then let loose a tiny bit so they can change their position a little and get a new grip. What you got to do, my granddaddy told me this, is hold on right behind the head and wait until you feel that little bit of loosen, then snatch him off you quick as can be."

Alex pondered this advice. He had no knowledge or expertise to think it wasn't true. It at least offered a small amount of hope.

"How long do you think it'll be before he loosens up again?" Alex asked. He very slowly rolled to the side, off the snake.

"They'll keep bit down for hours, maybe days. Bad as a snappin' turtle," Rafe said. "He's probably a rat snake. Thing I do know is that a snake bite'll bleed you like a stuck pig. Only good thing is if it was a rattler we'd a heard it, so we know it ain't poison. Probably. If it was, you'd be on your way to dead by now."

Alex clenched his fist and noticed that his left hand was slick and wet. He had thought it was snake shit, but realized now that it couldn't be. It had to be blood. If the snake had severed the artery in his wrist he would bleed to death. Alex pushed himself up on his elbow, waited a moment, then moved on into a sitting position. He felt the snake lift its body into a curl, hesitate as if waiting for the next onslaught, then settle onto his lap. It was as heavy as a small dog.

He had his breathing under control and the pain wasn't as intense as it had been. He wondered if the snake was getting tired of holding the bite.

"How'd this thing get down here?" Alex asked.

"Must be a hole in the walls or the roof," Rafe said. "If it was twisted, I mean the hole, we wouldn't see any light from the outside. Probably all kind of animals down here. Bugs, rats . . ."

"That's enough for me to hear," Walter said. "Snake's bad enough. No, snake's the worst, but bugs and rats is bad too."

Alex thought he felt the snake loosen his grip. He yanked on the head. The jaws closed even tighter. He couldn't stop a small surprised cry of pain.

The other two men held their breath. "It's . . . okay," Alex said, breathing through his mouth, trying to calm his racing heart. "I thought he was letting loose." He wiped his forehead on his sleeve, lifting the snake to do it. Even though the temperature was cool, he was sweating.

"Maybe we can smash its head up against the door?" Rafe offered.

Alex envisioned the result of that: the snake twice as pissed off as he already was. If he couldn't strangle it, and he couldn't, he certainly wouldn't be able to batter the reptile to death. "No. I'm just going to have to wait and try to get him off the way Rafe said."

They were all quiet.

"If that works," Walter asked, "then what you gon' do?"

chapter thirty-four

B IERCE STOOD AT the newspaper counter and counted out Molly's money: two dollars for a week's worth of daily advertisements plus one in the weekly issue. He had stood in line every day for more than a month and expected nothing more than the usual negative response from the clerk. "Four twenty-one," he said, as he slid the money toward the man, paying for the next week's ad. He turned to go. And felt a pluck at his sleeve. The woman behind him was tugging at him. "He wants you," she said.

Bierce turned back. The clerk was holding a piece of paper out to him. "Here you go, mister," the clerk said. Bierce took the paper. "It's an answer to your advertisement. It came in yesterday."

Bierce opened the slip of paper without thinking. It wasn't his advertisement, his money, or his answer. He read it anyway.

I am coming. Alex.

He slammed out of the newspaper office at a dead run.

He stood beside the love seat and held the slip of paper out to Molly. His hand was shaking. She glanced at him and took the paper and read it.

"Oh my God." She pressed her hand against her chest. "He's alive." She looked up at Bierce. "What did he say? The man at the counter."

"Not much. He said, 'It came in yesterday.' I left him immediately. I thought you should get the news as soon as possible."

"You're absolutely right. Thank you. I'll ask the man any questions myself. See if Ann will let us use the carriage. We're going to town."

Ned Rattle had worked for the newspaper for less than a year. His arm had been blown off at Gettysburg, and he supposed that the newspaper job had been offered out of guilt, or patriotism, or just plain pity. He didn't care which. It was far better than marching in the mud or being fired upon while charging across open fields into the face of enemy positions. He didn't even much miss the arm.

He tidied up his counter, enjoying a rare moment of peace between customers. He looked up and felt his heart quail like it had not done since the day he saw General George Pickett leading several thousand screaming Rebels across a field and up a hill straight toward him.

It was the lady who was with child, number 421, and the fellow who usually checked her account. The lady was red-faced, and looked extremely agitated.

Molly thrust the slip of paper at Ned. "Did you give my friend here this piece of paper?"

Ned glanced at it. He knew what it said. He read all the messages. He had thought the lady would be happy. He had seen so many of them, these women, coming in every day in their search for lost men, some of them in her same condition, searching and waiting. . . .

"Answer me!"

"Yes, ma'am!"

Molly made an effort to calm herself. She could see the counterman was terrified.

"The man who gave this to you. What did he look like?" she asked.

"Well . . ." Ned hesitated, not because he couldn't remember; he remembered very well. It was just that he sensed that the answer wasn't going to be the correct one, and this distraught lady seemed capable of violence. What if she had her baby here in his office out of sheer excitement? "He was an old man. With silver hair."

Molly looked astonished. "What?"

"Yes, ma'am. Quite a distinguished-appearing gent. In fact, if you turn around, you'll see him yourself. He's standing right by the door."

chapter thirty-five

THE ONE THING Alex felt he couldn't allow himself to do was fall asleep. His breathing and heart had slowed as his terror of the snake had lessened from the panic level of the first minutes.

He had Rafe on one side and Walter on the other, asking them to talk to him every few minutes to keep him awake.

He had no idea how much blood he had lost, but he thought that this was one reason why his head kept nodding forward. He kept his right hand on the snake's neck, with his left forearm, where the snake was attached, resting on his knee.

"Alex, don't sleep," Rafe said.

"Wake up, Alex," Walter said.

It was sometime after both of those men had fallen asleep when Alex, lost in a reverie that featured floating images of Molly and generic babies, felt the snake's grip loosen.

He yanked the snake off his arm.

The body whipped off his lap and slapped and curled against him. He fought the urge to throw the snake, and held the head at arm's length and endured the beating from the reptile's body.

"Wake up!" he shouted. "I did it. I got him off me." The snake curled around his right arm and tightened its coils.

"Don't turn him loose!" Walter shouted.

"I'm not going to turn him loose," Alex said. In the second he'd pulled the snake's head from his arm, he'd seen a plan unfold and take shape. "This snake is going to get us out of here."

Now Rafe and Walter took turns really staying up and keeping Alex awake. This time they had an added inducement. If Alex fell asleep, the snake would escape and be loose among them in the dark. So they sang, recited folk tales, and jabbered on, stopping only to ask, "You awake, Alex?"

"I'm awake," Alex replied. "Tell me about where you came from. Before you landed in here."

Walter was on duty. They could hear Rafe snoring softly.

"I was born," Walter began, "on a plantation down in Georgia.

Rafe here is my cousin. Our master, James Ogelthorpe, was not originally from those parts. He came from New England. He married a local lady and inherited her daddy's property when the old man died." Alex tried to lean back against the sloping door and decided against it. Better to stay uncomfortable and awake.

"About the time I was born," Walter went on, "the mistress had a baby boy named Johnny, after her daddy. I was pretty much reared right along with that boy. They took me into the house and taught me to read and do a little writing. Taught me to talk white when I want to, be around white folks without much fear. Mr. Ogelthorpe never beat any one of us, and it was mostly a happy house and farm. There was about ten of us as slaves." Alex's hand ached where he clutched the neck of the snake. He knew the second he lessened his grip the snake would squirm away and all would truly be lost.

"When the war started, Johnny just had to join up. Both his mommy and his daddy were against it, but he was wild to go and there wasn't nothing to be done about it. He lasted a good long time until he got killed this winter up near Winchester. Some battle, I don't remember."

They waited in silence for a minute. "It wasn't Cedar Creek, was it?" Alex asked. After another few seconds Walter answered.

"That sounds right. Anyway, they mourned the boy, then last month General Sherman arrived in our vicinity. A bunch of soldiers come through and killed Mr. Ogelthorpe and stole near everything worth a hoot. Took all the food and all the livestock. We had enough hid away to keep us alive, but that was it. And they said me and Rafe and the others were free and could go if we wanted." He sighed heavily. "The mistress begged us to stay, said we'd be free and all work the farm together and share what we had." He fell silent. After a few minutes Alex shifted his position, trying to ease the pressure on his knees.

"Why did you leave?" Alex asked. "It doesn't sound like a bad proposition." Walter was silent for another minute.

"We left because we were free. We left because we could. I don't figure you to understand. No disrespect."

"None taken," Alex said, feeling himself blush with some secret shame that he could not put a name to.

And so it went till the next day. Alex held the snake's head close to one of the cracks in the door and saw, dimly, that it was truly a huge snake, with black and white triangle markings. Rafe confirmed the coloration to be that of a rat snake. Alex wanted to stretch out the body and have one of the other two men measure it, but they refused to come near him. It was only after they heard his plan that they agreed to be squatting next to him when they heard Marta, yelling at Hiram, approach.

The bar scraped back through the handles of the door.

The door pulled open and Alex leapt up and threw the snake into the air in the direction Marta had been standing the day before. Light-blind, he could only hope that the two captors had performed their ritual so many times they wouldn't have changed positions on this particular day.

Marta screamed as Alex lunged up and threw himself toward where her feet and legs should be. He knew she was not screaming because of him.

She fired the gun, hitting nothing.

Hiram got the words "What the hell! . . ." out before being hit in the face with a bucketful of piss and shit that Rafe threw all over him. Rafe and Walter clambered out and piled onto the man, who had just dropped his axe and was wiping his face with his sleeve.

Alex had the woman's legs, wrapped in faded calico, clutched in his arms. He tipped her over with a solid thump. She hadn't even tried to catch herself or fight him off, as both her hands were trying to claw the snake off her throat and face where it had whipped around her neck and clamped down on her cheek.

She screamed on and on.

Alex's eyes burned and watered, but he was starting to be able to see. He could hear Hiram grunting and cursing behind him as he wrestled with Rafe and Walter. He saw the pistol on the ground where Marta had thrown it, and made a dive for it. He came up with the gun, stood, and turned.

"Hold it!" he commanded. "I've got the gun!"

"Save me," Marta moaned. "Get this devil off me. I'm dying."

"Git the hell off me, niggers!" Hiram shouted. Rafe and Walter were holding him down, one on each side. All of them were gasping for breath.

Alex looked down at Marta, rolling on the ground. Then she went limp.

"She's dead!" Hiram shouted. "That snake's done killed her!"

"I think she's just fainted," Alex said. For a minute he wondered if the woman was faking it, trying to catch him off-guard. He decided a person would have to be superhuman to fake a faint and lay completely motionless with a six-foot snake clamped onto her cheek just inches away from her eye. For a moment Alex thought that in a way it was a blessing that his snake attack had occurred in near-total darkness. The snake was bigger than he had imagined it, with a bright black-and-white-checked pattern and a slick, evil head. "You so much as move, and I'll kill you," Alex said, turning to Hiram. "Stay on the ground." Hiram started to get up. "Stay on the ground!" Alex shouted. Hiram got back down. "Walter, Rafe, stand up and get away from him. Find some rope." Both men were staring at him.

"Go on," Alex said. "What's wrong?"

Walter said to Rafe, "You hold on to that man for a minute longer." Rafe twisted Hiram's arms behind him. Walter stepped to Alex's side and whispered, "That's a single shot pistol and she done fired off the single shot. Soon as Hiram figures that out he ain't gonna pay much attention to you pointing it at him."

Alex looked at the pistol without being too obvious about it and saw that Walter was right. He kept it pointed at Hiram. "Like I said, find some rope. You hold on to him, Rafe."

"You ought to take a look at yourself," Rafe said, as Walter hurried away. Alex glanced down. His clothes were filthy. His left arm was covered in blood from elbow to fingertip.

"You got blood all over your face," Rafe said.

"I'll be okay," Alex said. He looked closer at his arm where the snake had been. There were two perfectly cut semicircles on the forearm. Blood had clotted in them. "Most of this will wash off."

Alex held the gun trained on Hiram's midsection while Rafe held him tight. He decided as soon as they got Hiram tied up he would reload the gun, and if Hiram gave them any trouble at all he would shoot him, and do it without any compunction.

Walter came back holding six feet of rope and a knife. "Tie him up. Stay behind him where he can't get at you." Alex gestured to Hiram. "Roll over on your stomach!" Hiram rolled over and Rafe tied his hands behind him. They all looked at Marta. The snake had decided that she no longer was a danger and had released her cheek. They watched it slither away in the direction of the root cellar.

"What're we going to do with them now?" Walter asked. Both he and Alex looked at the root cellar. They could see the last two-foot section of snake as it slid down in through the open door.

"What do you think we should do?" Alex asked. Walter's eyes narrowed.

"Throw them in the cellar," he said. "Lock the door down. We'll give them the same chance they gave us."

The inside of the house was surprisingly clean and tidy. It was a one-room cabin with a plank table, kitchen gear, stove, two chairs, and a bed. There was a pot of beans, this one with a big chunk of pork fatback, bubbling on the stove. Cooling on the table was a pan of corn bread. Walter showed the other two his finds: three dollars in greenbacks, a few coins, a side of bacon, and two onions.

Alex found a jug of water and a clean towel. He went outside and washed the blood off his face and arms. There was a wide semicircle of angry gash where the snake had got him. The edges were beginning to flush pink with infection.

He went back inside. "Let's eat the beans and get out of here," Alex said.

As they rolled out of the yard in the shabby buggy, Alex heard screams coming from the root cellar, screams and a thumping from inside. He hadn't found anything to load into the pistol so he threw the gun and watched it thump off the cellar door. The screams stopped.

The horse lasted one day and a morning before he fell over dead. Now on foot they traveled slowly, mostly at night to avoid Army patrols, disaffected Southern sympathizers, thieves, or anyone else that might stop them or slow them down.

On the third day they stopped at a small crossroads where there was a run-down, hand-hewn plank store with almost nothing on the shelves. Alex bought a can of tomatoes, three tins of sardines, and some crackers.

"What's the date?" he asked the bent, bespectacled old man who stood behind the counter.

The old fellow took Alex's money while he thought about it. "I ain't sure," he said, "but I believe it's the thirteenth of April. We ain't had a paper in a few days. Last one come after old Lee surrendered, lessee, that was four days ago. That'd make it the thirteenth, like I said. Tomorrow's Good Friday. Yes sir, I believe that's right." The old man leaned forward and looked out the door to where Rafe and Walter were standing on the porch talking to another black man.

"The war's over," the old man said. "You're gonna have to give them niggers up now."

"They're not mine," Alex said, picking up his cans. "They own themselves. How far to Washington City? And how do I get there?"

"Depends, of course. You boys are riding shank's mare, so figure on a day and a half, at least. Probably two. You just keep on this road, it's pretty hard to get lost. You kin ask anyone, and they'll set you straight."

Alex thanked the man and went outside. He handed Rafe and Walter a can of sardines. "Eat up," he said. "We've got to get a move on."

"That man over there," Rafe said, nodding at the black man they had been talking to, "says that all travel restrictions are off now that the war's over. Or near enough over. We don't got to hide no more. He says we might can pick up a little work around here, take our time gettin' into Washington City."

"That sounds fine, but I have to keep going." They sat down on the edge of the porch and opened up their sardines with a knife that had belonged to Hiram. Alex handed around the crackers, and they ate in silence. After he finished eating, he wiped his hands on his pants and stood up.

"I've got to go," he said, holding out his hand. The other two looked at his hand for a moment, then took it and shook. "You take the tomatoes," he said.

"Maybe we'll see you in Washington City," Walter said. "You get there first, you look up Father Abraham and thank him for what he's done for us. You tell him we'll be there to thank him ourselves in a while."

Alex nodded. "I'll tell him." He started down the road, then stopped and looked back. The two men were still sitting on the porch, holding the can of tomatoes.

I'll tell him. If I make it in time.

chapter thirty-six

W HO ARE YOU?" Molly asked, turning from the counterman to the older man by the door. She walked closer. She had seen this man before, yes, a month or so ago. He had been in line behind her at this very office. She had felt a vague unease then, thinking that he had seemed familiar. She knew she didn't actually know him, but she had seen him, somewhere, in the past.

"You don't know me . . ." he began.

"You're Alex's father," she said, making the connection. Years before, she had seen a picture in *Newsweek* of Charles Ames Balfour, his wife, and their young son, Alex. The man looked much the same as in that picture, only older: the long hair swept back, the slightly arrogant stance and faint smile as if he was enjoying some small joke that no one else would understand.

"Did you leave this message?" Molly asked, her voice sharpening.

"Yes."

"Why did you pretend to be Alex? Do you know where he is?"

"I know where he was. I'm not sure where he is now. He told me to leave the message and then wait for you to show up."

Molly looked at Bierce. He was right behind her. "Let's get out of here," she said, and turned back to Alex's father. "Come with us. We need to talk."

They took him to Ann's house. Molly leaned back in her love seat. "Talk," she said. "Everything."

"I'm Charles Balfour, as you guessed. I'm the chief financial officer with the Sanitary Commission." He glanced at Bierce, who was sitting at the side of the room, arms folded over his chest.

"Is he another one?" Bierce asked Molly. "Like Alex? Like you?"

Alex's father raised his eyebrows.

"He knows. At least some of it," Molly said. "Alex told him."

"*He*," Bierce said, gesturing to himself, "has still not decided if *he* believes what *he* has been told. But there seem to be more and more of you all the time. Are there any others out there waiting to drop in on us?"

Alex's father shook his head. "Not that I know of. As for your disbelief, I don't blame you."

"Tell me about Alex," Molly said.

"I saw him just several days ago. He was well, or at least as well as a man can be after months in a prison camp."

"Prison camp! That was Baker's doing, I'm sure," she said. "At least he didn't have him killed."

"Lafayette Baker?"

Molly nodded. "We've had some trouble from that man."

"Yes, that sounds right. But if Baker is looking for him, as he will be, Alex must be extremely careful when he gets to the city. If he has escaped, and I think he has, Baker will find out. He probably knows already."

Molly shook her head in exasperation. "When he gets to the city? Where is he? Tell me what happened," she said. "All of it."

Charles Balfour gave her an abbreviated version of his time with Alex. And his guess as to what happened after. He had learned that there had been a riot, and a fire, and that several prisoners had escaped, but the newspapers had not been informed. He didn't have any names, but he thought one of them must have been Alex. He had driven from the camp to Washington, expecting at any time to find Alex on the road, but he didn't.

Molly sat, hands on her abdomen, watching Charles Balfour carefully. She knew quite well of Alex's distrust—no, it was more than that, his hatred of his father. They had discussed it on many occasions. "And now you say he's on his way here, to help you?" she asked. She found it hard to believe, but she wanted to think that it was true. At least the part that he was on his way.

"Well, I'm sure he's on his way here to find you. That will be his first priority. He and I have discussed something that we need to do. He has promised to help me. What I am not sure of is his ability to get here in time."

"Time for what?" Bierce asked from across the room.

"We are going to try, Mr. Bierce," Balfour said, "to save the greatest man of this age, Abraham Lincoln. We are going to stop his assassination."

"Not this talk of assassination again. How do you propose to rescue the president?" Bierce asked, exasperated. "When Alex explained this to me, I believe he rather improbably identified the actor Wilkes Booth as the assassin."

"That's right," Balfour said. "If I might explain?" he asked, with raised eyebrows. Bierce nodded.

"History's chief events," Balfour began, "can often be reduced to matters of inches or seconds and luck, both good and bad. In this case, if various people are in slightly different positions or had been a minute or two early or late, events will be radically altered. All I propose to do is to influence events in the smallest possible way, to induce the merest ripple of change, to modify circumstances so that the outcome will not be the death of the president, but his continued existence."

Bierce crossed his arms over his chest, looking unimpressed and unconvinced.

"It is for the good not only of your society but of our own," Balfour went on. "We are the ones who will inherit this historical disease of political violence. Would you not change the world to make it a better place if you were able, Mr. Bierce?"

"I have not your confidence that I would know what 'better' would mean or involve, Mr. Balfour."

"A perfectly valid point," Molly said. "How can you be so sure that the result will then be better than what will happen if we were not to intervene?"

"I know what will happen if we do nothing, as do you," Balfour said. "Some events are unequivocally wrong, no matter how you examine them. This assassination is one of them."

Molly believed that nothing in what they were doing could be considered unequivocal. But she wouldn't question him. Yet.

"When Alex arrives, he knows to look for me at the Willard," Balfour said. "When he contacts me, I'll contact you. But I can't be sure that he will be here in time to help us stop the assassination. We must prepare for the eventuality that we will be proceeding on our own. We *will* be proceeding together, won't we,

Mr. Bierce?" He and Molly looked at Bierce, who was slouched, frowning, in his chair.

Bierce sat up straighter but the frown stayed. "Molly, are you committed to this course of action?" he asked.

She looked away for a moment. "I'm committed to Alex. If he's agreed to help, then I will as well. Unfortunately, he's not here to assure us of his intentions."

Bierce waited for a moment, then nodded. "All right. I'll go along. For now." *For you, Molly,* he added to himself.

Molly nodded and turned back to Balfour. "What's your plan?"

"John Wilkes Booth, of course," he said, "is the key. For most of last year, 1864, Booth has been the ringleader of a plan to abduct Abraham Lincoln. It is unclear whether he has been working directly for the Confederate government, but it is quite possible. There have been other such plots that originated in the office of Jefferson Davis."

"How can *you* know that?" Bierce asked, the sarcasm evident in his voice. "Does the Sanitary Commission pay you to be a spy, as well as do your other duties? Whatever they may be."

Balfour turned to him. "Mr. Bierce, I respect your natural skepticism. And, in fact, one day you will be well known for it. But at this point, if we are to work together, I'll have to ask you to at least hear me out on matters on which I am tolerably conversant. History is one of these matters. It has been agreed that we will move ahead. We cannot do so if you are determined to continually question me." He waited, his eyes never leaving Bierce's.

Bierce appeared to be making a decision, then shrugged. "All right. Say your piece."

Balfour continued. "Up until now, that has been Booth's plan: Abduct Lincoln, carry him off to the South, and ransom him for all the Rebel prisoners held in Union camps and jails. They would then be released, join their brethren in the South who still have not surrendered, and fight on. In his mind, he is removing a tyrant, committing his despicable, but in his mind patriotic, act for the good of his country and his beloved South." He paused, drawing a cigar out of his breast pocket. "Do you mind if I smoke?" he asked Molly.

"Yes," she said. "I do mind. It's bad for the baby." She placed her hand protectively on her abdomen.

Balfour, with a small smile and a slight bow, reluctantly put the cigar back in his pocket.

"In the last year Booth has held several meetings with Confederate spies in Canada and has made a number of trips into the South, ostensibly to act in plays, but in reality as an agent. He has smuggled much-needed drugs into the South and carried messages. He has met with Dr. Samuel A. Mudd, conferring on the possibilities of using the man's house as part of his escape route."

"Excuse me," Molly said. "I thought Mudd will be proven to be an innocent bystander."

"Mudd's heirs have considered it their life's work to exonerate their ancestor, and have had a great deal of success in doing so. Unfortunately, the man was guilty as charged. It is known that Booth spent a night in his house a month before the assassination. He, Mudd, introduced Booth to John Surratt, who was also a Confederate spy, and Booth became a habitué at John's mother's boardinghouse in Washington. And while you might consider Booth's plot as untenable, you don't know him or the power of his personality. You have to realize that Booth is an extremely magnetic person, a true star, engaging and persuasive. The others have fallen easily under his spell."

"He lives in our hotel," Bierce said. "I've seen him and his adoring fans, most of them women, many times."

"Exactly. But the men in his group are equally starstruck. And remember, up until the fourteenth of April, the goal is to abduct the president, not kill him. On that date Booth changes his mind and decides to kill the president. He will spend the day preparing both himself and his compatriots. We will have to wait for evening, for him to begin the last act of his personal play, before we can intervene."

"Excuse me," Bierce said. "But why don't we just tell the police or the Army what he's going to do and have them stop him?"

"Because the authorities would assume that the person bearing such news is part of the plot. Otherwise, how would that person know that such a thing is going to happen? In our case, our knowledge cannot be verified. If you brought in Booth and all the conspirators right now they would simply deny everything and there would be no way to prove it. Any evidence is purely circumstantial: their renting of horses and buying of boats, the secreting of arms at Surratt's tavern in Maryland, their ties with the Confederate secret service, all of this is true—but none of these things have any direct connection with an assassination plot. And no one knows it except us. The conspirators would be turned loose to go ahead and implement their plot, and we would probably be in jail. Besides, the authorities are already aware that there are any number of threats on the president's life. Lincoln has a drawer full of these threats; they come to him at the rate of two or three a day. His best friend and greatest protector, Lamon Stewart, who unfortunately is out of town, has told him repeatedly he must not attend the theater and he should not go out walking by himself. Yet he can be seen every day walking to the War Department or strolling through the park with no guards. The newspapers alert the populace to every appearance he is to make at the theater. No, we cannot go to the authorities. We must do this on our own."

"And what is it, exactly, you would have us do?" Bierce asked.

"Nothing violent. Nothing dramatic. We must simply delay, simply inconvenience Booth. And the others as well, but primarily Booth. I feel that if this particular coming together of circumstances is thwarted, he will give up the idea. The war is finally over. In a week or less, even zealots like Booth will understand that there is nothing any of them can do to change the course of history. The South has lost, and the cause cannot be salvaged, at least in any physical sense."

"You still haven't answered my question," Bierce said. "What are we supposed to do?"

"I can only tell you what positions to be in to intersect with Booth. When and where. Your job will be to, as I have said, delay and deny him. Booth has a particular moment planned for when he will strike. If that moment is deferred, I think his entire plan will fold like a straw house in a high wind."

"And what positions do you want us in?" Molly asked. She shifted on the couch, trying to make herself comfortable. She felt a sharp pain ripple across her midsection.

Balfour turned to look at Bierce. "Mr. Bierce, I want you inside the theater, but I want you stationed in the lobby at ten o'clock. That's when Booth will have had his final shot of whiskey and come in for the last time. I want you to simply go up to him, quietly explain that you know what he is about to do, and tell him that you will stop him if he tries to follow through."

"At which point he will shoot me," Bierce said. "Oh, that is a wonderful plan."

"I think he will do no such thing," Balfour responded. "Remember the fragility, the impulsive nature of the man. It is only today that Booth has decided on assassination rather than abduction. What is the point of shooting you? Could he then run upstairs, battle his way into the president's box, and shoot the president? He has a derringer, Mr. Bierce; this particular model holds only one bullet. He has a knife as well, but could he use it against an entire theaterful of able-bodied men who have been alerted to trouble by a gunshot? Again, it is extremely doubtful. I think he will simply deny everything and go back to the saloon for another drink."

Bierce nodded, grudgingly. "Possibly," he said.

"And what about me?" Molly asked. "What's my part in all this? What if something happens and Booth gets by Bierce?"

"I hope there will be no part in it for you at all," Balfour said. "I hope Alex will be here in time and he will be stationed on the upper circle at the theater and physically stop Booth if he makes it that far. In the event that he doesn't get here in time, I want you upstairs, and when you see Booth heading toward the president's box, I want you to go into labor. That will be enough to bring the whole production, play and all, to a halt. There will be a certain amount of chaos, which will alert the president, his guard, and everyone else that things are not proceeding normally. It will disrupt everything, including Booth."

Molly swung her feet down off the couch and sat up. She could feel the blood tingling in her toes. She thought about Alex's father's plan, and couldn't come up with anything really wrong with it. One part might fail, even two, but the possibility of all three failing was remote. *It could work,* she thought.

"What do you think?" she asked, looking at Bierce.

"I still think I'm going to be shot or stabbed, but I'm game," Bierce said.

"All right," Molly said to Alex's father. "We're in. What are you going to be doing while all this is going on?"

"Excellent," he said, smiling. "I'm going to be making sure that

Secretary Seward is not killed. If we succeed in this, we leave our children a far better world than we had. Now all we have to do is wait for Alex. Are we agreed?"

They all nodded. Molly winced as another pain raced through her abdomen.

BOOK THREE

chapter thirty-seven

T HERE WAS A time when Alex could run. Races. Marathons. Sprint or jog, mile after mile. Tirelessly, joyfully. No longer.

His feet ached and blisters tore his skin. His socks were little more than tattered rags. His shoes had been handmade by a prisoner who had traded them for ten full-frame photographs. There was no left or right to the shoes, just straight ahead. His old wound ached. He half expected to pull up his pants and see blood spurting from the scar by his knee.

He would jog for a minute or so, then walk until he'd gathered enough energy to jog again.

The sun advanced through the sky, arcing through the afternoon. He knew that he needed to travel north and west, which was the general direction the road was headed. Until it ended on the banks of a river.

Alex stood, staring stupidly at café au lait–colored water streaming along the low, tree-covered banks. Broken branches floated by. An iridescent green kingfisher flashed through the sunlight. Red-winged blackbirds chattered among the reeds that grew on the banks. A long brown water snake undulated along the surface, working his way upstream. Alex stepped back.

"He won't hurt you," a soft voice said on his left.

An old black man sat on a rock, fishing. He was smoking a corncob pipe. Alex watched the snake swim by just below where the man sat. The old man picked up a rock and chucked it at the snake, which disappeared under the surface.

"He gone now."

Alex looked up and down the banks. The water lapped at his feet. There didn't seem to be any way across the river. His head ached, and the glare of the sun on the water made his eyes burn. He looked back at the old man, peacefully puffing on his pipe. Alex could smell the sharp bite of the tobacco smoke. The man was as dark as a blackberry, and he had a fringe of cotton-white hair circling a shiny bald head. He was wearing a much-washed, once-white shirt and a set of overalls. *Where's Huck?* Alex wanted to yell. *Where's your raft? How about a little help here!* He bent down, scooped up a handful of the water, and wiped his face with it.

"Don't drink it," the old man said sharply. "That there river water'll get your bowels in an uproar."

"Is there any way across?" Alex asked.

"Oh, yes, there's any number of ways across."

Alex waited to find out what those ways might be.

"What would those ways be?" he asked, after the man hadn't offered any suggestions.

"Well," the man took his pipe out of his mouth and knocked it out on the heel of his boot. "The best way, of course, is the ferry. But you'd a had to be here yesterday to do that. Young Buddy Spears was doin' the ferryin'; his daddy was the regular hand but he done got shot up and dead at Cold Harbor. Then Buddy heerd that the war was pretty much over, what with Marse Robert give up, so he went on into Washington City to see the celebrations. Then out of sheer devilment someone untied the ferry and darned if it didn't float away." He put the pipe back into his mouth and blew through the stem. Then he inspected it briefly and put it into his pocket. He looked at Alex.

"That's where I'm going. Washington City," Alex said.

The man nodded. "I reckon you could swim it. Many have before you."

Alex looked at the river. It wasn't a very big river, but the water was swift and he knew he was too weak to try.

"I'd never make it," he said. He felt everything dying inside him: hope, strength, courage. *So close.*

"Or if'n you got a dime, I could row you across."

Alex reached in his pocket and found a nickel. "I've got five cents," he said hopefully.

The man drew his line out of the water and rested the pole on the rock where he sat.

"What you goin' to that city for anyhow? See the celebrations, like Buddy?"

"No, I'm trying to get to my . . . my wife. I haven't seen her in a long time. And I guess I'm trying to get there to see the president. I've got to do something to help him."

The old man chuckled. "Father Abraham. Well, I guess that's worth five cents to me. You can just say thank you from me for all he's done."

"What's your name?" Alex asked.

"Oh, just tell him ol' Jim said thank you."

Jim walked downriver fifty yards and disappeared into a stand of trees. In a minute he reappeared pulling a rope attached to a small rowboat. He motioned for Alex to climb aboard, and they were soon out onto the river.

On the far side Alex turned to wave to Jim, but the man had the boat heading back cross-stream and was busy with the current.

• • •

In the early evening Alex came to the town of Upper Marlboro. A small wooden sign proclaimed it the county seat of Prince George's County, Maryland. He briefly considered going straight ahead and walking through the center of town and saving himself an extra mile or two, but decided against it. He couldn't take the chance. News of his escape might have reached the community. He started on a long circle around the town.

As he walked, the sun dipped with late-afternoon golden shafts of light behind the stands of oak and tulip trees lining the road. It had been a warm day, but it would be a cool night. He was fairly certain he was headed in the correct direction, but he was afraid to stop and pound on a door and ask to make sure. He walked for another several hours until it was too dark to see the ruts in the road. He found a haystack in an abandoned field, removed some hay on the side away from the road, and crawled into the interior of the stack. The dust tickled his nose and scratched his throat. As he lay in the hay, he listened to the rustle of insects and the scratching of mice as they gnawed their way through the grain. An owl hooted. Far away a dog barked. *And the caravan moves on. I can do this,* he thought. *I can make it in time. One more day. I can find Molly. So close.* He slept.

chapter thirty-eight

MOLLY LAY IN her bed, watching the dove-colored rectangle of the window through the white gauze of curtains as the sky outside lightened. She could feel the baby inside her as it moved, as if it too was waking to the new day. She tried to imagine the baby, born, lying in her arms, nursing, peering up at her. But it was out of her experience, and any mental image was of a made-up baby, any expression a made-up expression, taken from movies or pictures of other babies. *Soon enough. Soon enough.*

She was afraid. Of what they were to do that day. Of having the baby. Of Alex not getting to her in time. Of being alone.

Lafayette Baker stood and drew up his pants and affixed his suspenders. He sat on the bed and pulled on his boots. He glanced in the mirror over his wife's dresser and saw a gaunt, bearded man who needed more than the few hours' sleep he had managed last night.

He stood, walked downstairs, his boots heavy on the steps, and went into the mahogany-paneled dining room. His wife was seated at the end of the long walnut table, opposite his place at the head. Their cook, Regina, came through the swinging door to the kitchen with his breakfast: strong black coffee, porridge, and a plate of bacon. He sipped at the hot black coffee and waited for it to relieve the faint headache that thumped lightly behind his eyes.

"You came in late," his wife, June, said.

"I had to work. The job . . ." he said. He didn't bother going on. The words were the same as they always were. He remembered last night, Nellie Starr sprawled across the bed, face flushed with drink, naked, taunting him. When he looked at her, drunken, crude, lascivious, he thought only of her sister Ella—proud and elegant. Too sophisticated for the likes of him. Booth's woman. He would see about that.

"She's been crying again," his wife said. "Your daughter is still crying."

He wiped his hand over his face and looked at the bowl of faintly steaming porridge. His stomach roiled and he tasted, faintly, the cheap bourbon he had drunk last night. "When's she going to quit?" he asked. "What more can I do? I'm sorry about the arm, she knows that. What more can I do? Ask Alison what it is that I can do."

"Ask her yourself. I'm sure you've done enough," his wife answered. "Quite enough."

Ambrose Bierce lay in bed and stared at the ceiling. Beside him, Marie slept deeply. *Exhausted,* he thought, *after a hard night of whoring.* He wondered what he had gotten himself into, not only with Marie, but with what he had promised to do today. Tonight. *For Molly.* He climbed carefully out of bed and walked to the window. The tall tree with the fan-shaped leaves outside his window seemed to tremble for a moment in a faint dawn breeze. Small nodes of pearlescent green fruit hung from the branches. Marie said the lovely tree produced this fruit in the springtime, and that after ripening, it dropped to the ground and stank like an outhouse until it rotted away. He knew, suddenly, that he would be gone from this place, one way or another, before the fruit dropped to the ground.

He turned and watched Marie another moment while she slept. Then he quietly dressed and left the room.

Charles Balfour fastened the last button on his silk vest and looked at himself in the mirror as he ran a brush through his hair. He glanced at the empty carpetbag that sat on the floor just under the dresser. He had looked at the nondescript bag many times in the last several weeks. At first it had drawn his gaze because it had been stuffed with two hundred and fifty thousand dollars of the Sanitary Commission's money. He had never grown used to handling huge amounts of cash, even though he had been doing it as part of his work with the commission throughout the war. But the cash was gone now, safely in the bank on its way to being transformed into gold. Soon enough it would make its way back into cash and reside, at least for a while again, in the carpetbag. Or in two carpetbags. Maybe three if everything went as planned. He checked his reflection one last time and went to eat his breakfast in the hotel restaurant.

As he limped down the steps, what remained of his leg shot with pain, which, as always, reminded him of Alex. Alex would be too late to make it back to Washington in time to participate in the evening's events, which was just as he had planned. And if by some miracle he did make the trip in time, it wouldn't really matter.

Walt Whitman rolled over and looked at the small open window in his childhood bedroom. He was visiting his mother on Long Island in New York. From his position on the bed he could see only the overcast, calcareous sky. He knew the high thin cloud cover would blow away as the sun rose and the day would be fine, blue-skied and green with the growing spring leaves and flowers and grass. It was early, earlier than he usually awoke, and for a moment he wondered what had brought him out of sleep. Then he noticed the smell of lilacs, blooming sooner than usual this year, just outside, and thought that it must have been this fresh sweet odor that had called to him. He lay in bed and thought that this evocative sense image, the lilac, might work well in a poem. He tried to think of a line or two, but nothing came.

He rolled his big frame out of bed and thought not of lilacs, or poems, but of breakfast.

• • •

Alex crawled out of the haystack and sat for a minute. The sky was black, the sun several hours from rising. There was a mist over the field, and it was cold, as he expected it to be. His burrow in the haystack had kept him and any number of mice, lice, and other creatures warm all night. He began walking. He had the whole day to make it to Washington. If nothing happened he would be there by dusk.

After an hour's walk he came to a fast-flowing stream where he stopped, knelt, then worked up his courage and dunked his head beneath the icy cold water. He didn't hear the horsemen coming up behind him. Until Chaney King, now a corporal in the Third Maryland Negro Regiment, sent to capture the men who had escaped three days before, shouted the order, "Seize him!"

And Alex was taken.

He was tied at the wrists and then roped with a lead to the pommel of King's saddle.

There were only a half-dozen men in the search party, including King, who strutted self-importantly, barely glancing at Alex as he issued his orders. Evidently a total of four men had run off the night Alex escaped, each seizing the same opportunity that had presented itself. The charred corpse of one had been recovered still in the camp, but besides Alex there were two more to be found. King announced that he would take responsibility for getting this particular prisoner back to camp. Several hours were taken up with making and drinking coffee as the Union soldiers decided how their expedition would proceed. None of them seemed to be in a hurry, especially King.

They broke camp and headed in separate directions. King rode, Alex walking beside him—tethered to King's saddle—headed back in the direction of Upper Marlboro. Alex limped along on the right side of the horse. King was armed with a Winchester repeating rifle, a sign of his status, and all the self-importance he could muster. The rifle was in a scabbard on the left side of his saddle. The morning sun burned the mist off the fields.

"They probably ain't gonna find those two other boys without me. They ought to go back the way we came," King said. "They'd head south, those other two that got loose; they were regular infantry soldiers. But I figured you to head in this direction since this is where you come from. Washington City, am I right?"

"That's right," Alex said. "Because I'm not a Rebel. As I've told you any number of times." He had been walking for two hours. Huge black flies buzzed around the horse's sweaty flanks and landed on Alex's neck and face. He waved them away with his tied hands. Every time he raised his hands to do so, King watched him carefully. Alex scanned the road, the trees, and the lone farmhouses in the distance. He'd made up his mind in the last hour: He was not going to let King take him back. He might die, but he would not go back to prison. Not with Molly waiting. When an opportunity came, he would seize it.

"Oh, lots of Rebels go to Washington City. I hear the town's full of 'em. Spies, stumblebums, loafers, deserters, all manner of Southern riffraff. But you ain't no riffraff, are you?" He laughed. "I don't know what the hell you are. 'Cept my prisoner."

"King, the war is over. Why are you doing this?"

"That's just it. The war ain't over till they tell me it's over. Meanwhile, I've got a duty and I am going to do that duty. I was ordered to find the ones escaped and I have done so. At least partly. I don't much care about the others, but I'll track them down as well."

A fly, and it must have been a particularly big one, bit the horse savagely on the right flank. The horse jumped, and shied away from Alex. In the second it took for King to regain control of the horse, Alex threw his entire weight on the rope connected to the pommel of the saddle. At the same time he spun to the side and kicked the horse in the rear leg as hard as he could.

Underneath the saddle blanket the horse was slick with sweat. The saddle rotated toward Alex as the horse jumped to get away from the kick. King, thrown off balance, tipped to the left and began to fall off his mount.

As quick as a cat, King levered his feet free of the stirrups, threw his right leg over the pommel and leapt to the ground. He landed on both feet, and was reaching for his rifle when the horse kicked him in the kneecap. The blow from the hoof sounded like a sledgehammer connecting with a wet cinder block. King fell down in the dirt and rolled onto his back, and the shying horse stepped on the leg it had previously kicked. King shouted and squirmed to the side, trying to dodge the bucking animal.

Alex danced away from the horse as it skittered back and forth in the road. He grabbed the bridle and tried to calm the animal. He saw King reach for his pistol, which was still in its holster, so he pushed the horse toward where the man lay on the ground, trying to interpose the horse's body between his own and King's pistol. The horse stepped on the already-broken leg once again. King screamed. Alex tried to reach down under the horse and grab King's gun, but the tether rope to which he was still attached was too short. He changed tactics and went instead for the Winchester that was hanging out of the scabbard on the still-twisted saddle. He got the rifle out and pointed it at King.

"Don't!" Alex shouted as King tried to roll over and get to his gun. "You move and I'll blow your fucking head off!" Every time the horse shied it pulled his aim away from King. Alex could see the other man trying to decide, between waves of pain, if he had enough time to get his pistol free. And every time it seemed as if he would try, Alex would get the rifle back on target, pointed at King's midsection.

"Easy. Easy," Alex said to the horse.

He steadied the rifle on King. The horse blew through his nose and stomped a foot but remained still.

"My leg's broke," King said, his voice strained. "Broke bad."

"Good," Alex said. "That's the least of your problems."

"You gonna kill me?"

Alex made himself think about it. Had King died while he was wresting with the horse, had the horse stepped on King's head, he would not have regretted it. Shooting the man as he lay on the ground was another matter. But if he left him alive, he would surely tell the nearest authorities where he was, and the whole county would be after him.

King grimaced in pain. He tried to sit up, then fell back. "If you don't kill me, this leg is gonna do the job. Go ahead and shoot me, get it over with."

Alex glanced up and down the road. They were still alone, but there was no telling how long that would last.

"Drag yourself off into those trees," he said.

"I cain't . . ."

"Just do it! Or I'll shoot you right here and drag you in there myself."

The man began to pull himself to the side of the road and then into the brush that fronted the line of trees. Alex followed slowly along, leading the horse. Twenty feet into the trees King stopped. "That's it," he gasped. "Go ahead and put me through if you're gonna. I cain't go no farther."

Alex looked back. They couldn't be seen from the road. He supposed if King yelled loudly enough he would be heard. And if he had dragged himself this far, he could drag himself back.

"Listen," Alex said, bringing the rifle to bear on King's gut. "I'm not going to kill you. I should—it would increase my chances of getting out of this—but I can't."

"Don't do me no . . ."

"Just shut the hell up for once. I'm going to tell you this one more time. I understand why you hate me, or if not me, Southerners and Rebel soldiers. I've tried to tell you that I am neither, that I was thrown into prison by mistake. I bear you no ill will, even though you've earned a fair share of it. In exchange for your life, I'd like to ask you for a favor, as ridiculous as that sounds under the circumstances." He waited but King didn't say anything. "When someone finds you," he went on, "tell them you were thrown from your horse and the animal ran off. Forget about me. I pose no harm to you or anything you believe in. I'll be gone, out of your life in a matter of minutes. The war will officially end in a few days. There's no need to continue your own personal feud." King didn't reply. Alex knew that he could expect nothing more out of the man.

Alex, with his hands still secured, loosened the bellyband on the horse and got the saddle back up into position. He tightened it and swung up into the saddle, from where he could easily untie the lead from the pommel. Using his teeth, he untied the rope from his wrists. He rubbed his rope-burned skin.

He listened to see if he could hear any movement from the direction of the road. He heard nothing. "Good luck," he said to King, and clucked to the horse to get him moving. The horse turned and stepped toward the road.

King drew the pistol Alex had forgotten to take away from him, aimed, and pulled the trigger.

The horse threw his head back as his hindquarters buckled under him. Alex was able to jump off as the animal rolled, kicking, onto his side. The horse snorted and blew in pain, his head thrashing from side to side. Alex looked back at King. The pistol was pointed at his midsection.

"Now we're even," King said. "Except your leg is in better shape than mine. Get the hell out of here."

The delay of his capture and march in the wrong direction turned what was a possibility into a probable impossibility. He now had lost a half day's worth of precious time.

He traveled off the main road whenever possible, cutting across cleared fields and hiding in the woods whenever there was any traffic. He once hid for an hour in the trees after nearly being surprised by a small troop of soldiers headed in his direction. After they had gone he made his way back to the road and continued on.

He ran when he could and walked when he couldn't. He thought about the past, the present, and the future, trying to place himself in all of them, until a kind of, if not peace, but a zone of acceptance came over him. He would do what he had to do, knowing he was now in the hands of fate and could do little or nothing to escape whatever was in store. He was moving forward toward Molly, and beyond that he refused to speculate. He dealt only with pain, the road, and the hours as they slipped by far too quickly.

chapter thirty-nine

AT FIVE O'CLOCK in the afternoon Preacher leaned against the trunk of an oak tree on the south side of Pennsylvania Avenue at Sixth Street, across from the National Hotel.

Preacher stepped out of the shadows. Colonel Lafayette Baker rode slowly down the avenue toward him. Baker continued half a block beyond Preacher, then guided his horse to the side and dismounted. He tied the horse to a hitching post and walked back up the block. No one looked at the two men as they stood beneath the trees and talked.

"He's been a busy boy, Colonel," Preacher said.

"I was afraid he would leave town."

"Maybe he will. John Wilkes has been up and down the avenue all day. He's been drinking pretty heavily."

"When you going to do it?"

Preacher snorted. "Sure as hell not gonna do it while it's daylight. There's time enough. He and I both got all evening."

"Remember. The newspapers say he's the handsomest man in America. When you get done I want him to be the ugliest. Permanently. But don't kill him."

Preacher spit into the dirt. "You already told me."

Baker nodded. "Good. We'll see how Ella likes him after tonight."

Preacher gave Baker a puzzled look. "What's that, Colonel?"

Baker shook his head, surprised at himself for voicing aloud what he was thinking. *I must be damn tired.*

"Nothing," he said. "I'm going home. You come by in the morning and we'll settle up."

Molly sat in front of the mirror, looking at her puffy, blotchy face. Her hair was stringy, but she had no energy to wash it. *Well, it's off to an evening at the theater,* she thought. *And hopefully nothing exciting will happen, Booth will be deterred, and history will be changed forever.* She pushed a strand of hair behind her ear and grimaced. *No, my problem isn't the theater or Lincoln, God help him. My problem is Alex. He has not come.*

There was a knock at the door.

"I hate to keep harping on this, my dear," Ann Benton said, coming into the room, "but I really don't think you should be going to the theater. Think of your condition."

Molly rested her hand on her protruding belly. She felt as if she needed a grocery cart to haul it around. "I'll be all right," she said. "It's important that I go. It's a favor for a friend. After this I'll stay right here and not move until the baby is born, I promise."

Molly didn't tell Ann that she had thought the same thing several times that day—that she shouldn't be going to the theater. She was torn between trusting Alex's father when he said Alex was going to help him, and remembering Alex when he would tell her how much he distrusted and hated his father. But there was also the matter of the assassination. Could she help save Lincoln? No matter what Charles Balfour's motives might be? Could they really change history for the better? She would go and find out.

Ann stood behind her and lifted Molly's hair from her shoulders while they both looked into the mirror.

"Well," Ann said, "if you're determined, the least we can do is to make you presentable. A nice hairdo will make your problems rest a lot lighter."

Molly laughed and leaned her cheek on Ann's hand. "All right," Molly said. "Do what you can. Make me presentable. If that's possible."

Preacher watched the front door of the National Hotel. A fine mist had settled over the evening, adding a hazy, globe-like glow around each of the gas streetlights. He shifted his weight and leaned against the tree. He didn't mind waiting, didn't mind the mist, didn't mind the colonel telling him what to do. As long as he was paid well, he was content to wait and watch. When the time came, he'd do what he was being paid to do.

An hour later, a parade of men, most of them drunk, marched down the avenue toward the capitol. Smoking torches illuminated their red, laughing faces as they sang patriotic songs and cheered for Lincoln, Grant, Sherman, and every other Union general they could think of. Preacher went around the corner and swung up on his horse so he could see over the heads of the marchers. Between the dark and the mist, it was getting harder to keep an eye on who came and went through the door.

Soon after the last of the parade staggered by, Booth came out the front door of the hotel. He was dressed in black. He mounted his horse and rode up the avenue and turned on Tenth. Preacher stayed half a block behind, unseen in the dark. He could still hear the marchers, farther away now, singing and cheering. Booth dismounted in front of Ford's Theatre and tied his horse to a railing. Preacher sat on his horse and watched Booth go into a tavern right next door to the theater. He swung off and tied his horse up as well. He could walk from here.

In the darkness, Alex limped toward the sentry post at the near end of the Navy Yard Bridge. He was dirty and exhausted. His arm throbbed where the snake had bit him. But he was almost there. Across the river he could see the flicker of gaslights in Washington. The heavy mist, which never became a real rain, had faded away. He shivered. Ahead, in a pool of light from a hanging lantern, Alex could see a soldier standing guard on the bridge. He knew, for the course of the war, all the bridges into Washington had been heavily guarded and anyone using them had to have either a pass or a damn good reason for crossing in either direction. He had no pass, but surely with the end of the war so clearly in sight the restrictions had to have been loosened. Because, save stealing a boat or swimming the river, this was going to be the only way he was going to get into the city.

He walked toward the pool of light.

"I'm drunk," Alex said to the soldier on guard. Alex slurred his words. "I admit it, Colonel. Take me to prison."

The soldier, a private, regarded Alex with a dubious smile.

"And why should I take you to jail?" the private asked.

"To shave my life," Alex replied. He staggered in a small circle as he pointed across the bridge into Washington. "For my wife will surely kill me if I make it home in this condition." He held out his two hands. "Tie me up and take me in."

"So you can tell your wife tomorrow that the reason you were out all night was that we stopped you and didn't allow you to cross the bridge?"

Alex frowned. "Someshing like that. Ain't it true?"

"We close the bridge at nine o'clock. I believe you've made it just in time." The soldier looked across the long wooden bridge at his counterpart on the far side. "Can you make it across by yourself?"

"Absholutely not."

The guard laughed. "Well, I've got no accommodations for drunken gentlemen. I'm afraid you'll have to try. If you fall off the bridge, don't expect me to dive in and save you."

Alex contemplated the long walk across the bridge. "Perhaps it would go better for me if I did fall in," he muttered, and started across.

Carter stopped the carriage in front of Ford's, leapt down, and opened the door, helping Molly haul herself out. The carriage was positioned right above a wooden ramp that led to the sidewalk, set in place so ladies alighting from carriages could get into the theater without muddying their long dresses. A slow-moving crowd of chatting men and women stood in line waiting to get into the theater, the hooped dresses of the ladies fighting for space amid the crowd. Alex's father had given her a ticket that he had purchased earlier. Inside, she was directed upstairs by the ticket taker to the dress circle, the second floor balcony. As she started up the stairs she looked over the heads of the crowd in the lobby and saw Bierce standing beside the ticket booth. He nodded at her and gave her a thin, nervous smile.

She knew that this theater, or a more modern version of it, was open as part of the National Park Service in modern Washington, D.C. And in fact was still used as a working theater. An usher showed her to her aisle seat.

She had the usual battle with her hoopskirt as she settled into her cane-bottomed chair. Being both massively pregnant and formally dressed was enough to defeat anything approaching normal movement on her part.

Her seat was on the aisle in the section farthest to the right in the theater. The two seats in front of her were empty. She was situated quite near the door that led into the president's box above the stage on the right. From where she sat she couldn't see into the box, but she had a general idea of what it looked like. She wondered for a moment if there was a modern American alive who couldn't summon at least a rough mental image of the scene of Lincoln's assassination. Every schoolchild at one time or another had seen a period engraving or drawing of the moment when Booth shoots the president in the back of the head. She was glad she was sitting where she was, unable to see the scene if it were to happen. *But it will not happen. That's why we are here.*

A chair, similar to the one she was sitting in, was placed by the door to the president's box. She assumed the presidential guard would sit there. For a moment she wondered why Alex's father had never mentioned a guard at the door. Why hadn't he stopped Booth?

The seats around her were all filled. The audience was an equal mix of men and women, many of the men dressed in military uniforms. Most of them were craning their necks to see who was in attendance, searching for famous generals and society ladies and stealing glances up at the president's box where they soon expected to see Lincoln.

The house lights dimmed and the audience fell silent. The play began.

Charles Balfour stood beneath a tree in the park immediately across from the White House. He was watching the house where Secretary of State William Seward was lying in an upstairs bedroom, recovering from injuries suffered in a recent carriage accident. There were lights on throughout the secretary's house. He checked his watch but couldn't read the numbers in the dark. He shivered. He checked his watch again, realizing it had been only a minute since he last looked at it, and that he still couldn't read the face. He tucked it firmly into the watch pocket of his vest. He looked up and down the dark street in front of him. The assassin Lewis Paine and his guide Davey Herold should be arriving at any time now. He allowed himself a moment's qualm, a slight thrill of fear, then pushed it away. He knew what he had to do, though it was not quite what he had told the others. He didn't care if the secretary of war lived or died on this night or any other. It was the secretary's *son* who had to be saved. He didn't know if his intervention would have any effect at all on the course of events—again, no matter what he had told the others—but he couldn't take the chance that it wouldn't. He waited.

. . .

Bierce stood by the ticket office and watched the last of the late-arriving patrons enter the theater. The ticket taker looked at him questioningly.

"Waiting on someone," Bierce said. "A woman. You know how women are."

The ticket taker smiled and nodded.

Actually, Bierce thought, *I don't have any idea how women are.* He thought about Molly. She had destroyed any notions he had formed over his lifetime about women. He had been engaged, informally, to a young woman back in Ohio before he left for the war, but that relationship had dissolved in acrimony, leaving him bitter and cynical on the subject of women. Until he met Molly. There was Marie, of course, but his attraction to the octoroon whore was more elemental than romantic. Both of them were well aware of that. But Molly was . . . different. To say the least. His intellectual equal, if not his better. He wondered, if circumstances had been different, if there were no Alex, could he have formed a serious friendship with Molly? He shook his head in exasperation at his own presumption, knowing that the answer was yes, if she would have allowed it. *But circumstances are never different. They are what they are.*

He looked around the now-empty lobby. The ticket taker was adding up the night's box office receipts. He could hear a coach outside as it pulled up in front of the theater. The front door was opened by a man wearing a bowler hat and a black suit. He held the door, and Mrs. Lincoln, followed by the president, entered.

From the end of the alley Preacher stood in deep shadow and watched Booth and another man at the back entrance to the theater. He had no idea what the men were discussing, but he could see it was Booth who went inside, leaving the other man holding the horse. Preacher wondered if this meant that Booth was going to be inside for only a short time. He waited several minutes then decided to walk around to the front of the theater to see if Booth was in the lobby, or if he had stopped off for another drink. Taltavul's, next door, seemed to be the man's favorite saloon.

He was pleased that Booth had decided to leave his horse in the dark alley. This was an excellent place, dark and lonely, to do what Baker wanted done.

The play had been going for fifteen minutes when Molly looked over to see a man walk down the aisle and open the door to the president's box. Then Mary Lincoln swept by, her dress brushing Molly's arm, followed by her husband, who towered over his wife. Another man and a woman entered the box behind them. The door was closed and a thickset man wearing a bowler hat sat down in the chair by the door.

Onstage, Laura Keene, the star of the play, stopped in mid-sentence and began to applaud. The audience, turning in their seats to peer into the president's box, began to stand and applaud. Molly tried to lever herself out of her chair and decided it wasn't worth the effort. No one was looking at her. All eyes were on the president of the United States. The orchestra in the pit began to play "Hail to the Chief." After several minutes of applause, the band finished, the audience sat back down, and the play resumed.

Molly felt a stirring inside her as she realized that, whatever was going to happen, there was no turning back for any of them. The play, both onstage and in time, was in motion.

John Wilkes Booth stepped quietly out from a side door next to the ticket booth. Startled, Bierce felt a sharp jolt of pain to his head. He instinctively reached up and lightly touched the scar where the bullet had hit him. His head began to ache.

"Evening, Mr. Buckingham," Booth said to the ticket taker. He glanced at Bierce.

"Ah, Mr. Booth," Buckingham said. "Nice to see you this evening. Have you come to see the play or the president?"

"Oh, the president," Booth said, smiling. "I've seen the play many times."

"He and his party have just gone up. That's what the applause was for, I've no doubt. If you slip inside, you can get a look at him."

"Plenty of time for that, Buckingham. I'm just stepping next door to Taltavul's for a drink. Care to join me?"

"No, thank you, Mr. Booth. I've got to see to the evening's proceeds. Maybe another time."

"Perhaps," Booth said, smiling again. He walked out the front door. Bierce hesitated, then followed. On the wooden sidewalk outside the theater he saw Booth as he went into the saloon next door. The rain had stopped, so Bierce decided to wait and watch for Booth outside. He took a deep breath of the fresh air and felt the ache in his head ease a bit. He leaned against the brick front of the theater. Three or four soldiers loitered nearby, waiting for the play to end so they could get a glimpse of Lincoln as he left. A light carriage driven by a tall cadaverous black man pulled up, and two Army men in uniform climbed out. One of them said something to the driver, who nodded, while the other, a large man with an elaborate uniform, stood reading the notice on the wall of the theater. He seemed familiar, and Bierce reflected for a moment on how many men one saw in an Army at war, and wondered how many of the soldiers he had seen over the last several years were now dead.

Bierce could tell from the stars on the large officer's shoulders that he was a general. The man stepped forward further into the light, and Bierce felt the pain in his head ratchet upward as he recognized him. Bierce rubbed his head. Small lights were beginning to flicker at the corners of his eyes. *General Holt. Coulter's Ridge.* He remembered telling the story to the men in the hospital, months ago, about the general—this general—who had ordered the artilleryman Coulter to shell his own house, killing his wife and child. And he remembered how he had vowed to punish the man who had issued that terrible order if he were ever to see him again.

Bierce stepped forward before he could think, before he could change his mind. *There are some deeds that must not go unpunished.* "General Holt," he called.

The general looked over at him. "Yes. Who is that? Who's there?" The general's aide turned, frowning, toward Bierce.

"You, sir, are a monster," Bierce said. A red haze slid down over his vision, and for a moment he heard the booming of cannon, the harsh cawing of crows, the snap of flames. He stumbled toward the general, shouting. "You are a man with no morals. Do you remember the name Coulter? Do you remember what you did to Coulter!" As he raised his fist, the general's aide hit him with the flat of his ornamental sword. Bierce felt not the sword but the bullet that had wounded him months ago, felt it again pierce his skull as pain lanced through his head, his body. He crumpled to the ground in front of the astonished general.

Two of the soldiers who had been standing nearby ran up and stood over Bierce.

"What the hell was he shoutin' about?" one of them asked. "What happened to him?"

The general looked down at Bierce, who was unconscious, then at his aide. "I have no idea what this man was raving about. Obviously he is a lunatic."

"Someone should get him to a surgeon," the soldier went on. He nudged Bierce with his boot.

"I have no interest in what you do with him. He can lay in the gutter, as far as I am concerned," Holt said. He turned to his aide. "Good man, Crowell. Let's go in, we're late as it is." The two of them went into the theater.

The soldiers looked down at Bierce. "We can't just leave him here. He'll get run over, sure as hell," one of them said.

"Let's drag him over against the wall. If a policeman comes along, we'll turn him over to him. He'll know what to do." They each took an arm and dragged Bierce to the wall of the theater. They sat him up and leaned him against a building, folding his hands in his lap.

"Maybe he's just drunk."

"He don't smell drunk."

"Probably crazy, like that general said. War done that to a lot of men. Drove 'em crazy."

They walked back up the block to wait for Lincoln to leave the theater.

chapter forty

MOLLY LOOKED AT the guard who sat in the chair outside the president's box. He stood up, pushed his hat back on his head, and moved to where he could peer over the railing and see the play. After watching for a minute he went back to his chair.

I don't blame you, Molly thought. *This may be the dumbest play I've ever seen.*

Two military men, one with an elaborate uniform with stars on his shoulders, came down the steps and sat in the seats in front of her. After they got themselves situated, she noticed that the guard at the door was not in his seat. She twisted around to see where he had gone, but couldn't find him in the dark.

Come back. Don't leave him.

As if in answer, the guard appeared again, wiping his mouth as he came down the steps and settled back into his chair.

Continuing his drunk act, Alex stumbled away from the guard at the city side of the bridge after having undergone a conversation much like the one he'd had with the soldier on the other side. He wandered into the shadow of a nearby building. As soon as he thought the guard could no longer see or hear him, he started to run.

His father had said that Molly and others were helping him with his plan to save Lincoln. That meant Molly was probably at Ford's Theatre.

Everyone around Molly was laughing at the antics onstage, when her water burst. She felt the startling surge of warm fluid as it flowed down her legs, soaked her dress, and dripped through the woven cane-bottom chair. She gasped, involuntarily, and pressed her abdomen as pain clenched her insides and squeezed and rippled through her.

Booth stepped out of Taltavul's Saloon after having downed

several whiskeys. He was usually a brandy drinker, but the occasion seemed to demand something stronger. He looked up at Ford's front door, where a number of soldiers were milling about. A man, evidently drunk, was seated against the building. He would go around the back way through the alley, check on his horse, and then go in. It was time.

Preacher, standing in the shadows, touched his pistol and made sure it was loose in the holster and followed Booth into the alley.

Charles Balfour blew on his cold hands. He leaned forward and listened. Two horses were approaching. He held perfectly still.

The two horsemen trotted up to the house, stopped, and climbed down off their mounts. One of the men was huge, the other small. They conversed for a moment, and then the big man handed the reins of his horse to the smaller and walked up the path to the house.

Standing in the dark alley behind the theater, Peanut John, a black man so named because he sometimes sold peanuts to the crowds at Ford's during intermission, heard someone approaching. It was so dark he couldn't tell who it was until the man was beside him.

"Hello, Mr. Booth. You come to take this horse off my hands?"

"Soon, Peanut. I just have to do something inside. I'll only be a few minutes."

Booth opened the door and stepped into the theater.

Preacher had hung back and listened to the conversation between Booth and Peanut John. *Soon,* he heard Booth say. *Good,* he thought.

Alex, running, crossed Pennsylvania Avenue, his feet skidding on the cobblestones beneath the layer of mud and horse droppings. Men stared at him as he continued up Twelfth and then turned right on E Street. His heart was pounding and he was winded, but he seemed to have entered some zone beyond fatigue and pain. With every step he felt he was coming closer to Molly, that some invisible band that connected them was drawing him to her, that all the months and months of pushing away his memory of her so he would not die of the weight of it could now be released.

Charles Balfour heard the first shouts from inside the house. Outside, the man holding the two mounts pulled at the bridles as the horses, frightened by the shouts, moved uneasily.

A woman screamed. Balfour began to creep forward through the bushes in the park.

A man inside the house cried out, "Murder! Murder!"

The fellow holding the horses dropped the reins of one of them and swung up onto the other. One more shout from inside, and he turned the horse and with a clatter of hoofs spurred him down the empty street.

Balfour walked quickly across the now empty street, up the path, and pushed open the front door.

He was blinded by the lights. Two men were fighting on the stairway leading to the second floor. He limped forward and began to climb the stairs.

Paine, the giant among the Booth conspirators, stood on the steps clubbing another man, who was on his knees. Charles Balfour knew that the downed man must be Seward's son. Balfour pulled himself up by the banister, unnoticed by the two struggling men. When he was close enough, he lifted his cane and brought it smashing down with bone-cracking force on Paine's back. The big man whirled around. Balfour whacked him again, this time on the leg. A look of confusion and indecision floated across Paine's face. Paine kicked away young Seward and dashed up the steps. Seward slumped to the ground and Balfour caught him as he began to roll down the stairs. Seward's eyes seemed to register Balfour's face then flickered closed.

Balfour held him beneath the arms and laboriously pulled him down the steps and around the corner into the hallway. More screams, this time from upstairs. Paine must have found the older Seward's bedroom. Balfour checked the younger Seward's pulse and found it irregular but strong. He would live.

Balfour picked up his cane from where it had rolled down the stairs, limped out the door, and closed it behind him.

Molly stood up and steadied herself by the back of her chair. The guard by the door of the president's box stared at her as she started up the steps. She stopped at the top as another wave of pain gripped her. She understood now why the pains she had experienced in the weeks before had been called false labor. They were nothing compared to this. This, she knew, was the real thing.

She staggered into the back of the balcony behind the rows of seats. Her dress was soaked with water, which in the dim light looked like blood.

The man guarding the president's box watched her painful ascent of the stairs. He stood up.

Booth hurried through a long basement hallway beneath the stage and moved up the darkened aisle that led to the back of the theater. He then entered the lobby and started up the stairs to the dress circle.

. . .

Alex turned up the low hill of Tenth Street and ran toward a knot of soldiers standing outside Ford's Theatre. He slowed, panting, as he approached them. He saw Bierce leaning against the building. He knelt at Bierce's side. There was blood leaking from the man's head wound. Alex touched his shoulder. Bierce opened his eyes.

"Coulter?" Bierce said.

"It's Alex. Where's Molly?"

Bierce's eyes seemed to focus. He looked at Alex. "Inside," he said.

Alex pushed open the theater door, crossed the lobby, and started up the steps.

The ticket taker looked up from a stack of greenbacks and frowned as the disheveled man passed him and ascended the steps. "You must have a ticket!" he shouted. He started to leave his booth, then realized he couldn't abandon his post while the evening's proceeds were still sitting on the counter.

Alex walked behind the last row of seats. On his left he was aware of the audience as they laughed. He heard, and registered in some part of his brain, the words of the actors on the stage.

"What!" a woman onstage shrieked. "No fortune?"

Ahead of him Alex could see a woman leaning against the wall.

"Nary a red," a man onstage said. "It all comes from their barking up the wrong tree about the old man's property."

The woman leaning against the wall slumped to the floor.

From the stage: "Augusta, to your room!"

Alex reached the fainting woman's side, bent, and turned her head. "Molly!"

She looked up at him. She smiled. "Alex."

Another man bent down beside them. "Is she hurt?" he asked. Molly recognized the guard by his hat. She could smell the liquor on his breath. "I'm having a baby," she said. "Don't leave your post. Booth. Booth."

"What the hell is she talking about?" the guard asked.

Booth walked behind the audience in the upper circle. Ahead of him, he could see two men bent down beside a woman lying on the floor. One of the men was the guard he had seen earlier beside the door to the president's box. He turned left down the aisle beside the box. The two military men in the aisle seats, laughing, glanced at him as he opened the door to the president's box and went inside.

From the stage: "Well, I guess I know enough to turn you inside out, you sockdologizing old mantrap!"

Great laughter.

From the president's box: a gunshot.

Silence.

Booth leapt from the box and landed, stumbling, on the stage. He held up a knife and shouted, "I have done it! *Sic semper tyrannis!*"

Pandemonium. Women screamed. Men shouted. The house lights came up. Chairs were knocked over as the audience began to mill about in confusion. A woman pointed to the president's box. Lincoln sat slumped over in his chair. Mary Todd Lincoln screamed.

The guard helping Alex stood up as he heard the pistol shot, looked around, and dashed away down the hall. Bierce suddenly appeared by their side. His head was bleeding. "Oh, Alex, the president," Molly said. Bierce helped Alex lift her up. She put her arms around their necks. "Too late," Alex said. "We have to get out of here."

Preacher flinched as the back door to the theater smashed open and Booth leapt onto his horse, kicking Peanut John in the head and turning the animal in one movement. Preacher pulled his gun and stepped out of the shadows and raised the pistol, centering it on Booth's back. In his mind he heard Colonel Baker's instructions: *Don't kill him!*

He lowered the pistol and watched Booth gallop down the alley.

Alex and Bierce quickly walked Molly down the hallway, down the steps, and outside before the audience had gathered itself together to escape the theater. One of the soldiers stood, puzzled. "Where's the president?" the soldier asked.

"The president's been shot," Alex said. "Get inside and see if you can help."

Carter came running to them, helping them up the street to the waiting carriage. They pulled Molly inside. On top, Carter snapped the reins, and they moved off with a jolt.

Alex looked at Molly. Her mouth opened, and she gasped as a labor pain held her in its grip, then released her. She squeezed his hand, looking at him. She touched his rough growth of beard, his tangled hair, his gaunt face. "What have they done to you?" she said.

"I'm all right," he said. "You'll be all right."

chapter forty-one

W HEN THEY ARRIVED at Ann Benton's, Molly insisted on walking from the carriage to the house.

Three of Ann's girls undressed Molly and put her into bed while Alex and Bierce waited outside the room. Dixie, the maid, had dashed out to fetch her mother, the midwife.

Alex was pacing in the outer room. He and Bierce had not really talked; there was too much to say and not enough time. Outside, even in this quiet neighborhood, they could hear crowds passing as people ran from house to house spreading the news of Lincoln's shooting.

"I can hardly believe it," Bierce said, shaking his head. He gently massaged his temple. "When your father explained it, the enterprise seemed unreal, like a story being told to children. I felt as if we were taking part in a game or a play." He shook his head. "Which I guess it was, for all the good we did."

"It wasn't your fault," Alex said, not really paying attention. His mind was on Molly in the next room. He stopped and looked at a picture on the desk. It was the portrait of Molly and Lincoln. He picked it up. "Oh my God," he said.

"What's the matter?" Bierce asked.

Alex looked at the picture and thought back. When he had appeared, so briefly, back in the present and seen Molly, he had snatched the newspaper-wrapped photograph from the table by the couch. The picture of Lincoln and Molly. This picture. *No, not this picture, there's nothing written on this one.* He'd taken the other picture and sewn it into the lining of his knapsack, which he had

324

last seen in Baker's hand as he was arresting Alex in their room at the National Hotel.

The bedroom door opened. "You can come in now," Ann Benton said. Every time she looked at Alex she frowned. He didn't blame her. He had glanced, once, into the large mirror over the mantel and had been shocked by his appearance. He'd seen homeless men in Manhattan with all their possessions packed into grocery carts who looked far more prosperous—and cleaner—than he did. He hesitated a moment and went into Molly's bedroom.

He had been afraid that he would turn the corner and she would not be there. That once again he would have slipped into some other place or time. But it was not so, she was there, and his breath caught in his throat as he looked at her.

"Girls," Ann said, "why don't we leave these two alone until Dixie gets back with her mother? The birth will not be for some hours, I believe."

The girls gave Molly pats on the shoulder and left the room. Alex moved to the chair by the bed.

Molly had on a loose shift. Her face was washed, and she was smiling.

"You look like hell," she said. She reached out. He took her hand.

"Thanks," he said, smiling back at her. "I've been on the road for the last couple of years. I haven't had time to clean up."

"How long has it been for you?" she asked.

"A couple of years? Eighteen months? I'm not sure."

"It's only been seven months for me. Has it been . . . terrible?"

He didn't answer. Her hand was soft and warm. He leaned over and kissed her. When he sat back in his chair her eyes were wide, her cheeks ruddy.

"Oh my," she said.

"Me too." He felt her hand clutch his. She trembled slightly for half a minute.

"We're going to have a baby," she said.

"So I noticed. I think it's wonderful. I'd like to assume I've only been gone nine months or so back where you're from."

She laughed. "That's right. It's yours. There's a part of you in me. Soon it will belong to both of us." She was quiet for a moment. "We screwed it all up, didn't we, Alex? Lincoln. He wasn't supposed to die," she said. "Your father . . ."

"My father. We'll get to him eventually. As far as screwing it up, I don't think it could have happened any other way. But we had to try."

"Your father said . . ."

"He said a lot of things. Who knows what to believe? We'll work it out later. Let's get this baby born first. Are you all right?"

"You mean in general?" she asked. He nodded. "I was examined by a lady doctor who wore a man's uniform, and she said I was healthy. Do you know why I'm here? In this time?"

He shook his head. "No. I've never even understood how it works with me. Your being here throws everything I thought I knew out the window. The one law that I thought I was sure of was that you have to be there, in the future, to draw me back."

"But I *was* there. You didn't come! I waited and waited."

He could see the pain in her eyes. He couldn't tell her. Not yet. *The reason I didn't come back is because you were dead. I saw you die. In Japan. I held you in my arms, and you were gone. We were in another time.*

"And then this lawyer showed up with the picture and the story of how you set everything up to send it to me—"

There was a knock at the door. Ann came in with Dixie and

an older black woman. The older woman was dressed all in white and carried a small bag. Her hair was done up in a white kerchief.

"Shoo," she said to Alex. "Corina is my name, and everything gonna be all right."

"This my momma, Molly," Dixie said. "She gonna help you have the baby."

"And we don't need no man in here," Corina said, putting her bag on a table.

"I'm staying," Alex said.

"Fine. You do your staying in the next room. Git."

Molly squeezed his hand and nodded at him. He stood, and said, "You know, Corina, someday the father will not only be around, he'll actually help out with the birth. He'll be there from beginning to end."

Corina laughed. "Bad enough I got to put up with those men surgeons, now you telling me I got to look after you at the same time? Get out of here with your stories."

Alex leaned over and kissed Molly, and went to the sitting room next door.

Several hours passed while a stream of women came and went from the room, carrying fresh clean white cloths and hot water, occasionally stopping to reassure Alex that everything was proceeding quite normally. Bierce slept in his chair.

Alex was dozing when it came to him, when the words slid together with an almost audible mental click. *The picture. Don't go to Japan. There's a part of you inside me. And then the man showed up with the picture and the story of how you set everything up.* His eyes opened.

Alex went to the desk and picked up the framed picture. He

took the photograph out of the frame. He went to the door to Molly's bedroom, opened it, and went in.

The women around the bed looked at him, frozen in a shocked tableaux at his intrusion. Molly was being supported by one of the girls as she grimaced and pushed, blowing in and out in great puffs.

"Now, I told you . . ." Corina began.

Molly looked up. "It's all right," she gasped. "It's all right. Let me down." Marie put a pillow behind her and eased her down. She was sweating and flushed, but she gave him a weak smile.

"I'm sorry," he said, glancing at the women who surrounded Molly, "but this can't wait. Is there a pen and ink here?" Molly nodded.

"In the little desk," she said, indicating a small walnut writing desk. Alex went to it, opened a drawer, and took out a pen and a bottle of ink with a cork stopper. He came back to the bed and held out the picture of Molly and Lincoln.

"I figured it out," he said. He knew he probably shouldn't be talking about it in front of the other women, but he didn't think they would understand anyway. They seemed to sense something of this and moved away from the bed, busying themselves with small tasks.

Alex went on. "You have to write on the picture, 'Don't go to Japan.' "

"Like on the other picture," Molly said, taking the photograph.

"There is no other picture. This is the picture! And you have to write on it if we're going to save your life."

She looked at him as if he had become unhinged, but she took the pen, dipped it in the ink he held out to her, and holding the photograph on her knee, wrote what he told her.

"It all came together while I was in the next room," he said, blowing lightly to dry the ink. "You said there's a part of me in you. That's the answer, that's why you're here. Because I'm here. The baby is part of me, so he, or she, is here. He traveled through time, and you were drawn with him."

She stared at him, assimilating what he had just told her. "And I just came along because I'm the carrier?" she asked, exasperated.

He shrugged, sheepishly. "Something like that. We're all connected. By blood, by time."

"What happens," she asked, slowly, "when the baby is born? When it is no longer inside me?" He could see the fear in her eyes as she began to understand.

"I can't know for sure," he said, taking her hand. "I think you'll go back to the future. And the baby will too. And then so will I. I just don't know when it will happen, how fast."

"That would be a good thing, right?" she said.

"Of course it would be. As long as you and the baby are all right when it happens. It might happen as soon as the birth is over, which would have you back there when you might be in trouble, medically. I . . . I don't know. What I do know," he said, "is that I have to get this picture to the people who safeguard it for the next 138 years before I'm taken back and it's too late." *Otherwise you will die in Japan.* "Who brought it to you?"

A labor pain seized her. He saw her grit her teeth and fight against it while she tried to speak.

"Jay Cooke," she gasped. "Get it to Jay Cooke's bank."

Alex pulled Corina to the side of the room as Molly pushed against the pain.

"How long," he asked, "until the baby comes?"

"You be a daddy 'fore noon," Corina said.

Bierce looked up from the desk when Alex came back in the room.

"You're leaving, aren't you?" Bierce said.

Alex nodded. "In a minute. I have to go out. I hope you can stay with her. I may need some money. Can I borrow some?"

"Is whatever you have to do really so important that you're going to leave your—" He stopped for a second, trying to check his anger. "You're going to leave Molly while she's having her baby?" He took his wallet out of his pocket and drew out a single bill.

"I have to. Her life depends on it. I can't explain. Maybe in time I'll be able to explain everything."

"Time," Bierce said, handing the bill to Alex, shaking his head. "Always time. I have twenty dollars, that's all."

Alex took the bill. "Thank you. I'll pay you back as soon—" Bierce stopped him with a raised hand.

"No need to worry about it," Bierce said. "Are you going back"—he waved his hand uncertainly—"there? And is she going as well?"

"Yes. I think so. Soon."

Bierce laughed shortly. "Too bad. She never finished helping me with my Owl Creek hanging story. I wanted to tell her I've turned it into a tale where the man who's being hung travels through time. If I don't see her again, you'll tell her that?"

"I hope you'll be able to tell her yourself." Alex went to the door. He couldn't help smiling. "Travels through time?"

"Yes. Except it doesn't work out too well for him in the end. Think I should change it?"

"No, it sounds fine. Just leave it like it is." He started to leave, then turned back around. "You've been a good friend, Bierce. You're going to be a famous man, a famous writer. Your Owl Creek story will be read by men and women and American schoolchildren for hundreds of years."

"Now I'm sure you're the one with the head wound," Bierce

said, holding out his hand. Alex shook it, turned, and left the house.

Dawn was beginning to lighten the sky. Alex was walking. The streets were mostly empty. Lincoln had finally died after lingering for hours. Those who had stayed awake to hear the terrible news were now home in bed, and those that did not yet know were just getting up.

Squads of soldiers trotted by in the street, eyeing him and all other lone males suspiciously. Rumors about assassins were flying, and the police and the military were looking for anyone to blame, arrest, and throw in jail.

A man with a ladder was extinguishing the gas lamps. The man yawned. He was quite probably the same fellow whose job it was to light the lamps at night. He nodded at Alex as he walked by. "Heard the news?" the man asked.

"Yes," Alex answered.

"Terrible."

The street in front of Cooke's bank was busy with men and women who were on their way to the park to stand in front of the White House. Across the park a squad of cavalrymen sat on their horses, guarding the Seward residence.

Alex pushed open the heavy door to the bank.

"Bank's closed," a guard inside said. "Out of respect for the president."

"I need to see Mr. Cooke. It's urgent."

"Everything's urgent today. Mr. Cooke is seeing no one."

The guard was a stout man with General Burnside's whiskers, which were becoming something of a fad. Alex reached into his pocket and pulled out the twenty-dollar bill that Bierce had given him. He handed it to the guard, whose eyes widened at the amount.

"Please," Alex said. "All I want is a few minutes of his time. I'll be sure to tell him that you tried to stop me."

The guard put the twenty into his pocket. "Here now!" he shouted. "You can't go in there!" He opened the door for Alex. "This bank is closed!" He pushed Alex inside and slammed the door.

Two men sat in the empty bank. The cavernous marble room was dark, lit only by two gaslights on two desktops and the silvery dawn that had just begun to lighten the tall narrow windows. The men looked at him.

"What is the meaning of this?" one of the men asked. He was tall and austere-looking, with a spade beard.

"I need to see Mr. Cooke," Alex said.

"I am Mr. Cooke, and this is my associate, Reginald Lambert. The bank is closed for business on this sorrowful day. Who are you, sir?"

"My name is Alex Balfour. Abraham Lincoln told me that he would inform you that I required an interview. This was several months ago, but—"

"I have never heard your name before in my life. Particularly from the lips of our late president. And believe me, I have remembered everything that great man ever said to me. Now, sir, you will please leave us before I call the guard."

"It is a matter of great urgency—" Alex began.

Cooke shook his head. "I'm sorry. We really do not have the time."

"But—"

"I am quite out of patience. Guard!" Cooke shouted. The bank door opened and the guard stood at attention.

"Yes, Mr. Cooke?"

"Please remove this gentleman." The guard nodded, stepped

forward, and took Alex by the arm. At the door, Alex turned back and pulled free of the guard.

"Now that's enough from you—" the guard began.

"John Jordan!" Alex shouted. "My name is Lieutenant John Jordan!"

"Come on now," the guard said, catching Alex's arm again. "Mr. Cooke says—"

"Just a moment!" Cooke shouted. Everyone froze. "Lieutenant John Jordan? Why did you not say so in the first place? Why did you give that other name?"

Alex wasn't quite sure what he was going to say until it came out. "My real name is Alex Balfour. I left a difficult situation in the town where I lived before I went to join the Army. I felt a new name, a new identity, would be useful. President Lincoln knew me by that name, John Jordan."

"And what is your connection to the president? Why was he willing to do you a favor?"

"Well, I guess I saved his son Tad from being run over by a herd of cows."

Cooke nodded. "Yes, the president explained it to me, though his rendition was a bit more dramatic than that. The president was certain that you saved his son's life. He said you wished to see me and gave you the highest recommendation, but you never appeared."

"I was sent out of town. I only recently returned."

After a moment's silence, Cooke sat forward in his chair. He gestured for Alex to approach. "And just what is it that you wish from us?" he asked. Alex walked to where the men were sitting.

"What I need is going to seem unusual, at the very least. And I don't have any money to pay for it. I hope I can convince you that some financial information I can suggest will more than make up any costs and inconvenience." Alex produced the photograph of Molly and Lincoln. "I want this picture delivered to someone in New York City approximately 140 years in the future. I'll write down all the specifics, the name, address, and exact date. Do you think it can be done?" he asked. "Can this picture be delivered so many years in the future? With so much precision?" Cooke stood up.

"This is not that unusual a bequest, Mr. . . . Balfour?"

"That's the name I prefer."

"The only unusual aspect is the length of time involved. As for the precision, I think you will find us, and those like us, to be most precise in all things. We can accommodate you, and the cost will be of no concern. On this day at least, we can honor the memory of our late president in many ways; let this be one of them. Reginald," he said, turning to the man who had remained silent, "draw up the necessary papers for Mr. Balfour. You can take all the particulars. I have other matters that need to be dealt with." He turned back to Alex. "Are you by any chance related to a Charles Balfour?" he asked.

"Yes," Alex said slowly. "He's my father."

"He is one of our clients as well. We have done quite a bit of business with him."

"We are not close," Alex said. "I would prefer that none of this be discussed with him."

Cooke gave a small bow. "Of course. We never discuss the business of our clients with anyone outside the bank." He extended his hand, Alex shook it, and Cooke turned and went to a row of offices at the back of the room.

Alex found Reginald Lambert quite willing and able to set up the bequest, as the banker called it, just as Alex wanted it. The picture would go, on October 20, 2002, to one Molly Glenn at his address in New York City, to be delivered by whatever employee of the Jay Cooke bank would be assigned the task.

In payment, Alex made several suggestions: to examine in great detail a small entry in the 1876 World's Fair to be found among the steam engine exhibit. This engine, labeled "Internal Combustion Engine," would utilize petroleum as fuel. He suggested that the inventor and all patents be acquired and extensive investment be made in oil wells and petroleum research. That material would soon be good for something far beyond its present use in medicines and as axle grease. He also told Lambert that railroads were great investments until that particular bubble and indeed the entire market would burst in 1873, before which it would be smart to have invested all equity monies in gold or bonds.

He also left a list of stocks that did not currently exist but should be passed down and bought over the years: IBM, Apple, General Electric, the blue chips of the twentieth century. Reginald Lambert wrote down all the suggestions without comment.

Lambert slipped the photograph into a manila envelope, sealed it with a wax Cooke and Company seal, then stood up and shook Alex's hand. The deal was done. Alex hurried out the door, past the now-glowering guard, and into the arms of two men in police uniform.

"That's him," the guard said to the policemen. "Busted in here earlier, shoutin' at Mr. Cooke. He's got somethin' to do with the killin' of the president, I'd wager my life on it."

The two policemen nodded their thanks and took Alex away, across the street, past the White House—already draped in black— and into the War Department building.

Alex knew where they were headed. The basement. Lafayette Baker's realm. He thought about struggling, breaking free, running, and knew it would be useless. His only hope was to talk his way out of trouble.

They put him in a room with a desk and two chairs and locked the door. He slumped into a chair and held his head in his hands. He thought he had finished with all of this, had completed the last task, and was ready to go back to Ann Benton's and see his child be born, to go back where he belonged.

The door opened. Lafayette Baker entered. "Ah," he said, "my escapee. The man who predicted President Lincoln's death. I've been wanting to talk to you."

chapter forty-two

THE BABY SLID out into Corina's waiting hands and Molly let out a whoop as the old midwife lifted the bloody squirming child up for all to see.

"It's a boy," Corina said. "A big boy. And he's got everything God meant for him to have. Dixie, fetch a clean towel and one of them little blankets." The baby began to cry.

"What's his name gonna be, Molly?" Dixie said, handing her mother a towel.

Molly couldn't take her eyes off her new son. Corina cleaned him up, wrapped him in a blanket, and handed him to her. She was trembling from exhaustion.

"Max," Molly said. The baby was warm. "Maxwell Bierce Balfour." The baby opened his eyes and blinked and squinted against the light. "He's named for an old friend of Alex's, and a new friend. Hello, Max."

In the next room, Bierce stopped writing when he heard Molly's shout and then the baby crying. The door opened. Dixie put her head out and said, "It's a boy. Everyone is fine." Bierce looked down at the paper on the desk in front of him as Dixie closed the door. He picked the paper up and reread it:

DEAR MOLLY,

IT IS WITH SOME TREPIDATION THAT I PEN THESE WORDS, BUT I FEEL IT WOULD BE THE GREATER COWARDICE ON MY PART TO LEAVE THEM UNSAID. IF THEY ARE UNSEEMLY, AND I FEAR THEY ARE, I CAN ONLY THROW MYSELF ON THE MERCY OF YOUR GOOD NATURE.

THESE LAST MONTHS HAVE BEEN WONDERFUL FOR ME AS WE WORKED TOGETHER. YOU HAVE ELEVATED MY POOR EFFORTS TO PUT WORDS ON THE PAGE TO THE LEVEL OF ACTUAL COMPETENCY. I INTEND TO CONTINUE YOUR LESSONS UNTIL I AM SATISFIED THAT YOU WOULD FIND WHAT I DO GOOD. I HAD NOT THOUGHT IT POSSIBLE TO COMMUNE WITH A MEMBER OF THE OPPOSITE SEX ON SUCH A LEVEL OF INTELLECTUAL EQUALITY. I HAVE ALSO BEEN SURPRISED TO FIND THAT EQUALITY EXTENDS TO THE SPIRITUAL LEVEL AS WELL. MY FORMER EXPERIENCE WITH WOMEN I NOW KNOW TO BE A SHAM, IN THAT IN THOSE INSTANCES MY EMOTIONAL INVOLVEMENT HAS BEEN OF THE SMALLEST NATURE AND CONCERNED PRIMARILY WITH AMUSEMENT AND

FEELING OF THE SHALLOWEST KIND. IT HAS NOT
BEEN SO WITH YOU, MOLLY.

BUT I KNOW THAT MY FEELINGS TOWARD YOU CAN
HAVE NO LOGICAL CONCLUSION OTHER THAN MY SEP-
ARATION FROM YOUR PERSON. TO DECLARE MY TRUE
FEELINGS, UNDER THE CIRCUMSTANCES, WOULD . . .

He studied the rest of the blank page. He stood, crumpled the letter, and put it into his pocket. He gathered his pen, ink, and paper and placed them into his writing case.

"You're still not answering my question," Lafayette Baker said. "You did not answer it some months ago and you know where it got you. If you do not answer it now, events will go far harder on you than it did then. I am filling my jails with possible conspirators; you will take your place at the head of them. Again: How did you know the president was going to be assassinated? Where did you obtain that printed material that foretold the assassination?"

"It's a newspaper, but I can't explain it to you." *At least that part of it is true,* Alex thought. He had to get out of here, had to get back to Molly. Baker had been questioning him for an hour.

"You know things because you're part of them," Baker countered. "You escape from Point Lookout, and a few days later someone kills the president of the United States. On the date you predicted in your so-called newspaper. Now I want to know who else was in on it. If you don't tell me, I'm going to have my men go to work on you."

Why not? Why protect them? Why not use them?

"If I tell you, if I tell you everything about the assassination, will you let me go?"

Baker studied him. "Tell me something I can check right now. Then we'll see."

"The assassin is John Wilkes Booth," Alex said. Baker laughed.

"Everyone knows that Booth fired the shot. He was recognized by hundreds of people at the theater. Where is he now, that is the question."

Alex thought. Years ago when he lived in Washington he and his mother used to eat at a Chinese restaurant on the corner of Seventh and H Street. There was a small plaque near the door proclaiming it to be the old Surratt house, where the Lincoln conspirators gathered to plan the assassination.

"Let's begin this way," Alex said. "Go to the corner of Seventh and H, on the south side of the street. There's a boardinghouse that is owned by a Mrs. Surratt. Arrest everyone you find there and question them."

Baker went to the door. "If there's any merit to this, I want to hear it all. Then you can go."

Alex nodded. "All right. Just hurry."

Molly held the baby. Corina had cut the umbilical cord and tied it off. The baby was dry now. Ann Benton had told her that Alex had not yet come back.

"We ain't done here," Corina said. "We got to get the cord and the blood out of you. Then everything got to do with the birthin' be done."

Molly barely heard her.

"Come on," Corina said. "You got to push some more. Everything that was in there got to come out."

Bierce stood in the teahouse where he had been staying, behind Ann's, and finished packing his carpetbag. After he closed the clasp he thought briefly of saying good-bye to Marie, then decided against it and walked around to the front. On the sidewalk he found Charles Balfour limping toward the house.

"Mr. Bierce," Balfour said. "Are you leaving?"

"That's right," Bierce answered.

"I thought we might talk. To see what went wrong last night. Are the others here?"

"Molly is here. The baby was just born. Alex is gone." He stopped. He saw something like fear in the older man's eyes.

"Alex was here? He was here last night?"

"He arrived at the last minute. Too late to stop the assassination. We all failed."

"And where is he now? When will he be back?"

"I don't have any idea," Bierce said, pushing by the man.

"But I need him," Balfour said. "I need to see him."

"You're out of luck," Bierce said. "Good-bye."

Balfour stood on the paving stones and watched Bierce walk away. He turned, walked to the house, and knocked on Ann Benton's door.

Baker was gone for an hour. When he came back into the room he was dusty and sweating. "All right," he said, wiping his forehead with a handkerchief. "We arrested your Mrs. Surratt and a man named Paine who claimed he was a workman there to dig a ditch. He was dressed in ordinary clothing, has no calluses on his hands, and cannot account for his whereabouts last evening. We've also brought in several of the boarders who say they have information to give. I asked them about you, but no one admits to knowing who you are. Now, what else can you tell me?"

"They don't know me because I had nothing to do with the plot."

"Where's Booth?" Baker asked.

"I'm not exactly sure, but I can give you enough information so you'll know where he will end up. He spent last night at a doctor's house in Maryland, a Dr. Mudd. Now he's on the run. He thinks if he can get far enough south he'll be hailed as a hero."

"Fool. It will go ten times as hard on the South as it would have if this had never happened."

"What about our deal? You'll let me go?"

Baker waved his hand. "Yes, yes, you've got your deal. Give me Booth."

"Get me a map," Alex said.

He used Baker's pen to trace the route as well as he could remember. He knew that people of his own time actually went on paid excursions to follow Booth's exact route by bus and boat, and wished he had that sort of exact knowledge. "It ends approximately here," he drew a circle on the map. "In Virginia, at the farm of a man named Richard Garrett. Booth, and his guide Davey Herold, who was in on the whole plot with him, will be in Garrett's barn on the twenty-sixth of this month. Now," Alex said, standing up, "can I go?"

Baker finished writing. He stood up without answering and went to the door. He opened it and called into the hall, "Sergeant!" When a policeman appeared, Baker opened the door all the way. "Put this man in a cell," he said. "Until further notice."

"Push!" Corina commanded Molly, tugging on the umbilical cord. With a soft plopping sound the placenta slid out.

And Molly, and the baby, disappeared.

Ann Benton stood at the front door, talking to Charles Balfour. "I'm sorry, Mr. Balfour, I really don't think she's up to seeing anyone quite yet. Perhaps you might call back in a few days?" From inside the house there were screams. Ann turned and looked at the steps to the second floor. Dixie appeared at the head of the stairs.

"They gone!" she shouted. "They gone!"

Ann turned back around. Charles Balfour had left the front door and was walking through the gate to the sidewalk, hurrying away.

Alex sat on the cot in his cell. He was surprised at himself for believing Baker would let him go. He tried to think of some way to get out of jail. He wasn't terribly afraid that he would be connected to the assassination, he'd never heard of an Alex Balfour as part of the conspiracy, but he had to get back to Molly.

Molly found herself on the floor of Alex's house in New York. She was clutching the baby. She sat up. She looked at the bottom of the white nightdress she was wearing. It was soaked with blood. She pulled herself to her feet. She reached for the phone on the end table and dialed 911.

"I need an ambulance," she said. The baby began to cry.

Preacher didn't like it when Baker gave him these jobs, but after last night he couldn't complain. He hadn't told Baker just how close he had come to capturing or killing Lincoln's assassin, but still it was clear he had failed. *Maybe this will make up for it,* he thought. He stood in front of the cell door and looked back down the empty corridor. The guards had been called upstairs for a meeting with Baker.

He checked the knife in his boot. He didn't really mind killing a man, especially one who had something to do with the assassination. He just didn't want to get blood on his clothing. He used the big key to open the door.

The cell was empty.

Alex fell to the floor. He felt carpet and pushed himself up, looking around. He was in the living room of his house in New York City. He listened. The house was quiet but he could hear sounds of traffic outside.

He stood up.

"Molly!" he shouted.

He looked back down and saw blood on the carpet. He bent and touched it. The blood was still wet.

He stood again, looking around frantically. On the end table was a note.

ALEX. WE HAVE GONE TO ST. VINCENT'S HOSPITAL. WE ARE ALL RIGHT! I LOVE YOU. MOLLY. AND MAX.

Alex hit the front door, jerked it open, and dashed out on the front porch. Once again, he began to run.

chapter forty-three

THE HOSPITAL KEPT Molly and Max for two days, then let them go home. The doctors were more concerned about Alex's infected snakebite than they were with mother and baby. Alex slept in a chair by her hospital bed for one of the two nights, then spent the next day running around buying baby supplies: a crib, stroller, diapers, changing table, and everything else the lady at the baby store said he would need.

For two more days they stayed inside. After the first day the antibiotics he'd been given began to work and the redness of the infection in his arm and the residual pain began to subside. Alex ventured out only for quick trips to the grocery store. Being outside was almost painful for him. Overwhelmed by the sights and sounds of twenty-first-century life, to him everything seemed to move at ten times the speed he had grown accustomed to. He was surprised by the sheer volume of *pictures* that surrounded him everywhere he looked, the visual weight of simple existence. He was also surprised to find how clean the air smelled, even loaded with exhaust, compared to where he had been. No horse manure, no coal smoke, no filthy streams polluted with the refuse from butcher shops or the carcasses of drowned animals.

He and Molly held Max and learned the necessary skills of caring for a baby. He had bought a shelfful of baby books, and the first line of *Dr. Spock* reassured both of them, as it had millions of other new parents: "You know more than you think you do." They did not turn on the TV. They did not answer the telephone the few times it rang.

"Let's go for a walk," Molly said. "We can try out that fancy stroller you paid too much money for."

"The saleslady said we had to buy the best one. It's a safety thing. Are you sure you feel up to it?"

"The saleslady racked up a hell of a commission the day you walked in. And yes, I feel up to it. I'm sore, but generally fine.

"For God's sake," Molly said as they negotiated the stroller down the steps to the sidewalk, "it's got a sound chip that plays ten different lullabies. Do we really need that?"

"I don't know," Alex said, as they turned left down the sidewalk. "Maybe. Let's go to the little park on the corner."

Molly steered the stroller around a pile of trash the neighbors had put out on the sidewalk. "The park. I hate to tell you this, but they put a building in where the park was."

Alex looked down to the next block. His gaze swept upward, from the base of the new structure to the sign on the top proclaiming it to be the Seward Building. And then to the skyline beyond. He stopped walking.

"My God," he said. "Where are the Twin Towers?"

Alex had never been particularly wedded to his computer for his research into the past. He sometimes thought it was the touch and smell of old books, newspapers, and magazines, the artifacts of another age that drew him away from the present, if not in reality then in his own mind. But after Molly told him of the attack on the Towers he spent two days reading everything he could find about it on the Internet.

Sated with the horror of that event, he slipped easily into researching their adventures in the nineteenth century in hopes that he might answer some of the questions that still kept him awake at night.

When he wasn't on the computer, he and Molly spent their time with the baby, the three of them together, lying on the living room floor on the quilt they would take off the bed. Molly had gone to the bookstore and bought a copy of the complete works of Ambrose Bierce and a biography of his life. She had finished the biography and was reading the works.

She called Tommy at the *Times*. He was relieved to hear from her and wanted to know everything that had happened. She put him off, saying that it would have to wait until she was not as sore and tired as she was at the moment. He told her he had made up a complicated lie for her boss about her having a medical emergency and having to take a leave of absence from work.

Alex was flat on his back, lying on the living room floor. Max was on Alex's chest, awake, looking at him with serious blue eyes. Molly put a bookmark into the volume of Bierce stories and rolled over. "There's a story in here I want you to read," she said.

"I intend to read all of them when you're done," he said.

"I know, but read this one now. It's called *Oil of Dog*. It's one of the most disturbing stories I've ever read." She laughed shortly. "Although there are number of others that could also qualify for that honor. Our friend Bierce developed quite a taste for the macabre."

Alex sat up, cradling Max on his lap. "Did he become as cranky, bitter, and difficult a person as I remember reading about?"

"According to his biographer, it sounds so. I think he was very unhappy about something and it came through in his work. His stories are full of horror. His characters kill their mothers and fathers and their children. And their pets. Wives kill husbands and vice versa. His columns are funny, but he was brutal to anyone he considered not quite up to his standards and ideals. Throughout all of it I sense a kind of emptiness, a feeling of a missed chance."

"Do you think it had anything to do with us?" Alex asked.

Molly shook her head. "I asked myself that question while I was reading the biography. The answer is, of course, who knows? We must have had some effect. But I think it's likely that his war wound accounted for more of his misery than we did. At least I hope so."

Molly watched Alex play with the baby. "You know, we haven't really talked about the past since we got back," she said. "Washington. What happened to us. Do you think we changed anything? All that we did with your father? And what ever happened to him? What did he get out of all of it?"

"I've been researching," Alex said. He touched Max's hair. "There's a lot of information to sift through. Eventually I'll figure at least some of it out."

"But did we change anything?"

"I don't know. Not as far as Abraham Lincoln was concerned. I'm not sure we'd even know if something *was* altered. Maybe it would be changed in our minds as well. Or maybe any alteration would be so small we wouldn't even notice it."

"But why did he do it? Your father. Why go to all the trouble?"

The baby smiled at Alex.

"Hey, look, he smiled at me!"

Molly shook her head, looking down at the baby. "He's too young to smile. I read that in a book. He's just passing gas."

"Bullshit. He smiled at me."

"Yeah, well, that's something else; you're going to have to start watching your language around the baby. We don't want his first word to be 'bullshit.' Anyway, you still haven't answered my question: Why would your father go to all that trouble? Finding you in the prison camp, organizing the others and me. And you know when he was at the prison camp and he told you he had contacted me, that I was going to help him, he hadn't. Up to then he'd only been following me at the newspaper when I checked my ad. He contacted me *after* he had seen you in the camp."

"I think he wanted to forge a bond between us all. So when we came back here we would be his anchor."

"Like I am for you."

"Yes."

"But I was here, and you didn't come back before, at least not before I was pregnant," she said.

"Remember, there was that brief moment when you were sleeping. When I picked up the picture of you and Lincoln."

"At the time I thought that was just a dream. I understand it was all somehow tied to the picture and me not going to Japan. But you never told me why I shouldn't go. When I was about to have Max I asked, but you didn't tell me."

"I didn't want to frighten you." He sighed, knowing he couldn't put it off any longer. "In my past, in another universe, you went to Japan to research your story. You were killed there. I was there as well, with you. After that happened, after I shifted back in time again, I knew that I had to get word to you to not go in the first place. I could do that because I was farther back in time, a hundred and fifty years before any of the other events had happened. But it didn't occur to me how to do it until I saw the picture of you and Lincoln at Ann Benton's and it didn't have the words 'Don't go to Japan' written on it. Not yet. The picture I picked up when I briefly went back to this house and you were asleep had the words written on it. I had to do what I did, because *I had already done it.*" She was frowning at him. "I know it's hard. There were two pictures, at least briefly: the one I first picked up, which I sewed into the lining of my knapsack, and the one Brady gave to you and you had framed at Ann's."

"Then where's the other picture?" Molly asked. "Where are any of the pictures, for that matter?"

"The picture, because there is really only one picture, must still be sewn into the lining of my knapsack. The last time I saw it Lafayette Baker was waving it around while he arrested me for plotting Lincoln's assassination. I'm sure it was eventually thrown out. I didn't want to tell you all of this because I didn't want you to get upset about the Japan incident."

Molly rolled her eyes. "The Japan incident. Of course I'm upset. What do you mean I was killed? By whom?"

Alex held up a hand. "I'm just going to have to say, that's another story. A very long one. And I will tell it to you, I promise, but not today. Let's go on to what happened in Washington." He waited. She nodded, reluctantly, and he went on.

"By sending you the picture with the note that you wrote on it when you were having the baby, by warning yourself *not* to go to Japan before you actually went, we short-circuited that event. That timeline, that universe, was changed because *you didn't go.* You were saved because you were not there to have the event happen to you. And because you were here, after Max was born, I was drawn back. Like I've always come back when you were here. But the pregnancy changed everything. Max went back, and I followed."

"Doesn't that mean events can be changed?" She asked.

He shrugged. "I guess it means that under certain circumstances events can at least be forestalled. I suppose that amounts to change. It did in this case. But the larger events in history?" He shrugged again. "I just don't know." The baby was asleep. They placed him on his back in his crib and put a light blanket over him. Then Alex and Molly stretched out on their bed, and Alex held her while they watched their son sleep.

The memory of the boy who had saved his life in the past still haunted Alex. He dreamt of him, holding the tin cup, saw him rising up out of the stormy night, slamming a club into the foraging pigs as they grazed among the living and the dead.

Alex began reading through histories of the Battle of Cedar

Creek. List after list of regimental roles were available, used mostly by people searching for Civil War soldier ancestors. He pored over the long lists of names until he found Lieutenant John Jordan listed as missing in the Battle of Cedar Creek. He sat for a moment, staring at the name, wondering if the Jordan family ever gave up hope that their son would be found alive.

He worked the lists of soldiers compiled by duty rosters, payment records, and by religion. He continued on, scrolling down screen after screen of names, hundreds of names, until . . .

Solomon.

And then he was back, lying beneath the bushes, looking out at the man dressed as a preacher. He saw again the boy caught and held, the burst of flame from the pistol, the wounded man slapped to the ground by the bullet and the boy shouting one word.

Solomon!

And here it was, in a list of the dead, organized by religious affiliation: *Solomon Baruch. Hebrew. 121st* New York Infantry.

He found a government roster for the 121st, all soldiers who were part of the unit for the year 1864, and pored over every name but found no connection to Baruch. He had thought that the boy might have been a brother, but Solomon was the only Baruch.

And then he found a picture of the boy.

He had been sitting at his computer. Molly was playing with the baby in the next room. Her voice was a low background murmur. He was almost idly following Booth's escape route through Maryland and Virginia to see how close he had come to reality with the crude map he had drawn for Colonel Lafayette Baker.

The article that showed the escape route map informed him that Colonel Baker had not physically participated in the capture of Booth, as Alex had thought, but instead sent his cousin Luther Baker in his place. Interested in the family connection, Alex followed a link to a book published years before by a vanity press, the author, now dead, being a distant relative of the Baker family. Another link showed that the New York state library system owned a copy, so over the computer he asked the system to send the book to the New York City branch on Forty-Second Street.

The next day he was handed a copy of *Lafayette C. Baker: Legendary Spymaster* by Anthony Blair Baker. He took it home to read. He sat on the couch, Molly and the baby on the quilt at his feet, and flipped to the back of the book to the section on the Booth escape and capture. He read how Baker's legendary prowess led him to catch Lewis Paine at Mrs. Surratt's boardinghouse, *yeah, sure, I'm the one who sent him to Surratt's,* and then to dispatch his minions unerringly to the Virginia farmhouse where Booth was cornered in a barn. *Yeah, right.*

Alex finished the section on the capture of Booth without learning anything new. The book went on to chronicle the rest of Baker's life, which was pretty much a descent into insanity. Alex flipped to the middle of the book where there were photo illustrations.

There was Lafayette Baker in powerful profile with jutting nose and forehead and thick full beard.

Mrs. Baker, looking plain, severe, and stern.

He heard Max make a noise. "He just said 'Daddy,' didn't he?" he called to Molly. And turned the page.

And there he was. The boy who had saved his life, who had watched in horror as his friend was murdered in front of him. Alex saw a picture of a woman dressed in a full skirt, her hair pulled back in a bun. A child, probably four or five years old, dressed in a sailor suit, stood in front of her. At first Alex thought the woman must be the water boy's sister, the resemblance was so uncanny, until he noticed that there was only one hand resting on the child's shoulders. The sleeve of the other arm was pinned up. The arm itself, missing.

Amputated, he thought.

The caption beneath the photograph read: *Alison Baker, only child of Lafayette Baker, with her son Solomon. 1869.*

And then he understood. There was no boy. Alison Baker was one of the many women who disguised themselves as men and ran off to war with their husbands or lovers. Solomon Baruch was probably her lover, and she had thrice damned herself: first for being with a man out of wedlock, for that man being a Jew, and for running away. All of which would have been enough for Baker, whose position gave him the power of life and death, to order Solomon Baruch killed and the girl brought home. Alex remembered lying behind a tree, watching as the preacher strode into the clearing, scooped up the boy Alex now knew was a girl, and shot the wounded man who lay on the ground.

The evidence was too strong to be coincidence. There were no other Solomons in the 121st New York Infantry.

Alex felt a flush as he realized that he had gone to Baker and told him the story of the murder at Cedar Creek. Told him of the man who had appeared in the woods and murdered the wounded Union soldier. Not knowing that it was Lafayette Baker who sent the man to do just that. No wonder Baker had sent him to the Point Lookout prison camp. The surprise was that Baker hadn't had him killed outright. Alex wondered if the guard at the prison camp, King, was part of it, if Baker had given him the job of antagonizing Alex until he struck out and forced the guard to kill him.

He heard a gurgling noise from the baby. Molly sat down beside him. "He just smiled at me!" Molly said. Alex came back from the past and looked at her.

"Oh, he smiles at me all the time," Alex said, tickling Max's tummy. "He loves my jokes. What he's doing now with you is probably just passing gas. That's what it says in the baby books."

Molly elbowed his leg, hard, looked up, and smiled at him.

"What's so funny?" Alex asked, rubbing his leg.

"Oh, nothing," she replied, sweetly. "I wasn't smiling, I was just passing gas."

A month passed and they found themselves in summer, content to live and love their baby and each other.

The morning sun glowed through the new bright white curtains they had hung over the bedroom windows.

He opened his eyes, hearing Molly stir beside him. She would rise, pick up Max, and bring him to their warm bed to lie between them.

"Alex!" Molly cried. "Alex! He's gone! Max is gone!"

chapter forty-four

THEY COULDN'T GO to the police. The facts were simple, the conclusion obvious. To them. It wouldn't be to anyone else.

The doors had been locked. They were alone. Nothing else was missing. No one had crept in while they slept and taken the baby.

The baby had gone into the past, and there was nothing they could do. Except wait.

The days passed. Nothing that Alex had ever undergone, no wound, no loss, was as painful as this. The image of their baby, lying somewhere alone in the past, was almost more than either of them could bear. The thought that he might be dead was indeed more than they could bear. They never voiced that possibility, and when it came to them, as it must, they pushed it away and closed their eyes.

Alex prepared meals, but they hardly ate. They slept, sometimes, usually not at the same time, one of them always awake, always watching.

At first they could not stop talking, thinking, frantically trying to come up with a plan. Then they gradually gave up all their attempts and fell silent. Each alone with their terrible longing.

He worked all day and most of the night on the computer, searching for something, anything that might help. He stood at the shelves of his father's library, now his library. He took down all those books printed during or about the Civil War, thinking that's where Max was, where he had to be. He held the old books, fingering their cracked leather bindings, inhaling their musty scent, running his hands over the pages, trying to will himself back.

One afternoon he looked up at Molly. She was standing in the doorway of the library. He put down the book he was holding. "Can't you do something?" she asked. She'd asked this before, but it was the tone of her voice that had changed. He felt the implied accusation.

He was shocked at the weight she'd lost in the week Max had been missing. She was dressed in jeans and a T-shirt, clothes that now hung slack, accentuating her angular collarbones, the thinness of her arms. She wore no makeup. She was pale, her eyes at the same time both feverish and yet flat and distant.

"I don't know what to do, you know that," he said. "It's not my fault, Molly."

She came into the room and slumped into a chair. She looked at him. "Yes it is, it's your fault." He started to protest, but she waved a hand to silence him.

"I know, I know, I'm sorry." She sat looking at the floor. "Maybe not your fault, exactly," she went on, "but it happened because of you. Because of this ability, this affliction you and your family have. It took our baby; now I want you to find him. I want you to find him!"

He went to her and knelt at her side. He took her hand. "I love him too, Molly. We've been over it and over it. I know what you must be feeling. I know what's driving you to talk this way. The only thing we can do is help each other to try and get through this. It's all I can do."

She pulled her hand away, covered her face, and wept.

And so they drifted through the house, coming together to eat on rare occasions, sleeping wherever exhaustion found them, though at some point each night they would gravitate to their bedroom where the crib sat empty beside the bed. And if they then could not sleep, they would lie on the bed and wait.

chapter forty-five

ALEX WOKE, GASPING, from a dream of loss. He was sweating, twisted in the unwashed sheets. Molly was sitting on the side of the bed with her back to him. She turned. The baby was cradled in her arms.

"He's back," she said. "He's back."

Molly passed the baby to Alex. Max looked at him, wide-awake. He waved his arms as if reaching toward Alex's face. Alex hugged the baby, pressing his face against the small soft body and smelling his sweet smell. He closed his eyes for a moment, then placed the baby carefully on the bed.

Max was wearing a long white nightgown with a matching cap. The material was lightweight cotton and it had delicate embroidery-work around the collar and on the cap.

"He seems healthy," Alex said. Molly got a tissue and blew her nose and wiped her eyes. Alex took the cap off Max and began to undress him.

Molly gasped. Underneath the nightgown Max wore only a cloth diaper, neatly tied on each side. There was writing on his chest.

In ink were the letters, neatly printed: *N.Y.C.W.H.S.* Below that was *F 50.* And below that, *C.B.*

Alex tried to ignore the writing as he examined the baby. He took off the diaper and rolled Max on his stomach. The baby made gurgling sounds and worked his arms and legs as if he were swimming. Alex turned him back over. "Not even a diaper rash," he said. "Let's get him dressed and take him to the pediatrician."

Molly got a disposable diaper and put it on the baby. Max started to cry, so she lifted him to her breast. He snuggled in and began to suckle. Molly rocked back and forth.

"Taking him to the doctor. I'm not sure that's a good idea," she said.

"Why? We need to make sure he's okay."

"He looks fine. In fact, that's the problem. Look at him, Alex, this is not a two-month-old baby. He's only been gone a week, and yet he looks more like four months. He's grown, put on weight, he's more advanced. The pediatrician is going to notice it. There will be questions that we can't answer."

"But . . ."

"Think about it," she said, raising her voice. "First of all, we showed up with this baby already born. There was no record of any prenatal care. All we had was that crazy story I told the hospital about being out of the country. There's still the problem of a birth certificate and how they're legally going to issue one. If we come into the doctor's office with what he's going to suspect is a different baby, there's going to be real trouble." She rocked back and forth and began quietly to hum a lullaby.

She was right. Max did appear bigger and heavier.

The baby finished eating and Molly laid him back down between them.

"All right," Alex said. "We'll just watch him closely. We can get another doctor, we'll just use the we-just-moved-to-town story again." He picked up a notepad and copied the letters that were written on Max's chest.

N.Y.C.W.H.S.

F. 50

C.B.

"Do you have any idea what it means?" she asked.

Alex tapped the pencil on the pad. "Well, of course I'm not sure, but I can guess. N.Y. is probably New York. C.W. could easily be Civil War. And H.S. is either High School or Historical Society, and I think we can safely say it's the latter. In research terms F usually stands for Folio. It's probably a reference to a specific batch of papers."

"And the C.B.?"

Alex looked at her. "Charles Balfour."

She looked up from the baby.

"No."

"It's the only thing that makes sense. Like it or not, his blood runs through Max's veins, just like it does mine. He's sent us a message. These are directions."

Her eyes were narrowed with anger. "I'm going to give him a bath. You figure out what Charles Balfour wants."

Alex tried the computer first. No New York Civil War Historical Society. Then he tried the telephone. It took the operator three seconds to find the number.

The phone was answered on the second ring by a man with a cheery, tenor voice.

"New York Civil War Historical Society, Daniel Jarvis, how may I help you?"

"Are you open to the public?"

"Yes sir, we are."

"What is the nature of your collection?"

"Well, despite our name, we are quite specialized. Our papers are specific to the United States Sanitary Commission for the year 1864. We have more than 3,000 documents but they are all within this time period and subject."

"That's quite unusual, isn't it?"

"Well, Mr. . . . ."

"Balfour," Alex offered.

There was a silence. "Isn't that interesting," Jarvis said. "Do you wish to see the collection?"

"Yes. Why did you say my name was interesting?"

"When would you be coming in?"

"Today? Right now?"

"Now would be fine, Mr. Balfour. We're located in the Flatiron Building, top floor. I'll be waiting for you."

. . .

The elevator creaked upward. The pale green paint was chipped and scarred. The car had been jammed with publishing types who got off at intervening floors as the elevator ground to the top. Alex found the Historical Society at the end of a long, dingy hallway.

The Society had two rooms filled floor to ceiling with gray, acid-free containers. Daniel Jarvis sat at a desk in the front office with his back to an incredible view of New York. He had white hair and a genial smile, though Alex would have been hard pressed to guess his age.

"We don't get many visitors," Jarvis said, shaking Alex's hand and gesturing to the only other chair in the room. "I confess, I'm quite discouraging to most callers. We get a dozen queries every day, but our scope is so limited we appeal only to the narrowest researchers. Civil War buffs and ordinary people doing genealogical research can be extremely persistent, but it's rarely worth their while to come here. The name of the Society draws them to us initially. Unfortunate in some respects, but we're stuck with it."

"Then why did you invite me to come in?" Alex asked.

"It was your name—Balfour. Our original benefactor was named Balfour; I thought there might be some connection." Jarvis swiveled his chair to the side and pointed to a framed picture on the wall. "That's our Mr. Balfour."

It was the photograph Alex had taken back at the prison camp.

"No connection," he said evenly. "Not to my knowledge, there isn't." The sight of the photograph seemed to reach out to him for just a second, to threaten to draw him back. He looked away. "Perhaps you can just tell me about the Society," he said. "Its origins, your benefactor, what you do day-to-day."

Jarvis had his elbows on his desk and his fingers tented. He nodded agreeably.

"Yes, yes, of course. Please stop me if I ramble on, I don't get much opportunity to talk to the public about our purpose." He leaned back in his chair, and frowned. "Actually, we don't have much of a purpose at all. In 1865 the Society was organized by the outgoing commissioner for finances of the United States Sanitary Commission. Medical facilities were almost nonexistent at the beginning of the war, so the Commission collected large amounts of money as donations from citizens and applied it to this problem. They built hospitals, hired nurses, gave soldiers a place to eat and sleep when on leave, and generally performed all the necessary services that the military did not seem able to supply. By war's end, the Commission was a huge organization with an extremely large income. The financial officer was responsible for the collection and disbursement of millions of dollars. In 1865, the outgoing financial officer, Mr. Charles Balfour, decided to preserve some of the documents of the Commission." He stopped talking and swiveled his chair so it looked out over Fifth Avenue. "I'll be frank with you, Mr. Balfour, there's really no good reason to have done so. In many ways the collection is quite haphazard. It's almost as if Balfour went through the records and dumped everything into boxes, set up the charter and funding for our organization, and went on his merry way." He turned back to Alex and spread his hands to indicate the space around him. "I am the sole employee. What you see is the entire collection, and to be honest, most of it is quite boring. Even the most persistent researchers leave after a few hours, saying there's nothing here to interest anyone. And having made a crack at organizing things any number of times, I'd have to agree with them." He laughed, and shrugged his shoulders. "There you have it, I'm afraid."

Alex nodded and tried to look wise. "Would it be possible for me to look at folio 50?"

Jarvis appeared surprised. "Of course. If you'll just fill out this form giving us your name and address."

He slid a small slip of paper to Alex, stood, walked around the desk, and went to a stack of boxes and pulled one from the pile. "They're all numbered. Very simple, really." He handed Alex the box, and Alex handed him the form he had filled out. "There's a table in the other room. Would you like my help going through the box?"

"No, thank you. I prefer to work alone." Jarvis led him into the other room and indicated the wooden table where Alex could sit. Alex put his briefcase and the folio box on the table and stood and smiled until Jarvis went back to his own desk. He pulled up the chair, sat down, and opened the box.

Inside was a smaller, black cardboard box, approximately sixteen inches by twenty inches and three inches deep, tied closed with a black ribbon. Alex untied the bow, opened the box, and found it crammed full of papers. The inside of the box smelled of dust and age. The papers were thin and brittle. There must have been five hundred sheets of varying sizes, all covered with careful hand-written script, most of them lists and tables of accounting. Alex felt his heart begin to sink—he had no idea what he was looking for—and then told himself to cut the crap and just get to work. He lifted each sheet out, read it, and put it facedown in a neat pile.

It took two hours before he found the message from his father. He was reading a letter the Commission had received thanking them for a donation of quilts. When he turned the letter over to place it on the pile, he recognized his father's handwriting. All of his father's books had been handwritten on legal pads, and Alex had grown up surrounded by drifts of these yellow tablets covered with his father's careful copperplate script.

· · ·

"Alex" the page began, "your patient researching skills have obviously brought you to this document. Amazing, isn't it, the way we are sending these messages over the years? I got the idea to do this from you, I confess, and the example of your little bequest at Cooke's bank. A word of advice: Never trust anyone to keep his or her mouth shut. Jay Cooke loves to gossip. He wouldn't tell me the exact nature of your transaction with the bank, but he told enough for me to discern the outlines of a message sent into the future. For his indiscretion I told him to disregard any financial advice you may have given him. This assures that he will declare bankruptcy in 1873, but more on that later.

"I hope you admire my method of sending you this rather lengthy message. I feel that this is the most boring collection of artifacts ever purposefully assembled, thus assuring that no one will look at them with enough interest to discover this letter. And even if they did, what harm would come of it? At any rate, it wasn't difficult to set up the basic structure of the Society. It's surprising how small an amount of money it takes, thanks to the miracle of compound interest, to assure the lifetime in perpetuity of an organization like the N.Y.C.W.H.S.

"And why am I bothering at all? First, I feel I owe you some explanation after the effort you and your friends put in with the Lincoln attempt. (It worked just as I planned.) But mostly, with the advent of the baby, it behooves us to stay in touch, as it were. If I had been taken back with you as I wished, we would not be in this position. But I wasn't, so here—or there—we all are."

Alex glanced up and saw Jarvis, standing in the doorway looking at him. "Find something interesting?" he asked.

"Not really," Alex replied. "Like you said, a pretty boring collection." He placed the letter on the pile and picked up another paper, pretending to read it.

"I just wanted to say that I'm going to lunch. Can I get you anything?"

"No, thank you. I'm about through here."

"I see. Well, if you finish before I get back, put the material in the box and place it on my desk. Pull the door closed behind you, it locks automatically. I realize this goes against the usual suspicious nature of your average New Yorker, but really"—he looked around the room—"what's to steal?"

He gave a small wave and left the room and the office. Alex heard the lock snap as Jarvis closed the outer door.

It took Alex all of thirty seconds to decide to steal his father's letter. He realized he was abusing Jarvis' trusting good nature, and his scholar's horror of document thievery raised its head briefly but was easily dismissed. The entire collection existed only to make this moment possible. By all rights, the letter belonged to him.

He checked the backs of successive pages of material and found where the letter ended, slipped the pertinent pages into his brief-case, then packed everything else up and put it on Jarvis's desk. He scrawled a quick thank you on a scrap of paper, and left it on the box. He made sure the door was securely locked behind him.

Max and Molly were lying in bed. The baby was curled up, chewing on his fingers.

"I gave him a bath. The writing washed right off."

Alex put the briefcase down and sat on the bed. "I was right," Alex said. "The whole place was a mail drop from my father to me." He reached down and retrieved the papers. As he started to hand the papers to Molly, Max made a grab for them. Alex carefully uncrumpled the pages from the baby's hand.

"I'll read it to you," he said. "I've only gone through the first page myself." He started from the beginning and read aloud till he got to where he had stopped at the Society office.

"From here on it's all new to me," he told Molly, and began reading aloud again.

" 'The attempt to stop the Lincoln assassination was less than an honest effort on my part. In fact, quite the opposite was intended. As far as Lincoln was concerned, I wished history to stay just the way we had both learned it. I have no idea if it is possible to change the course of events. I needed to be certain that history would occur as I knew it and as I needed it to, and I felt you would have not joined me in the endeavor had I not sounded sure of myself. My particular interest in the saving of the young Seward was accomplished, though would it have been so if I had not intervened? I don't know.

" 'Why my interest in not attempting to change the Lincoln end of things? As the financial officer of the Sanitary Commission I have the responsibility of, often, having to carry around quite absurdly large amounts of cash. Throughout the war I have made use of this task by "borrowing" this cash and investing it for short periods of time. Because I was aware of the outcome of certain major battles during the war, I was able to take advantage of the natural swing in the currency and stock markets. It was simple: If the North won an important battle, stocks would rise and the price of gold would go down. If a battle was lost, the opposite occurred. Rather than bother with different stocks, I simply put my borrowed money into and out of gold. While I was never positive how much I was going to make, I was always sure to make at least a small profit and often quite a large one. This was a sort of war profiteering, yes, but I was not alone in the business. Secretary of the Treasury Salmon P. Chase earned great sums of money using the same maneuvers. Because of Chase, and our friend Jay Cooke, who also benefited, Lincoln instituted a clever rule that ended that scheme immediately. The rule was that when you made any sort of a buy or sell on the gold market it did not become official for one week, and the price was based on the day it became official. And since no one could look a week into the future to predict the outcome of a battle, the profiteers were stymied. Except in my case.' "

Alex put the papers down for a moment. "I knew he had to be up to something."

"Read," Molly said.

He lifted the papers again.

" 'Two weeks before the assassination I put in an order to buy gold with money I was "borrowing" from the Commission. Because the war was nearly over and everyone knew it, stocks were soaring and gold was dropping. Then on the day my buy order became official, on the eighth of April when gold had reached a new low, I put in my order to sell, which under the rule would come into effect the day after the assassination, when stocks would have plummeted and gold would have been at an all-time high.

" 'And did it work? I could make you look up the newspapers of the period to find out, but I'll save you the effort: It didn't work very well at all. I made some money, a tidy sum for this time, I admit, but not the killing, excuse the word, that I had expected. It turns out that the American businessman has a solid sense of patriotism. The politicians appealed for calm in the markets on the day Lincoln died and that's what they got. Very few investors sold their holdings. Gold rose, but only modestly. So much for banking on a national tragedy.' "

Alex turned on the bed to face Molly. "Can you remember what happened to the stock market after the Twin Towers were hit?"

She laughed, cynically. "Of course I can remember. The president called for American investors to do their patriotic duty and not panic. To stand firm and not sell. And of course the day after the attack the market went into the toilet."

"So much for the patriotism of the American investor," Alex said. "Times change." He continued reading:

" 'As for the assassination itself, I have always felt that the most curious aspect of it was the mystery of why the guard left his place beside the door to the presidential box. Had he stayed, Booth would have been foiled, or at least had to fight his way inside, and those in the box would have been warned. And I believe that without all of you, Bierce, Molly, and yourself, he very well might have remained in his chair on guard. But each one of you offered just the sort of opportunity to disturb the normal course of events and cause the man to rise and investigate what the disturbance might be—thus freeing the way for Booth to enter the box unopposed and assassinate Lincoln. And subsequently cause the stock market to crash, gold to soar, and I would have emerged with a fortune. Had that aspect of my plan failed and Lincoln survived, I believe we all would have been reconciled, and I would have been drawn back to where you are right now. Either way I would have won.' "

"I knew it!" Molly interrupted. "I told the guard to get back to his post. He wouldn't listen! It was our fault!"

"No, it wasn't!" Alex said loudly. "We don't know that. We can't know what would have happened if we hadn't been there." They sat for a moment, neither of them looking at the other.

"Would you like me to hold Max for a while?" he asked gently. He could feel her body suddenly tense.

"No," she said quickly. She put her arms around the baby.

"Have you taken your hands off him since this morning? While I was gone?"

"No. Why should I?"

"I just thought you might need a break."

She shook her head in exasperation. "I don't need a break. I've already been implicated in causing Abraham Lincoln's death. What I need is for you to read the goddamned message from your goddamned father so I can understand what's happening to us. Why is he going on with the nonsense about the money? I need to know what's happened to Max."

Alex touched her arm. He could feel the muscles and tendons clenched rock-hard beneath his hand.

"He's probably lying about everything. With him it's never about information, only misinformation. And even if he's not lying—"

"Just read the letter!" Molly shouted. The baby looked up at her and crinkled his face, about to cry. "Please," she added, more evenly, soothing the baby. She took a deep breath, and said in slow measured tones, "I just want to hear what he has to say about Max."

" 'A last word about banks and bankers,' " Alex read. " 'You may have wondered about my concern over the young Seward. The night of the attack I made sure he saw my face as I aided him in his battle against Lewis Paine. It was only later that I revealed myself to him, and since then we have become business associates. In 1873, when Jay Cooke's bank fails, in part because Cooke will not be following any of your recommendations, young Seward will buy the bank on my recommendation, and I will become one of the directors. I have told you before, I do not wish to stay in this time, but if I must stay I will do so in style and comfort.

" 'And now, on to my grandson.' " Alex stopped. Reading the word *grandson* sent a chill through him.

"Go on," Molly urged.

" 'What a lovely baby Max is,' " he read. " 'After he "arrived" I went to Ann Benton's and had a conversation with that lady. I didn't tell her that Max was at my home, but I wanted to see how much she knew about him. She explained how terrible it was that all of you had simply disappeared. She told me that Molly had named the baby Max. I assured her that if I ever came across any of you again I would notify her immediately. The poor woman was distraught.

" 'I immediately hired a wet nurse, a very competent young woman, who has taken perfect care of him.

" 'What you must now understand, Alex, is that you can never again be rid of me. The ties of blood and the curse that runs through our family links us, all of us, whether you like it or not. Max will come to visit me again. You cannot stop it. Just as you will come to me again. And when you do, you will work to see that I return to your present. For you see, I may not need you to do me this service any longer. I now have Max. Perhaps not at this moment but soon. He will learn to love his grandfather. And then I will return with him. And then we will see whose child he has become.' " The rest of the page was blank.

Alex let the papers fall to the floor. Molly's face was set, cold and hard.

"Will he do what he says?" She asked.

"He's certainly capable of it. He tried to kill me at least once before when it suited his purpose." He was quiet for a moment. "I've told you I believe he killed my mother. Will he do what he says now? If he can."

"What can we do?" she asked. "Can we stop him?"

"I don't know. I don't know how to stop him."

She looked at him, and he could see the mother-rage that lay quivering just beneath her surface. He had never seen her like this, rigid with hate.

"I know how to stop him," she said, her tone perfectly even. "He is right, you will go back, sometime. You are drawn to him the same way Max now is. It will happen again. And when you go back, he will be there." She stopped, and for a moment he could feel her measuring him, weighing his strength, his purpose, his will. His love for his child.

She went on. "You will find your father, and you will kill him."

chapter forty-six

C HARITY PETTIBOW COMPOSED her plain but not unattractive face and knocked on the heavy oak door. The man's voice inside bade her to enter. She straightened her bonnet and opened the door.

Mr. Charles Balfour was seated behind his desk in his wood-paneled study. He peered at her over his spectacles.

"Ah, Mrs. Pettibow," he said. "You're leaving now?"

"Yes, Mr. Balfour. The man has put my things into the carriage."

"Well, I have your address. I'll be contacting you in the future."

"Do you think so, sir? I wish I had been able to say good-bye to little Max."

"Yes, that was unfortunate. As I said, his father came to pick him up unexpectedly."

She didn't believe it. If someone had come in the night, she would have heard, she was sure of it. But there was no other explanation.

"Do you know when he'll be returning?" she asked. It was a sad but not unusual story: the mother had died of childbed fever, leaving the father, Mr. Balfour's son, whom she had never laid eyes on, to take care of the baby. At least, that was what Mr. Balfour had told her.

"I can't be sure," Balfour said, taking his glasses off and laying them on the desk. "When he returns he may be past the stage where he needs a wet nurse, but I know he'll be back."

She nodded. That would be all right. She had enough milk for her own little Davey as well as Max if the baby came back before he was weaned. In the two months she had taken care of him there had been no problem.

"All right, the carriage is waiting. I'll be going."

Mr. Balfour smiled. She didn't like the way he smiled. It was just a little off somehow. The man himself was a little off, as if he didn't really belong here, and then there was that strange writing on the baby's body. She never understood that but he insisted on it. But she found she could overcome any uneasiness she had being around him as long as he had paid her such an excellent wage.

She gave a small nervous curtsy and turned to go.

"As I said, I'll be getting in touch," Balfour went on. "You did a splendid job taking care of our little Max." She looked back at him. His smile grew even broader, and she liked it even less. "He'll be back here before you know it," he said. "Max loves his grandpa. He won't be able to stay away for long."

acknowledgments

Thanks to my loyal editors, consultants and friends, Lloyd Davis, Syd Jones, Sherry Conway Appel, Sandy Fisher, and Bill Garrison, fine writers all. And I can't forget the boys down at Squatting Toad: Larry, Dan, John, Mark, and Allen. Special thanks to Philip Turner, the best book wrangler a writer could ever hope for.

ALLEN APPEL is a graduate of West Virginia University who has worked as an author, illustrator, photographer, and playwright. *Time after Time,* his first Alex Balfour novel, was published by Carroll & Graf in 1985 to wide critical acclaim, including praise from the *New York Times Book Review* ("A fine entertainment. . . . a ferociously paced adventure") and the *Washington Post* ("An absorbing novel . . . part history, part science fiction, part love story, *Time after Time* is total adventure"). *Twice upon a Time,* and *Till the End of Time* soon followed and the Alex Balfour series became what *Kirkus Reviews* called "a lightweight vehicle for historical fiction that works." Appel is also co-author of the thriller *Hellhound.* He lives with his wife and children in Upper Marlboro, Maryland.